MOON 月詠 PHASE 6

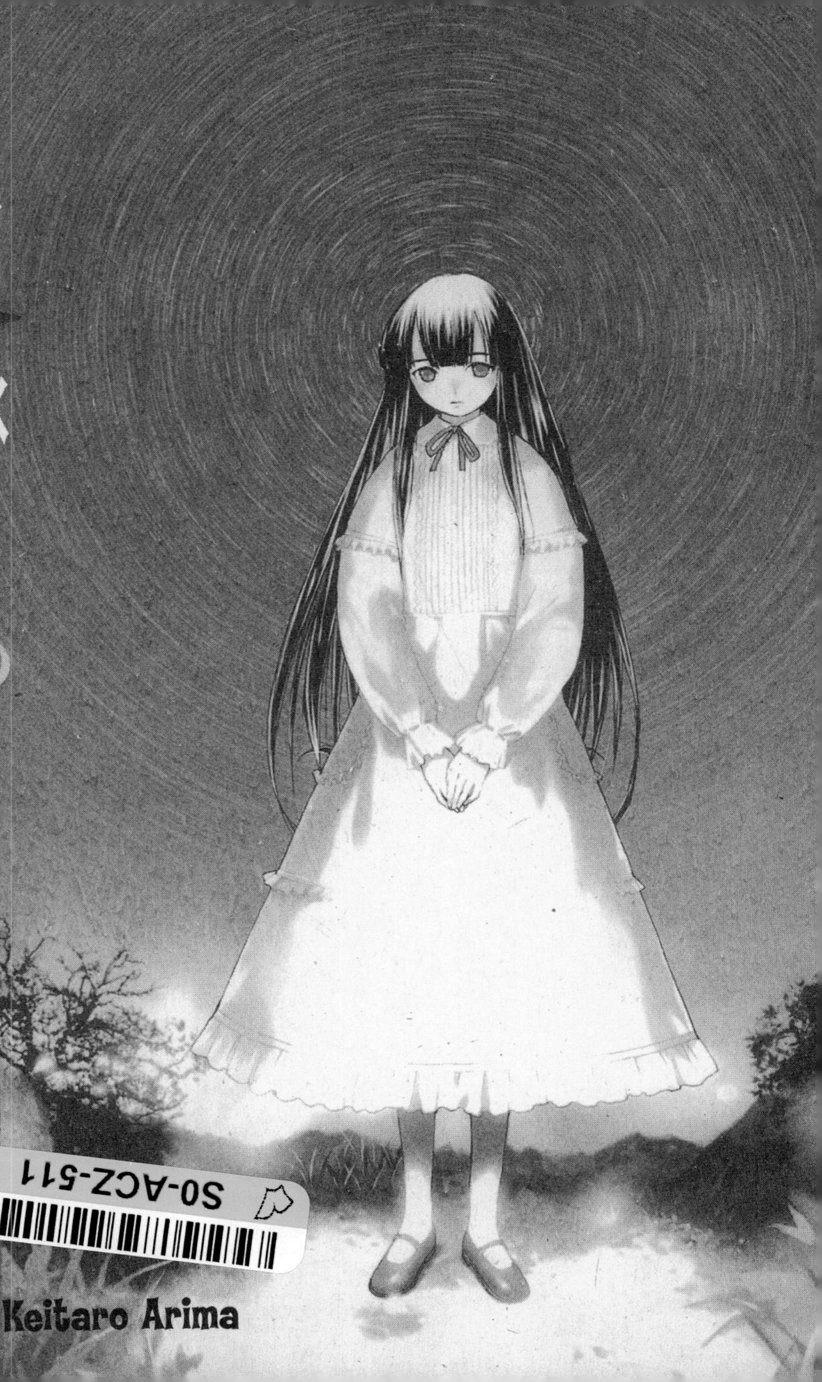

Keitaro Arima

STORY SO FAR

Kouhei Mido has never had an encounter with the supernatural kind, so why are ghosts showing up in every photo he takes? His biggest catch on film, however, has to be the cute but stubborn vampire girl Hazuki. And she's moved in with him and his grandfather in order to find her mother.

After a wild ride of defeating the evil vampire Count Kinkle and tackling his growing feelings for Hazuki, Kouhei wants to believe that all the pieces of the puzzle have finally fallen into place. But when they learn more of Hazuki's past with the help of her possessed cat Haiji, it looks like they've only begun to scratch the surface.

And behind closed doors, another menace will step into the ring... Mario, Hazuki's childhood guardian.

TSUKUYOMI

Moon Phase 月詠

CREATED BY: KEITARO ARIMA

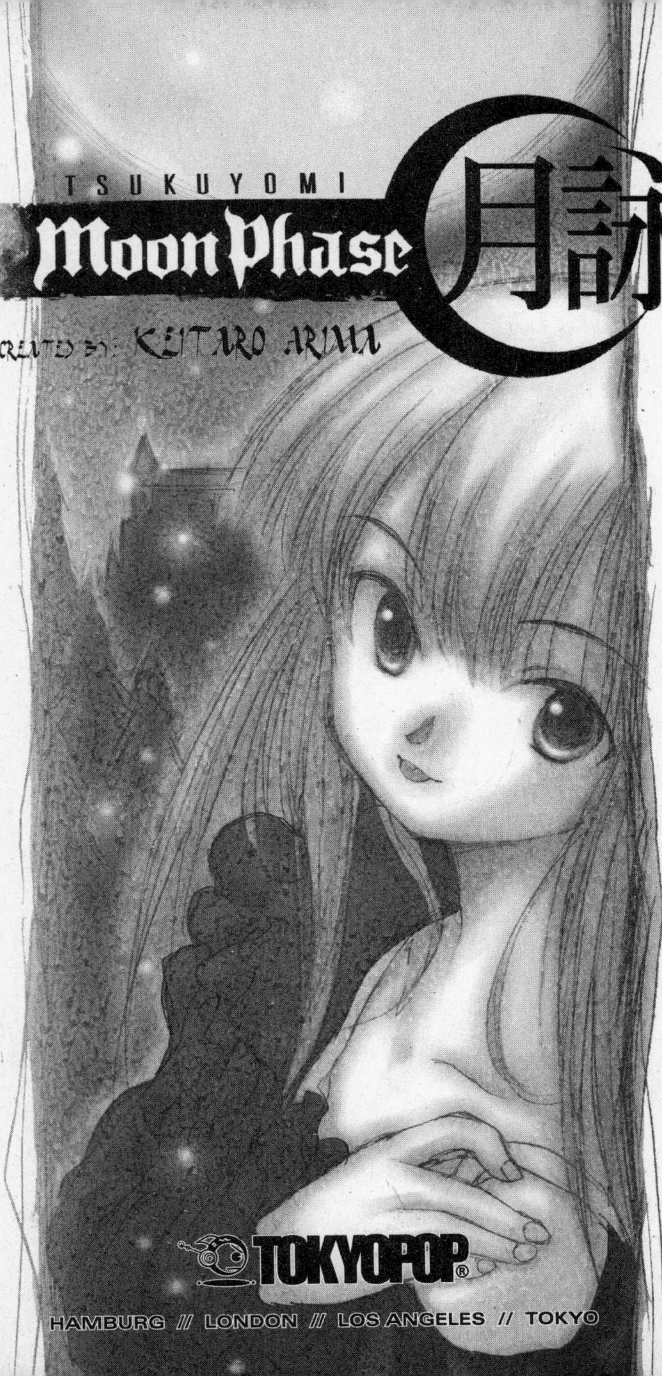

TOKYOPOP®

HAMBURG // LONDON // LOS ANGELES // TOKYO

Tsukuyomi: Moon Phase Volume 6
Created by Keitaro Arima

Translation - Yoohae Yang
English Adaptation - Jeffrey Reeves
Retouch and Lettering - Star Print Brokers
Production Artist - Courtney Geter
Graphic Designer - Monalisa De Asis

Editor - Katherine Schilling
Digital Imaging Manager - Chris Buford
Pre-Production Supervisor - Erika Terriquez
Art Director - Anne Marie Horne
Production Manager - Elisabeth Brizzi
Managing Editor - Vy Nguyen
VP of Production - Ron Klamert
Editor-in-Chief - Rob Tokar
Publisher - Mike Kiley
President and C.O.O. - John Parker
C.E.O. and Chief Creative Officer - Stuart Levy

A ⚆ TOKYOPOP® Manga

TOKYOPOP and ⚆ are trademarks or registered trademarks of TOKYOPOP Inc.

TOKYOPOP Inc.
5900 Wilshire Blvd. Suite 2000
Los Angeles, CA 90036

E-mail: info@TOKYOPOP.com
Come visit us online at www.TOKYOPOP.com

ISBN: 978-1-59532-953-0

First TOKYOPOP printing: March 2007
10 9 8 7 6 5 4 3 2 1
Printed in the USA

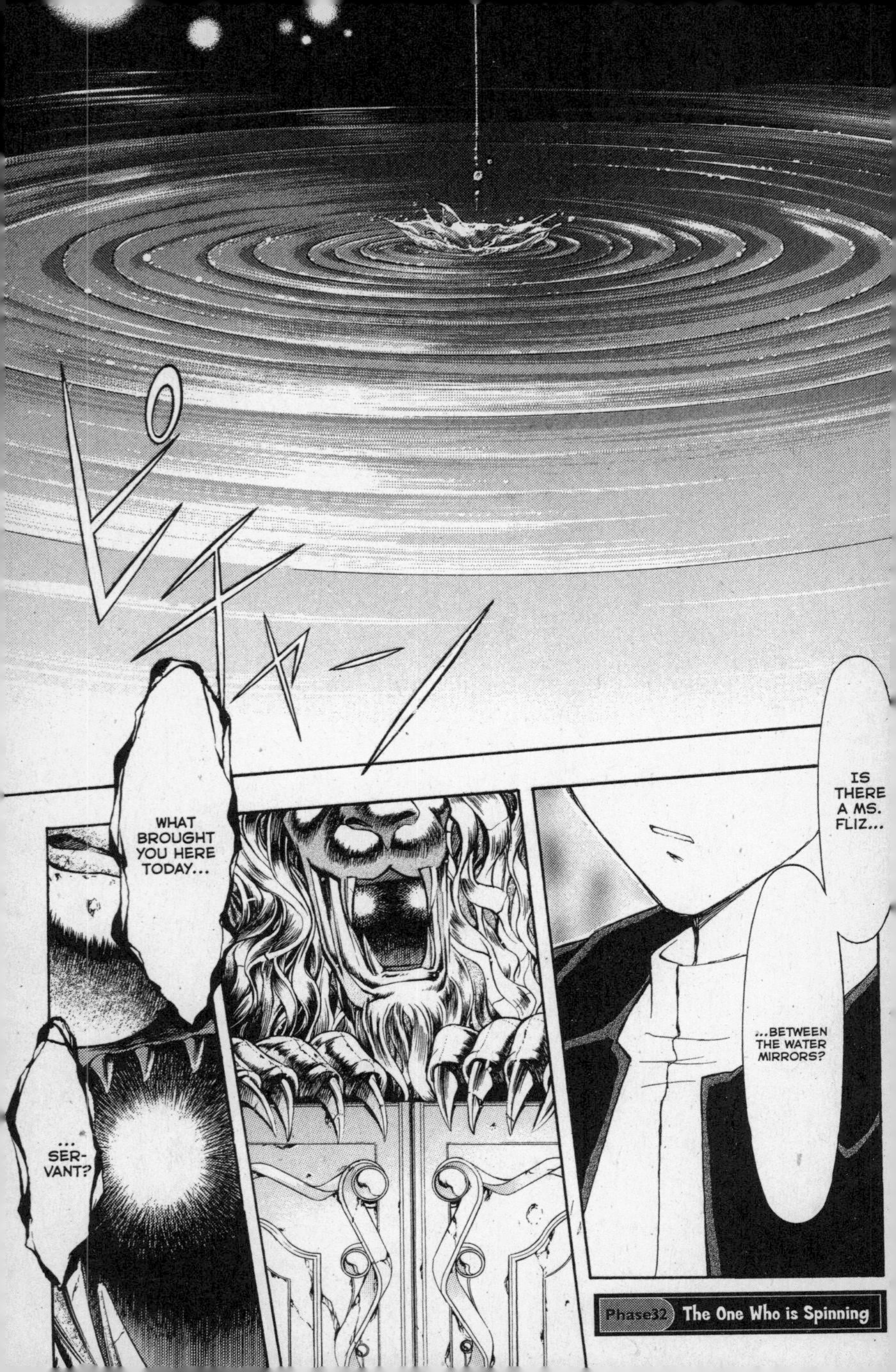
ピチャーン
IS THERE A MS. FLIZ...
...BETWEEN THE WATER MIRRORS?
WHAT BROUGHT YOU HERE TODAY...
... SERVANT?

Phase32 The One Who is Spinning

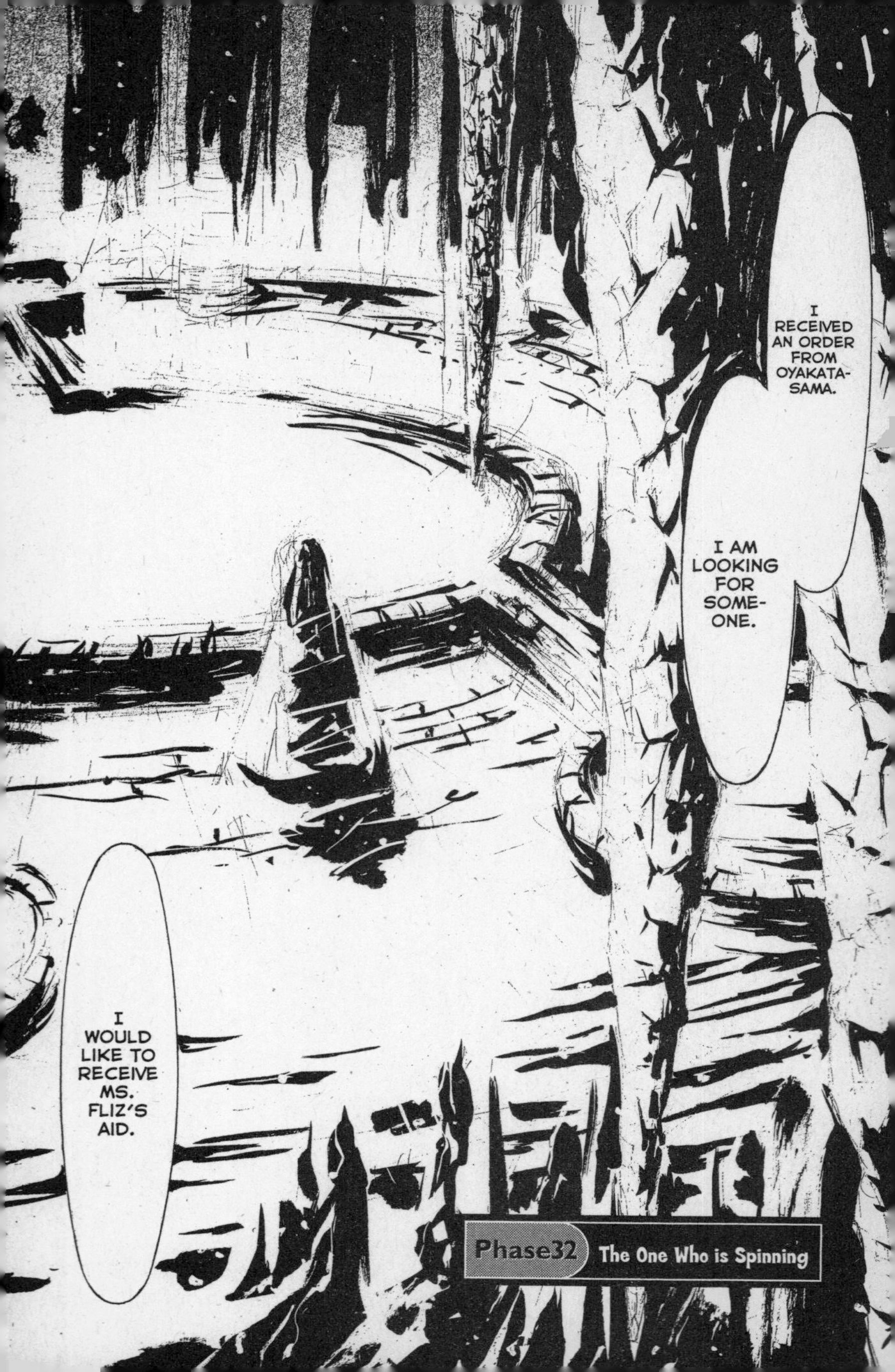
I RECEIVED AN ORDER FROM OYAKATA-SAMA.
I AM LOOKING FOR SOME-ONE.
I WOULD LIKE TO RECEIVE MS. FLIZ'S AID.
Phase32
The One Who is Spinning

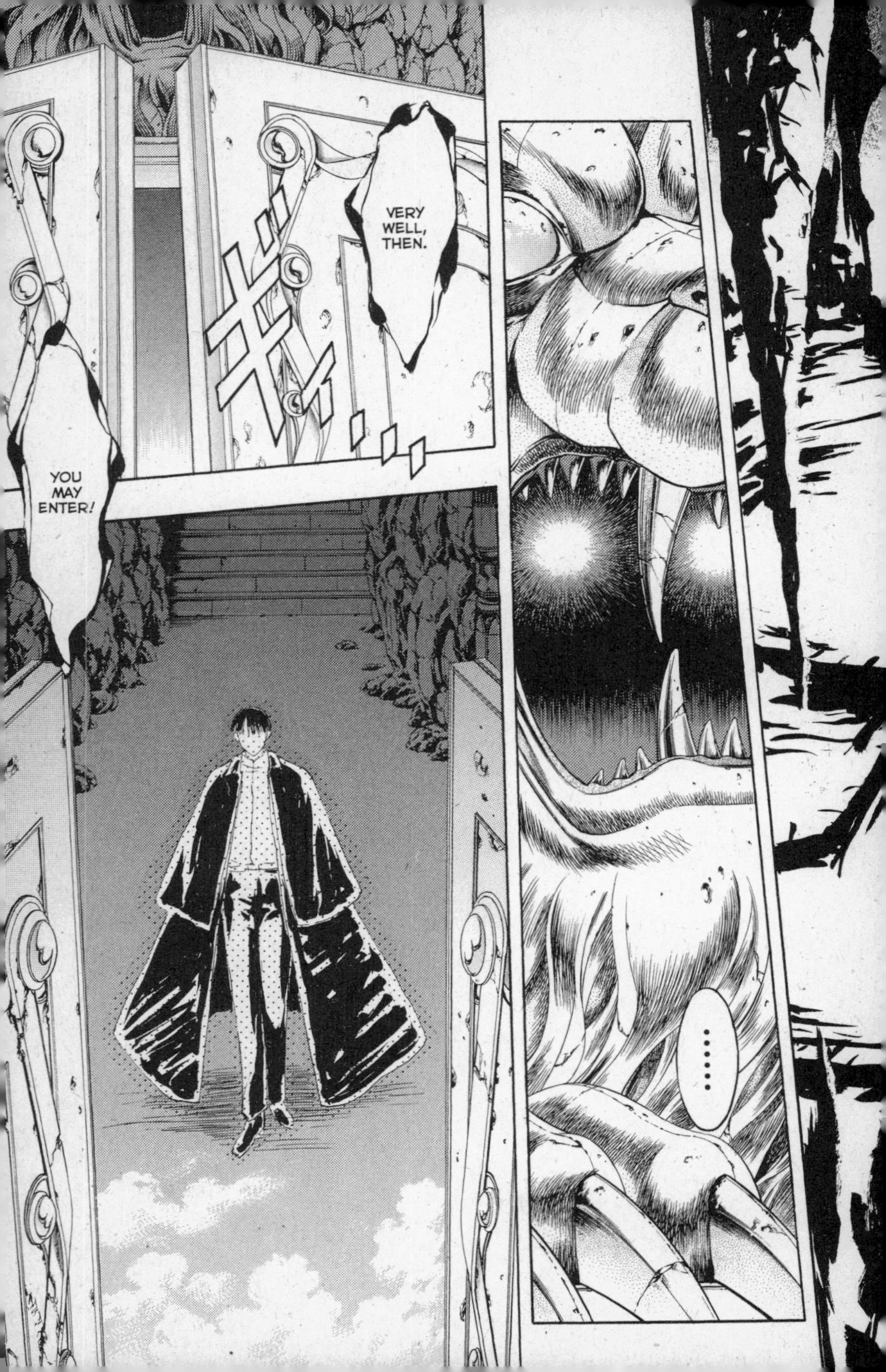
......
VERY WELL, THEN.
YOU MAY ENTER!

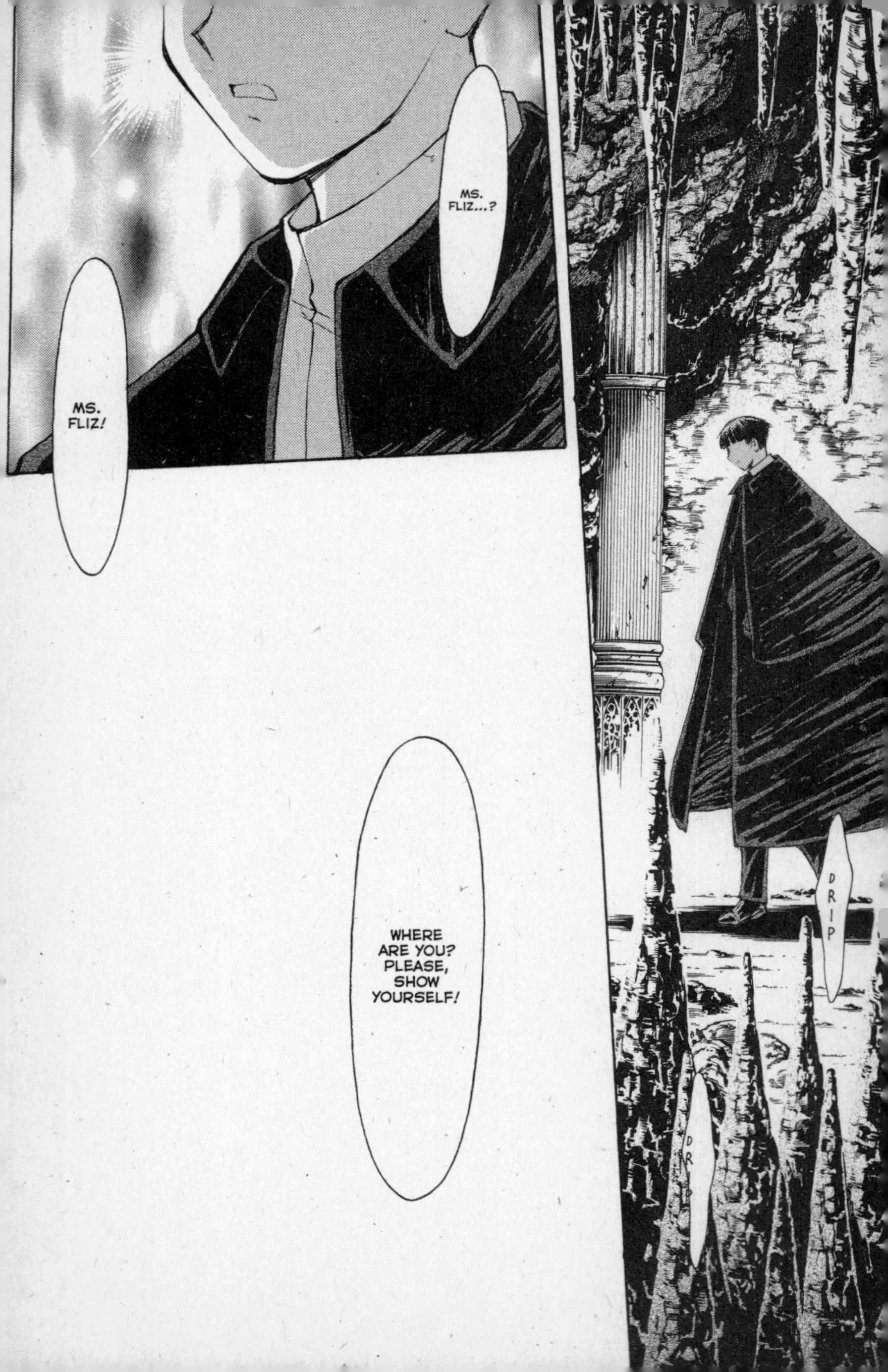
DRIP
DRIP
MS. FLIZ...?
MS. FLIZ!
WHERE ARE YOU? PLEASE, SHOW YOURSELF!

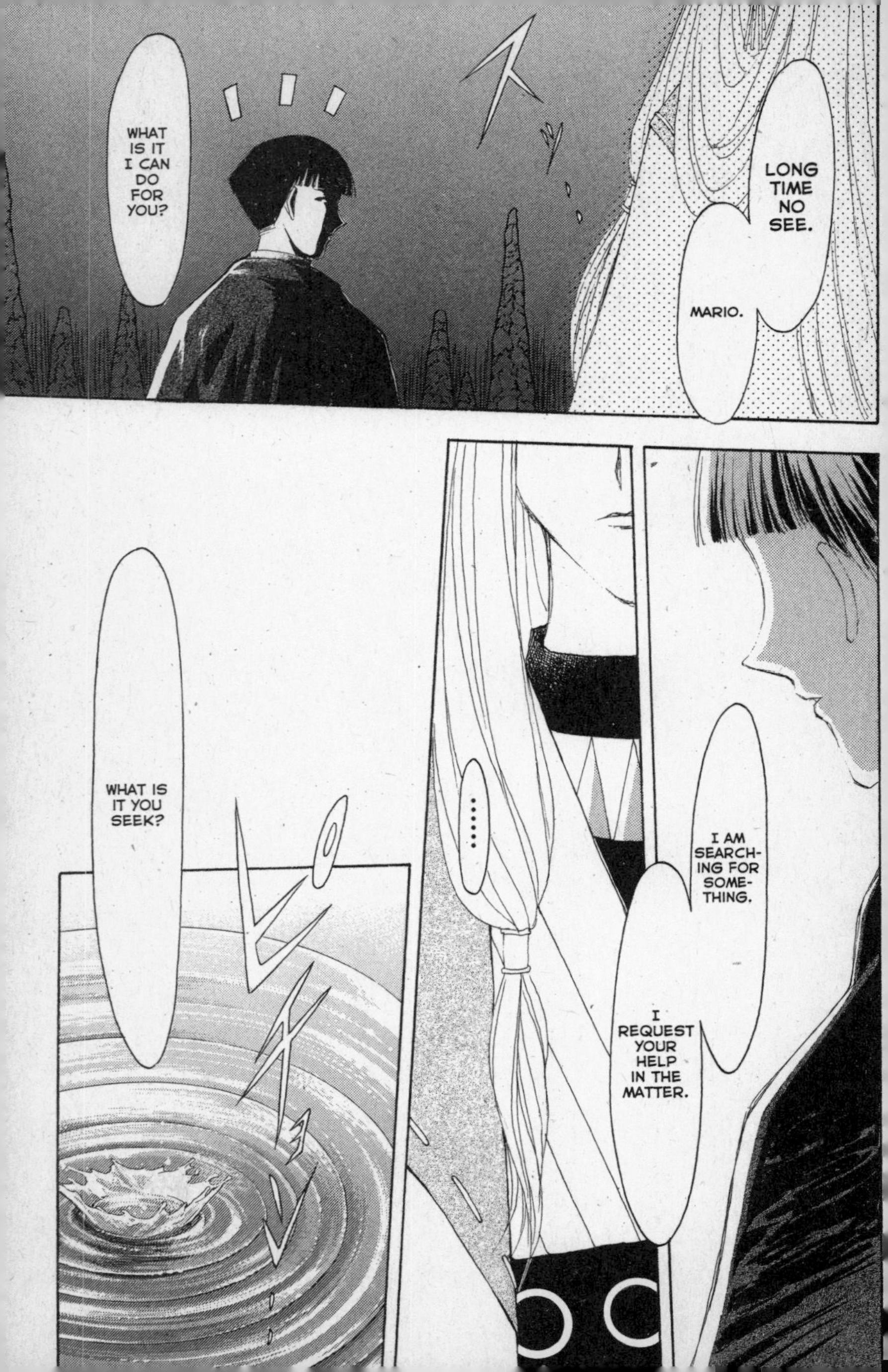
LONG TIME NO SEE.
MARIO.
WHAT IS IT I CAN DO FOR YOU?
I AM SEARCHING FOR SOMETHING.
I REQUEST YOUR HELP IN THE MATTER.
......
WHAT IS IT YOU SEEK?

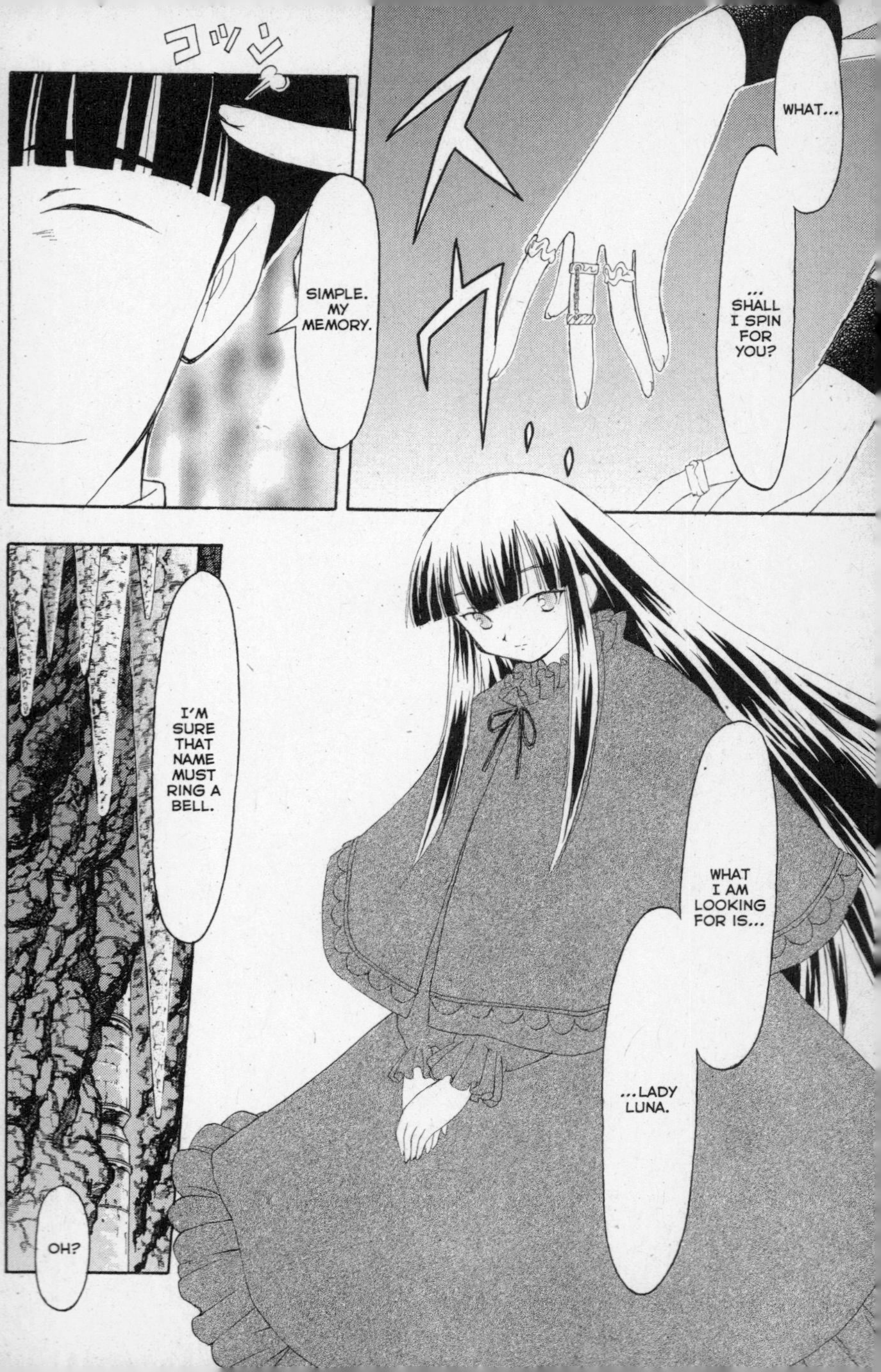
WHAT...
スッ
...SHALL I SPIN FOR YOU?
コツン
SIMPLE. MY MEMORY.
WHAT I AM LOOKING FOR IS...
...LADY LUNA.
I'M SURE THAT NAME MUST RING A BELL.
OH?

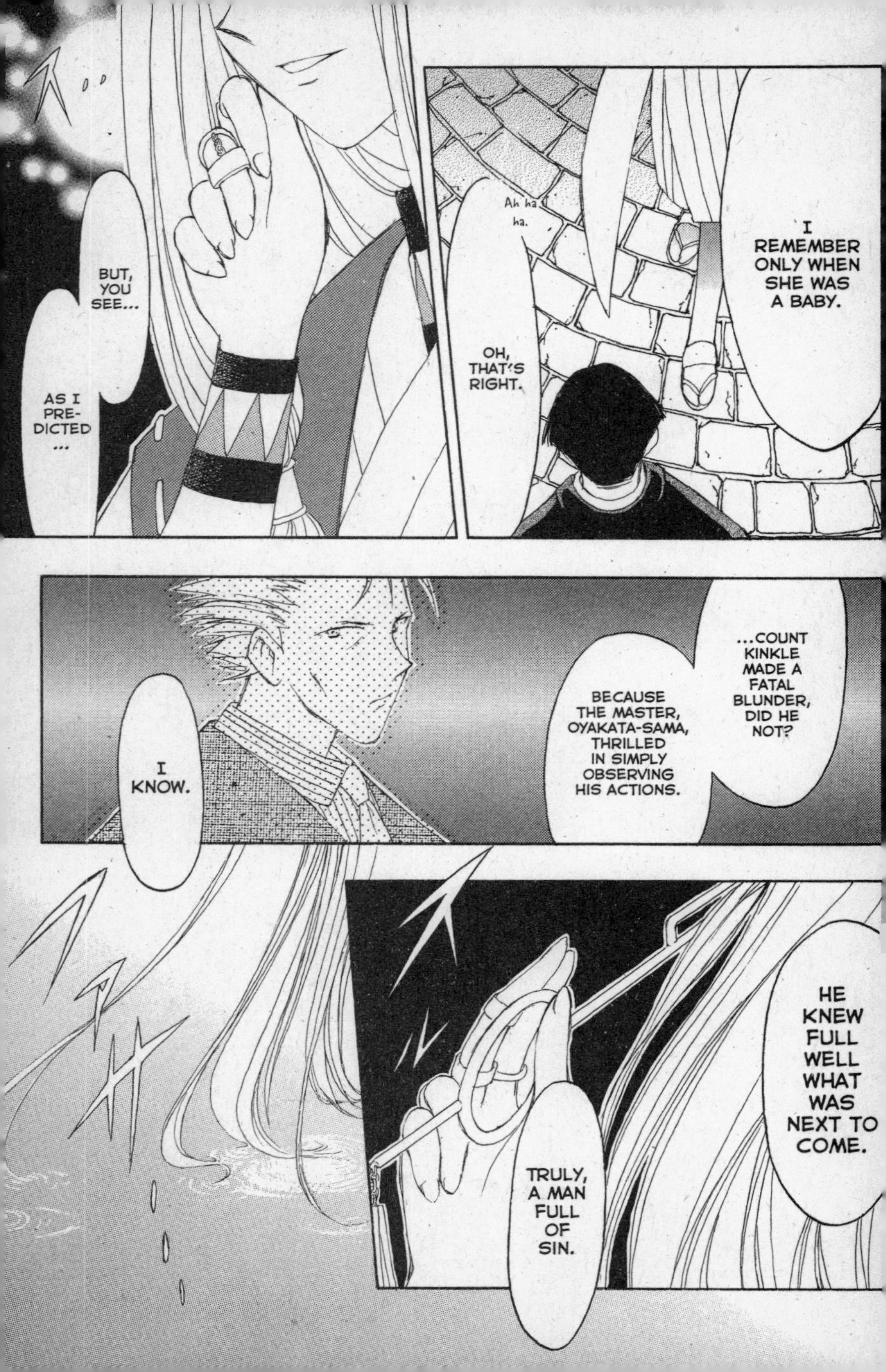
I REMEMBER ONLY WHEN SHE WAS A BABY.
Ah ha ha.
OH, THAT'S RIGHT.
BUT, YOU SEE...
AS I PRE-DICTED...
...COUNT KINKLE MADE A FATAL BLUNDER, DID HE NOT?
BECAUSE THE MASTER, OYAKATA-SAMA, THRILLED IN SIMPLY OBSERVING HIS ACTIONS.
I KNOW.
HE KNEW FULL WELL WHAT WAS NEXT TO COME.
TRULY, A MAN FULL OF SIN.

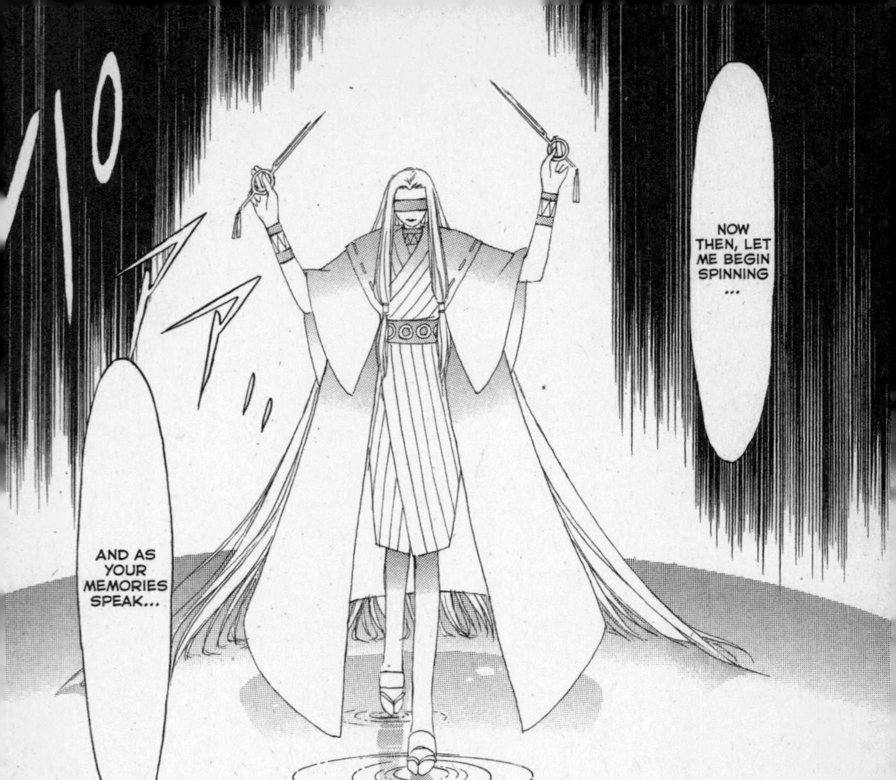
NOW THEN, LET ME BEGIN SPINNING ...
AND AS YOUR MEMORIES SPEAK...
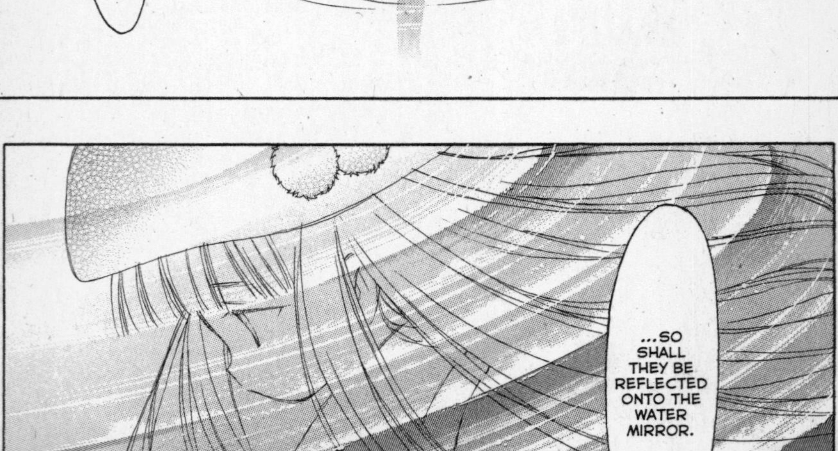
...SO SHALL THEY BE REFLECTED ONTO THE WATER MIRROR.

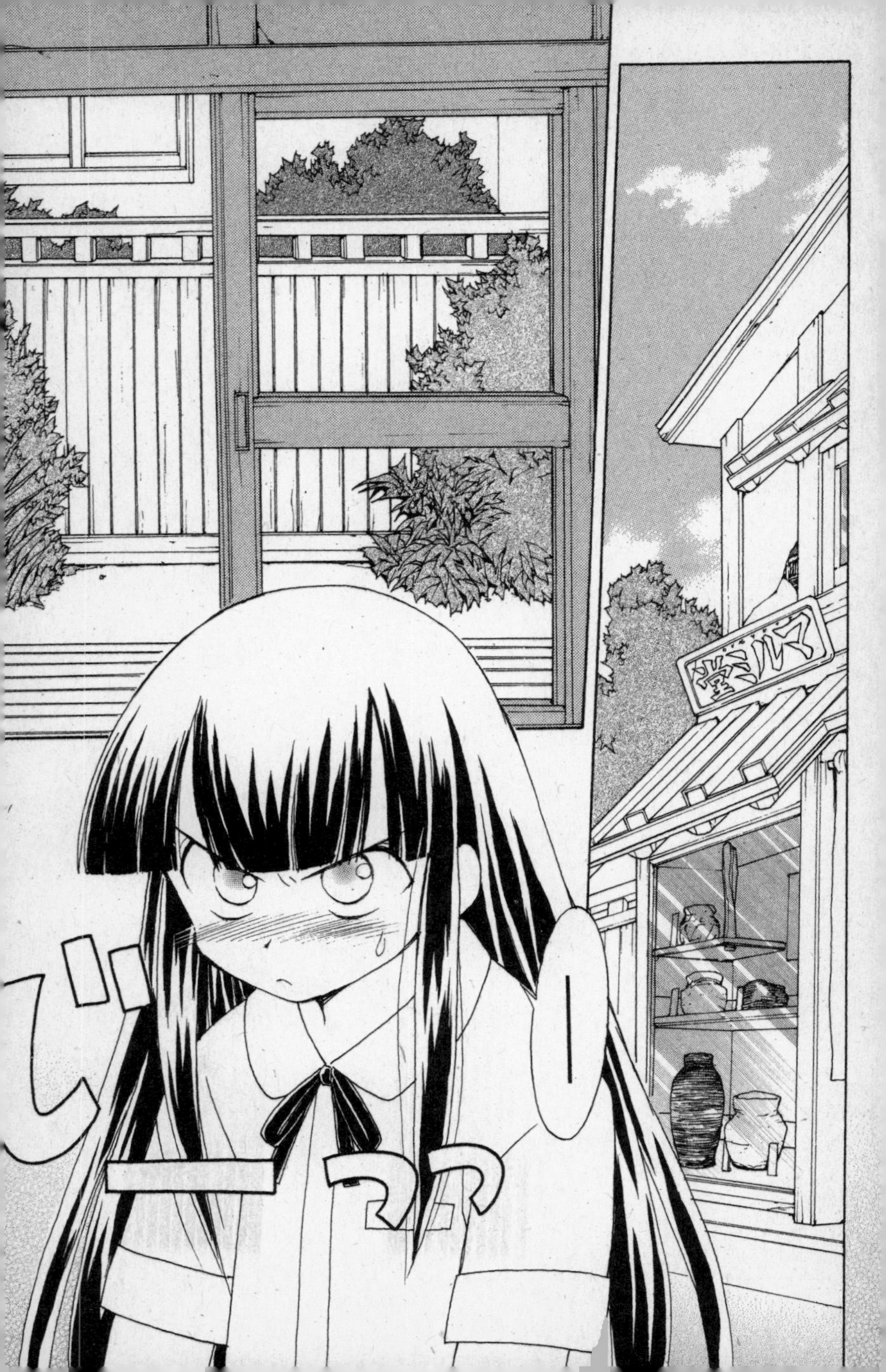
マルミ堂
じぃーーっっ

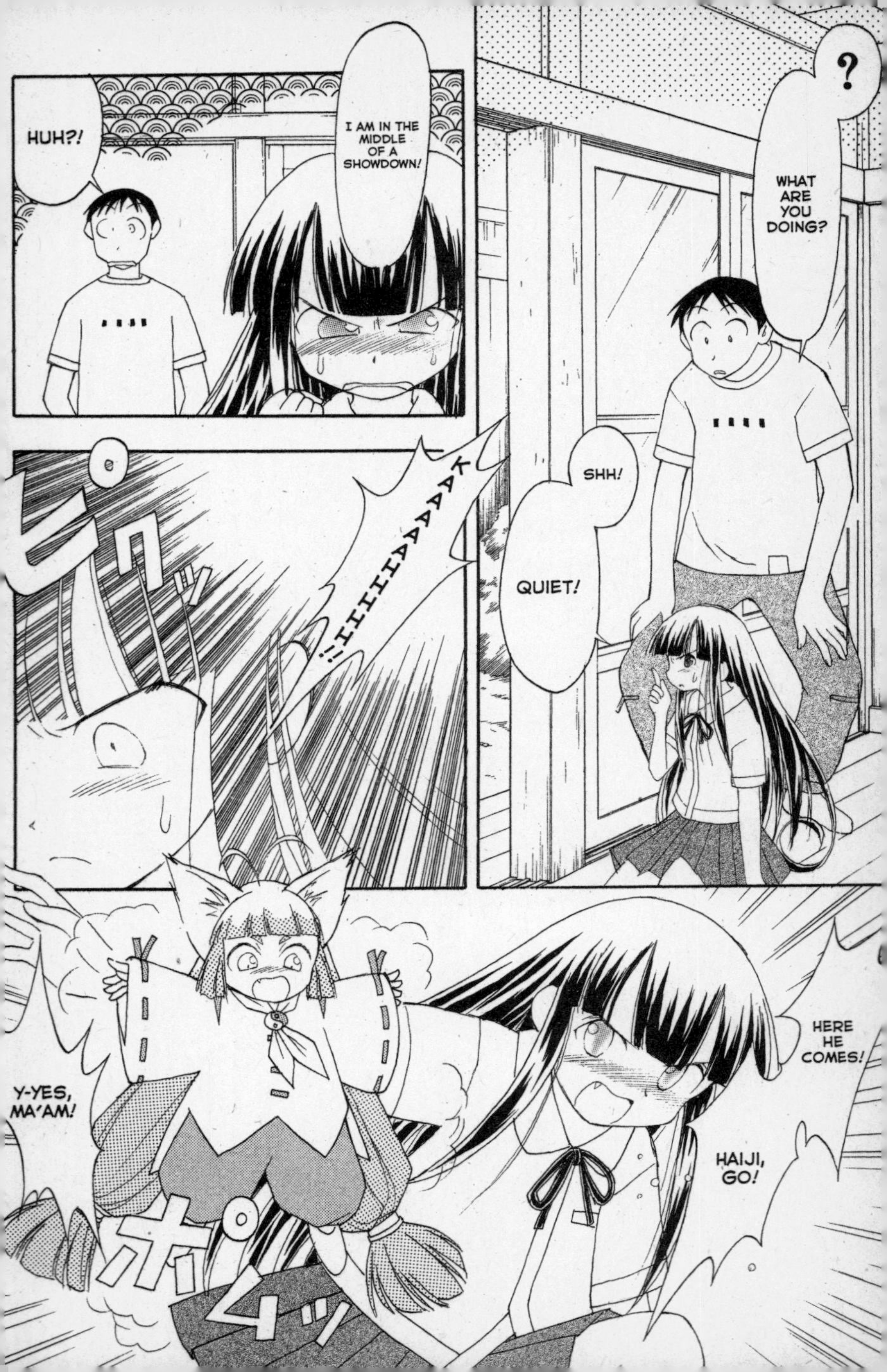
?
WHAT ARE YOU DOING?
SHH!
QUIET!
I AM IN THE MIDDLE OF A SHOWDOWN!
HUH?!
KAAAAAHHHHH!!
HERE HE COMES!
HAIJI, GO!
Y-YES, MA'AM!

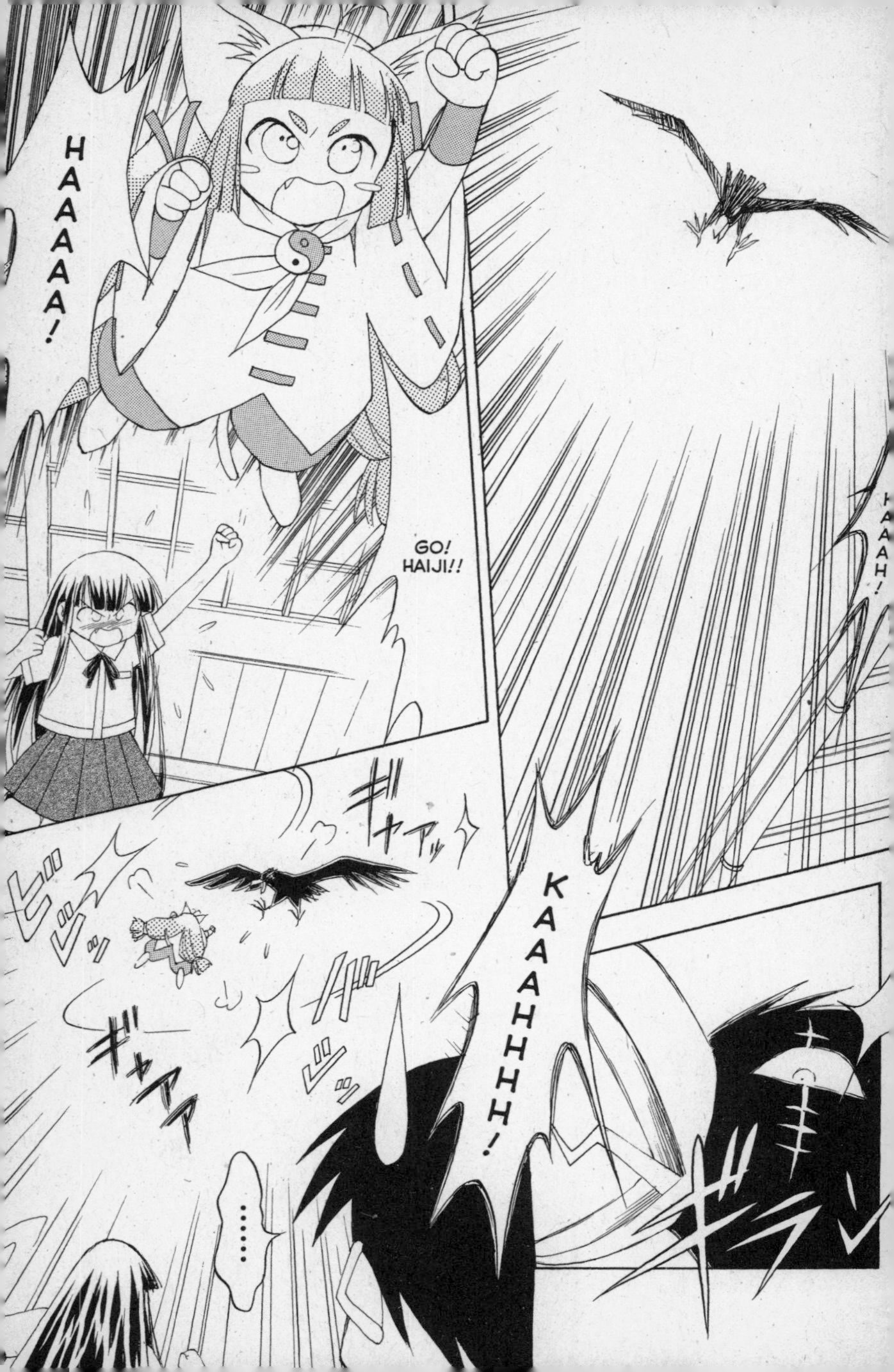
HAAAAH!
KAAAAHHHHH!
ギラン
HAAAAAA!
GO! HAIJI!!
ギャアッ
ビシッ
ギャアア
ジュッ
......

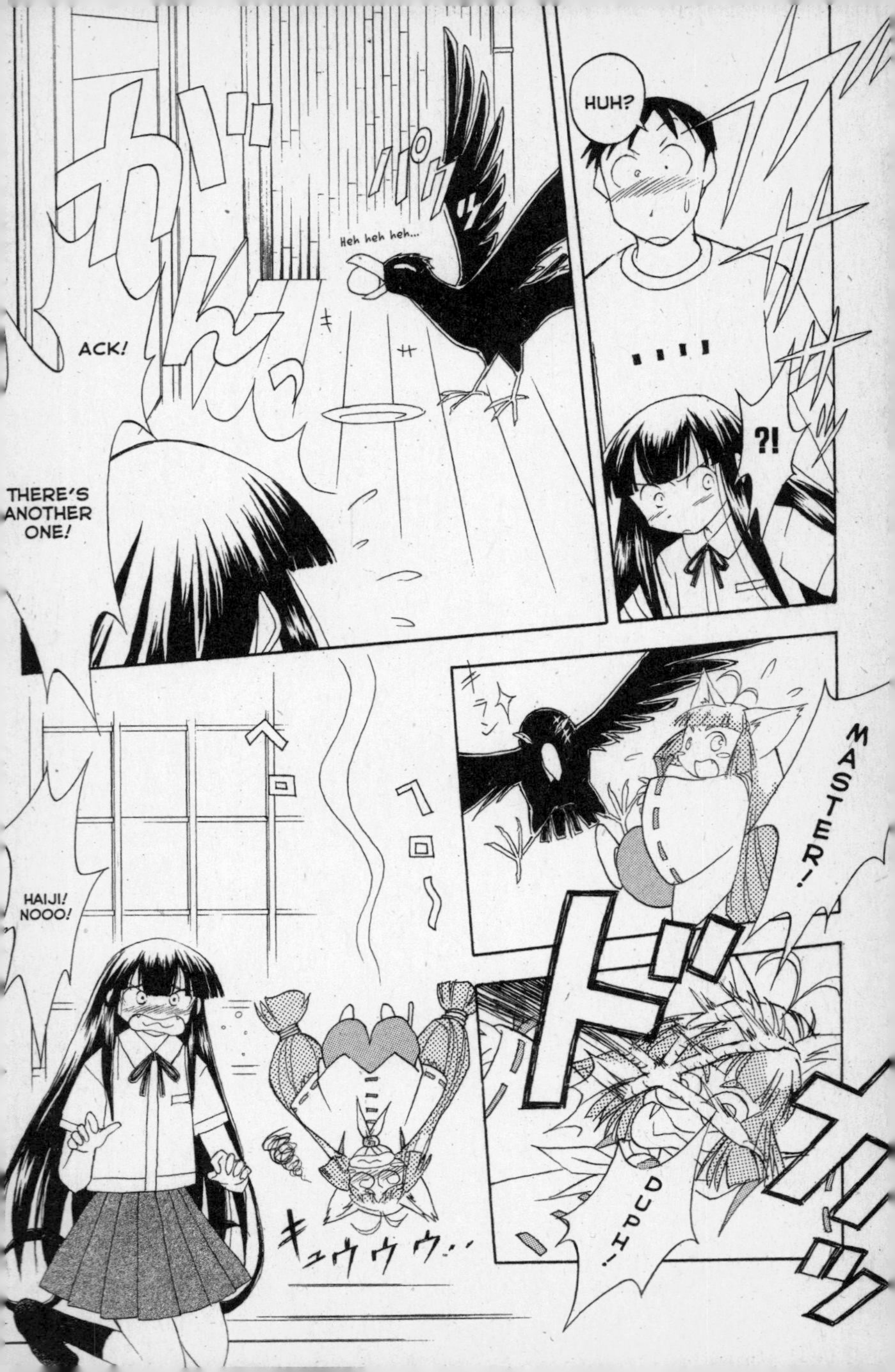
HUH?
....
?!
Heh heh heh...
ACK!
THERE'S ANOTHER ONE!
MASTER!
DUPH!
HAIJI! NOOO!

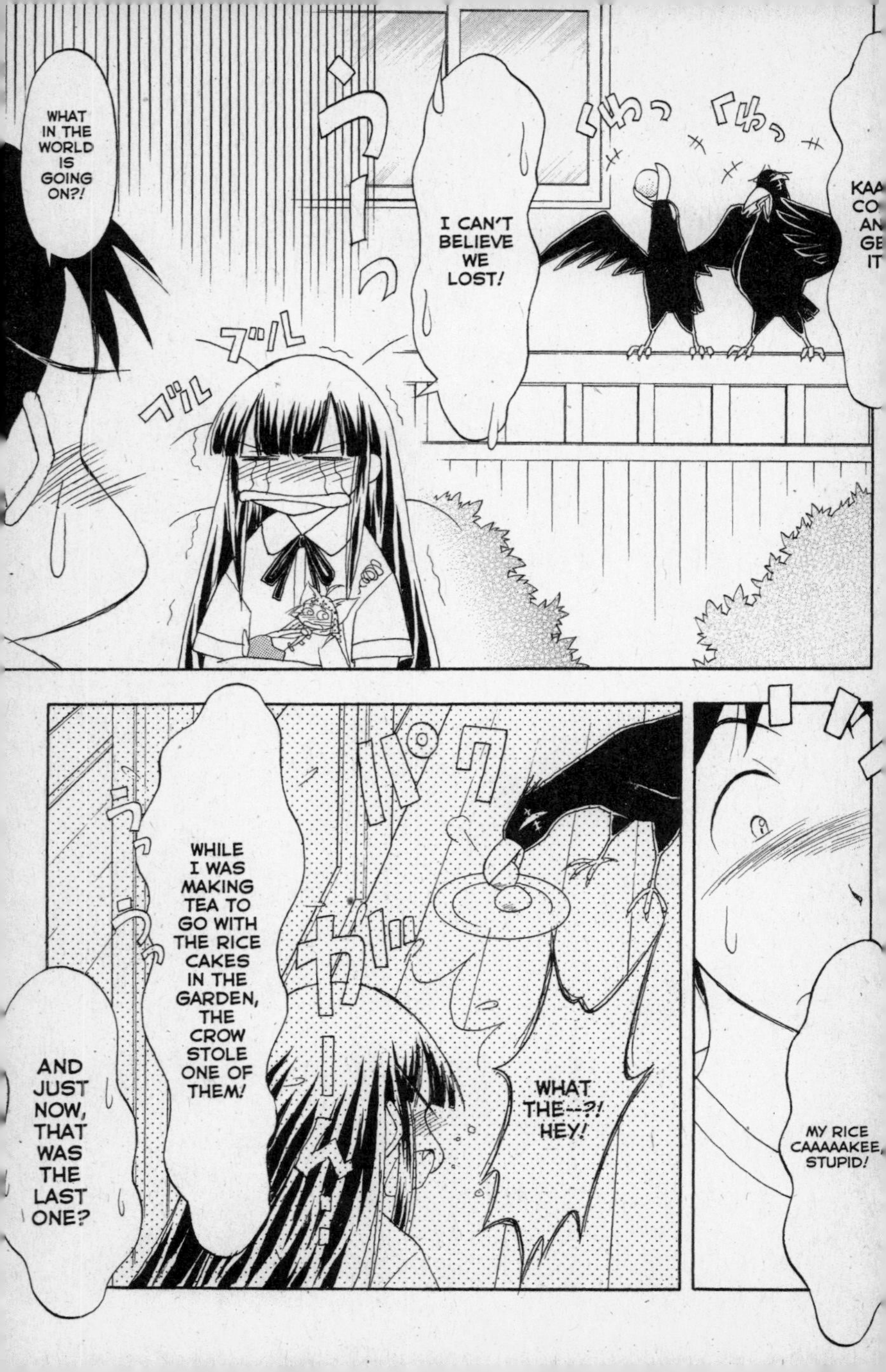
I CAN'T BELIEVE WE LOST!
WHAT IN THE WORLD IS GOING ON?!
MY RICE CAAAAAKEE, STUPID!
WHAT THE--?! HEY!
WHILE I WAS MAKING TEA TO GO WITH THE RICE CAKES IN THE GARDEN, THE CROW STOLE ONE OF THEM!
AND JUST NOW, THAT WAS THE LAST ONE?

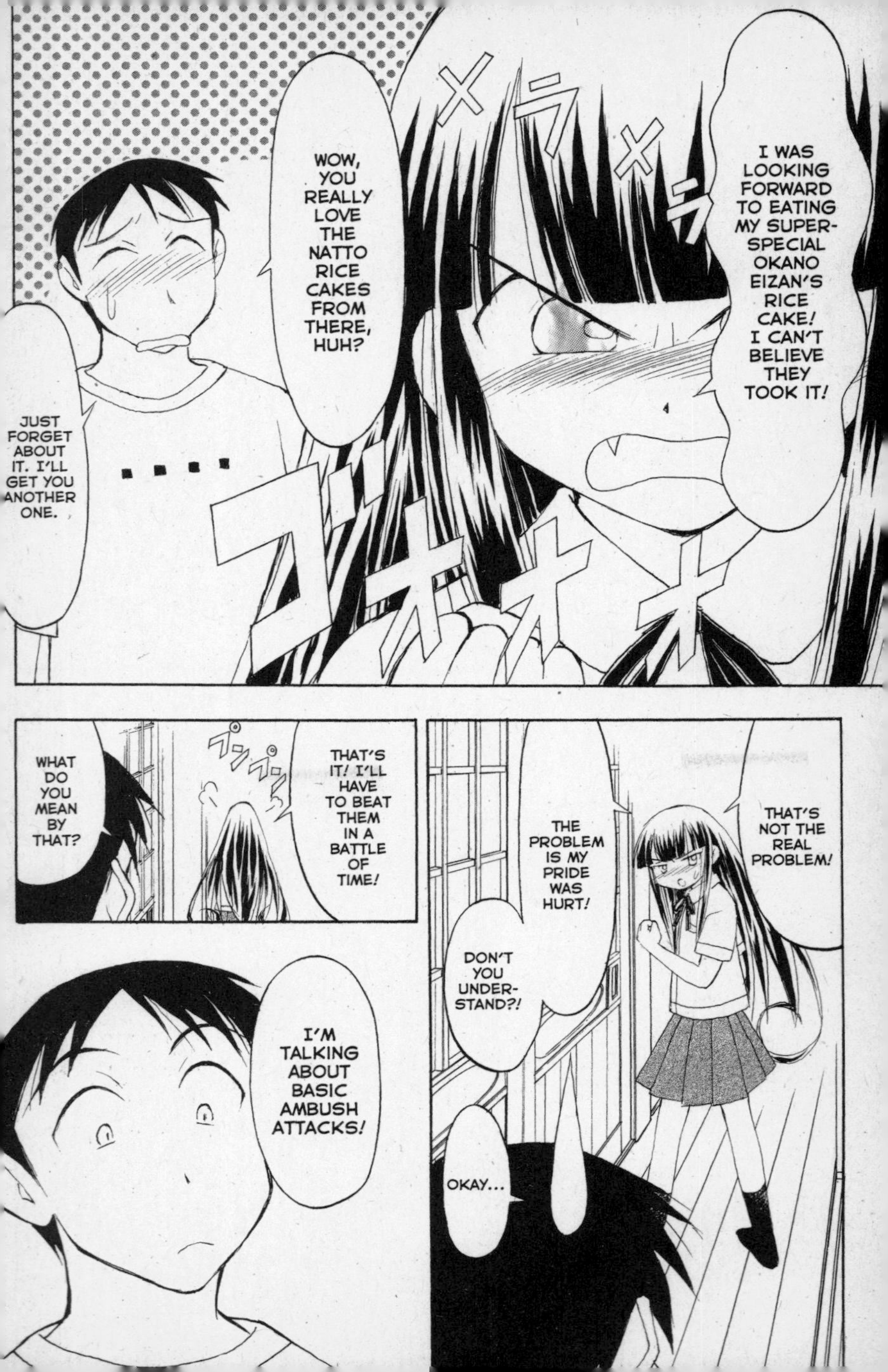

メラメラ
I WAS LOOKING FORWARD TO EATING MY SUPER-SPECIAL OKANO EIZAN'S RICE CAKE! I CAN'T BELIEVE THEY TOOK IT!
WOW, YOU REALLY LOVE THE NATTO RICE CAKES FROM THERE, HUH?
ゴオオ
....
JUST FORGET ABOUT IT. I'LL GET YOU ANOTHER ONE.
THAT'S NOT THE REAL PROBLEM!
THE PROBLEM IS MY PRIDE WAS HURT!
DON'T YOU UNDER-STAND?!
OKAY...
THAT'S IT! I'LL HAVE TO BEAT THEM IN A BATTLE OF TIME!
WHAT DO YOU MEAN BY THAT?
I'M TALKING ABOUT BASIC AMBUSH ATTACKS!

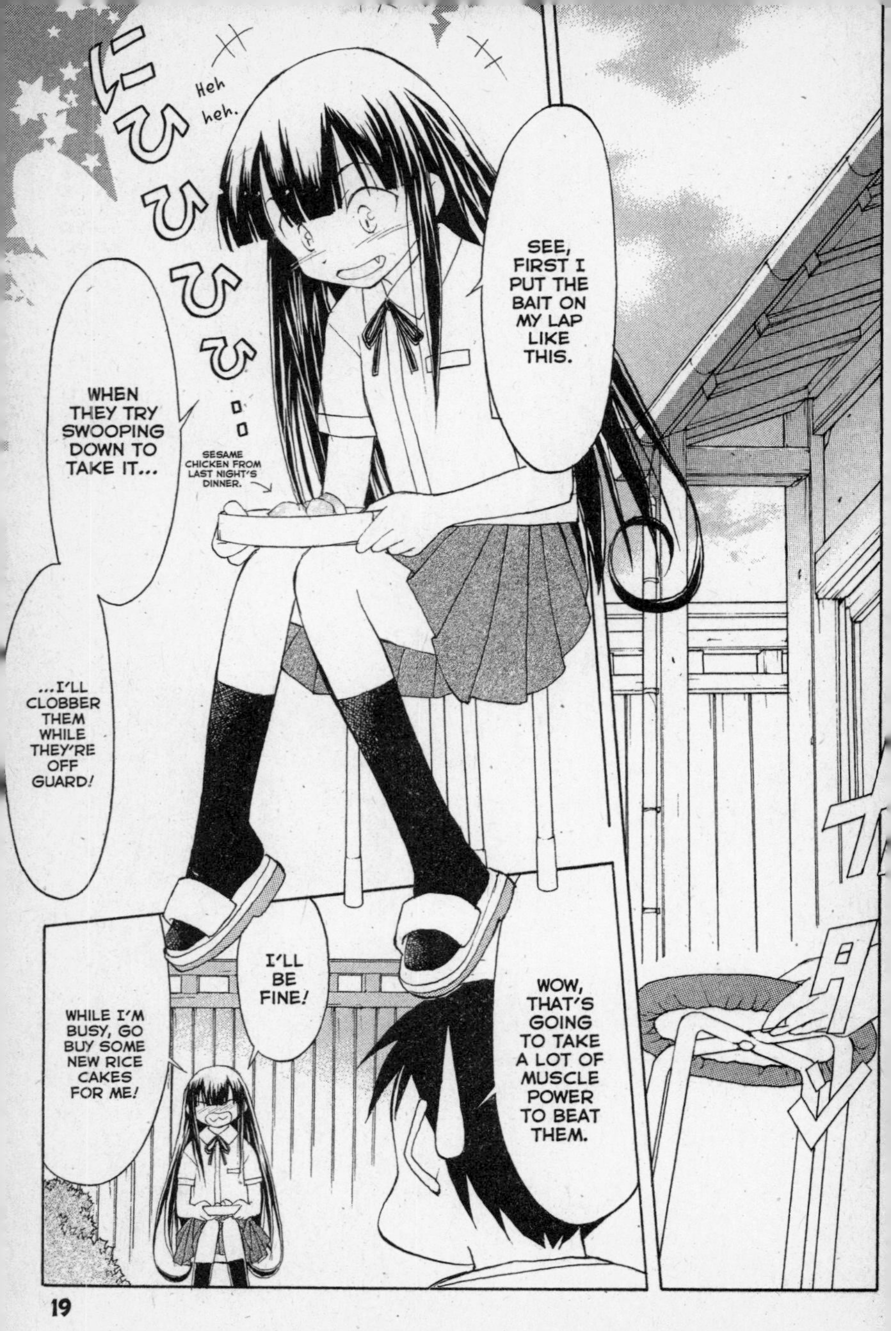
SEE, FIRST I PUT THE BAIT ON MY LAP LIKE THIS.
Heh heh.
にひひひひ
SESAME CHICKEN FROM LAST NIGHT'S DINNER.
WHEN THEY TRY SWOOPING DOWN TO TAKE IT...
...I'LL CLOBBER THEM WHILE THEY'RE OFF GUARD!
WOW, THAT'S GOING TO TAKE A LOT OF MUSCLE POWER TO BEAT THEM.
I'LL BE FINE!
WHILE I'M BUSY, GO BUY SOME NEW RICE CAKES FOR ME!

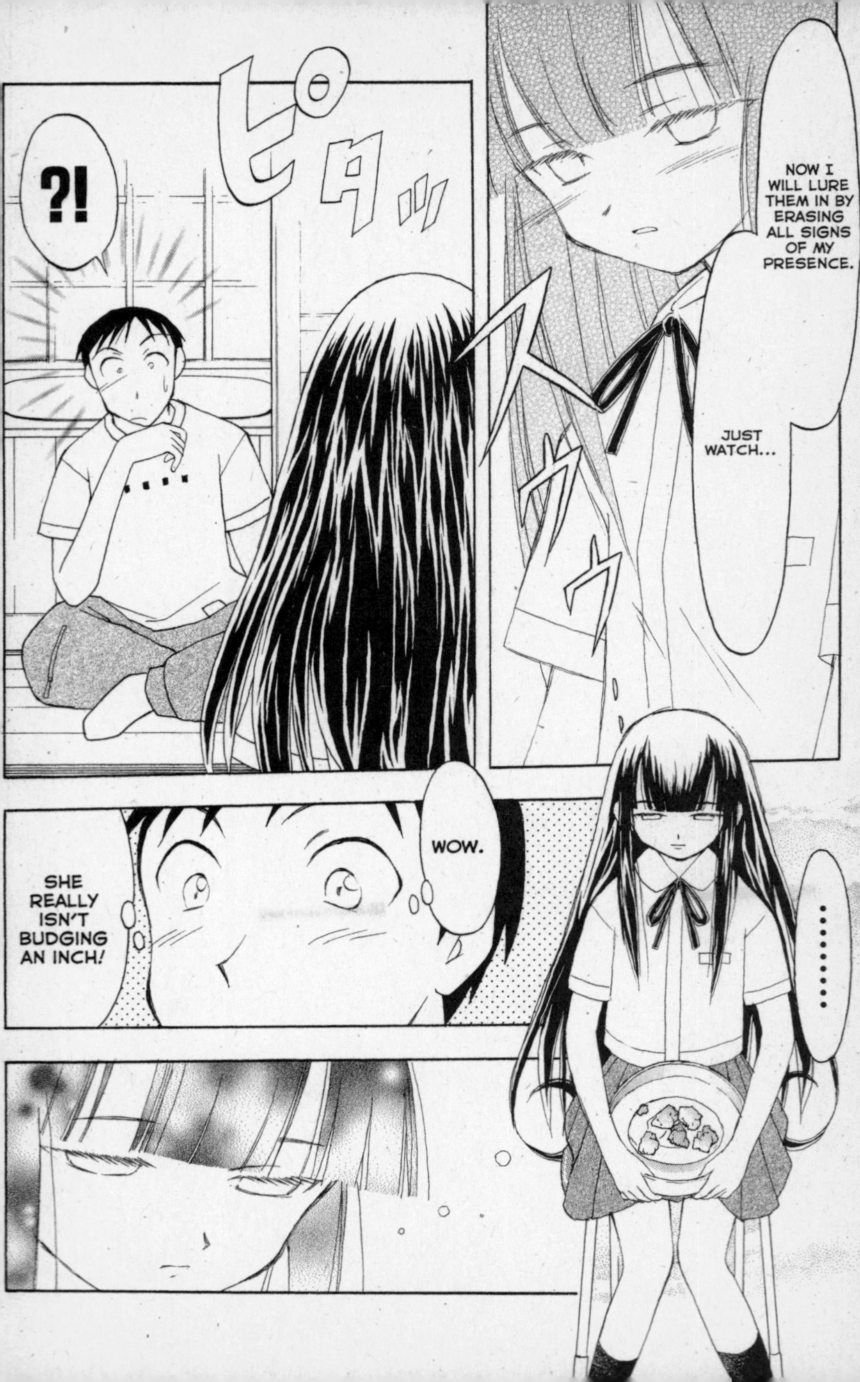
NOW I WILL LURE THEM IN BY ERASING ALL SIGNS OF MY PRESENCE.
JUST WATCH...
ピタッ
?!
......
WOW.
SHE REALLY ISN'T BUDGING AN INCH!

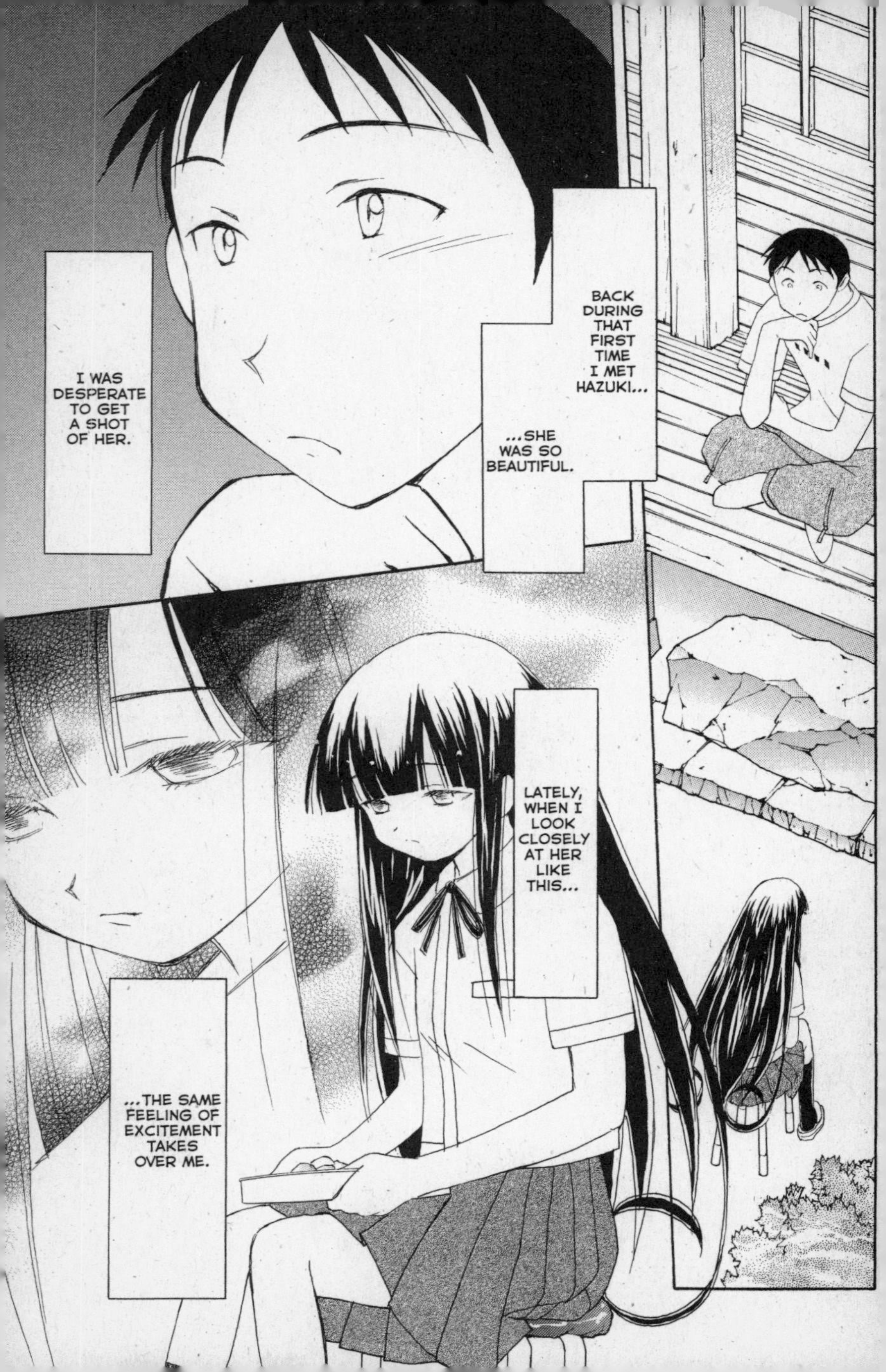
BACK DURING THAT FIRST TIME I MET HAZUKI...
...SHE WAS SO BEAUTIFUL.
I WAS DESPERATE TO GET A SHOT OF HER.
LATELY, WHEN I LOOK CLOSELY AT HER LIKE THIS...
...THE SAME FEELING OF EXCITEMENT TAKES OVER ME.

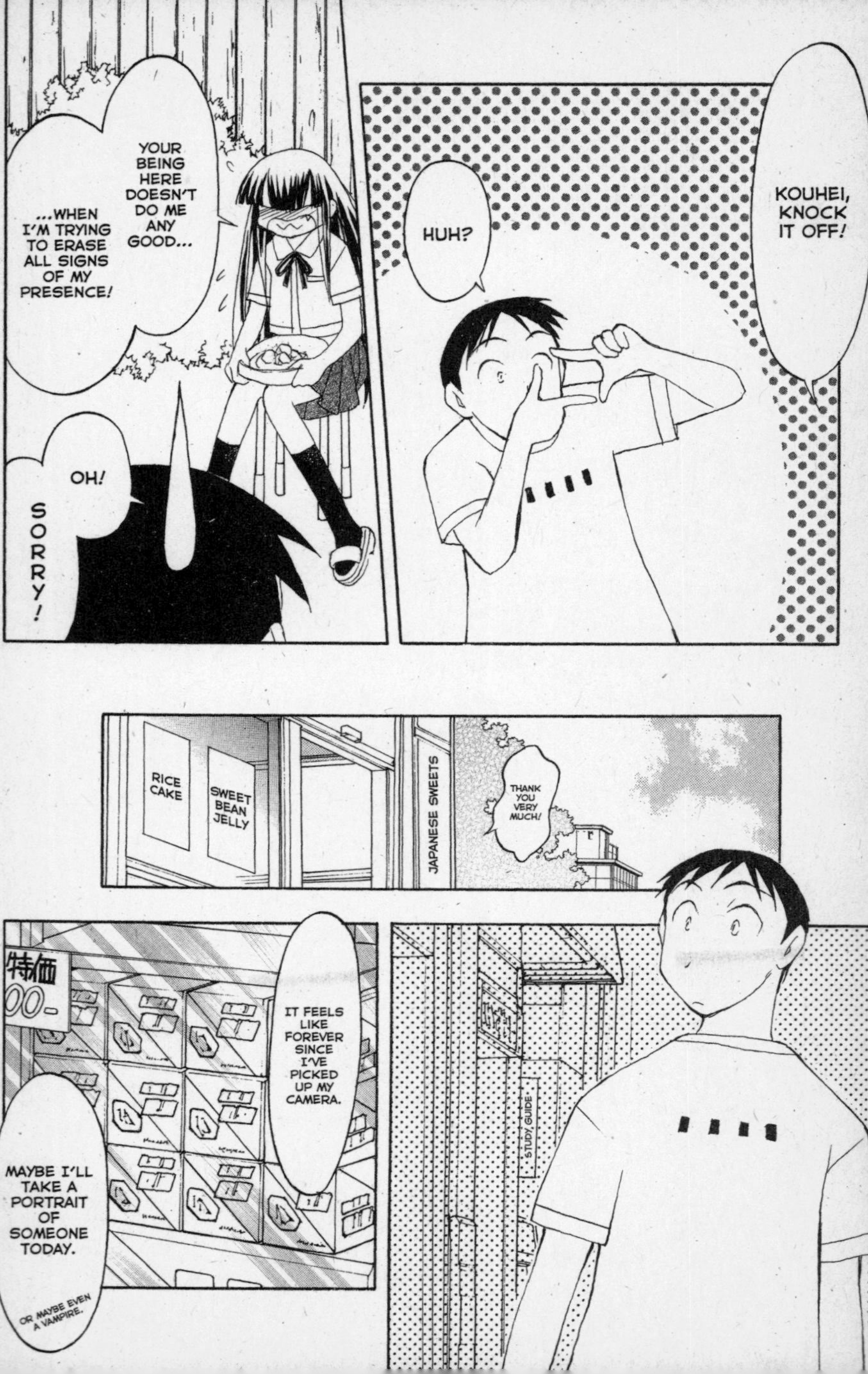

KOUHEI, KNOCK IT OFF!
HUH?
YOUR BEING HERE DOESN'T DO ME ANY GOOD...
...WHEN I'M TRYING TO ERASE ALL SIGNS OF MY PRESENCE!
OH!
SORRY!
JAPANESE SWEETS
SWEET BEAN JELLY
RICE CAKE
THANK YOU VERY MUCH!
STUDY GUIDE
IT FEELS LIKE FOREVER SINCE I'VE PICKED UP MY CAMERA.
MAYBE I'LL TAKE A PORTRAIT OF SOMEONE TODAY.
OR MAYBE EVEN A VAMPIRE.

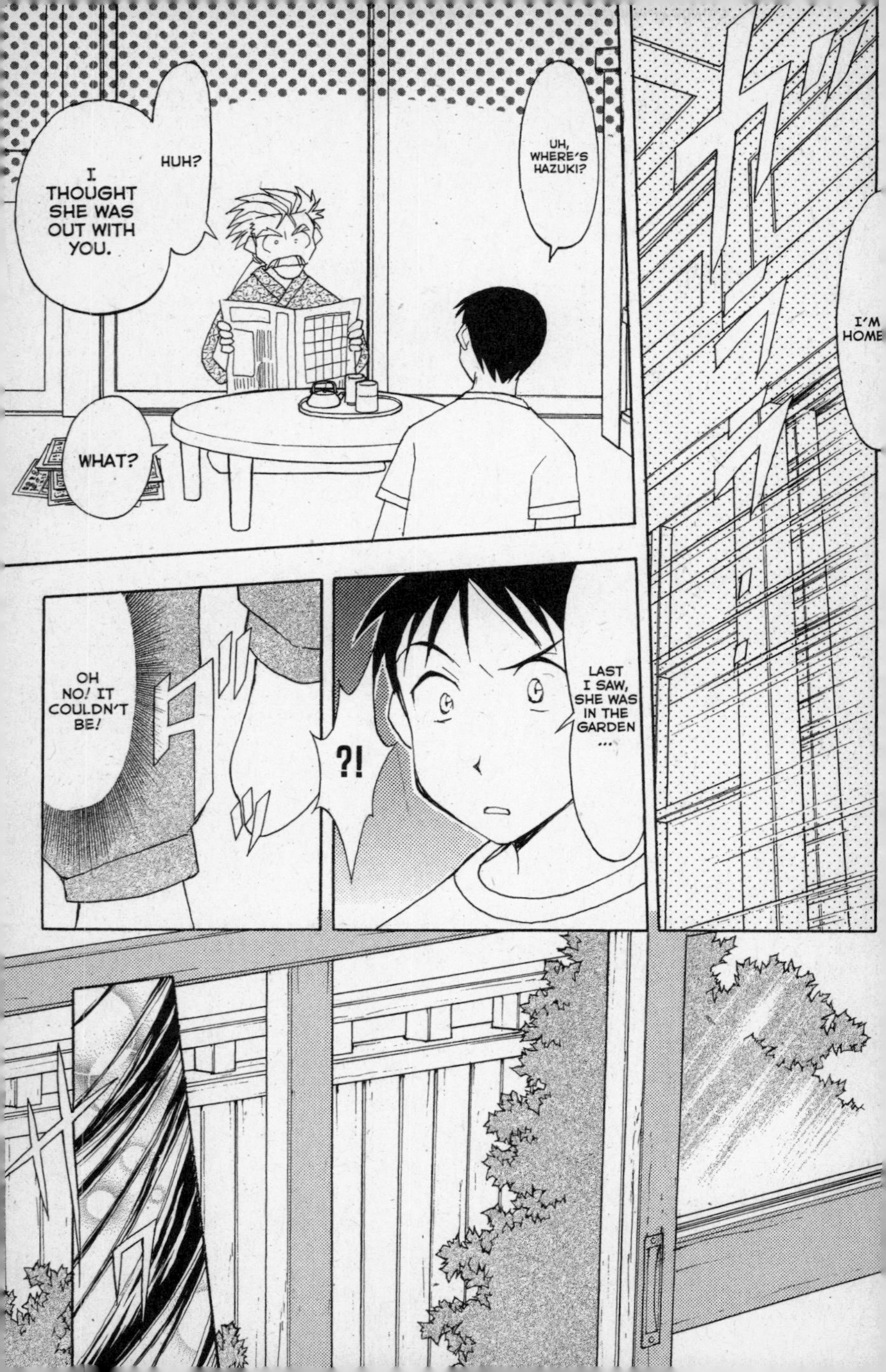
I'M HOME
UH, WHERE'S HAZUKI?
HUH?
I THOUGHT SHE WAS OUT WITH YOU.
WHAT?
LAST I SAW, SHE WAS IN THE GARDEN ...
?!
OH NO! IT COULDN'T BE!

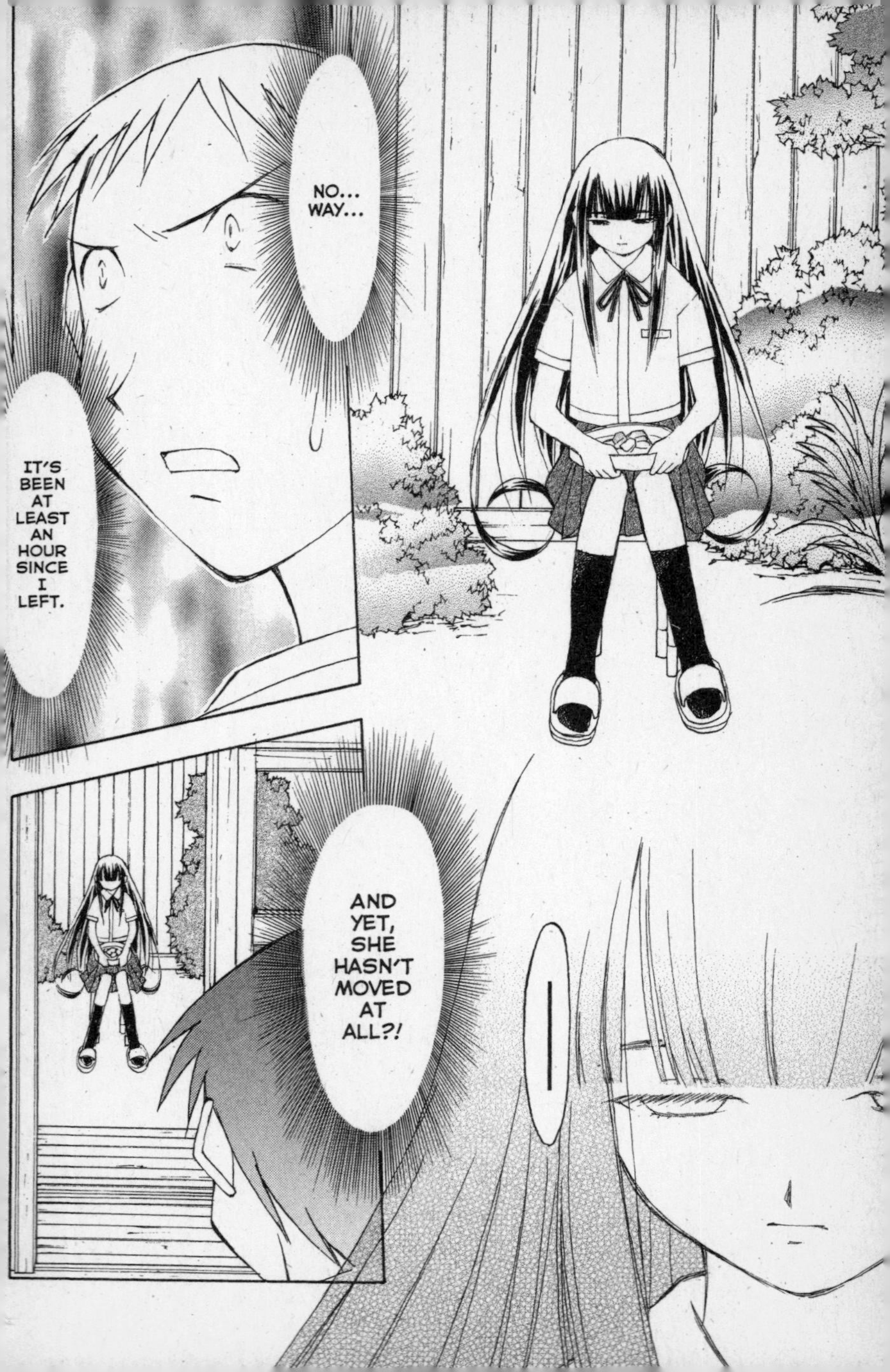
NO... WAY...
IT'S BEEN AT LEAST AN HOUR SINCE I LEFT.
AND YET, SHE HASN'T MOVED AT ALL?!

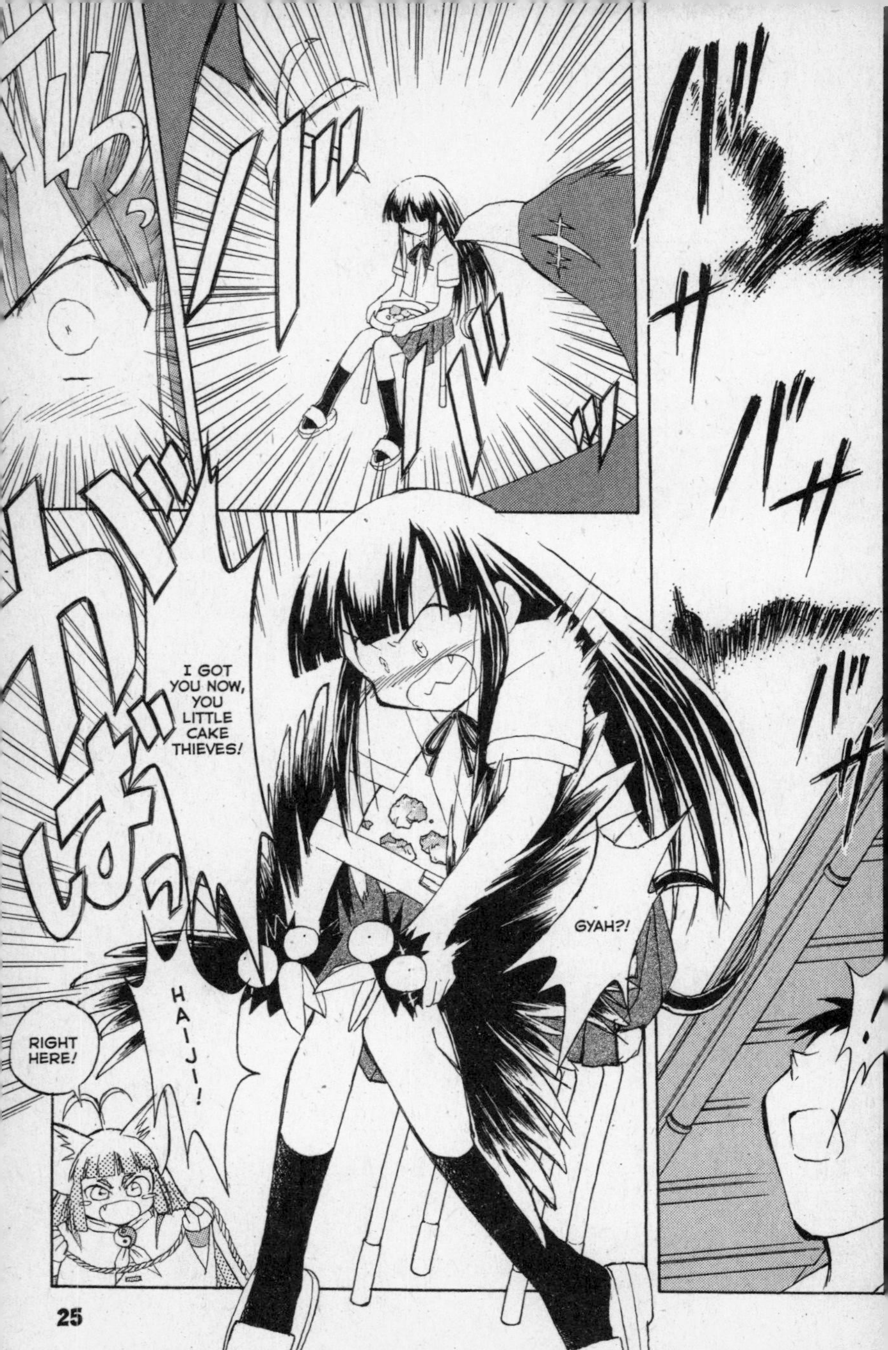
I GOT YOU NOW, YOU LITTLE CAKE THIEVES!
GYAH?!
HAIJI!
RIGHT HERE!

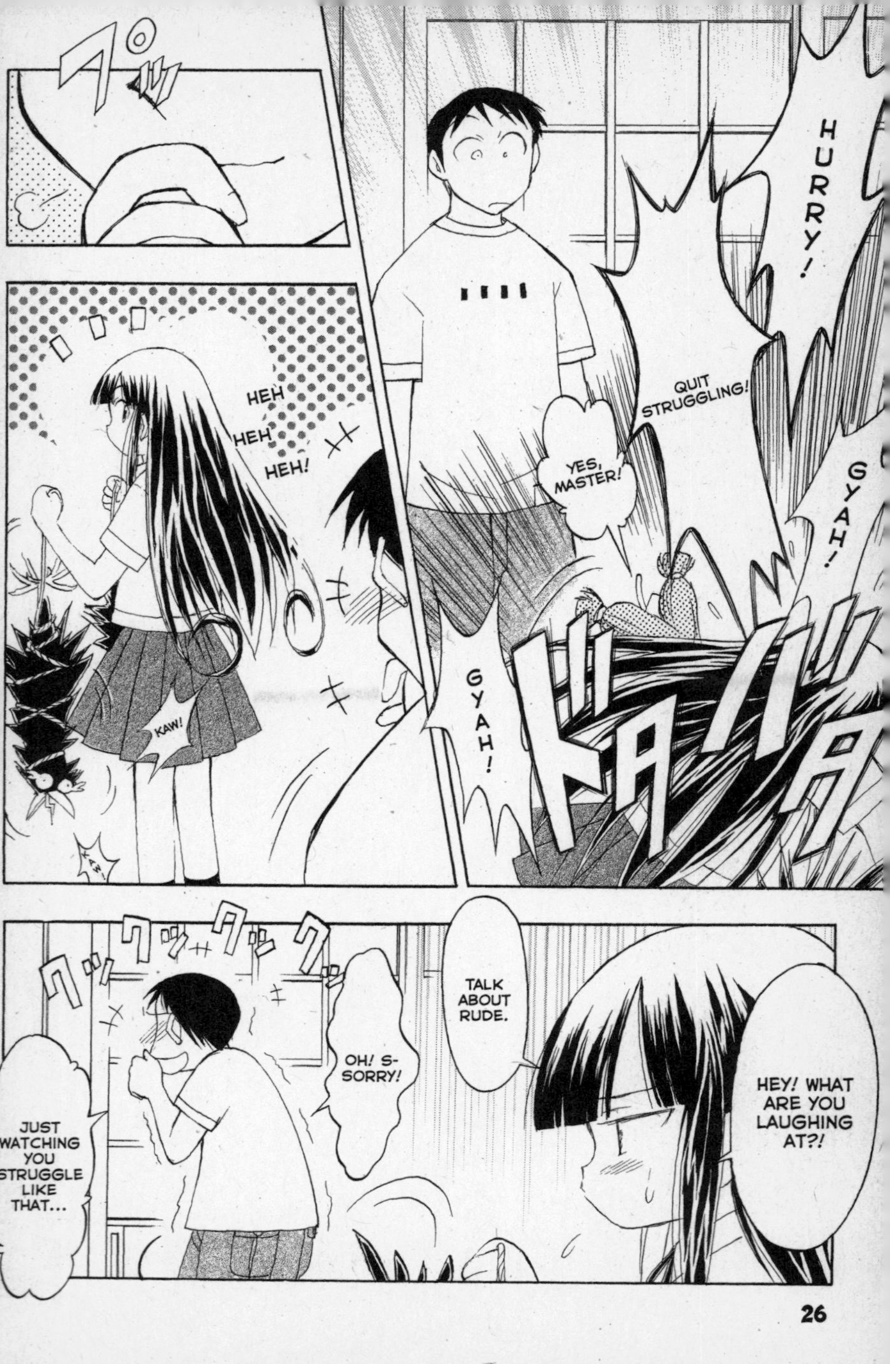
HURRY!
QUIT STRUGGLING!
GYAH!
YES, MASTER!
GYAH!
HEH HEH HEH!
KAW!
HEY! WHAT ARE YOU LAUGHING AT?!
TALK ABOUT RUDE.
OH! S-SORRY!
JUST WATCHING YOU STRUGGLE LIKE THAT...

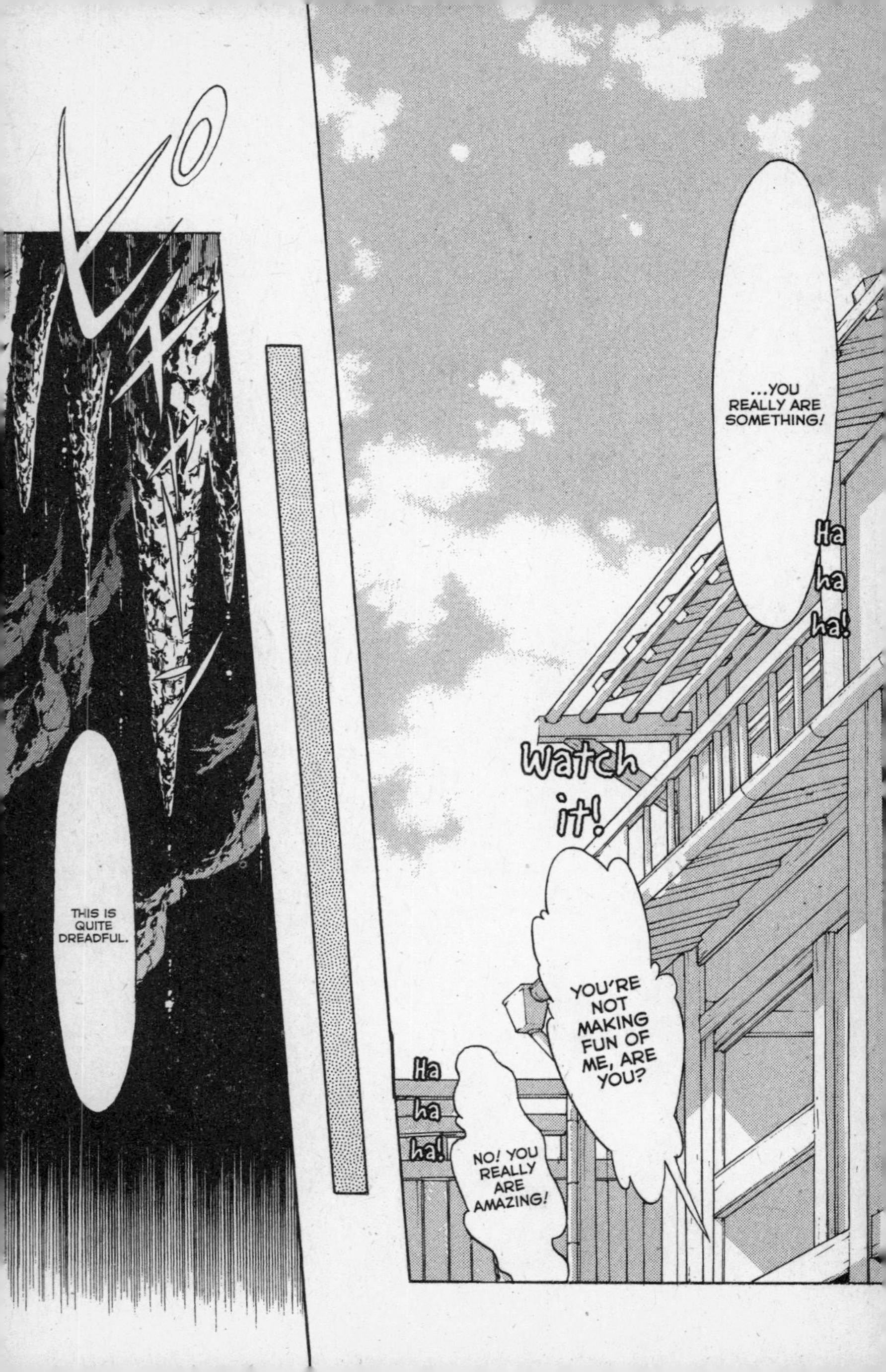
...YOU REALLY ARE SOMETHING!
Ha ha ha!
Watch it!
YOU'RE NOT MAKING FUN OF ME, ARE YOU?
Ha ha ha!
NO! YOU REALLY ARE AMAZING!
THIS IS QUITE DREADFUL.

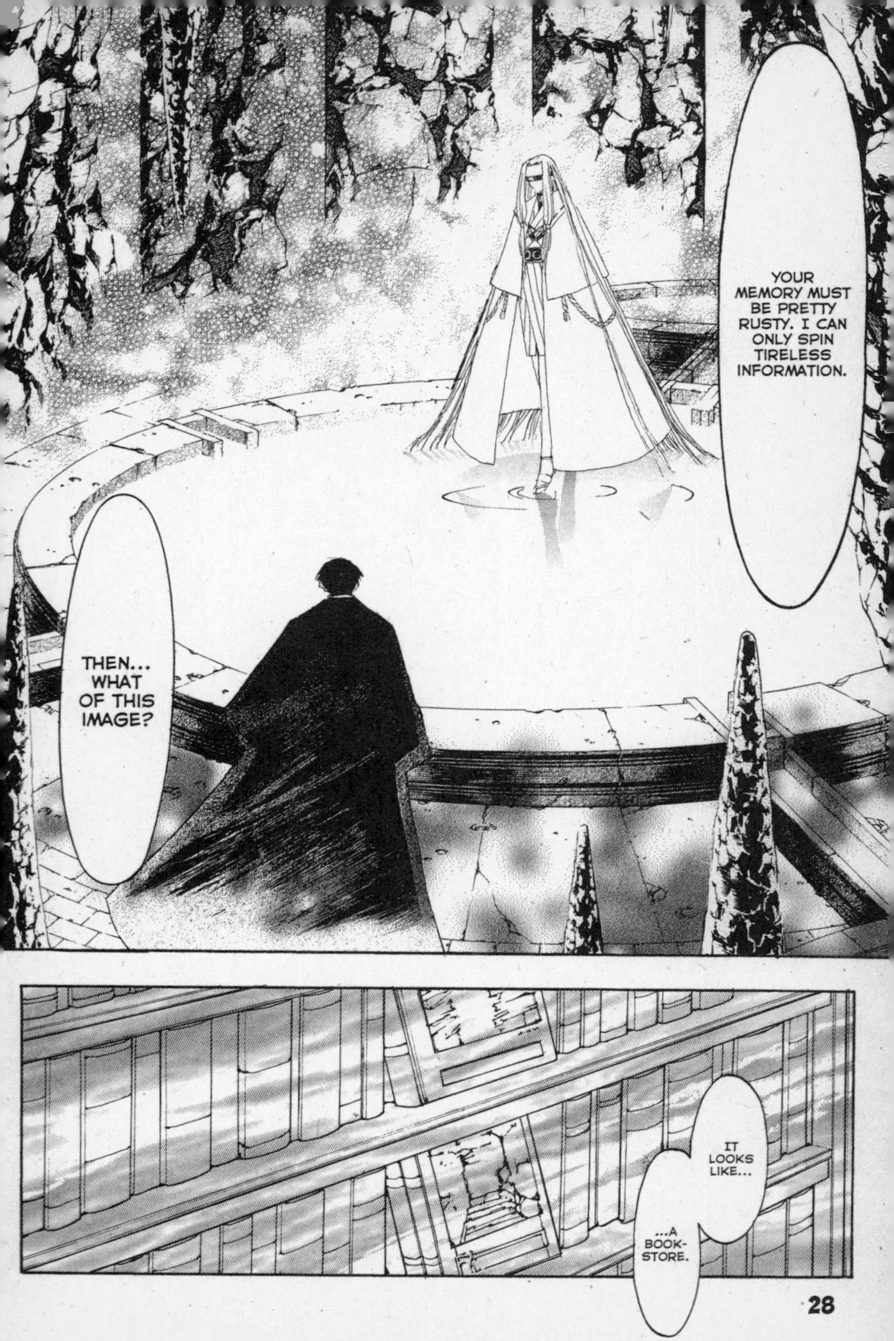
YOUR MEMORY MUST BE PRETTY RUSTY. I CAN ONLY SPIN TIRELESS INFORMATION.
THEN... WHAT OF THIS IMAGE?
IT LOOKS LIKE...
...A BOOKSTORE.

MOON 月詠 PHASE

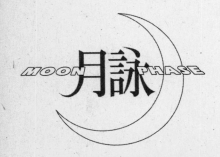

A HUMAN-FACED CAT I FOUND
IN A STRANGE TOWN.

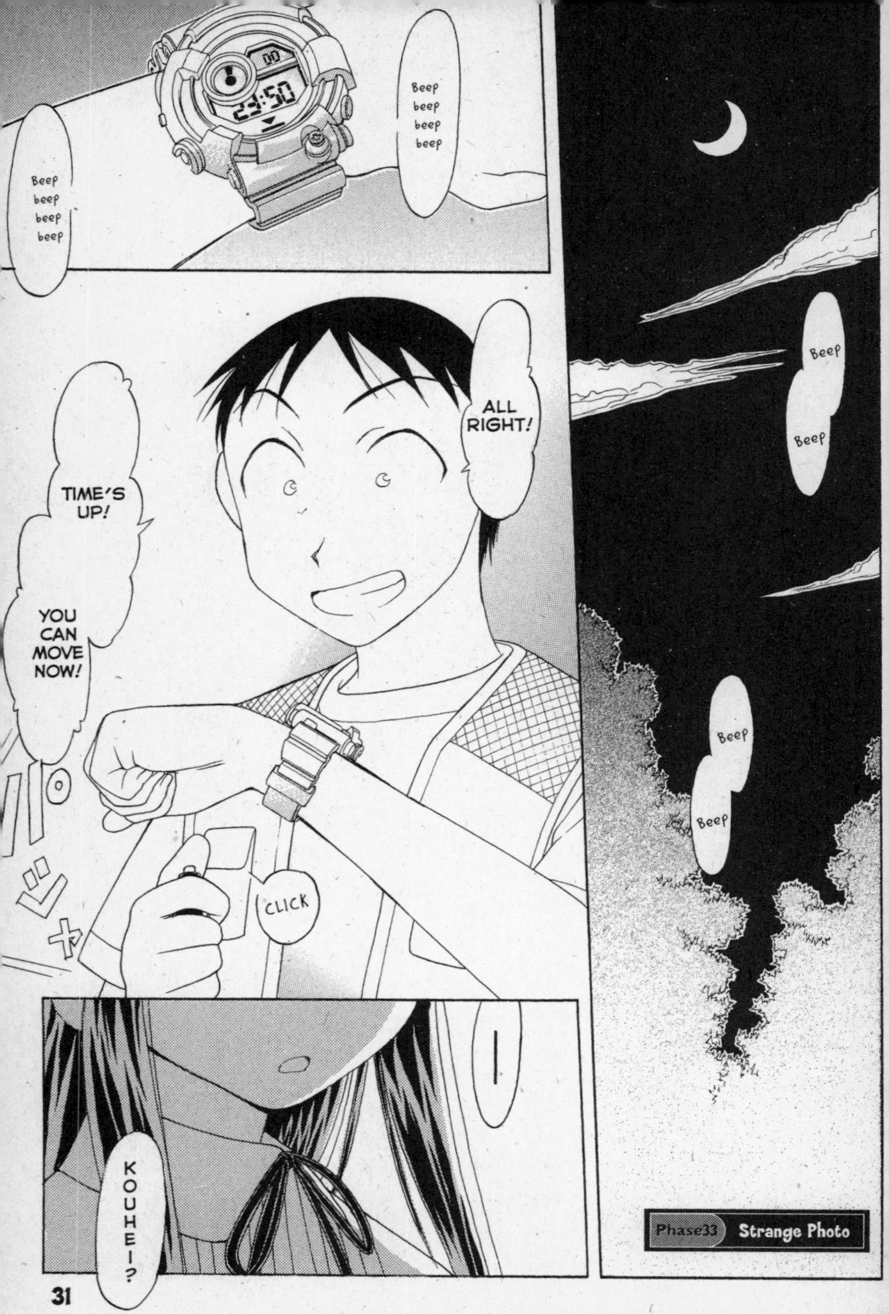
Beep
Beep
Beep
Beep
Phase33 Strange Photo
Beep beep beep beep
Beep beep beep beep
ALL RIGHT!
CLICK
TIME'S UP!
YOU CAN MOVE NOW!
KOUHEI?

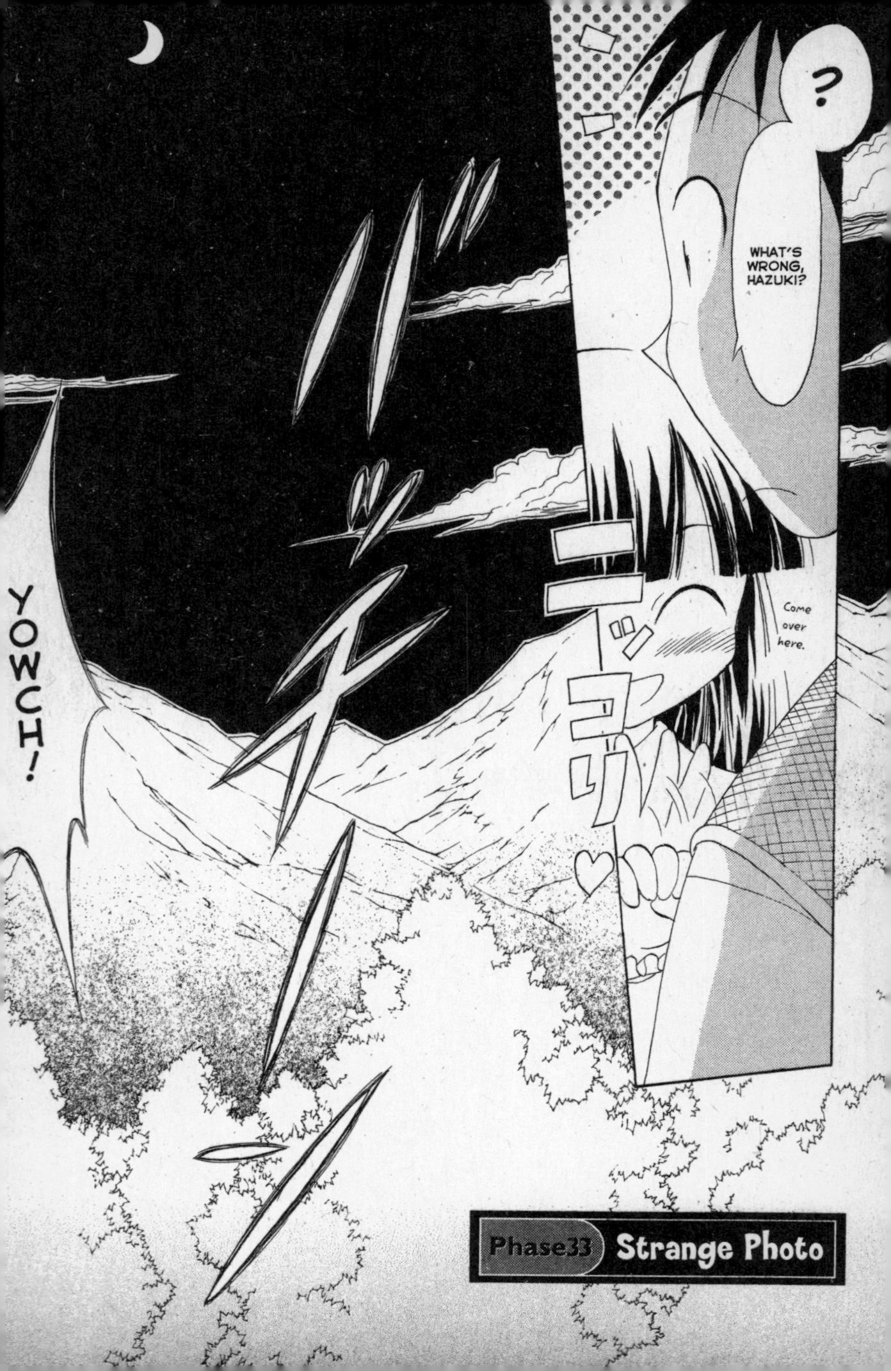
?
WHAT'S WRONG, HAZUKI?
Come over here.
YOWCH!
Phase33 Strange Photo

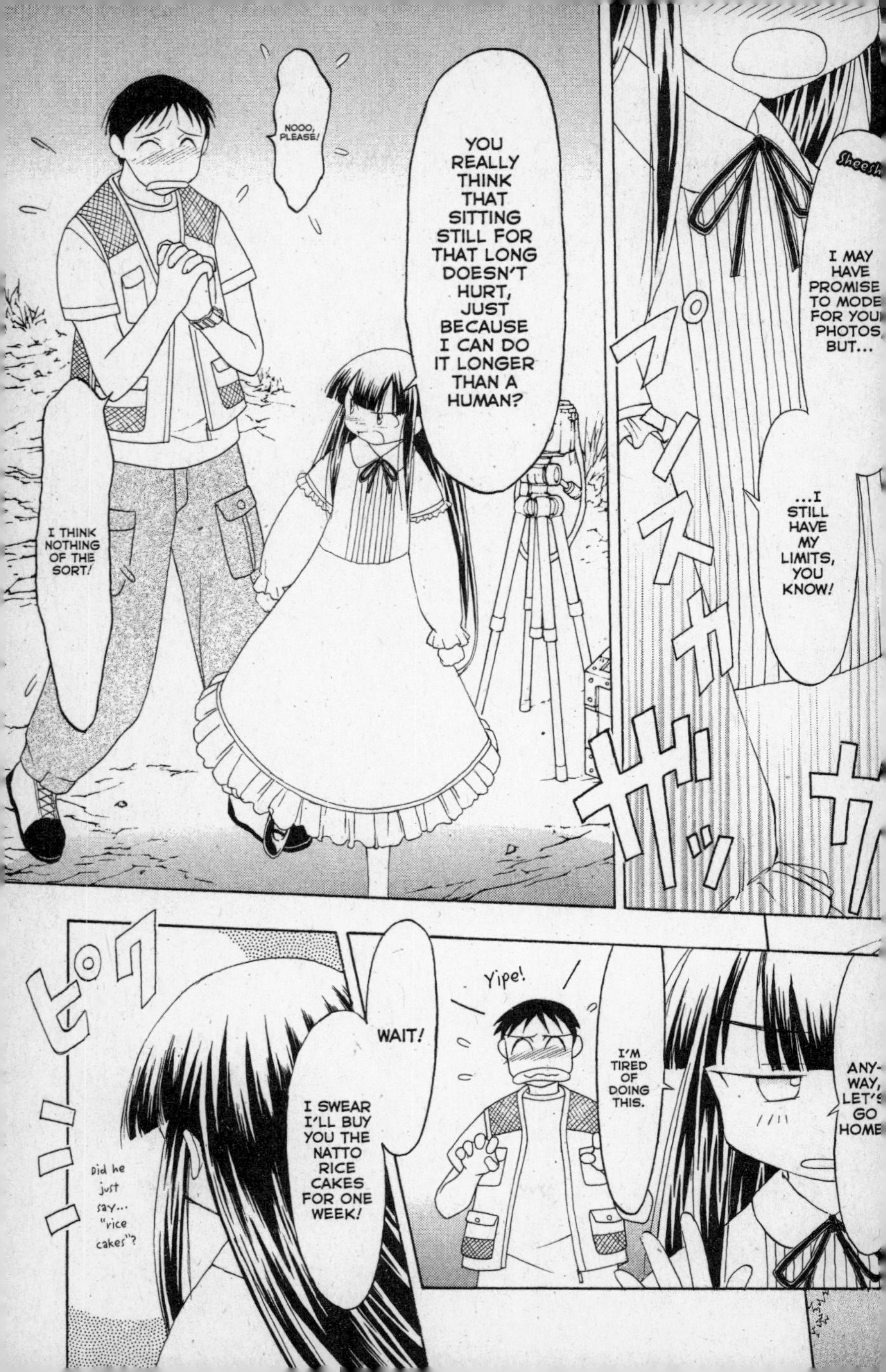
Sheesh
I MAY HAVE PROMISE TO MODE FOR YOU PHOTOS, BUT...
...I STILL HAVE MY LIMITS, YOU KNOW!
YOU REALLY THINK THAT SITTING STILL FOR THAT LONG DOESN'T HURT, JUST BECAUSE I CAN DO IT LONGER THAN A HUMAN?
NOOO, PLEASE!
I THINK NOTHING OF THE SORT!
ANY-WAY, LET'S GO HOME
I'M TIRED OF DOING THIS.
Yipe!
WAIT!
I SWEAR I'LL BUY YOU THE NATTO RICE CAKES FOR ONE WEEK!
Did he just say... "rice cakes"?

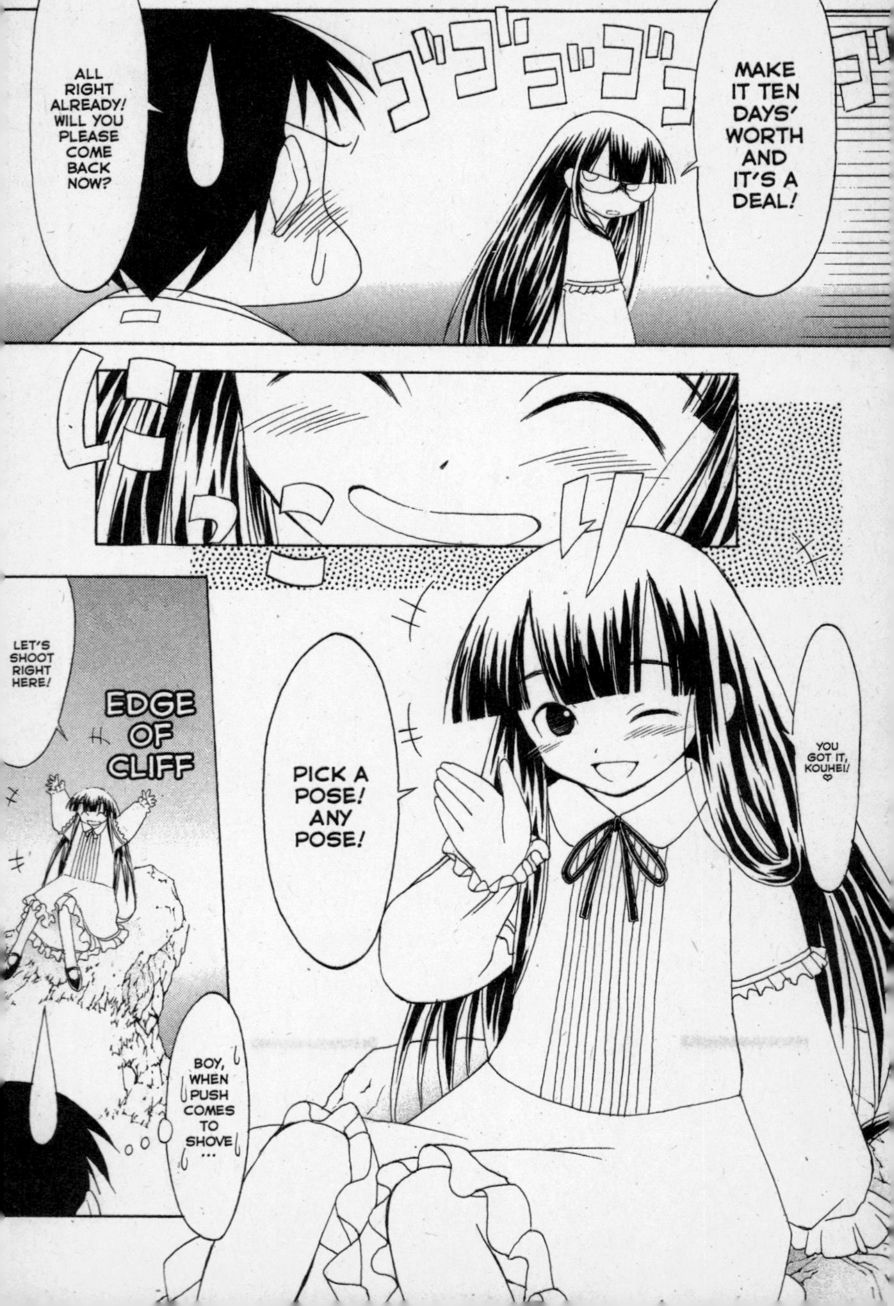
MAKE IT TEN DAYS' WORTH AND IT'S A DEAL!
ALL RIGHT ALREADY! WILL YOU PLEASE COME BACK NOW?
YOU GOT IT, KOUHEI! ♥
PICK A POSE! ANY POSE!
LET'S SHOOT RIGHT HERE!
EDGE OF CLIFF
BOY, WHEN PUSH COMES TO SHOVE...

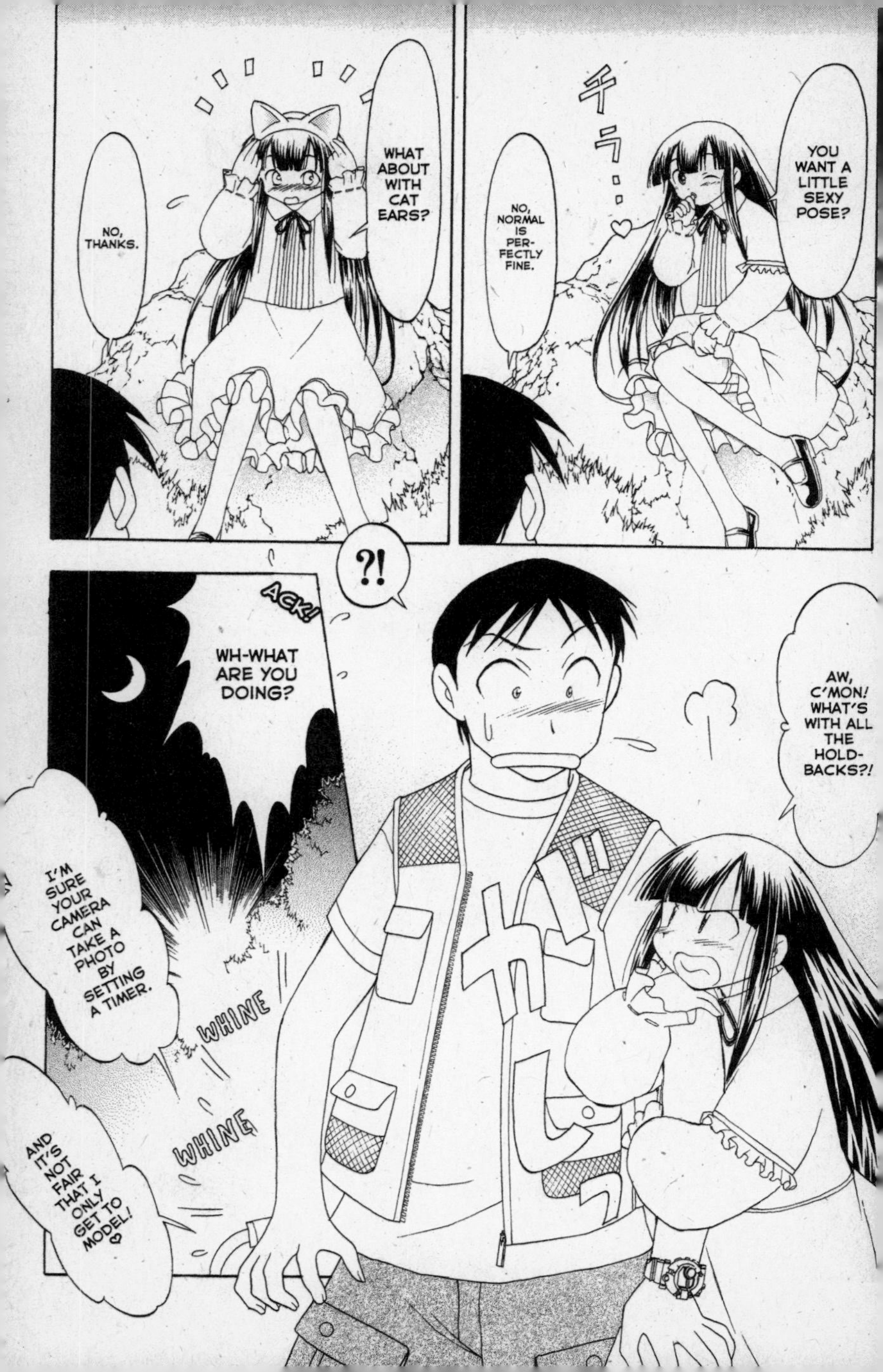
YOU WANT A LITTLE SEXY POSE?
チラ
NO, NORMAL IS PER-FECTLY FINE.
WHAT ABOUT WITH CAT EARS?
NO, THANKS.
AW, C'MON! WHAT'S WITH ALL THE HOLD-BACKS?!
?!
ACK!
WH-WHAT ARE YOU DOING?
I'M SURE YOUR CAMERA CAN TAKE A PHOTO BY SETTING A TIMER.
WHINE
WHINE
AND IT'S NOT FAIR THAT I ONLY GET TO MODEL! ♥

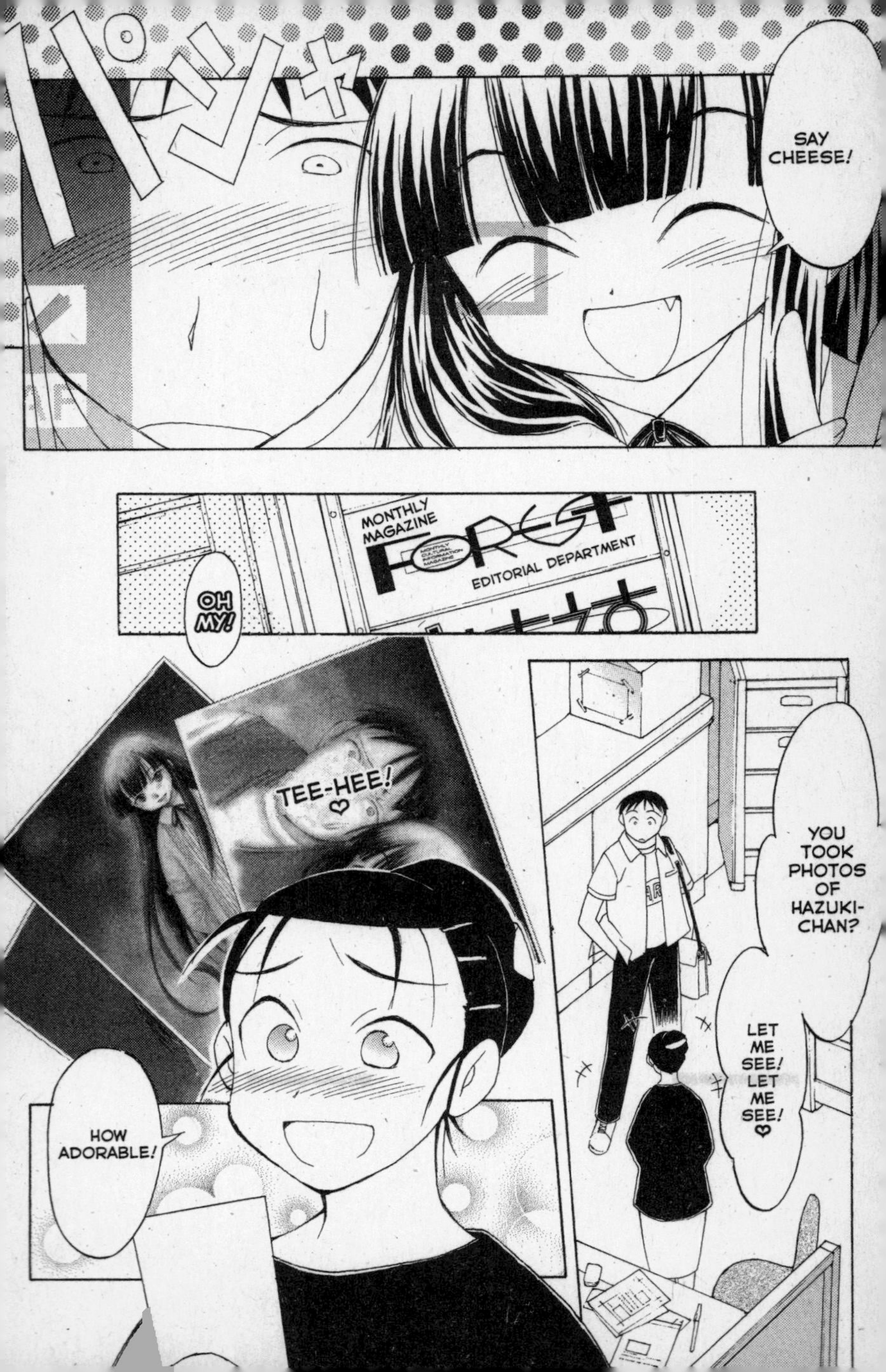
SAY CHEESE!
MONTHLY MAGAZINE
FOREST
EDITORIAL DEPARTMENT
OH MY!
YOU TOOK PHOTOS OF HAZUKI-CHAN?
LET ME SEE! LET ME SEE! ♡
TEE-HEE! ♡
HOW ADORABLE!

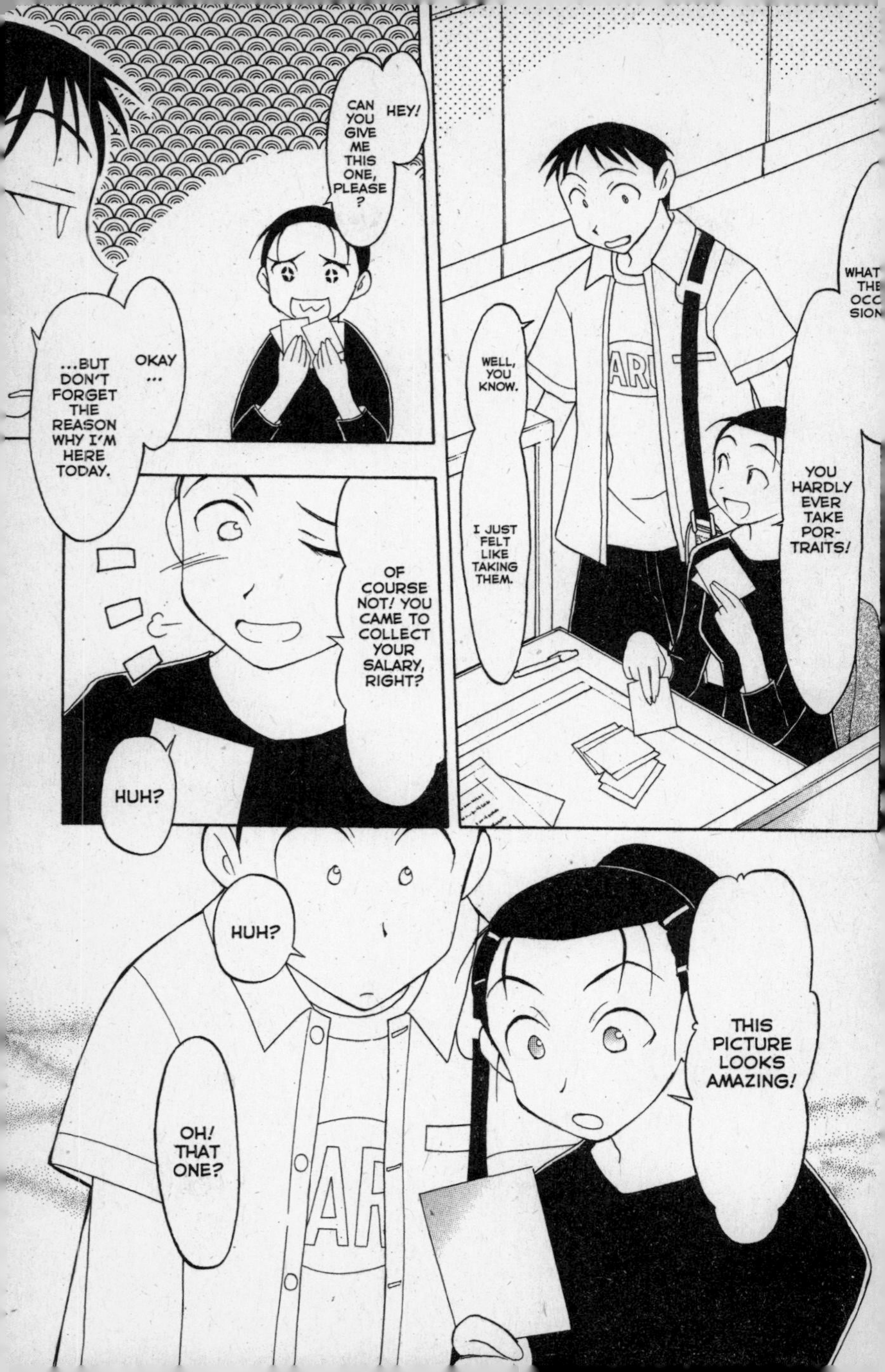
WHAT THE OCC SION
YOU HARDLY EVER TAKE POR-TRAITS!
WELL, YOU KNOW.
I JUST FELT LIKE TAKING THEM.
HEY!
CAN YOU GIVE ME THIS ONE, PLEASE?
OKAY...
...BUT DON'T FORGET THE REASON WHY I'M HERE TODAY.
OF COURSE NOT! YOU CAME TO COLLECT YOUR SALARY, RIGHT?
HUH?
THIS PICTURE LOOKS AMAZING!
HUH?
OH! THAT ONE?

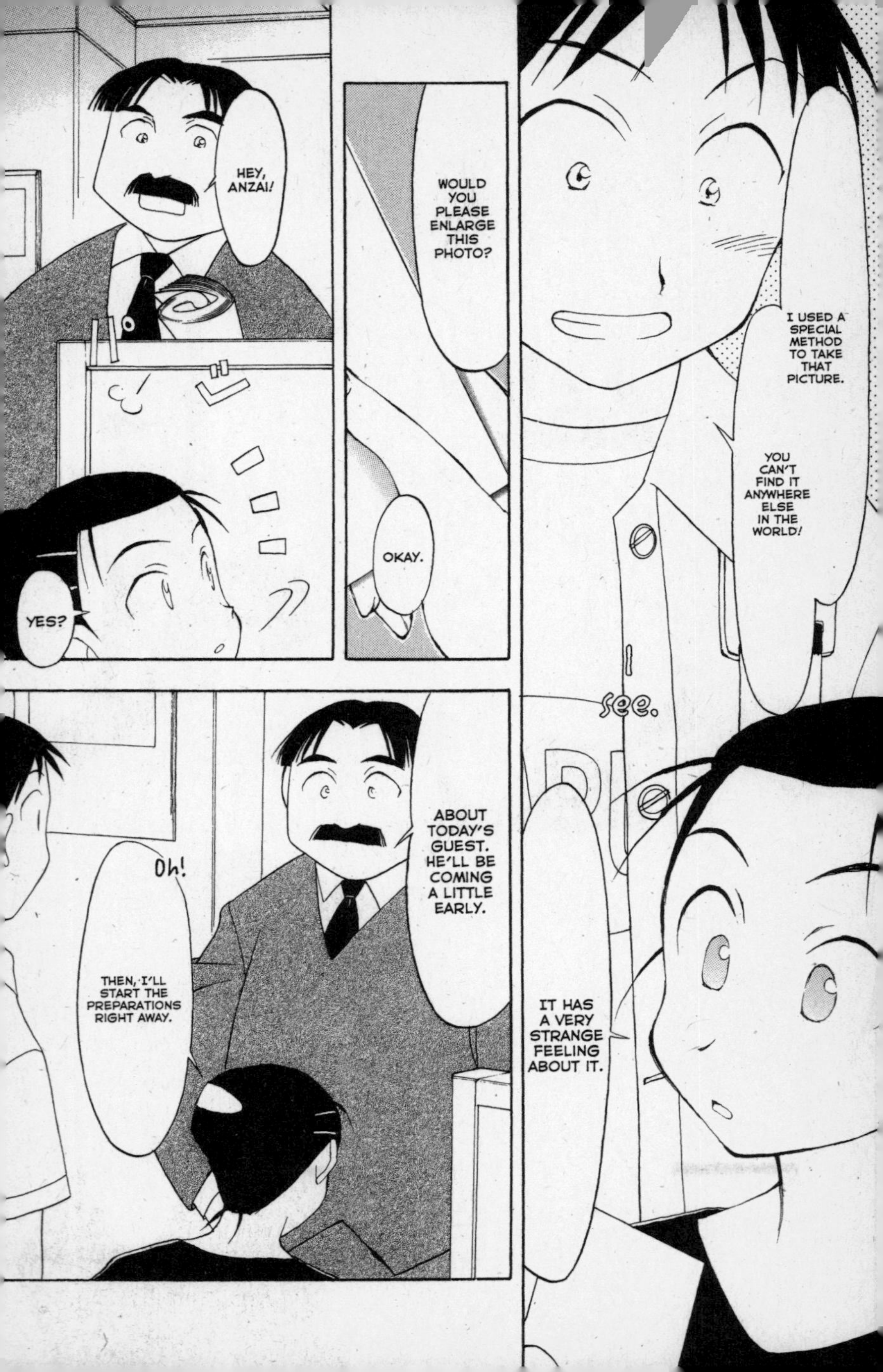
I USED A SPECIAL METHOD TO TAKE THAT PICTURE.
YOU CAN'T FIND IT ANYWHERE ELSE IN THE WORLD!
I see.
IT HAS A VERY STRANGE FEELING ABOUT IT.
WOULD YOU PLEASE ENLARGE THIS PHOTO?
OKAY.
HEY, ANZAI!
YES?
ABOUT TODAY'S GUEST. HE'LL BE COMING A LITTLE EARLY.
Oh!
THEN, I'LL START THE PREPARATIONS RIGHT AWAY.

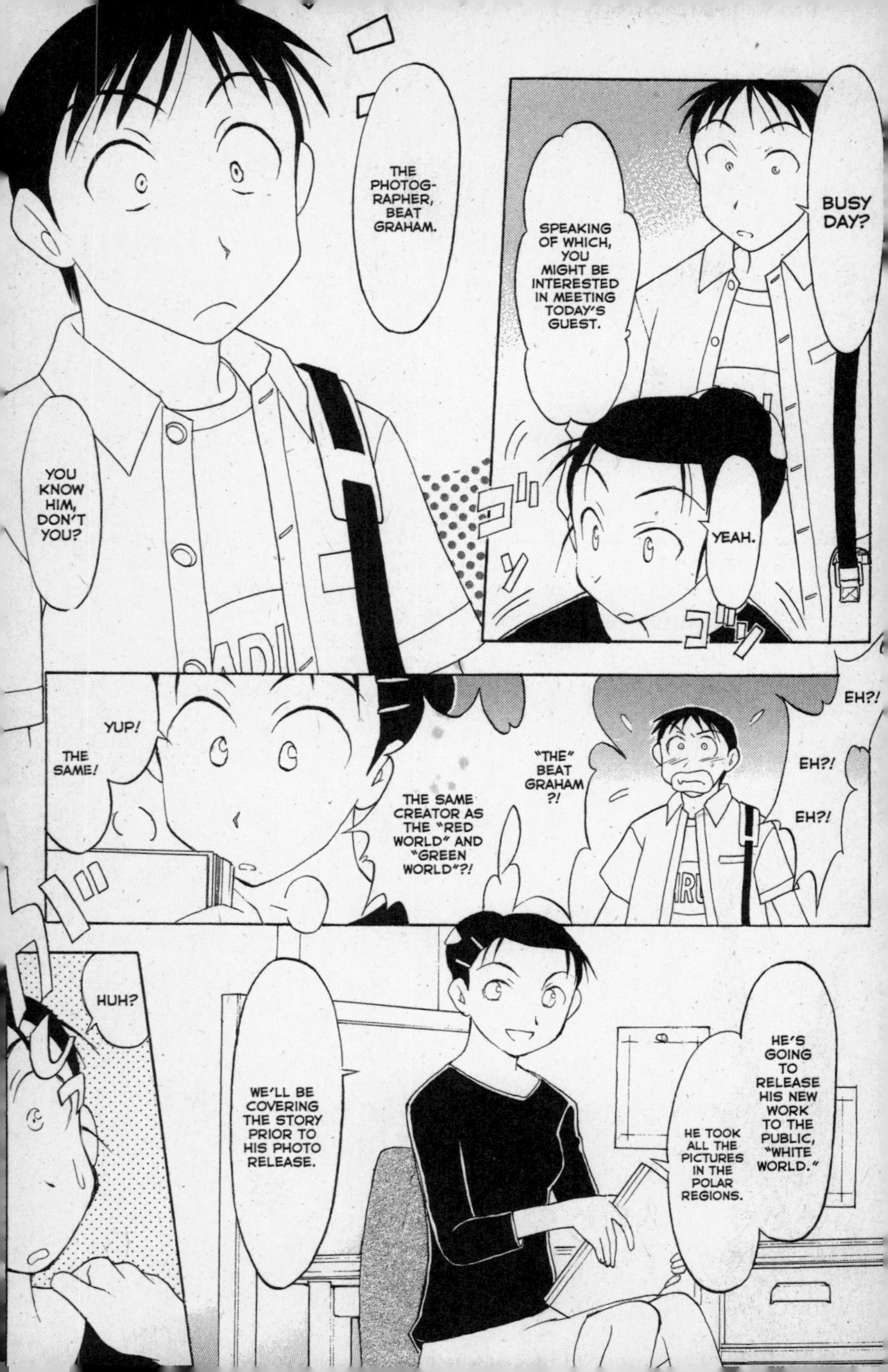
BUSY DAY?
YEAH.
SPEAKING OF WHICH, YOU MIGHT BE INTERESTED IN MEETING TODAY'S GUEST.
THE PHOTOG-RAPHER, BEAT GRAHAM.
YOU KNOW HIM, DON'T YOU?
EH?!
EH?!
EH?!
"THE" BEAT GRAHAM ?!
THE SAME CREATOR AS THE "RED WORLD" AND "GREEN WORLD"?!
YUP!
THE SAME!
HE'S GOING TO RELEASE HIS NEW WORK TO THE PUBLIC, "WHITE WORLD."
HE TOOK ALL THE PICTURES IN THE POLAR REGIONS.
WE'LL BE COVERING THE STORY PRIOR TO HIS PHOTO RELEASE.
HUH?

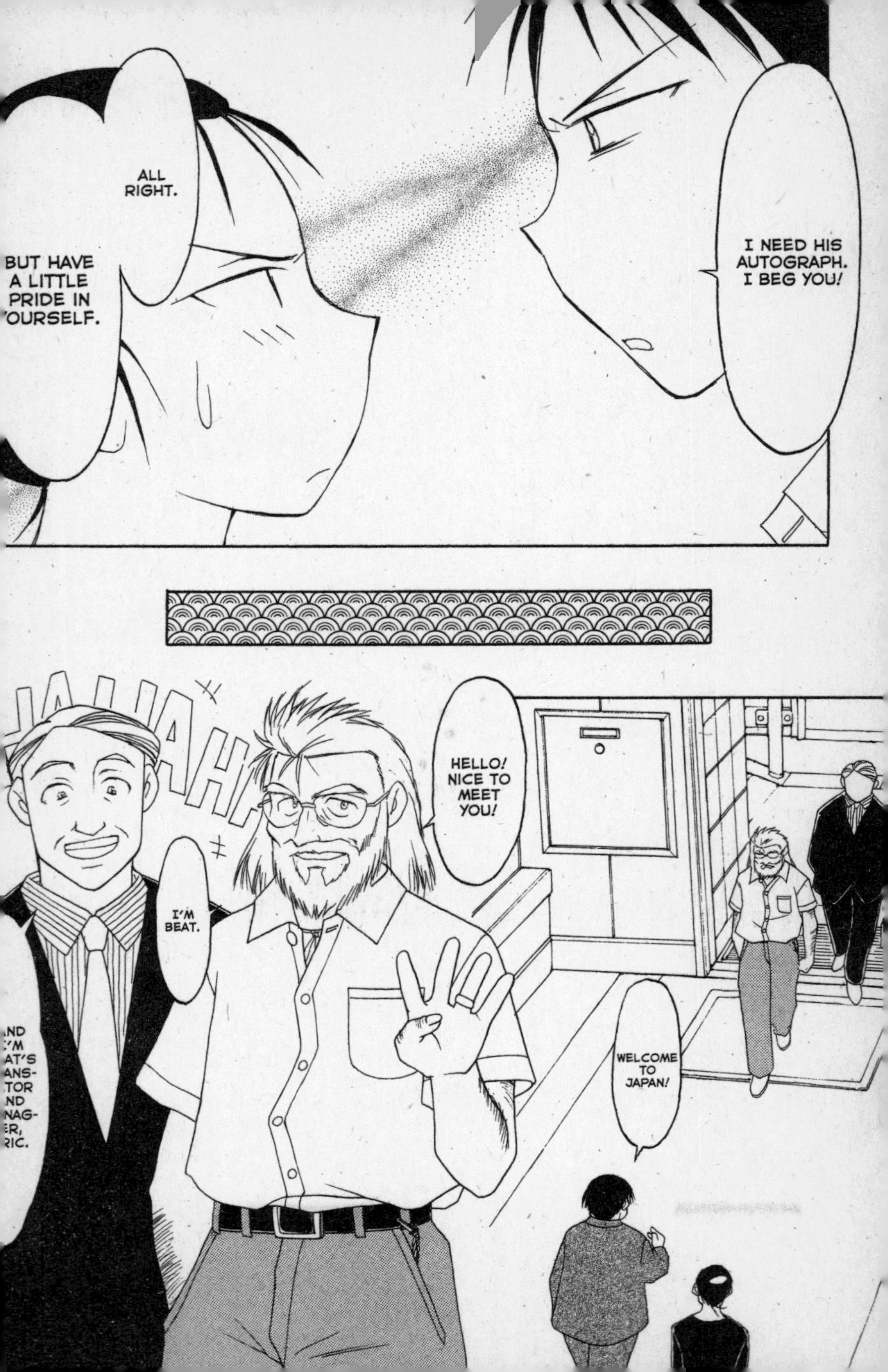
I NEED HIS AUTOGRAPH. I BEG YOU!
ALL RIGHT.
BUT HAVE A LITTLE PRIDE IN YOURSELF.
WELCOME TO JAPAN!
HELLO! NICE TO MEET YOU!
I'M BEAT.

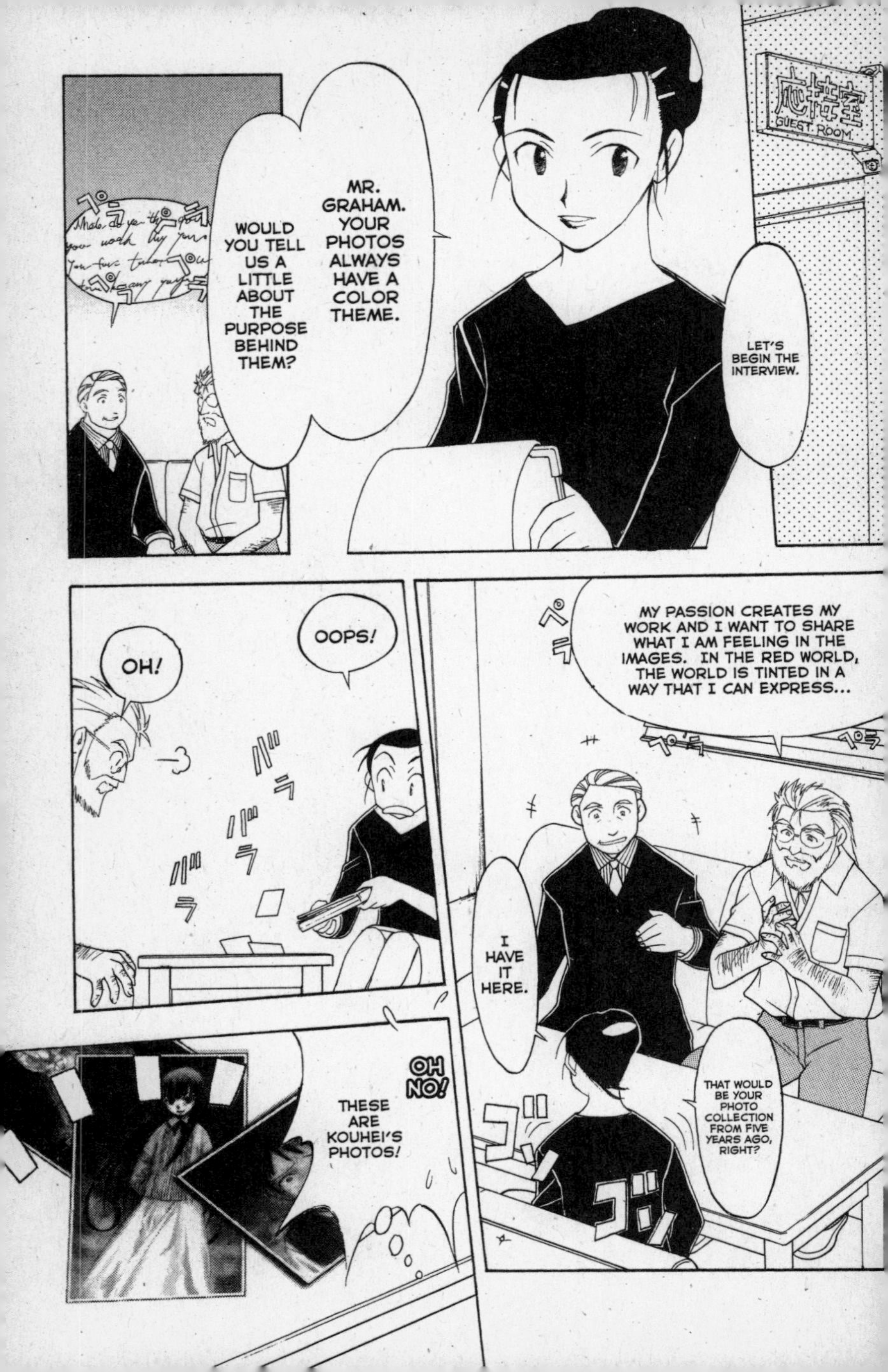

GUEST ROOM
LET'S BEGIN THE INTERVIEW.
MR. GRAHAM. YOUR PHOTOS ALWAYS HAVE A COLOR THEME.
WOULD YOU TELL US A LITTLE ABOUT THE PURPOSE BEHIND THEM?
MY PASSION CREATES MY WORK AND I WANT TO SHARE WHAT I AM FEELING IN THE IMAGES. IN THE RED WORLD, THE WORLD IS TINTED IN A WAY THAT I CAN EXPRESS...
I HAVE IT HERE.
THAT WOULD BE YOUR PHOTO COLLECTION FROM FIVE YEARS AGO, RIGHT?
OOPS!
OH!
OH NO!
THESE ARE KOUHEI'S PHOTOS!

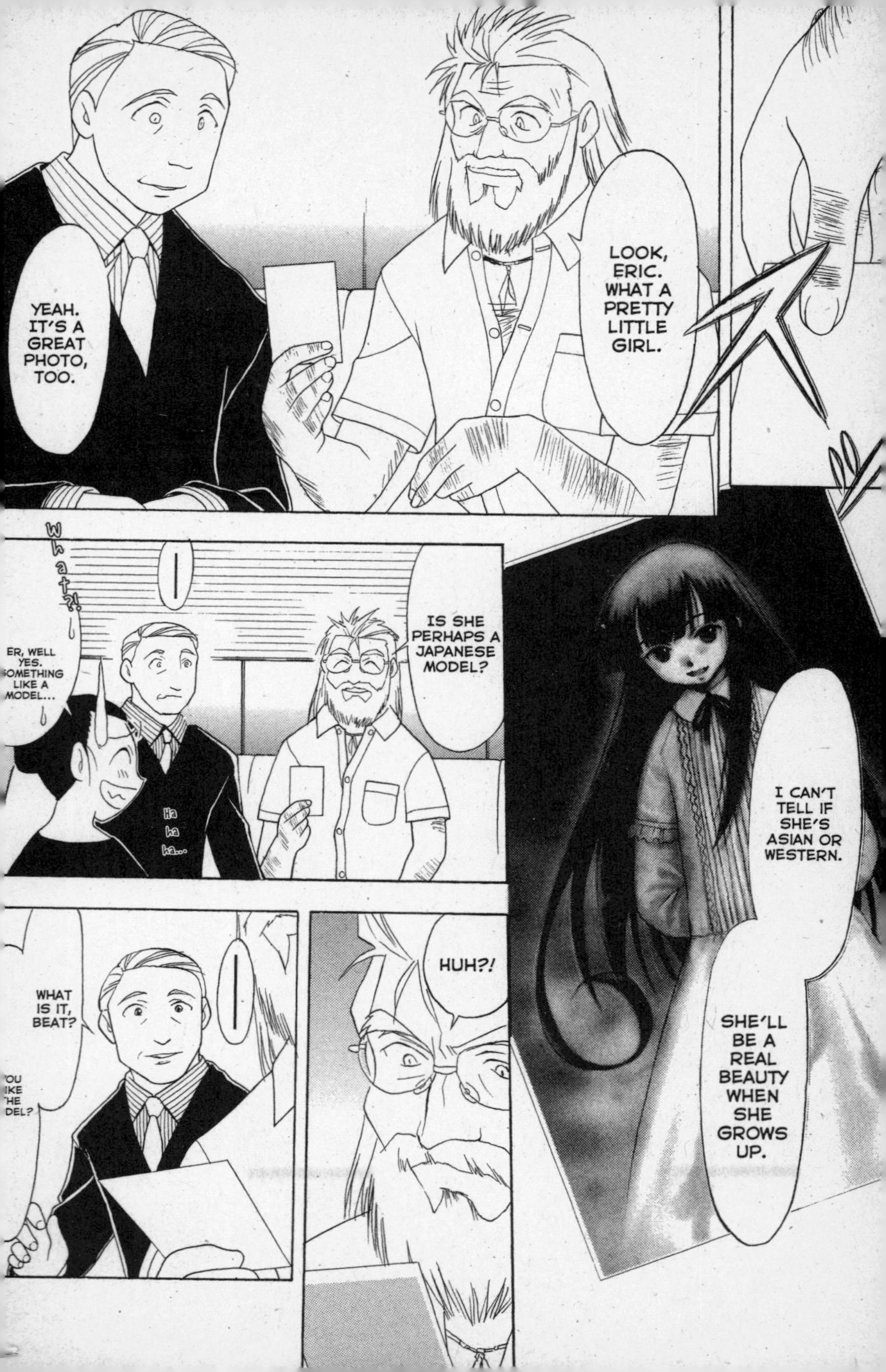
LOOK, ERIC. WHAT A PRETTY LITTLE GIRL.
YEAH. IT'S A GREAT PHOTO, TOO.
I CAN'T TELL IF SHE'S ASIAN OR WESTERN.
SHE'LL BE A REAL BEAUTY WHEN SHE GROWS UP.
IS SHE PERHAPS A JAPANESE MODEL?
What?!
ER, WELL YES. SOMETHING LIKE A MODEL...
Ha ha ha...
HUH?!
WHAT IS IT, BEAT?

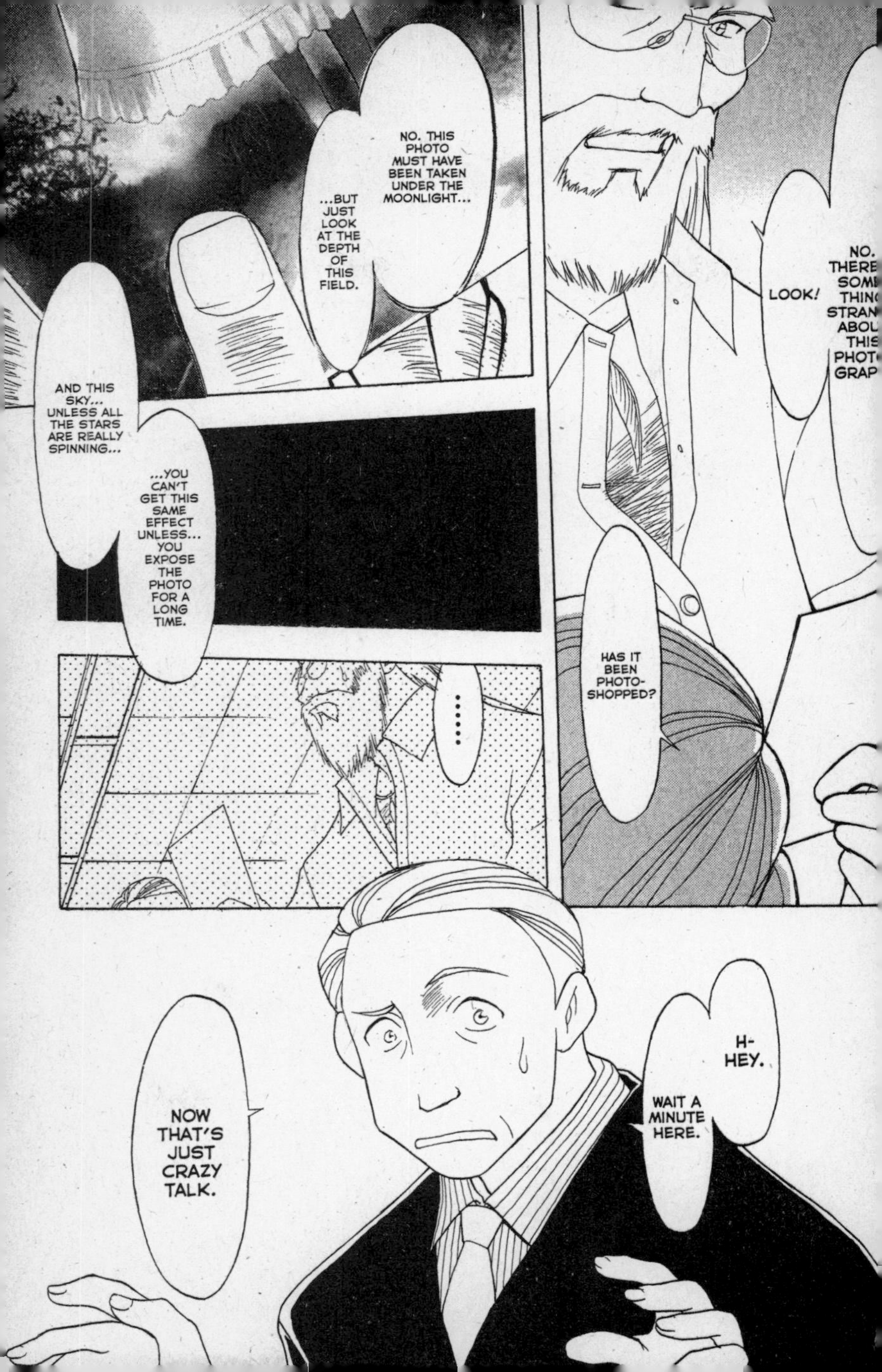
NO. THERE SOME THIN STRAN ABOU THIS PHOT GRAP
LOOK!
NO. THIS PHOTO MUST HAVE BEEN TAKEN UNDER THE MOONLIGHT...
...BUT JUST LOOK AT THE DEPTH OF THIS FIELD.
AND THIS SKY... UNLESS ALL THE STARS ARE REALLY SPINNING...
...YOU CAN'T GET THIS SAME EFFECT UNLESS... YOU EXPOSE THE PHOTO FOR A LONG TIME.
HAS IT BEEN PHOTO-SHOPPED?
......
H-HEY.
WAIT A MINUTE HERE.
NOW THAT'S JUST CRAZY TALK.

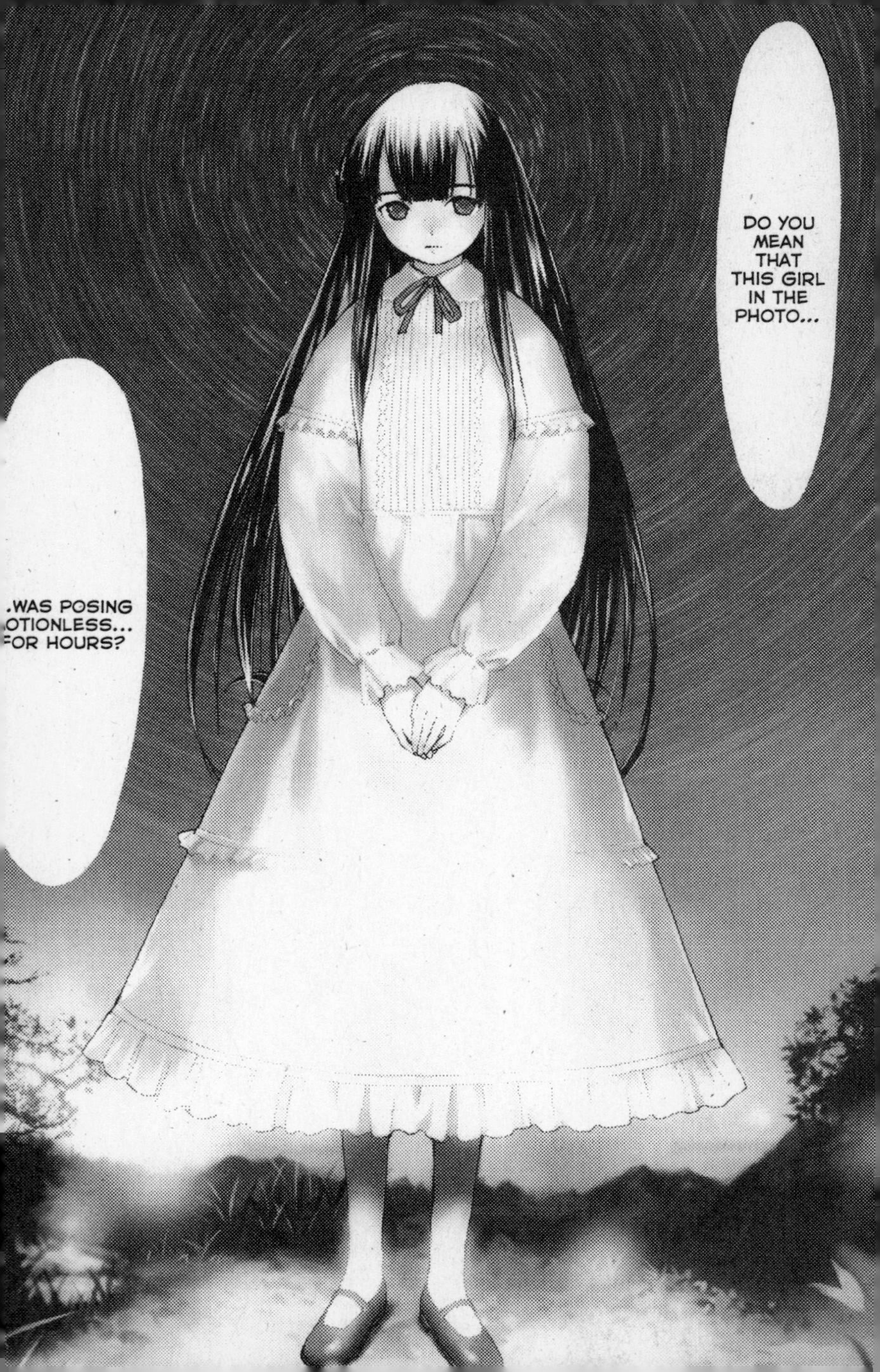
DO YOU MEAN THAT THIS GIRL IN THE PHOTO...
.WAS POSING OTIONLESS... FOR HOURS?

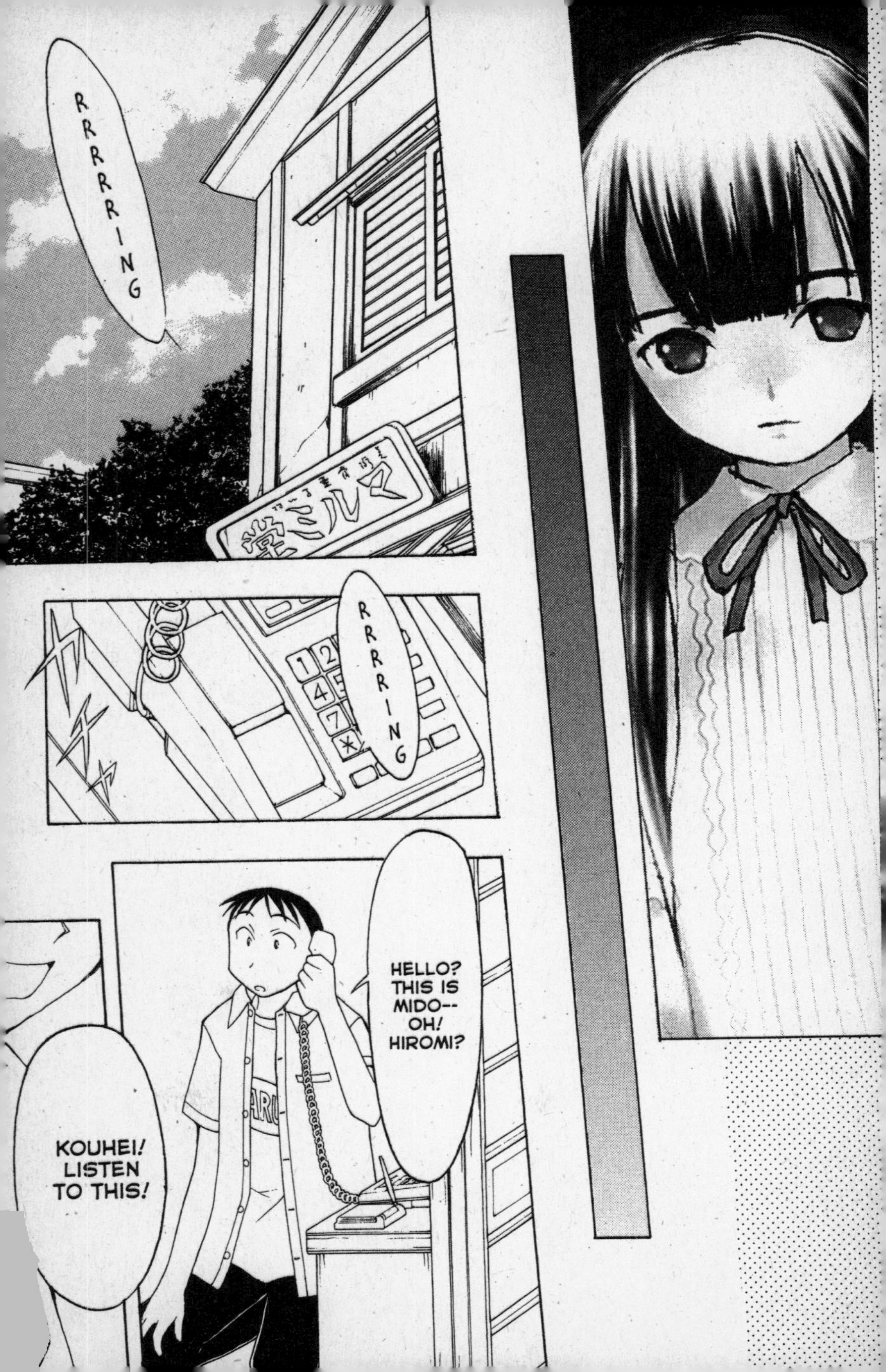
RRRRRING
RRRRING
HELLO? THIS IS MIDO-- OH! HIROMI?
KOUHEI! LISTEN TO THIS!

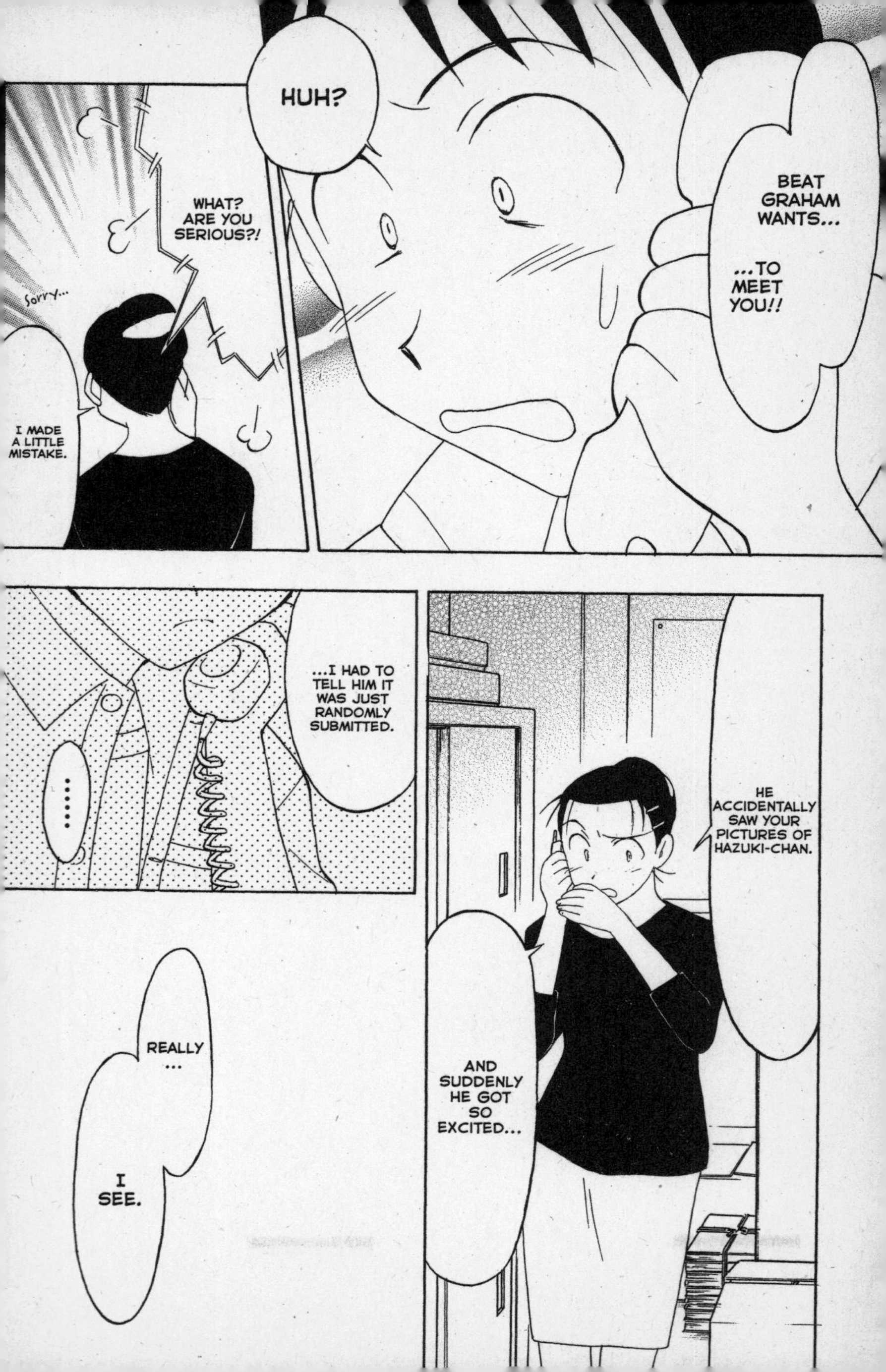
BEAT GRAHAM WANTS...
...TO MEET YOU!!
HUH?
WHAT? ARE YOU SERIOUS?!
Sorry...
I MADE A LITTLE MISTAKE.
HE ACCIDENTALLY SAW YOUR PICTURES OF HAZUKI-CHAN.
AND SUDDENLY HE GOT SO EXCITED...
...I HAD TO TELL HIM IT WAS JUST RANDOMLY SUBMITTED.
......
REALLY ... I SEE.

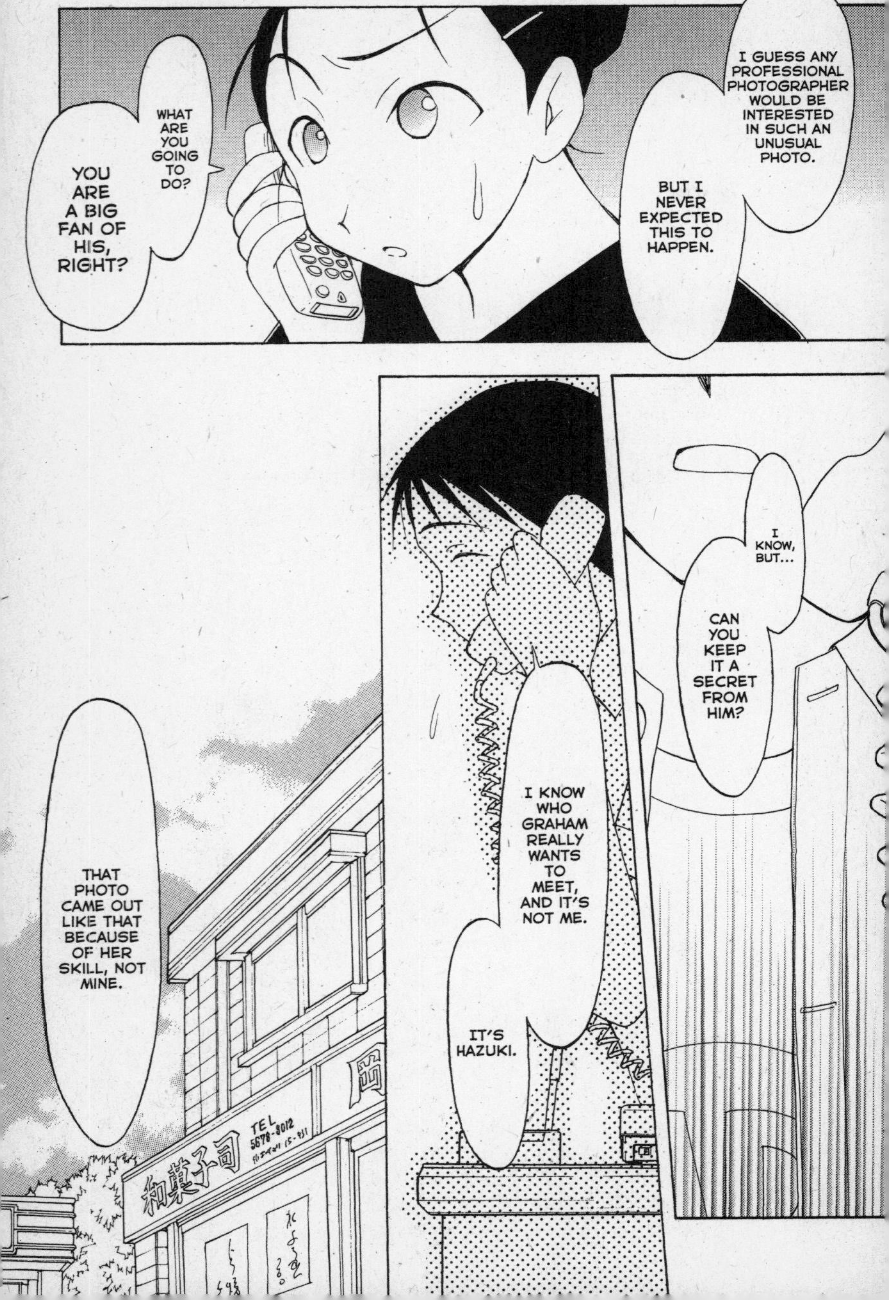
I GUESS ANY PROFESSIONAL PHOTOGRAPHER WOULD BE INTERESTED IN SUCH AN UNUSUAL PHOTO.
BUT I NEVER EXPECTED THIS TO HAPPEN.
WHAT ARE YOU GOING TO DO?
YOU ARE A BIG FAN OF HIS, RIGHT?
I KNOW, BUT...
CAN YOU KEEP IT A SECRET FROM HIM?
I KNOW WHO GRAHAM REALLY WANTS TO MEET, AND IT'S NOT ME.
IT'S HAZUKI.
THAT PHOTO CAME OUT LIKE THAT BECAUSE OF HER SKILL, NOT MINE.
TEL 5678-8012
和菓子司

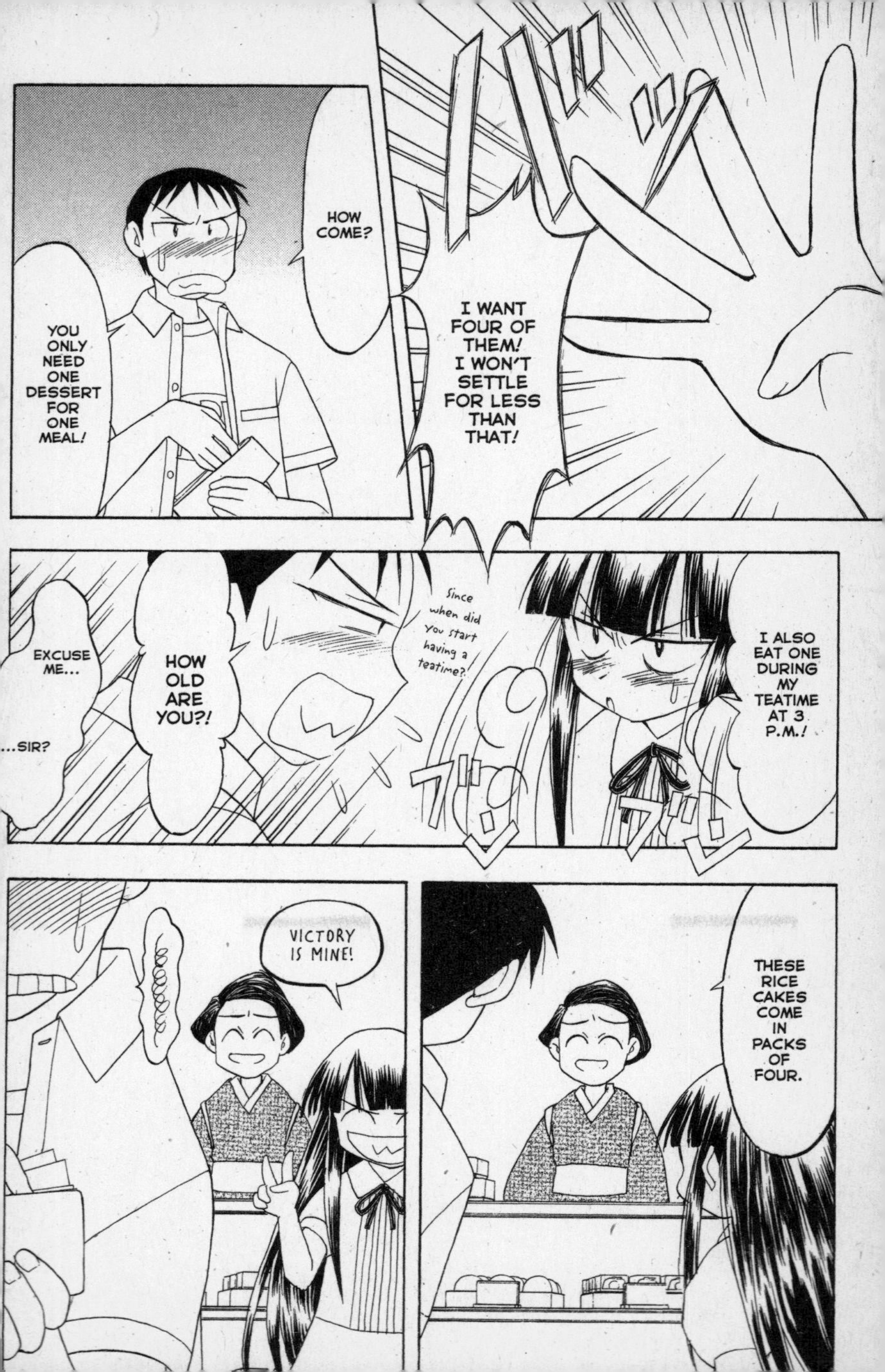
I WANT FOUR OF THEM! I WON'T SETTLE FOR LESS THAN THAT!
HOW COME?
YOU ONLY NEED ONE DESSERT FOR ONE MEAL!
I ALSO EAT ONE DURING MY TEATIME AT 3 P.M.!
Since when did you start having a teatime?
HOW OLD ARE YOU?!
EXCUSE ME...
...SIR?
THESE RICE CAKES COME IN PACKS OF FOUR.
VICTORY IS MINE!

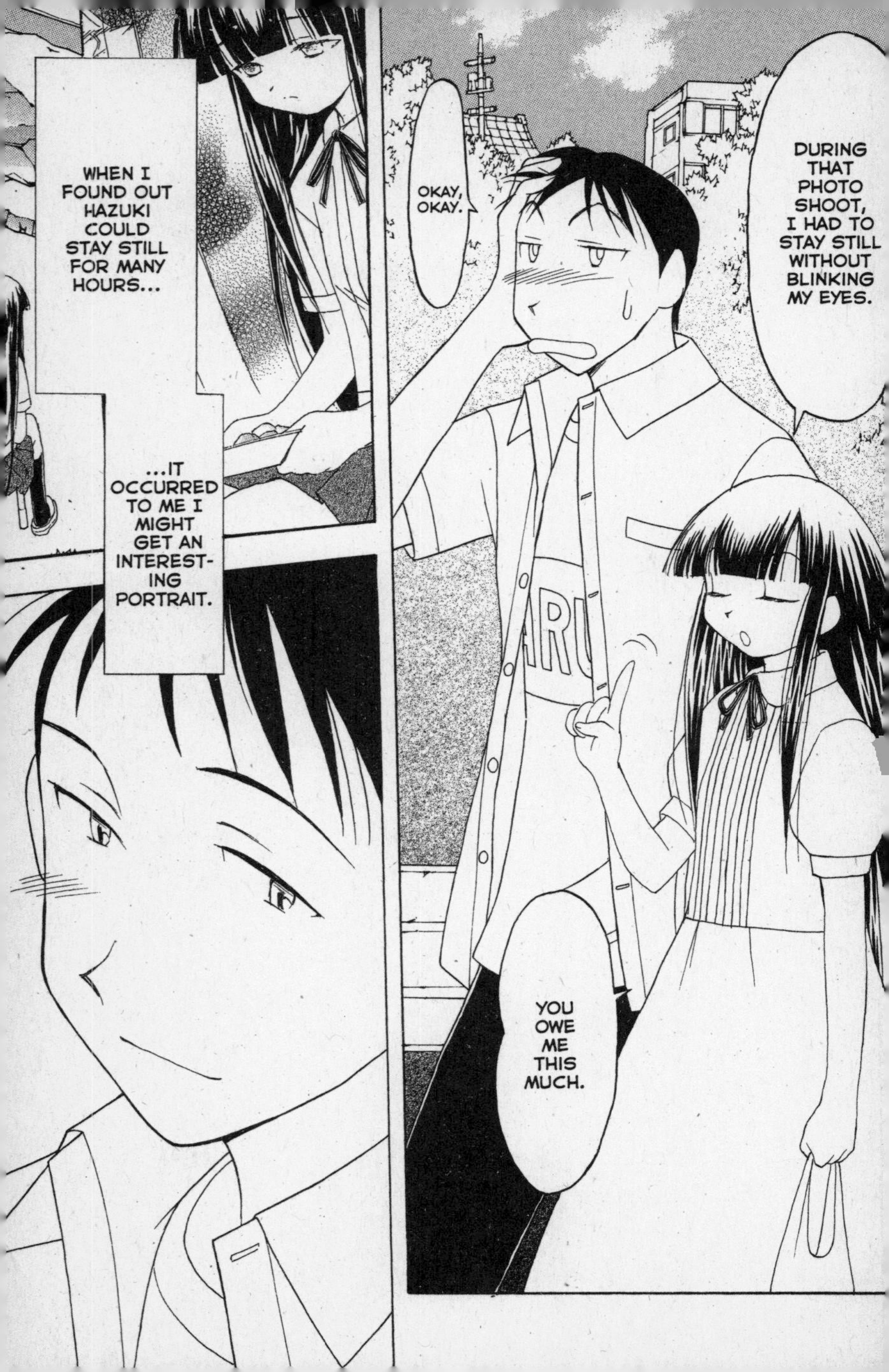
DURING THAT PHOTO SHOOT, I HAD TO STAY STILL WITHOUT BLINKING MY EYES.
OKAY, OKAY.
YOU OWE ME THIS MUCH.
WHEN I FOUND OUT HAZUKI COULD STAY STILL FOR MANY HOURS...
...IT OCCURRED TO ME I MIGHT GET AN INTERESTING PORTRAIT.

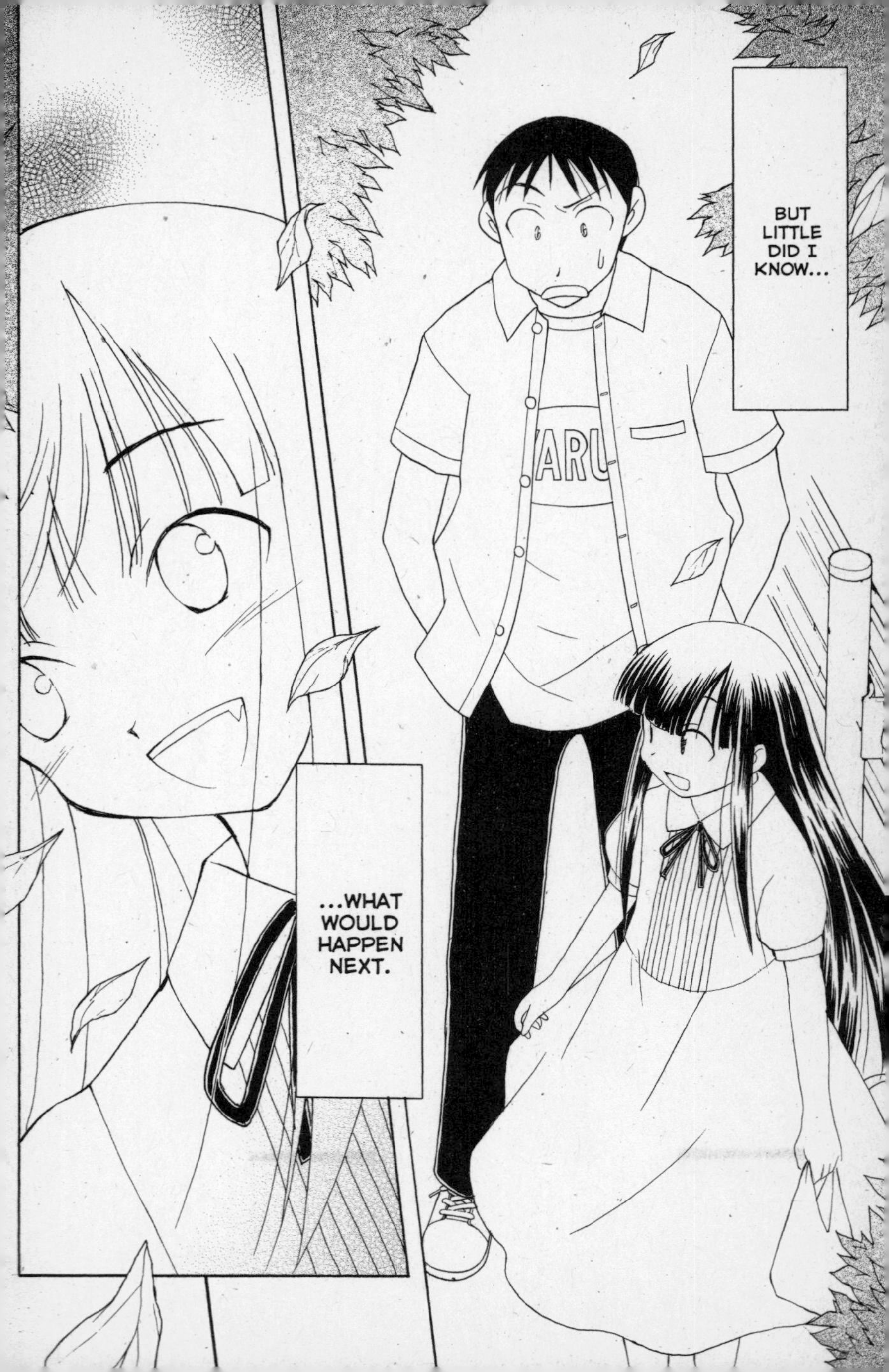
BUT LITTLE DID I KNOW...
...WHAT WOULD HAPPEN NEXT.

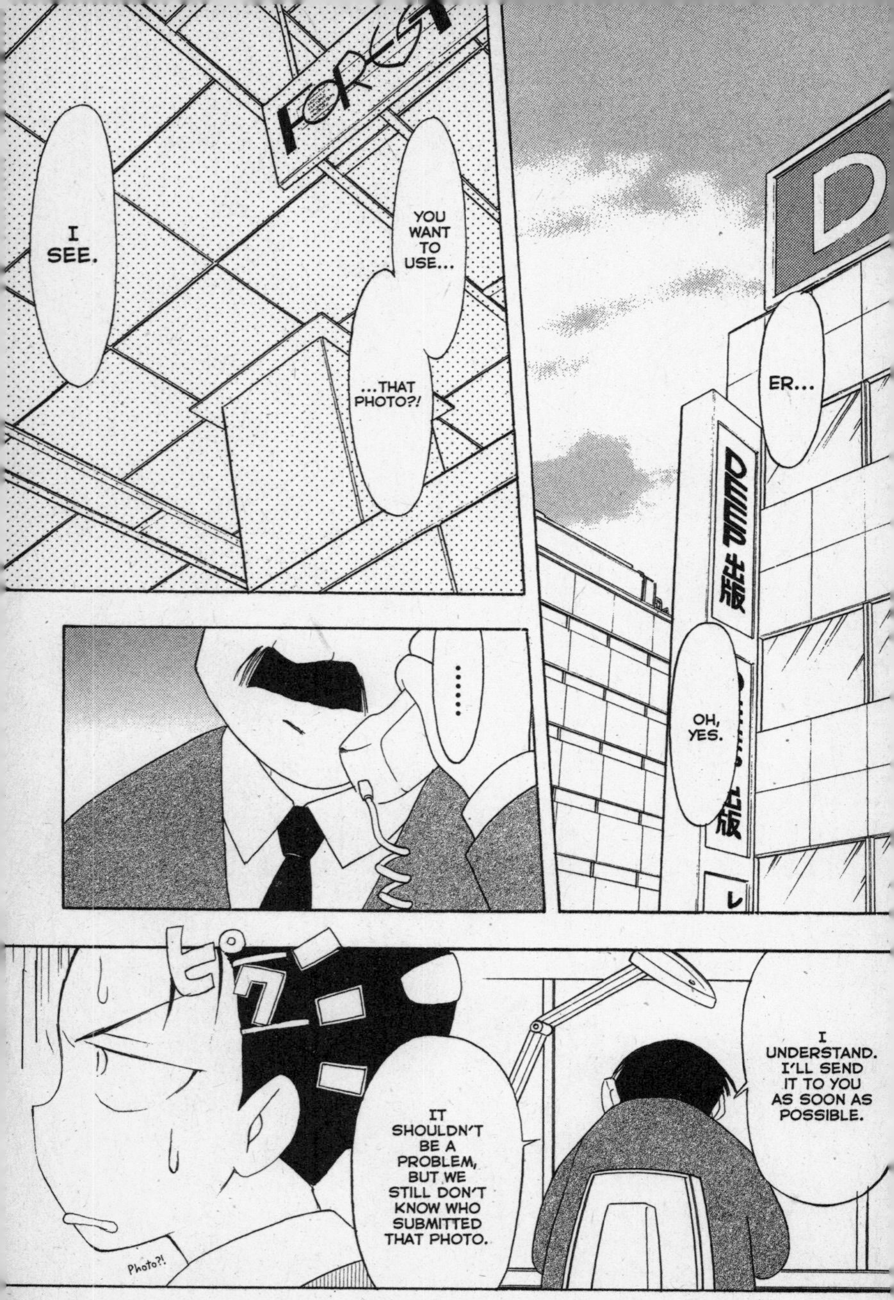
ER...
OH, YES.
YOU WANT TO USE...
...THAT PHOTO?!
I SEE.
......
I UNDERSTAND. I'LL SEND IT TO YOU AS SOON AS POSSIBLE.
ピクッ
IT SHOULDN'T BE A PROBLEM, BUT WE STILL DON'T KNOW WHO SUBMITTED THAT PHOTO.
Photo?!

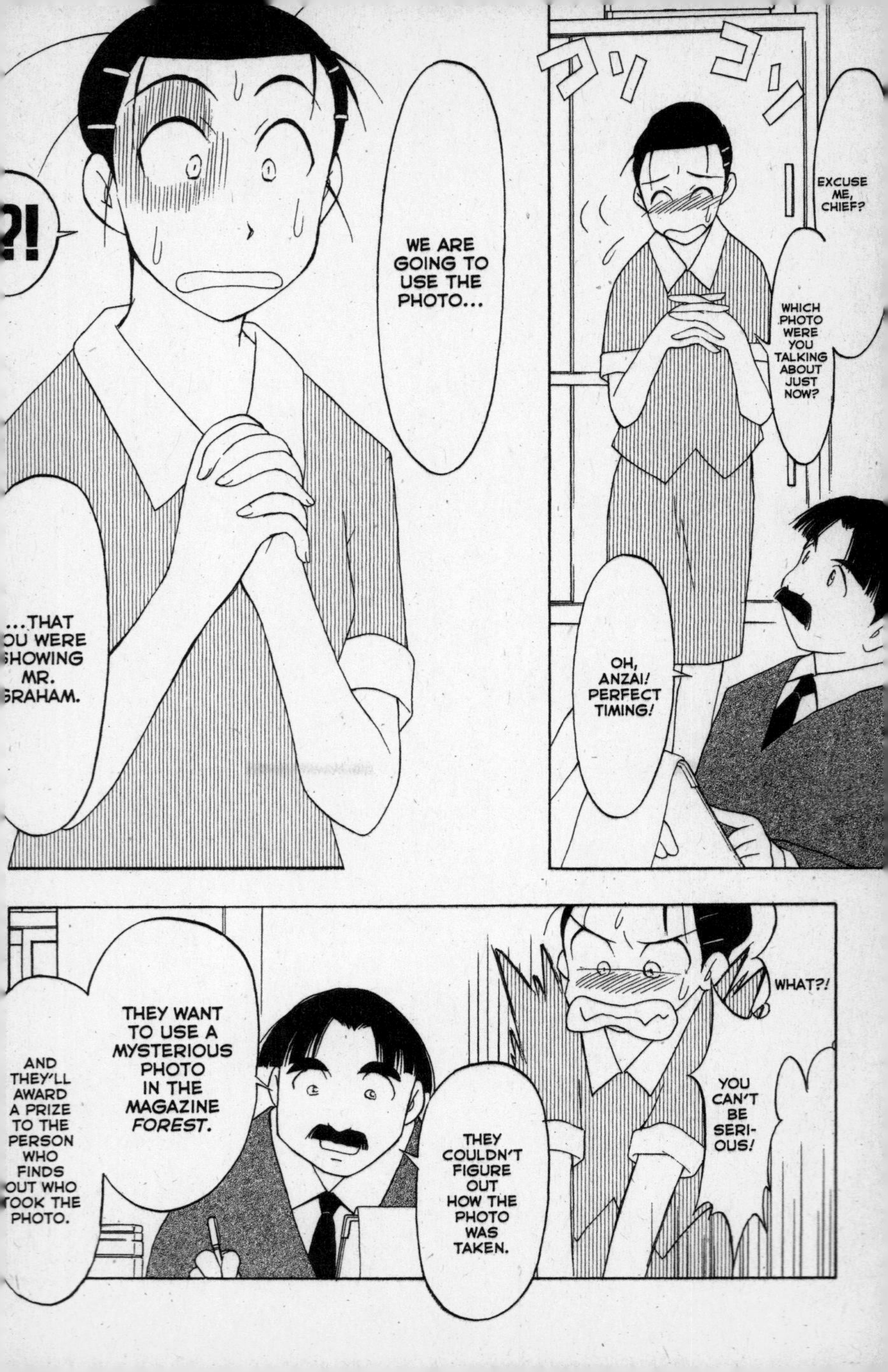
EXCUSE ME, CHIEF?
WHICH PHOTO WERE YOU TALKING ABOUT JUST NOW?
OH, ANZAI! PERFECT TIMING!
WE ARE GOING TO USE THE PHOTO...
...THAT OU WERE SHOWING MR. GRAHAM.
?!
WHAT?!
YOU CAN'T BE SERI-OUS!
THEY COULDN'T FIGURE OUT HOW THE PHOTO WAS TAKEN.
THEY WANT TO USE A MYSTERIOUS PHOTO IN THE MAGAZINE *FOREST*.
AND THEY'LL AWARD A PRIZE TO THE PERSON WHO FINDS OUT WHO TOOK THE PHOTO.

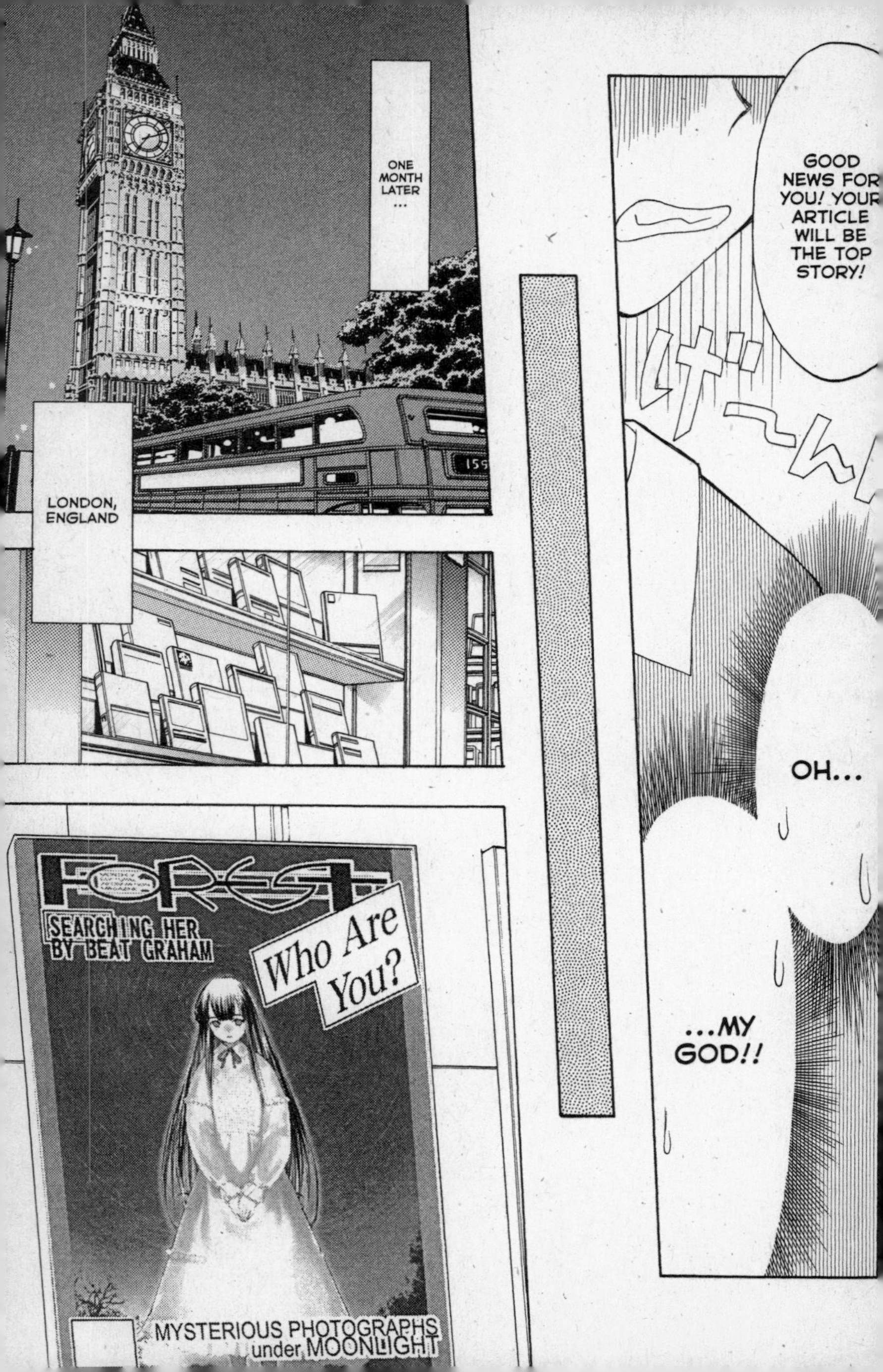
GOOD NEWS FOR YOU! YOUR ARTICLE WILL BE THE TOP STORY!
げ〜ん
OH...
...MY GOD!!
ONE MONTH LATER ...
LONDON, ENGLAND
159
FOREST
SEARCHING HER BY BEAT GRAHAM
Who Are You?
MYSTERIOUS PHOTOGRAPHS under MOONLIGHT

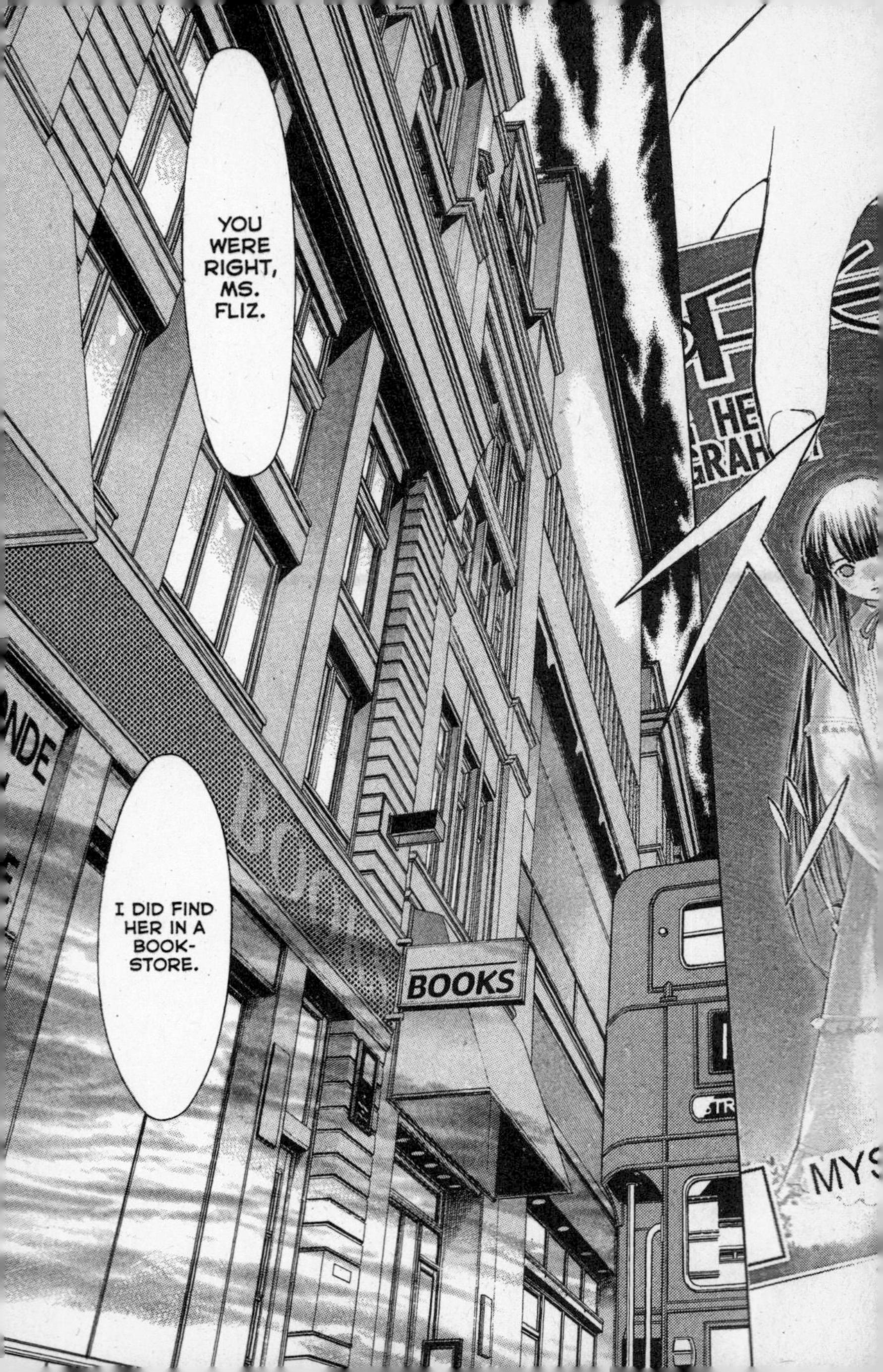
YOU WERE RIGHT, MS. FLIZ.
BOOKS
I DID FIND HER IN A BOOK-STORE.

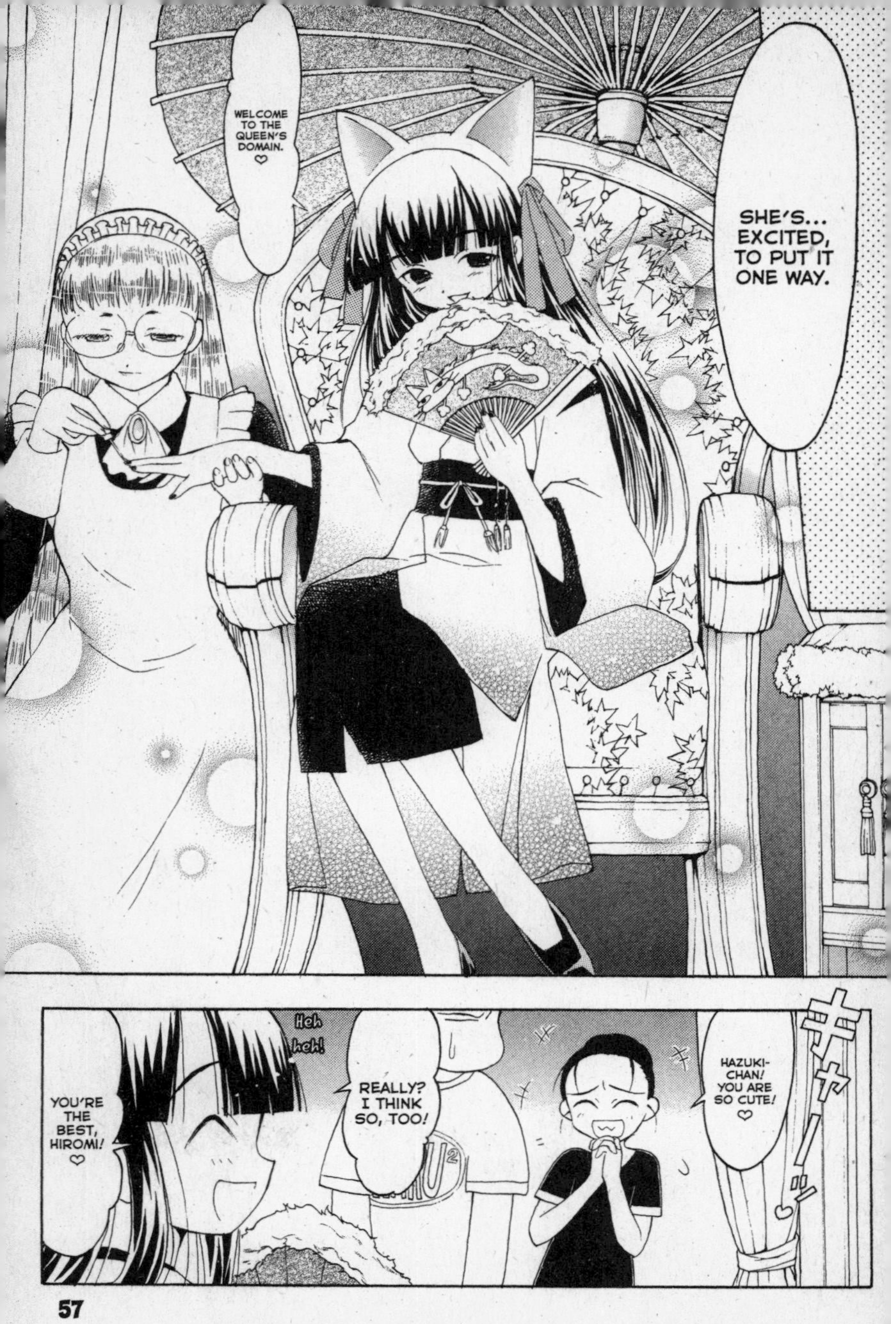
SHE'S... EXCITED, TO PUT IT ONE WAY.
WELCOME TO THE QUEEN'S DOMAIN. ♡
HAZUKI-CHAN! YOU ARE SO CUTE! ♡
REALLY? I THINK SO, TOO!
Heh heh!
YOU'RE THE BEST, HIROMI! ♡

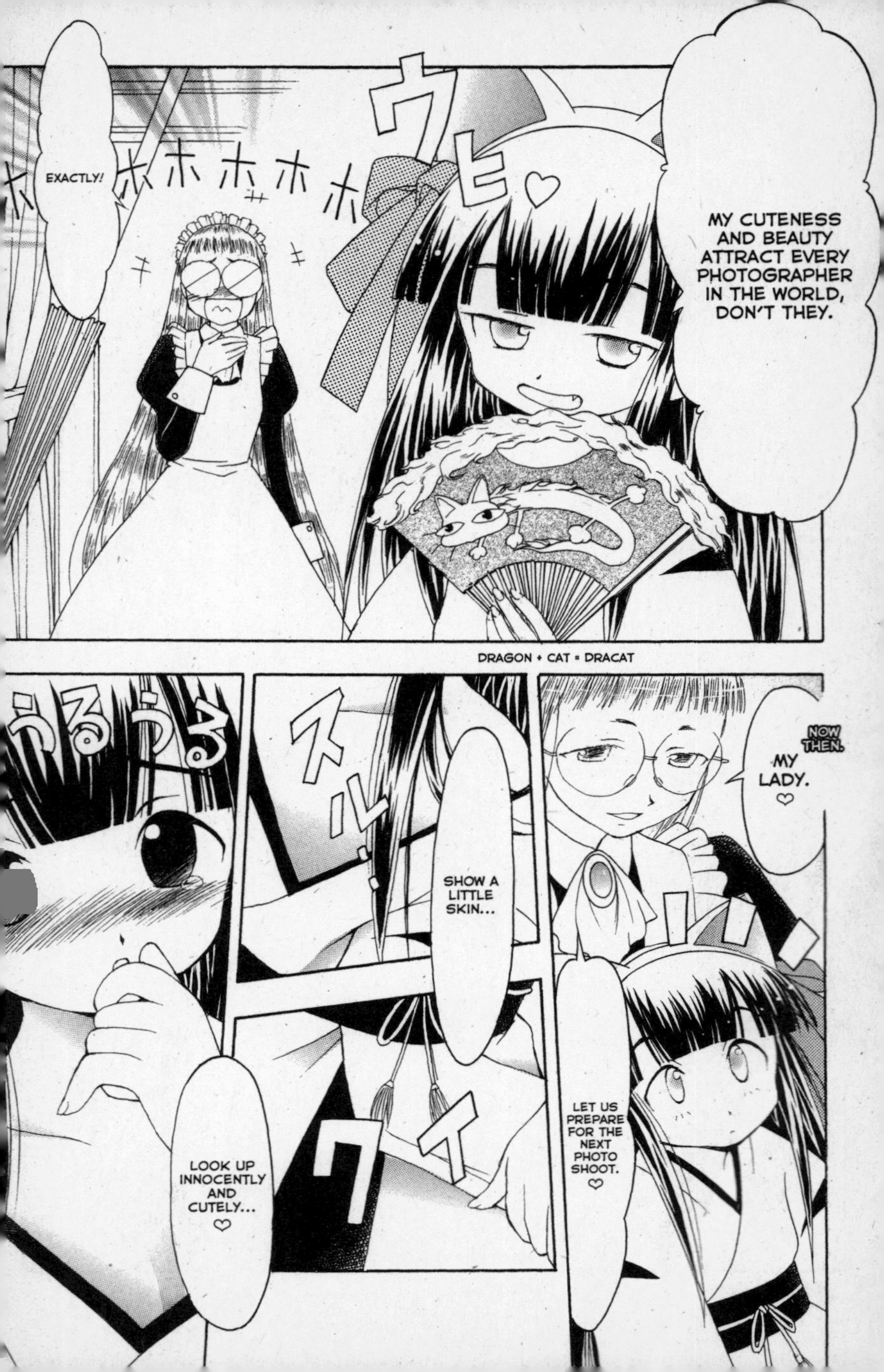
ウヒ♥
MY CUTENESS AND BEAUTY ATTRACT EVERY PHOTOGRAPHER IN THE WORLD, DON'T THEY.
EXACTLY!
DRAGON + CAT = DRACAT
NOW THEN.
MY LADY. ♡
LET US PREPARE FOR THE NEXT PHOTO SHOOT. ♡
スル
SHOW A LITTLE SKIN...
クイ
うるうる
LOOK UP INNOCENTLY AND CUTELY... ♡

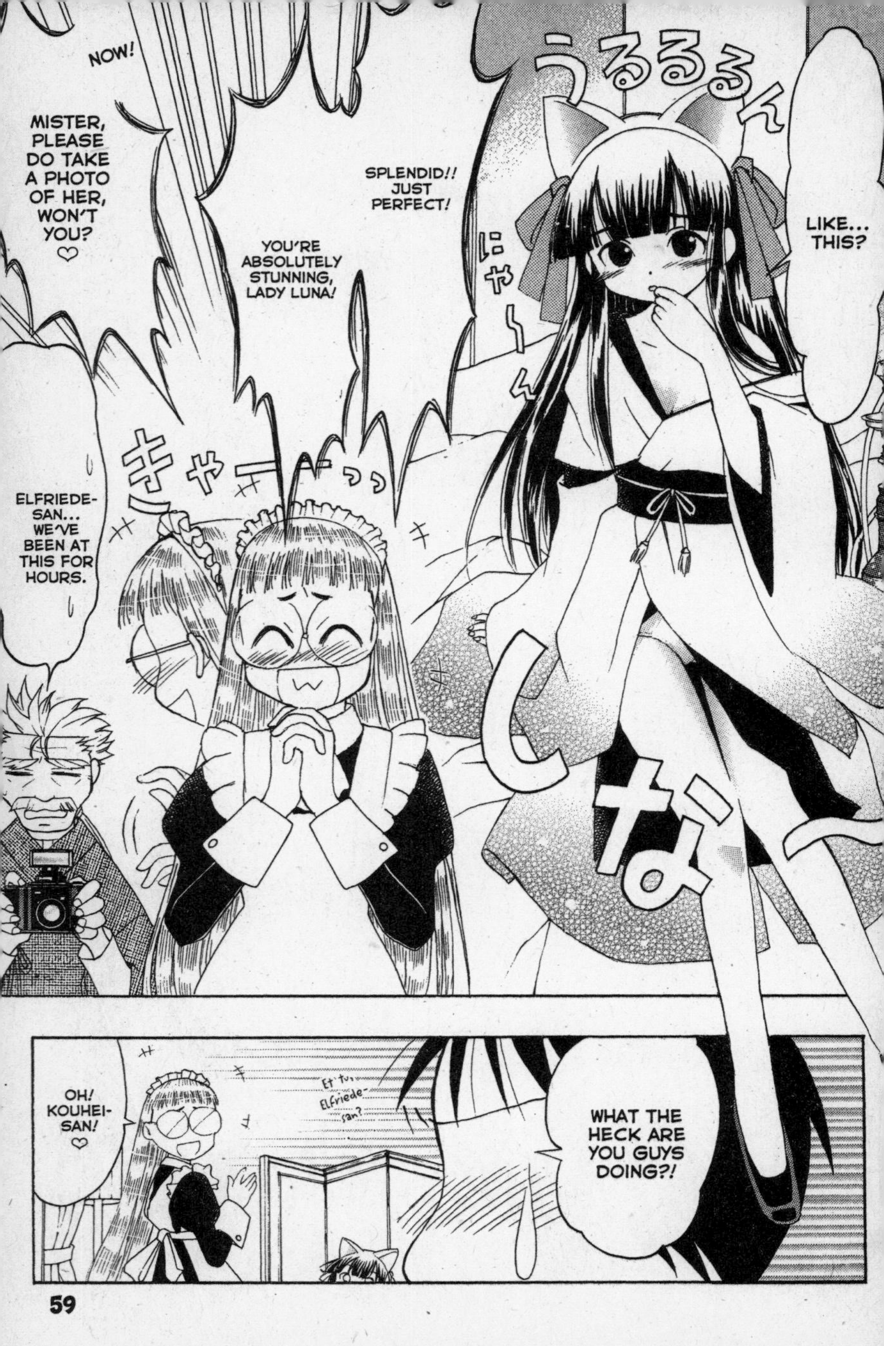
うるるるん
LIKE... THIS?
にゃ～ん
こんな
SPLENDID!! JUST PERFECT!
YOU'RE ABSOLUTELY STUNNING, LADY LUNA!
キャーっっ
NOW!
MISTER, PLEASE DO TAKE A PHOTO OF HER, WON'T YOU? ♡
ELFRIEDE-SAN... WE'VE BEEN AT THIS FOR HOURS.
WHAT THE HECK ARE YOU GUYS DOING?!
Et tu, Elfriede-san?
OH! KOUHEI-SAN! ♡

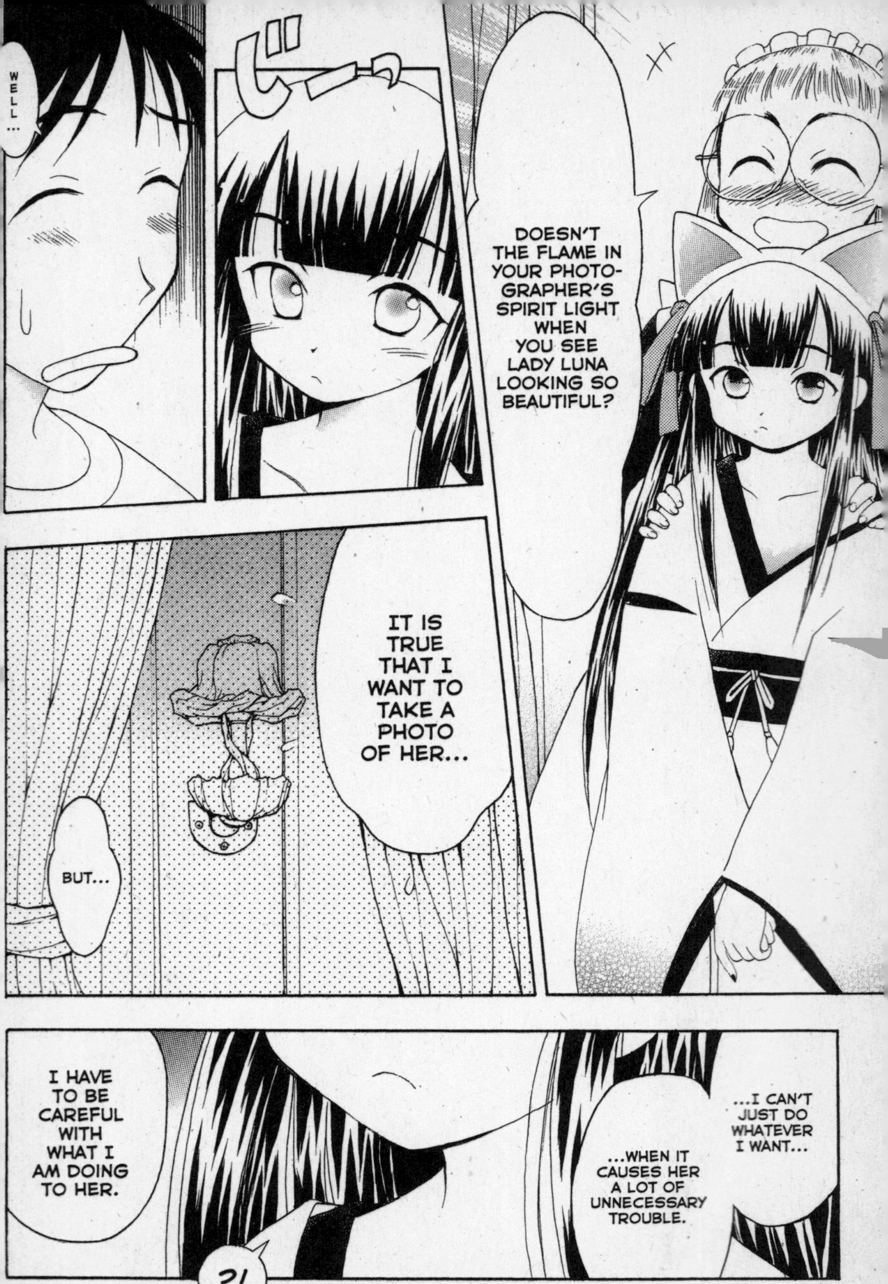
DOESN'T THE FLAME IN YOUR PHOTO-GRAPHER'S SPIRIT LIGHT WHEN YOU SEE LADY LUNA LOOKING SO BEAUTIFUL?
じーっ
WELL...
IT IS TRUE THAT I WANT TO TAKE A PHOTO OF HER...
BUT...
...I CAN'T JUST DO WHATEVER I WANT...
...WHEN IT CAUSES HER A LOT OF UNNECESSARY TROUBLE.
I HAVE TO BE CAREFUL WITH WHAT I AM DOING TO HER.
?!

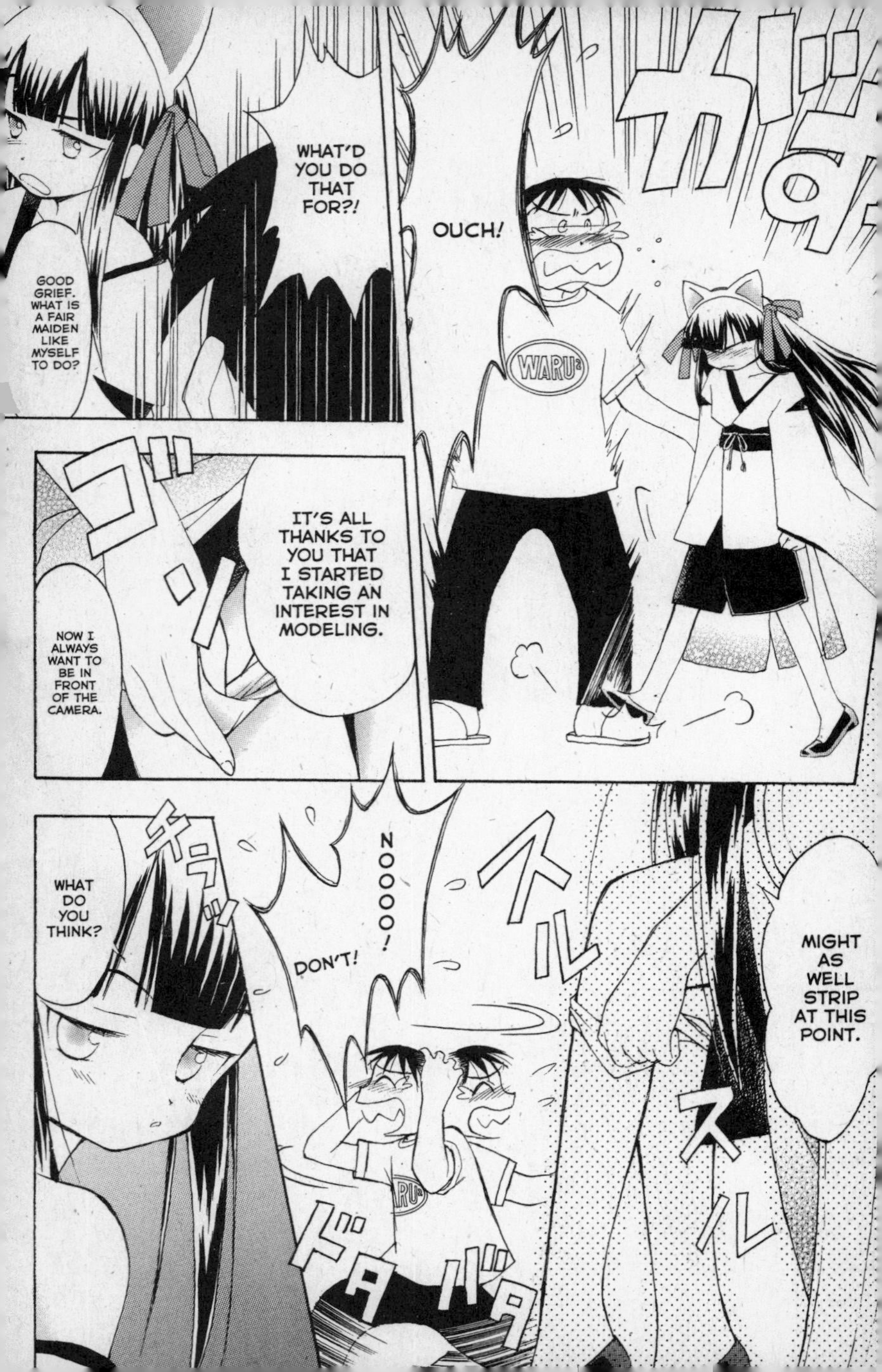
OUCH!
WHAT'D YOU DO THAT FOR?!
GOOD GRIEF. WHAT IS A FAIR MAIDEN LIKE MYSELF TO DO?
IT'S ALL THANKS TO YOU THAT I STARTED TAKING AN INTEREST IN MODELING.
NOW I ALWAYS WANT TO BE IN FRONT OF THE CAMERA.
MIGHT AS WELL STRIP AT THIS POINT.
NOOOO!
DON'T!
WHAT DO YOU THINK?

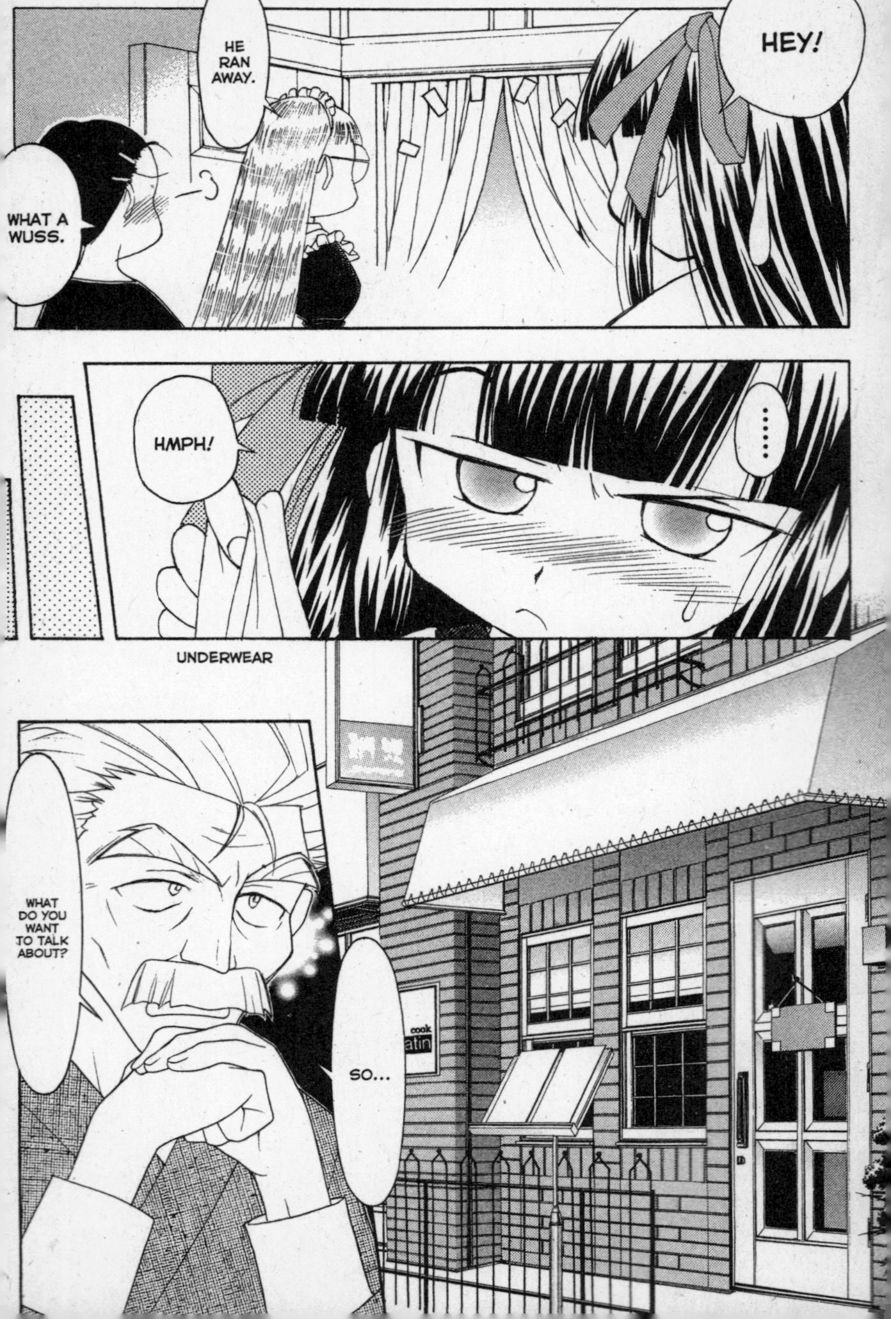
HEY!
HE RAN AWAY.
WHAT A WUSS.
......
HMPH!
UNDERWEAR
SO...
WHAT DO YOU WANT TO TALK ABOUT?

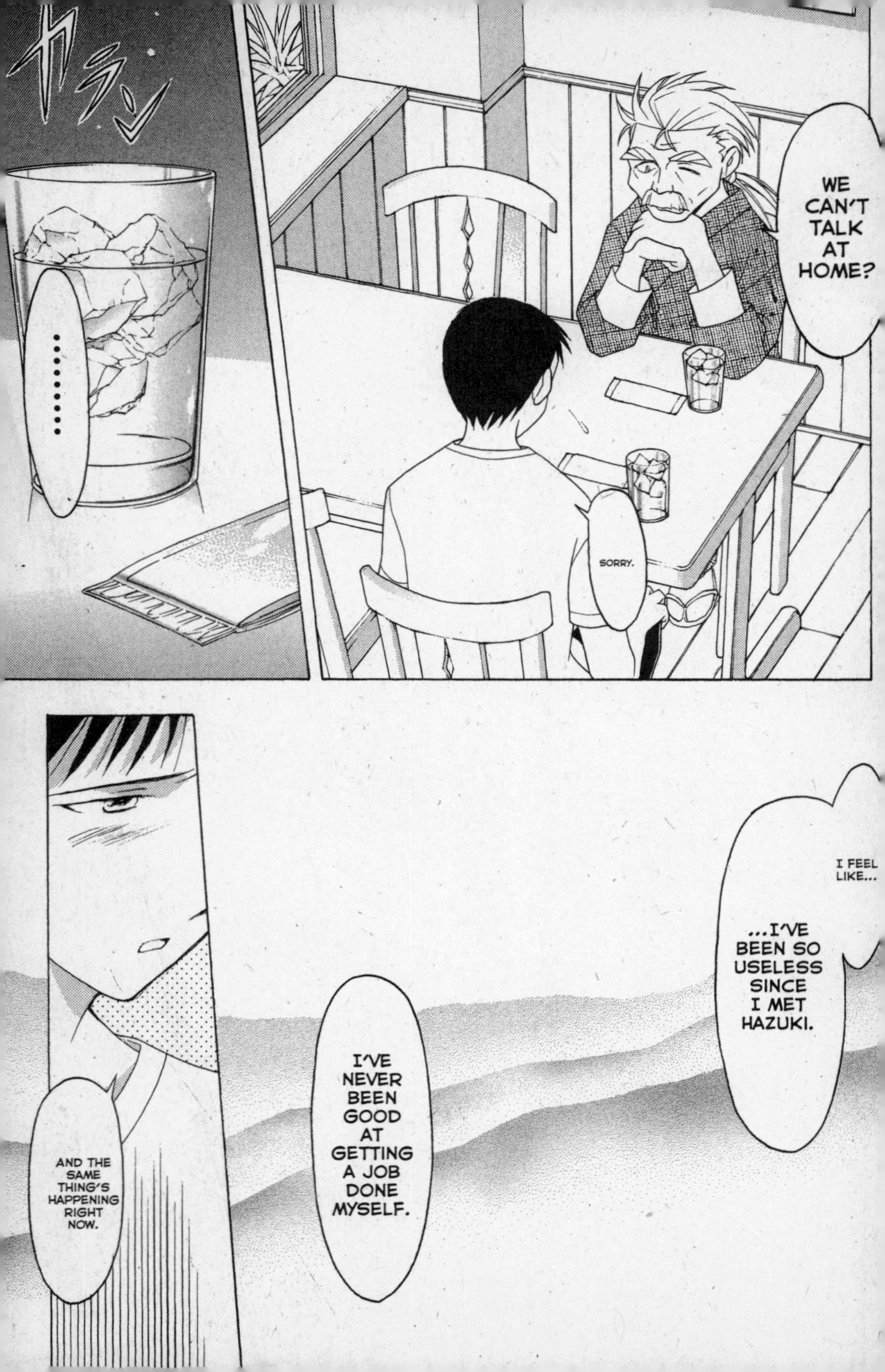

WE CAN'T TALK AT HOME?
SORRY.
カラン
......
I FEEL LIKE...
...I'VE BEEN SO USELESS SINCE I MET HAZUKI.
I'VE NEVER BEEN GOOD AT GETTING A JOB DONE MYSELF.
AND THE SAME THING'S HAPPENING RIGHT NOW.

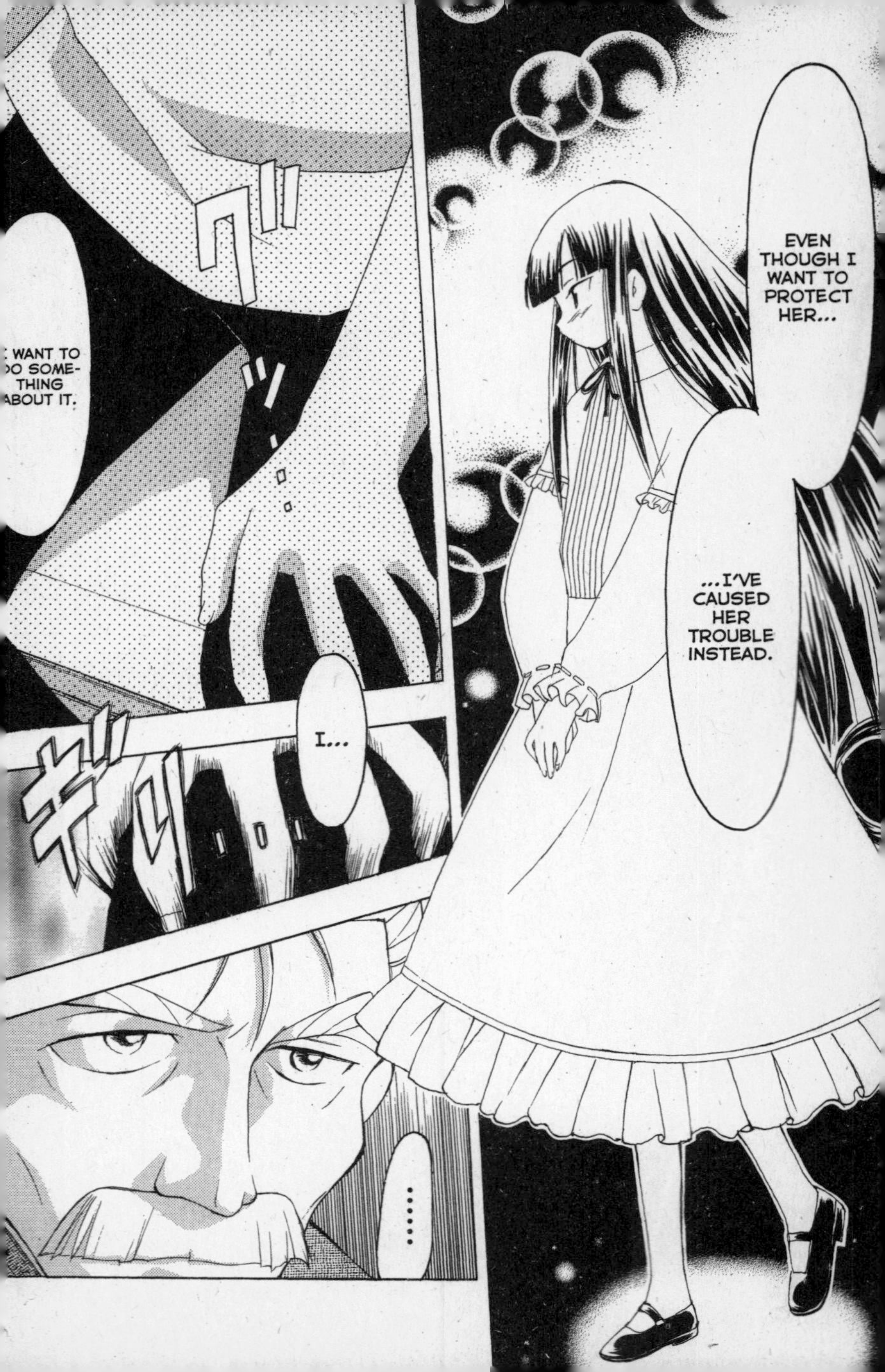
EVEN THOUGH I WANT TO PROTECT HER...
...I'VE CAUSED HER TROUBLE INSTEAD.
WANT TO DO SOME-THING ABOUT IT.
I...
......

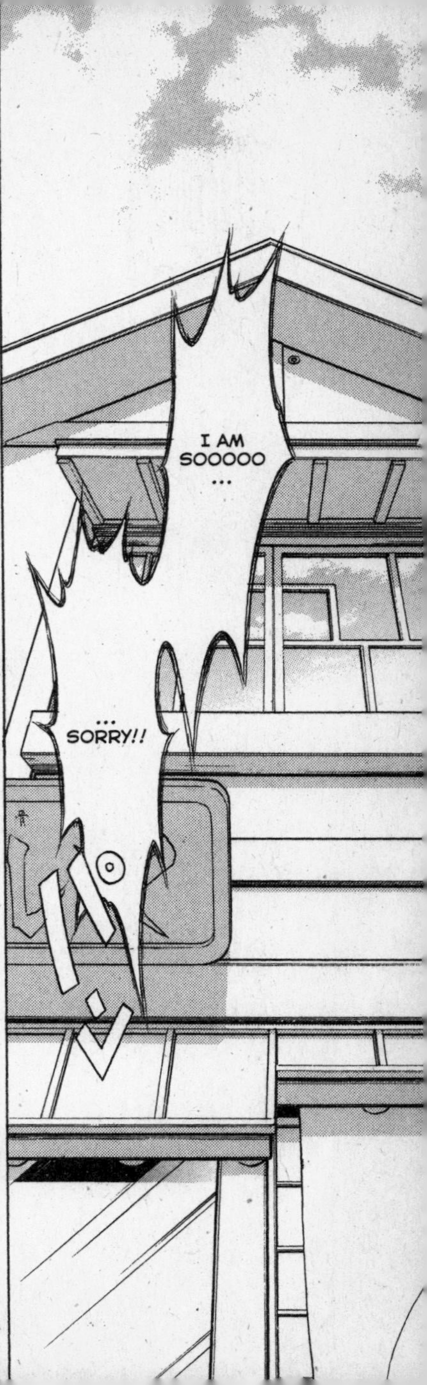
I AM SOOOOO ...
... SORRY!!

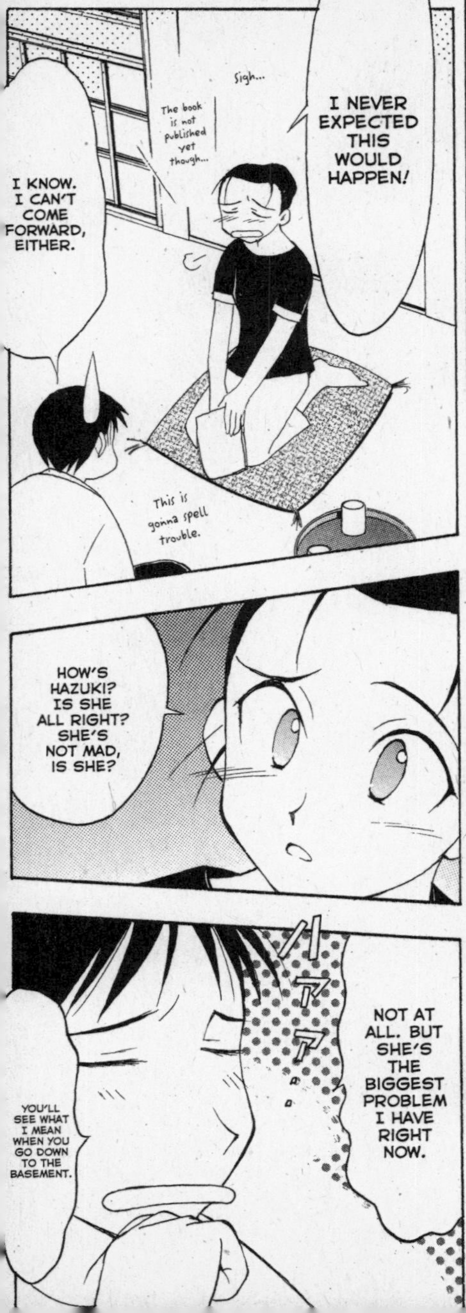
I NEVER EXPECTED THIS WOULD HAPPEN!
Sigh...
The book is not published yet though...
I KNOW. I CAN'T COME FORWARD, EITHER.
This is gonna spell trouble.
HOW'S HAZUKI? IS SHE ALL RIGHT? SHE'S NOT MAD, IS SHE?
NOT AT ALL. BUT SHE'S THE BIGGEST PROBLEM I HAVE RIGHT NOW.
YOU'LL SEE WHAT I MEAN WHEN YOU GO DOWN TO THE BASEMENT.

Phase34 Kouhei's Decision

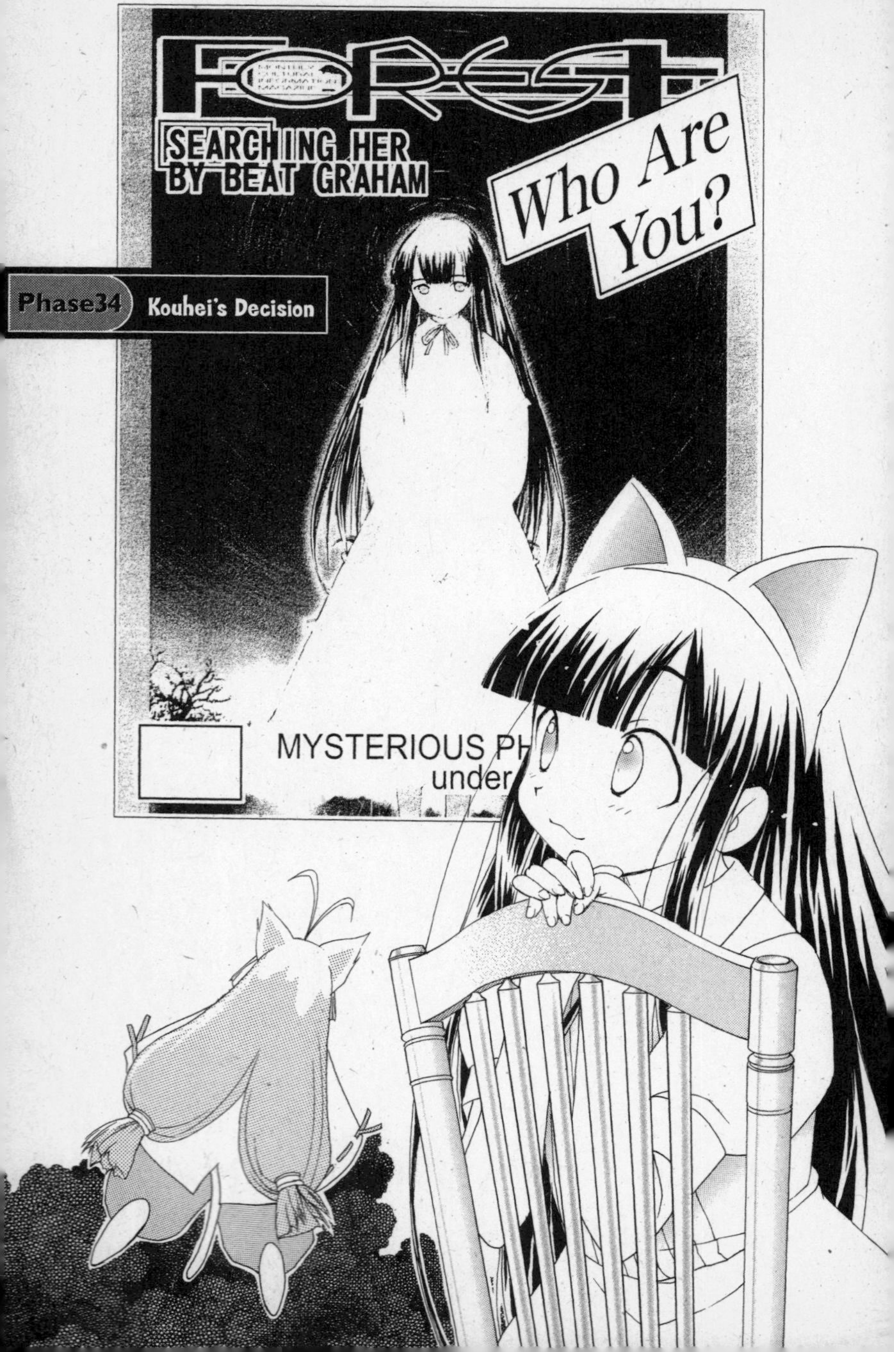
FOREST
SEARCHING HER
BY BEAT GRAHAM
Who Are You?
MYSTERIOUS PH
under

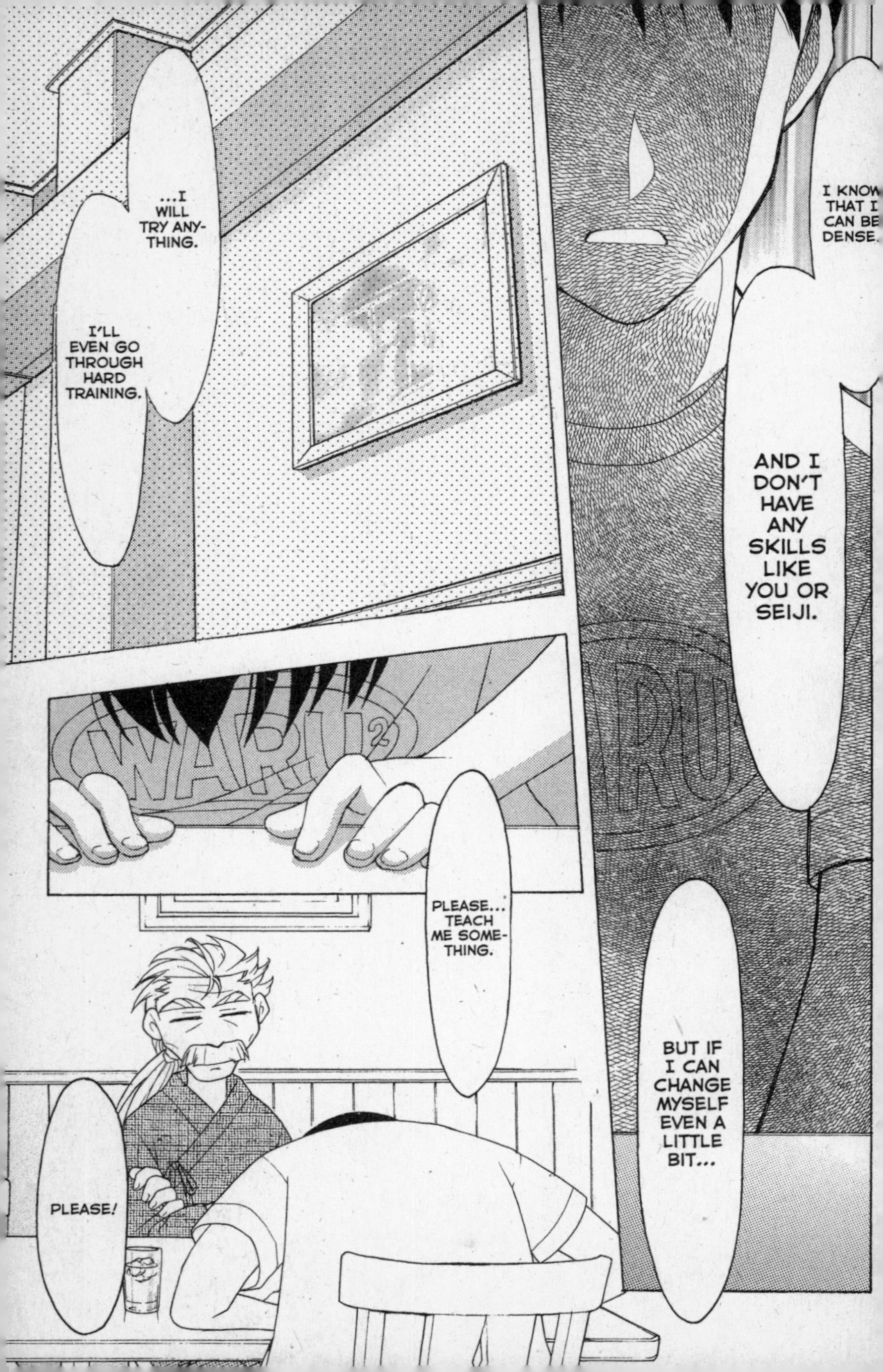
I KNOW THAT I CAN BE DENSE.
AND I DON'T HAVE ANY SKILLS LIKE YOU OR SEIJI.
BUT IF I CAN CHANGE MYSELF EVEN A LITTLE BIT...
...I WILL TRY ANYTHING.
I'LL EVEN GO THROUGH HARD TRAINING.
PLEASE... TEACH ME SOMETHING.
PLEASE!

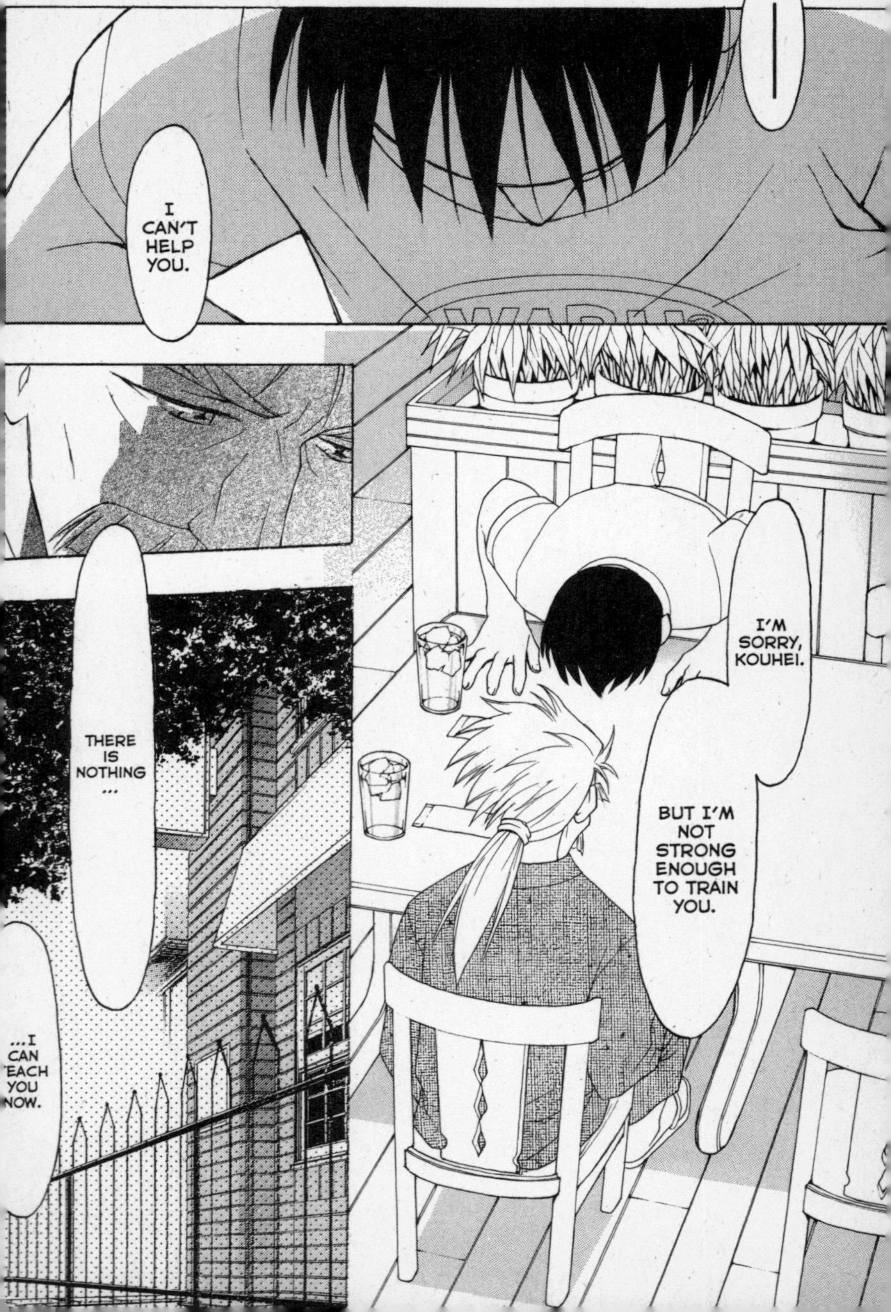
—
I CAN'T HELP YOU.
I'M SORRY, KOUHEI.
BUT I'M NOT STRONG ENOUGH TO TRAIN YOU.
THERE IS NOTHING ...
...I CAN EACH YOU NOW.

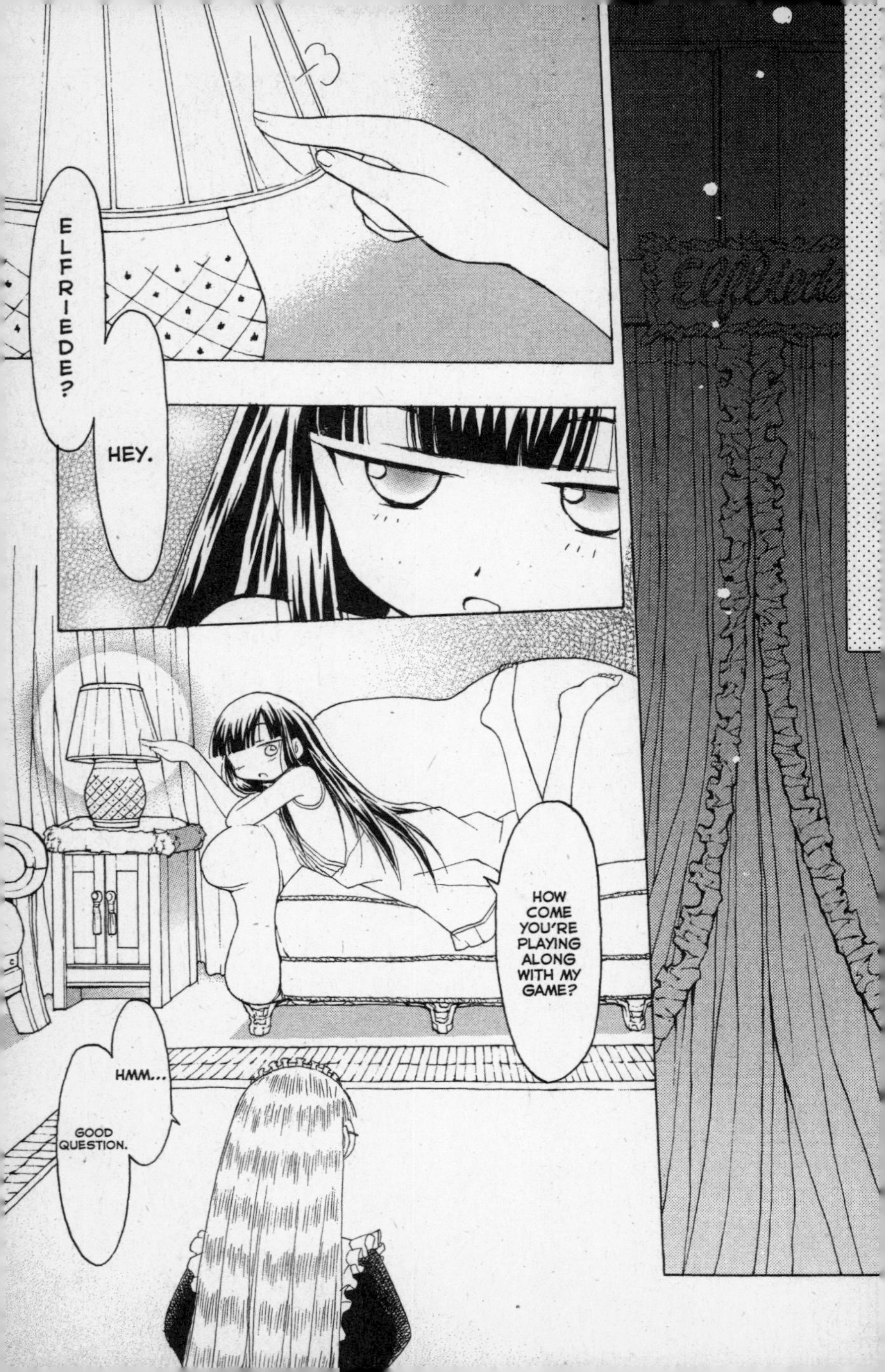
ELFRIEDE?
HEY.
HOW COME YOU'RE PLAYING ALONG WITH MY GAME?
HMM...
GOOD QUESTION.

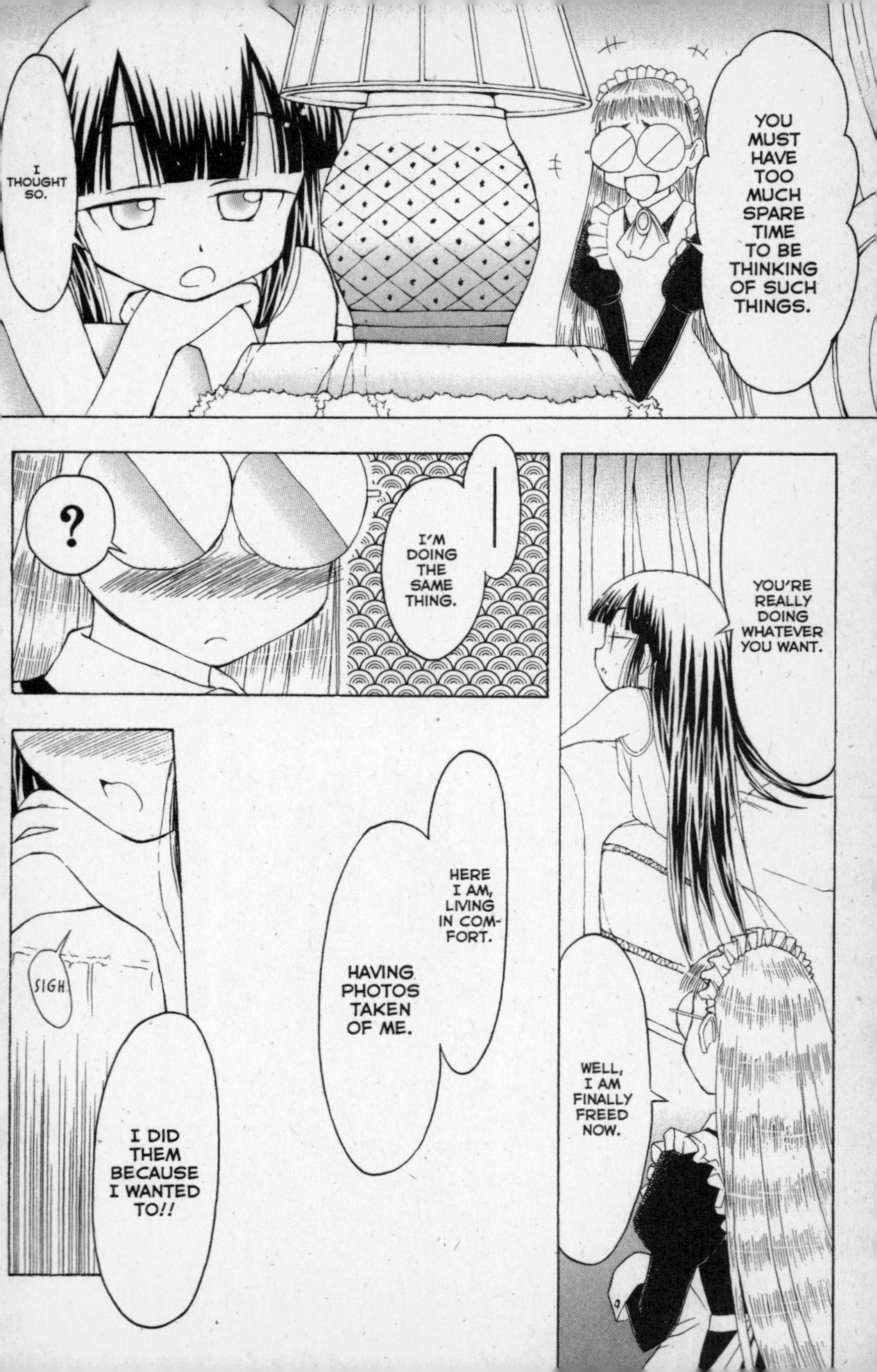
YOU MUST HAVE TOO MUCH SPARE TIME TO BE THINKING OF SUCH THINGS.
I THOUGHT SO.
YOU'RE REALLY DOING WHATEVER YOU WANT.
WELL, I AM FINALLY FREED NOW.
I'M DOING THE SAME THING.
?
HERE I AM, LIVING IN COMFORT.
HAVING PHOTOS TAKEN OF ME.
SIGH
I DID THEM BECAUSE I WANTED TO!!

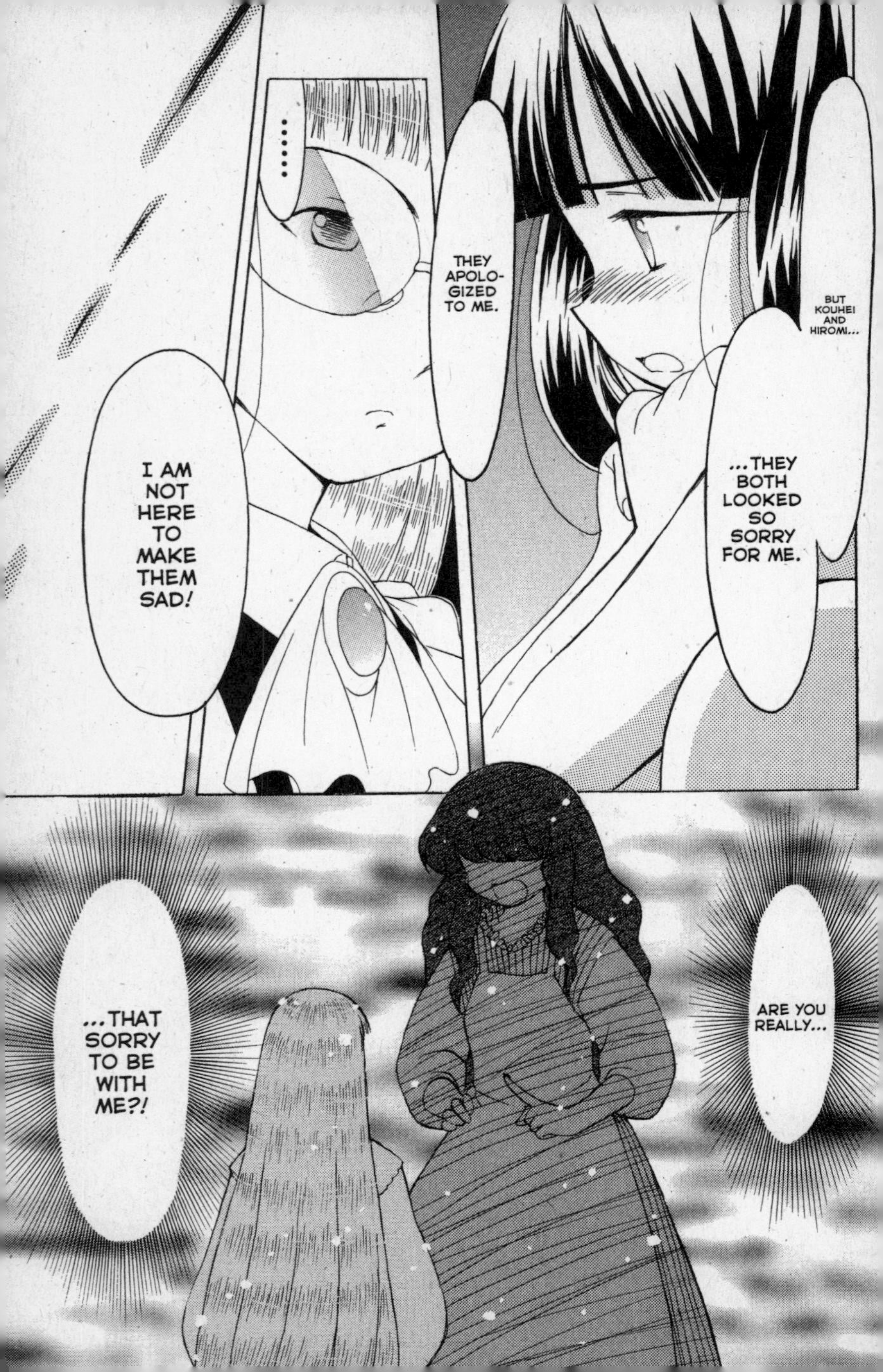
BUT KOUHEI AND HIROMI...
THEY APOLOGIZED TO ME.
...THEY BOTH LOOKED SO SORRY FOR ME.
......
I AM NOT HERE TO MAKE THEM SAD!
ARE YOU REALLY...
...THAT SORRY TO BE WITH ME?!

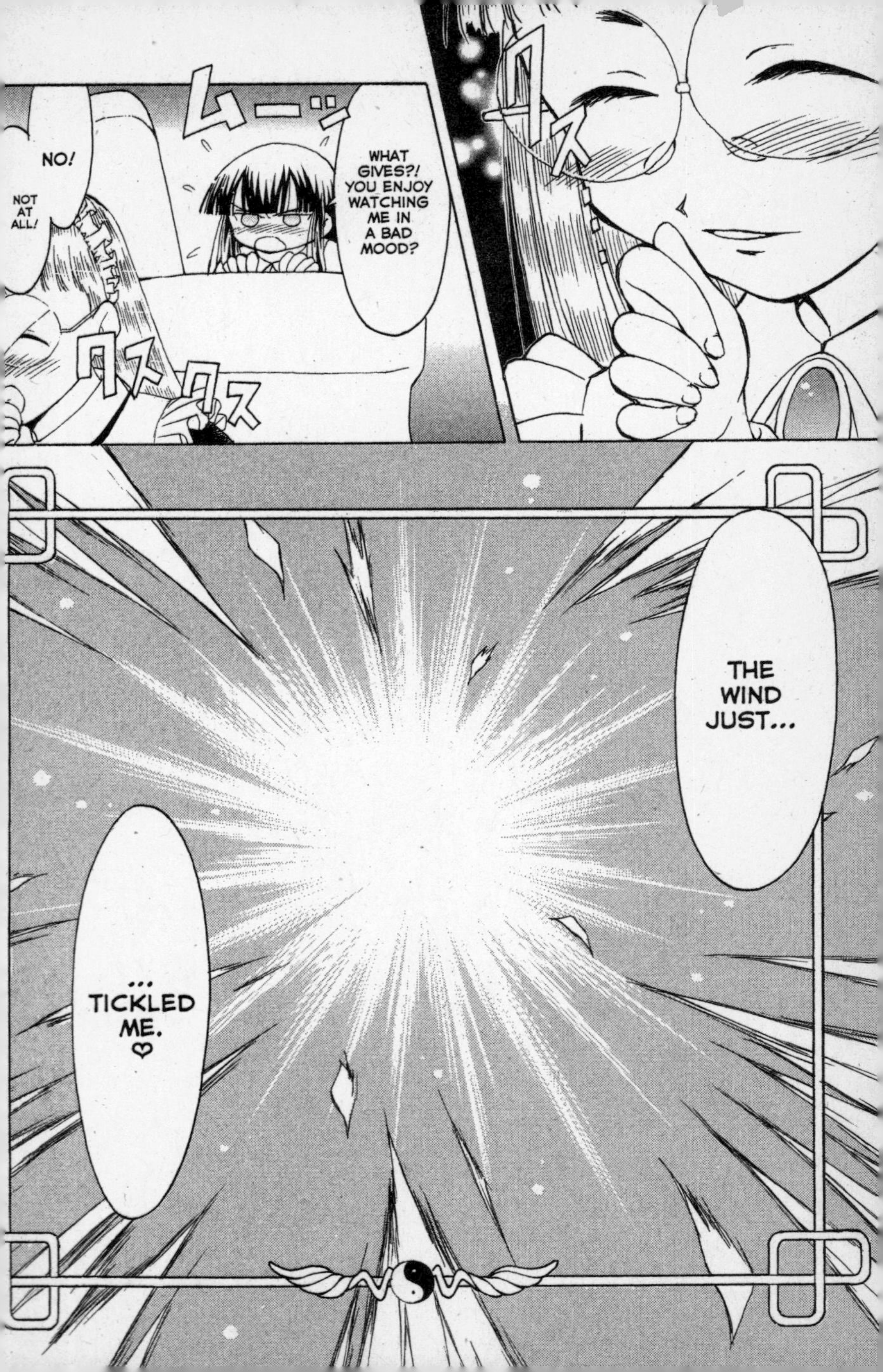
クス
WHAT GIVES?! YOU ENJOY WATCHING ME IN A BAD MOOD?
ムーッ
NO!
NOT AT ALL!
クスクス
THE WIND JUST...
... TICKLED ME. ♡

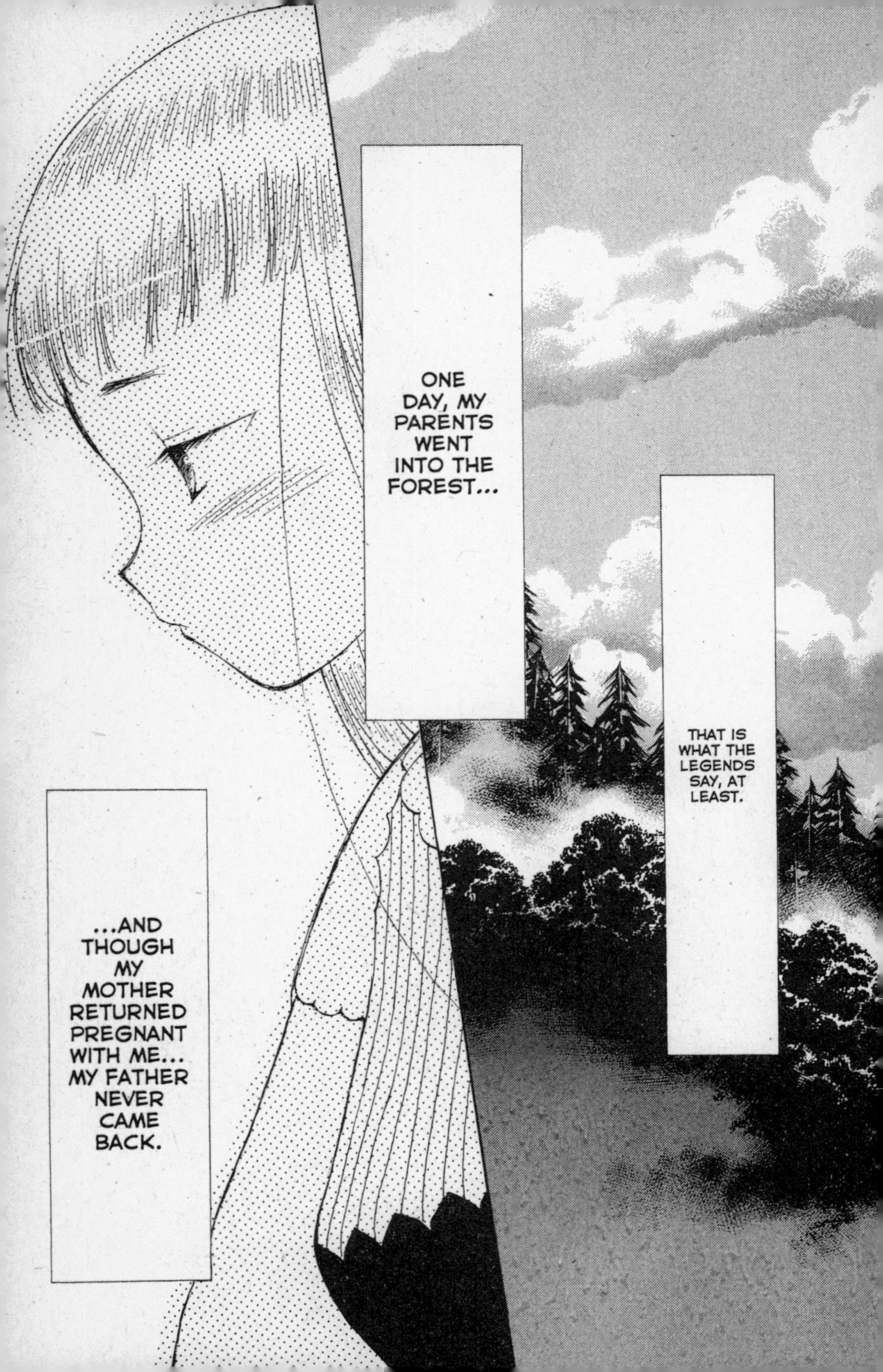
ONE DAY, MY PARENTS WENT INTO THE FOREST...
THAT IS WHAT THE LEGENDS SAY, AT LEAST.
...AND THOUGH MY MOTHER RETURNED PREGNANT WITH ME... MY FATHER NEVER CAME BACK.

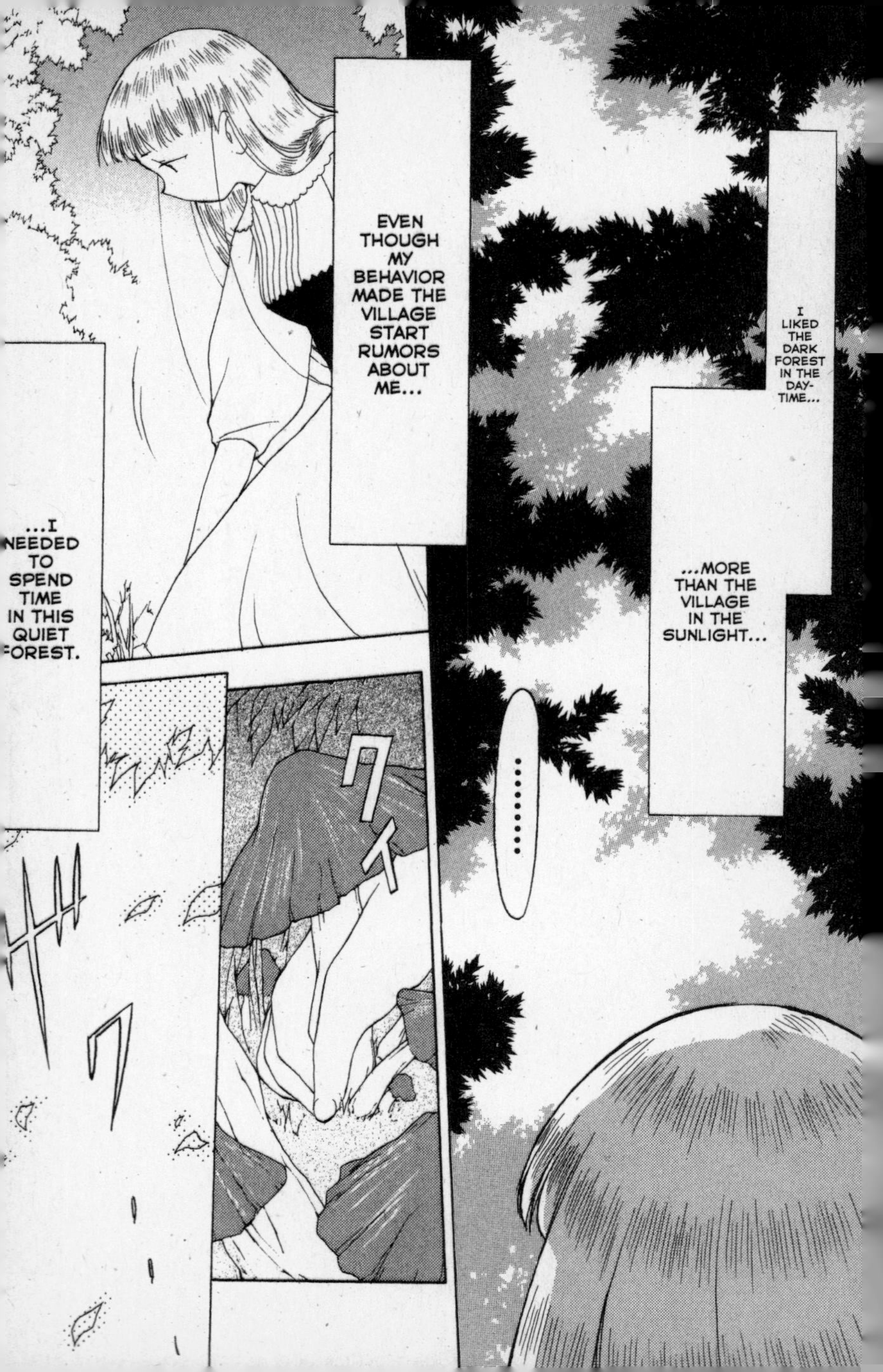
I LIKED THE DARK FOREST IN THE DAY-TIME...
...MORE THAN THE VILLAGE IN THE SUNLIGHT...
......
EVEN THOUGH MY BEHAVIOR MADE THE VILLAGE START RUMORS ABOUT ME...
...I NEEDED TO SPEND TIME IN THIS QUIET FOREST.

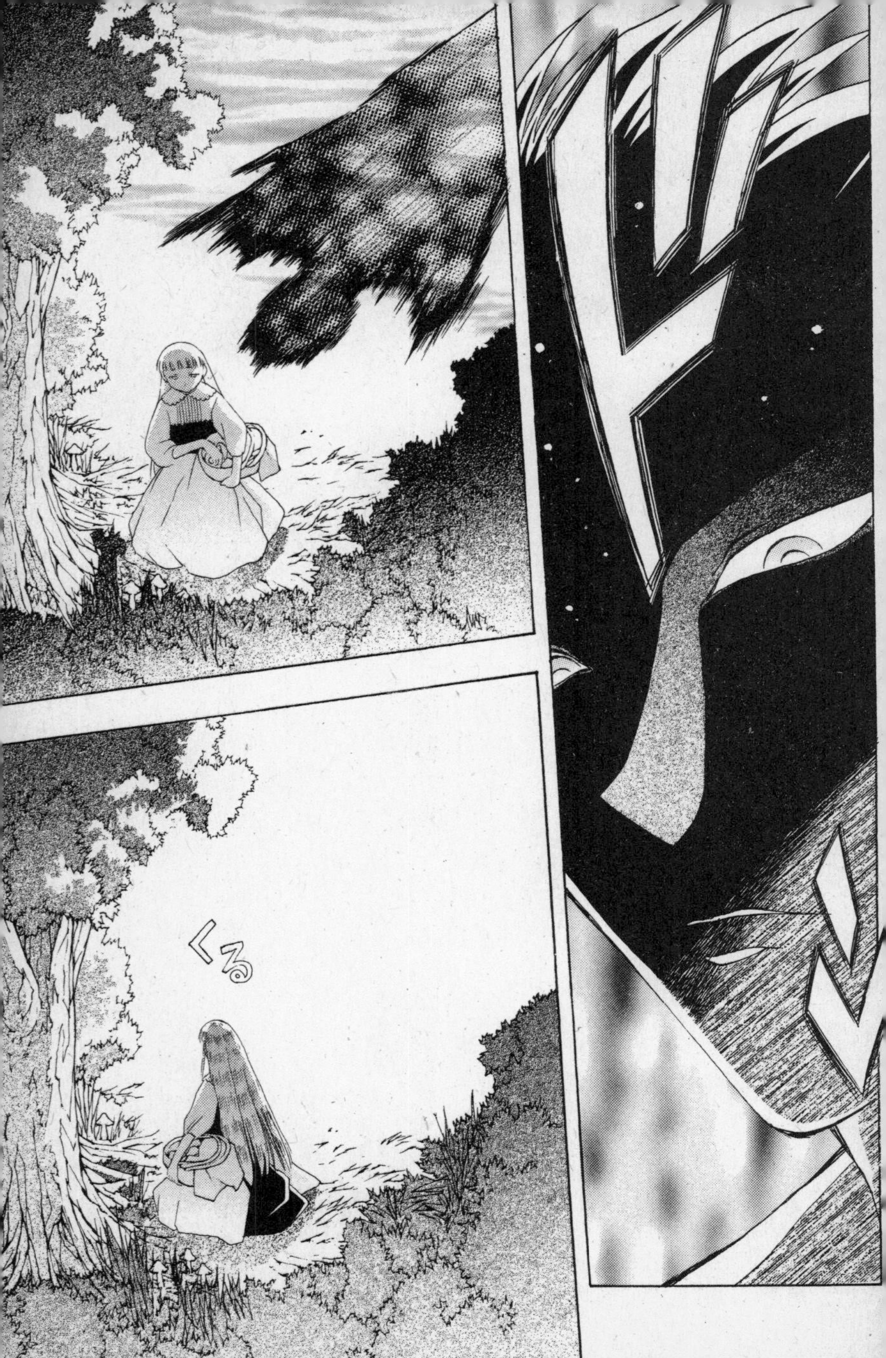
くる

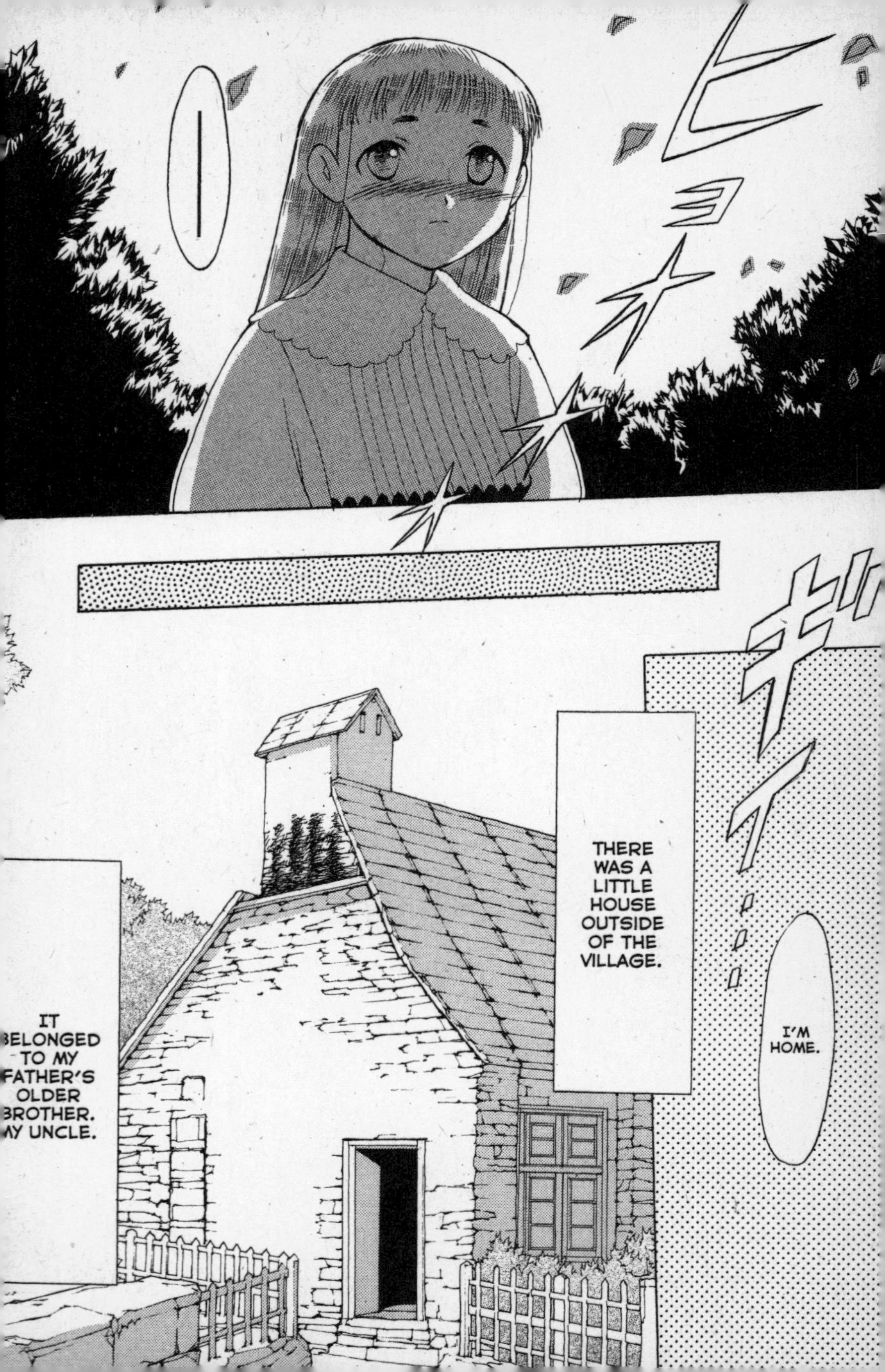
THERE WAS A LITTLE HOUSE OUTSIDE OF THE VILLAGE.
I'M HOME.
IT BELONGED TO MY FATHER'S OLDER BROTHER. MY UNCLE.

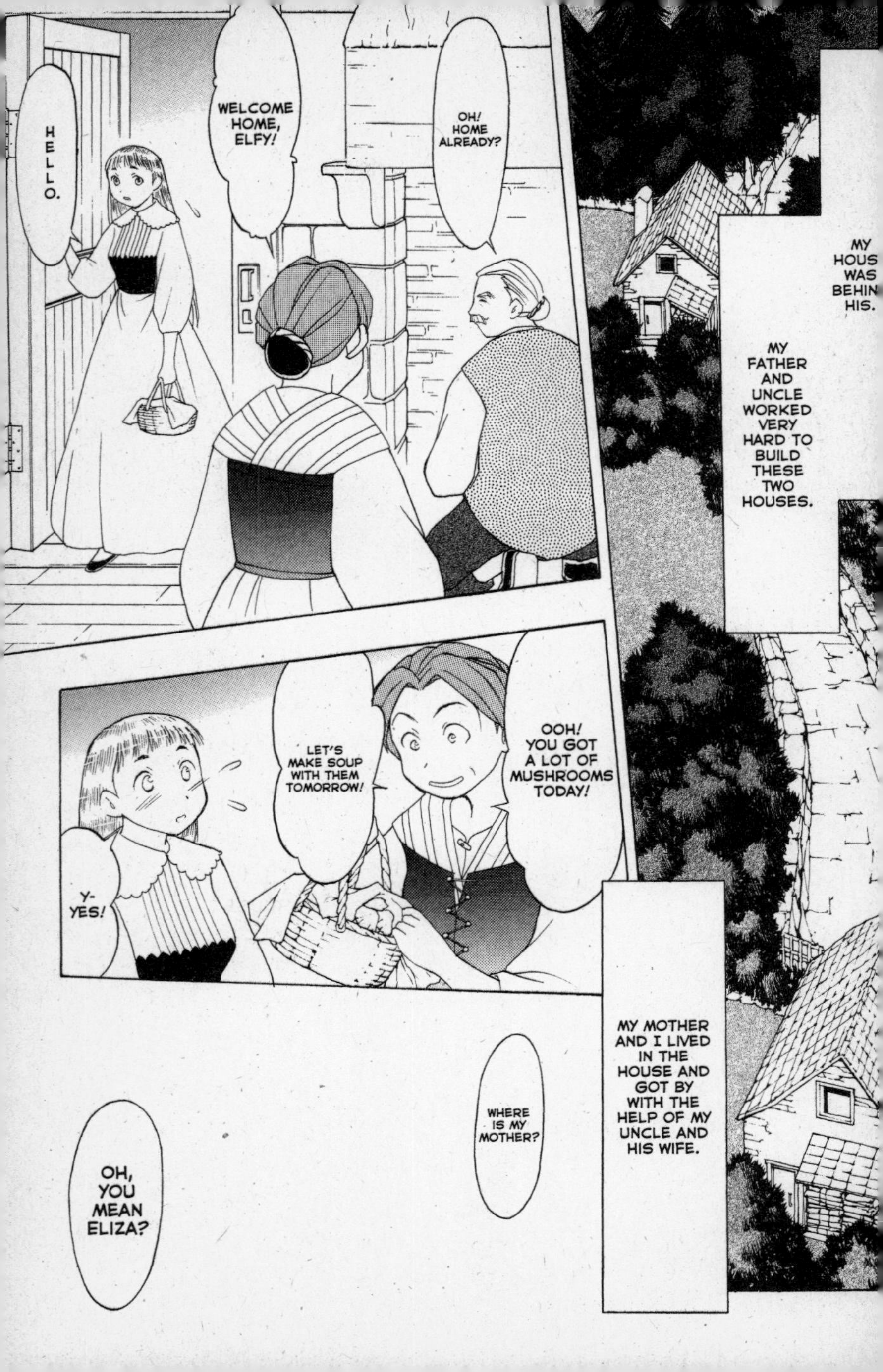
MY HOUS WAS BEHIN HIS.
MY FATHER AND UNCLE WORKED VERY HARD TO BUILD THESE TWO HOUSES.
MY MOTHER AND I LIVED IN THE HOUSE AND GOT BY WITH THE HELP OF MY UNCLE AND HIS WIFE.
OH! HOME ALREADY?
WELCOME HOME, ELFY!
HELLO.
OOH! YOU GOT A LOT OF MUSHROOMS TODAY!
LET'S MAKE SOUP WITH THEM TOMORROW!
Y- YES!
WHERE IS MY MOTHER?
OH, YOU MEAN ELIZA?

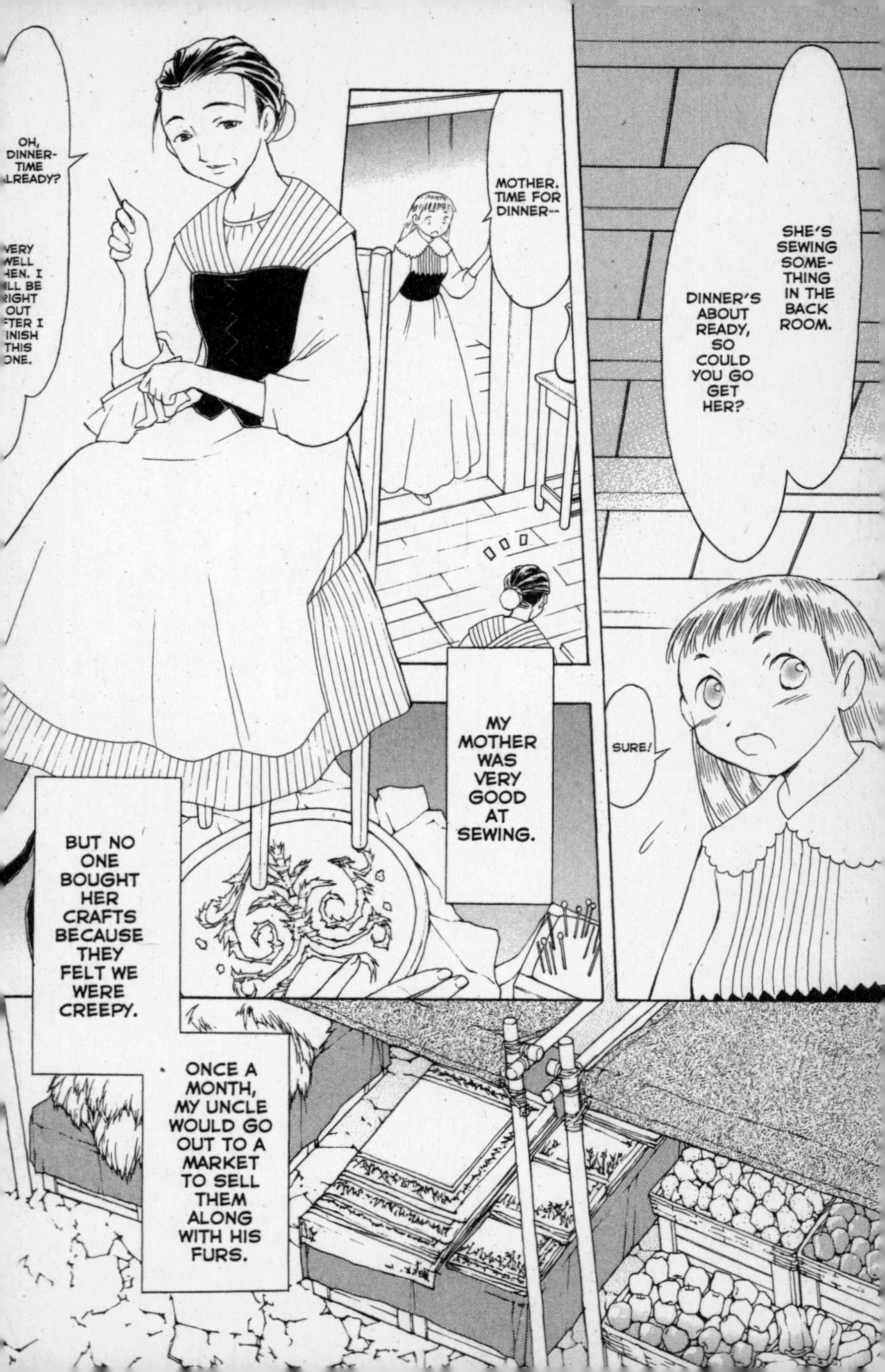
SHE'S SEWING SOME-THING IN THE BACK ROOM.
DINNER'S ABOUT READY, SO COULD YOU GO GET HER?
SURE!
MOTHER. TIME FOR DINNER--
OH, DINNER-TIME LREADY?
VERY WELL HEN. I ILL BE RIGHT OUT FTER I INISH THIS ONE.
MY MOTHER WAS VERY GOOD AT SEWING.
BUT NO ONE BOUGHT HER CRAFTS BECAUSE THEY FELT WE WERE CREEPY.
ONCE A MONTH, MY UNCLE WOULD GO OUT TO A MARKET TO SELL THEM ALONG WITH HIS FURS.

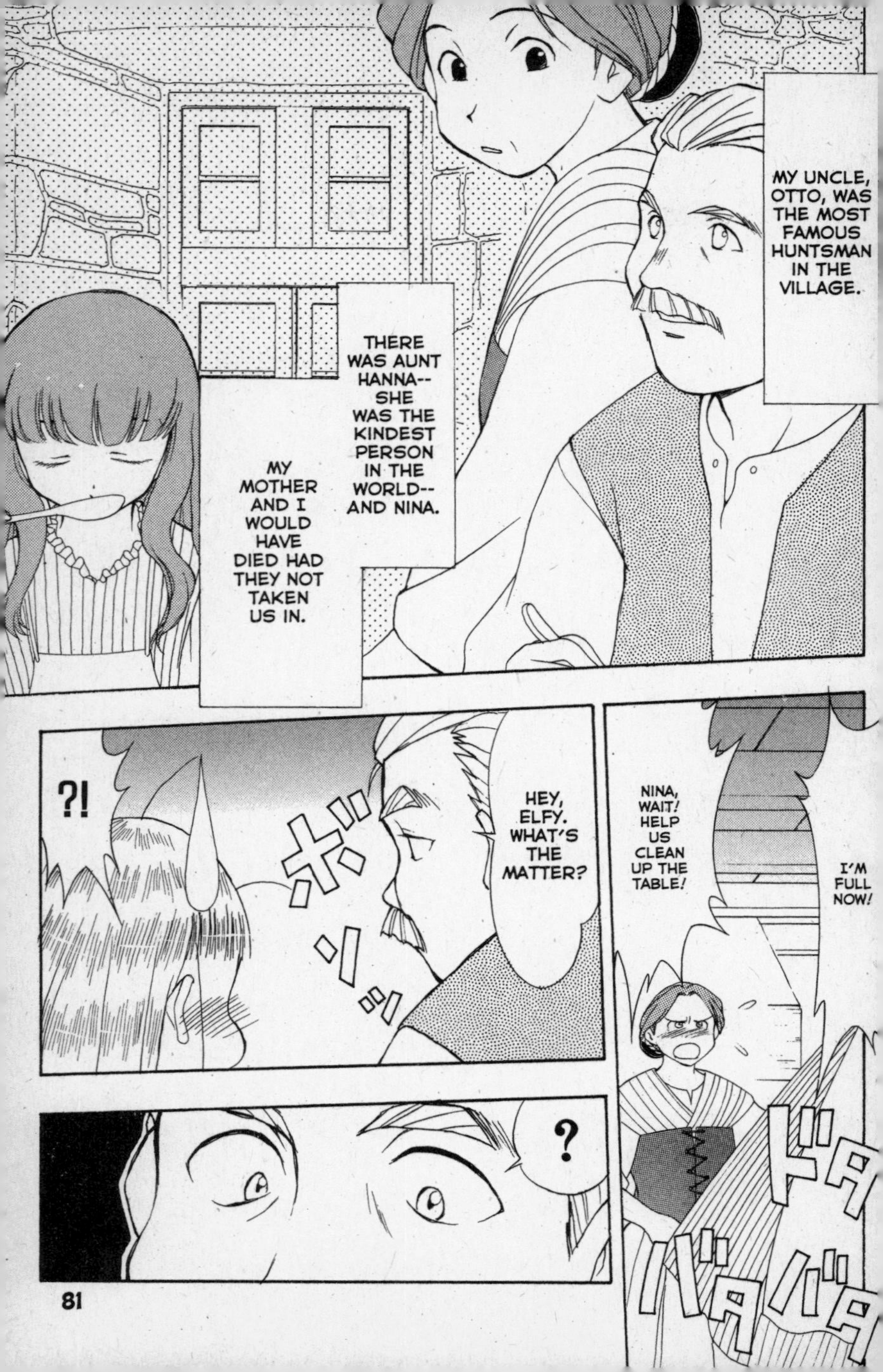
MY UNCLE, OTTO, WAS THE MOST FAMOUS HUNTSMAN IN THE VILLAGE.
THERE WAS AUNT HANNA-- SHE WAS THE KINDEST PERSON IN THE WORLD-- AND NINA.
MY MOTHER AND I WOULD HAVE DIED HAD THEY NOT TAKEN US IN.
I'M FULL NOW!
NINA, WAIT! HELP US CLEAN UP THE TABLE!
ドタ
バタバタ
HEY, ELFY. WHAT'S THE MATTER?
?!
?

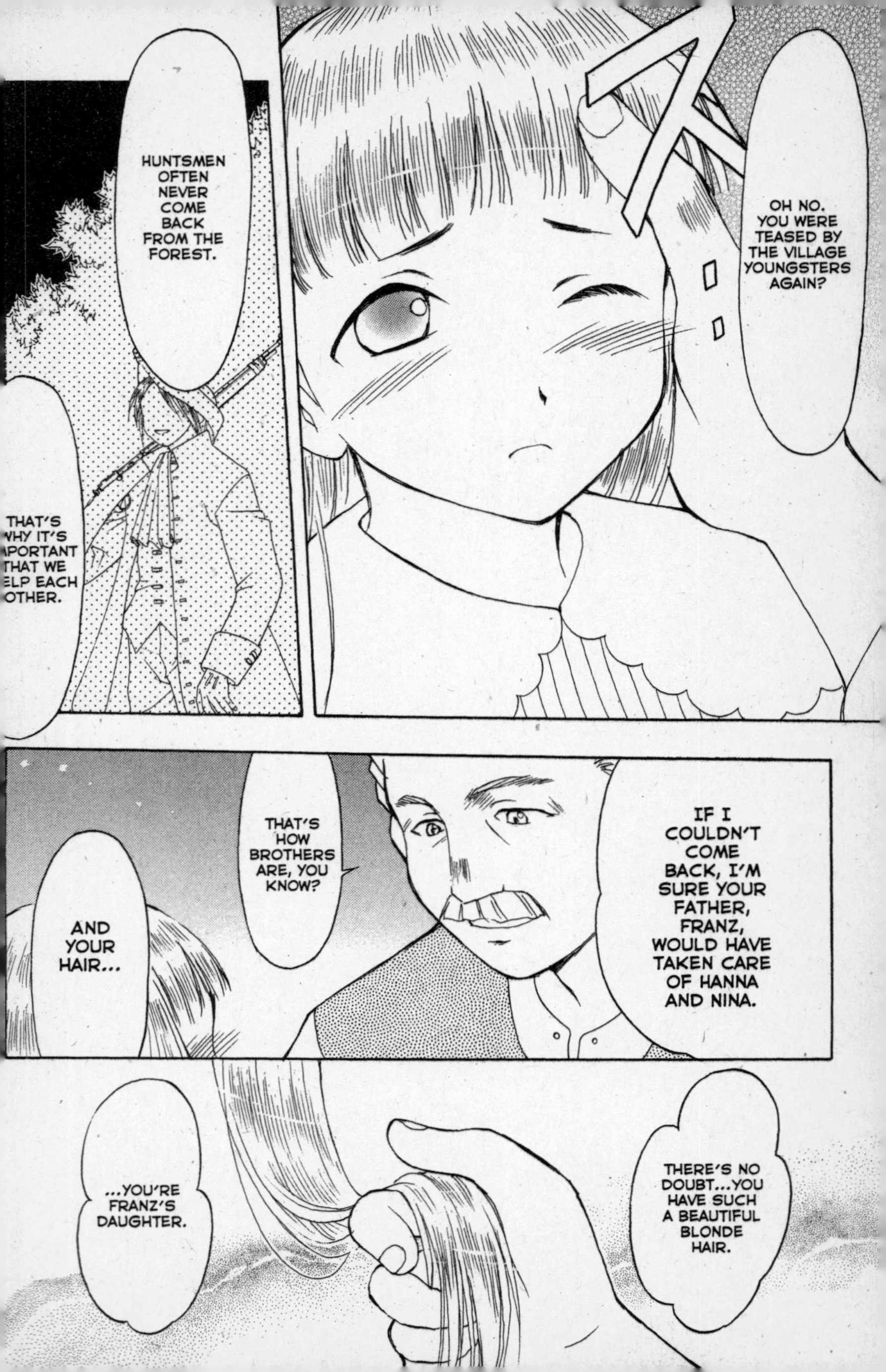
OH NO. YOU WERE TEASED BY THE VILLAGE YOUNGSTERS AGAIN?
HUNTSMEN OFTEN NEVER COME BACK FROM THE FOREST.
THAT'S WHY IT'S IMPORTANT THAT WE HELP EACH OTHER.
IF I COULDN'T COME BACK, I'M SURE YOUR FATHER, FRANZ, WOULD HAVE TAKEN CARE OF HANNA AND NINA.
THAT'S HOW BROTHERS ARE, YOU KNOW?
AND YOUR HAIR...
THERE'S NO DOUBT...YOU HAVE SUCH A BEAUTIFUL BLONDE HAIR.
...YOU'RE FRANZ'S DAUGHTER.

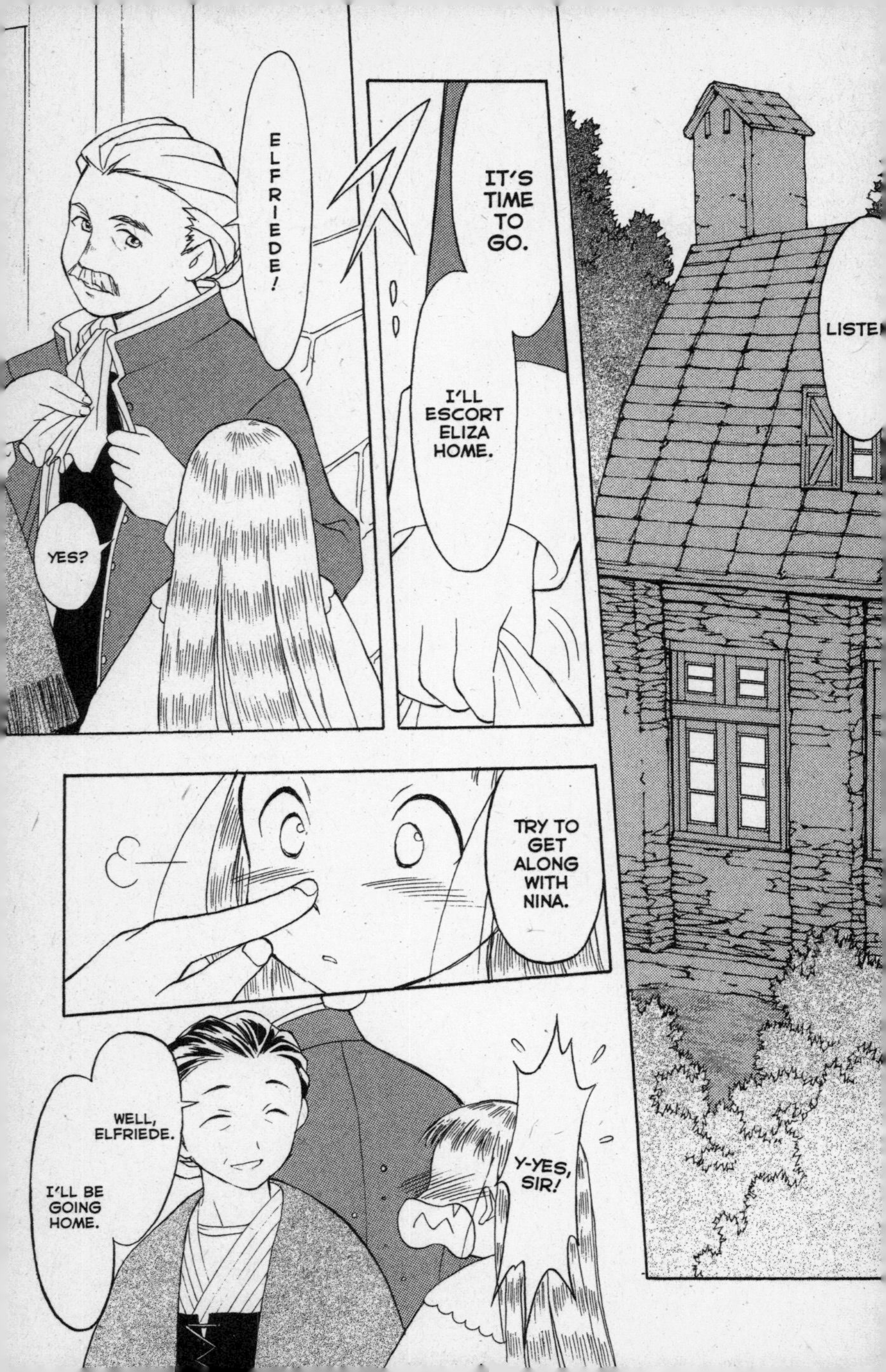
LISTE
IT'S TIME TO GO.
I'LL ESCORT ELIZA HOME.
ELFRIEDE!
YES?
TRY TO GET ALONG WITH NINA.
WELL, ELFRIEDE.
I'LL BE GOING HOME.
Y-YES, SIR!

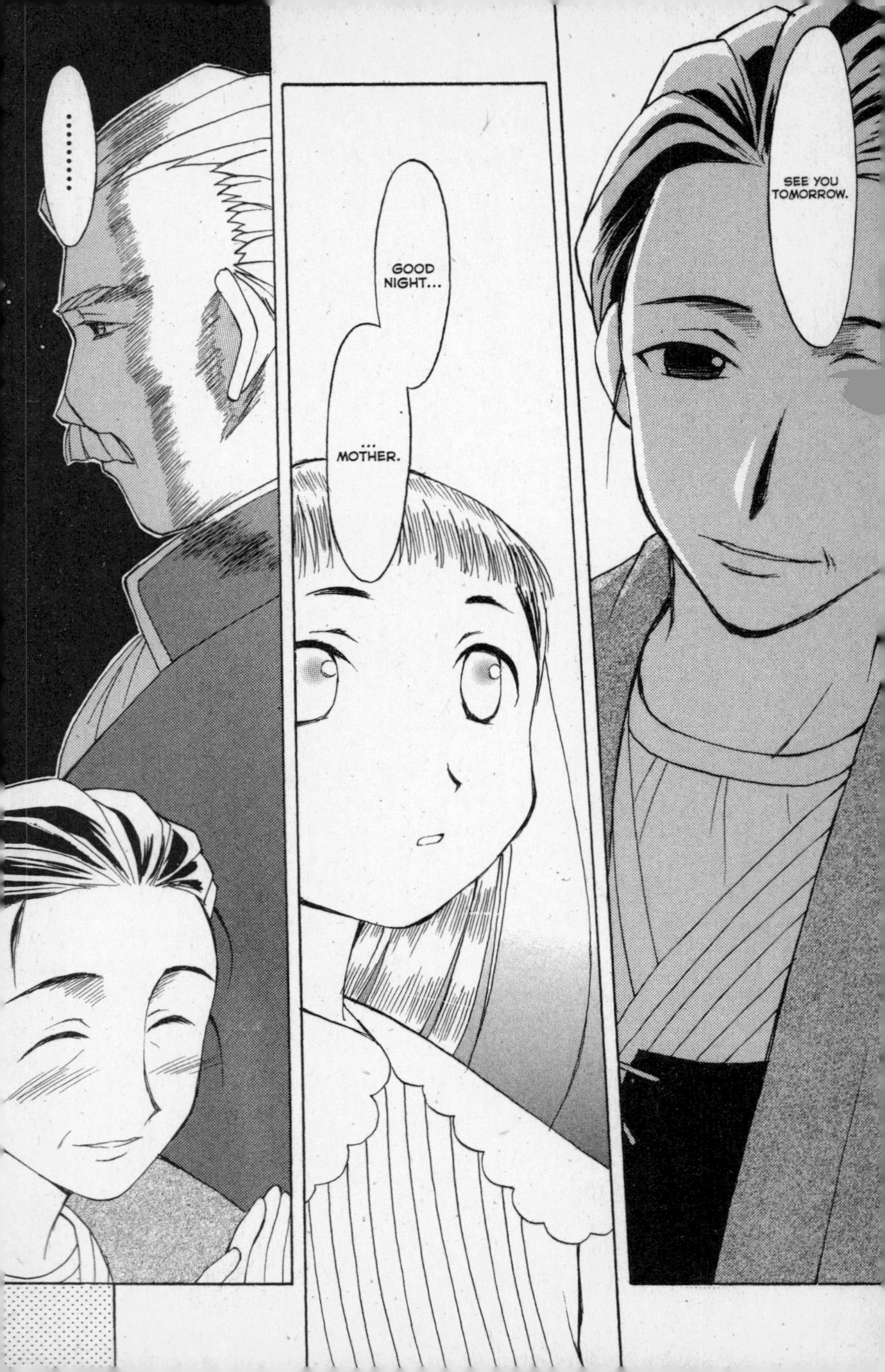
SEE YOU TOMORROW.
GOOD NIGHT...
...MOTHER.
......

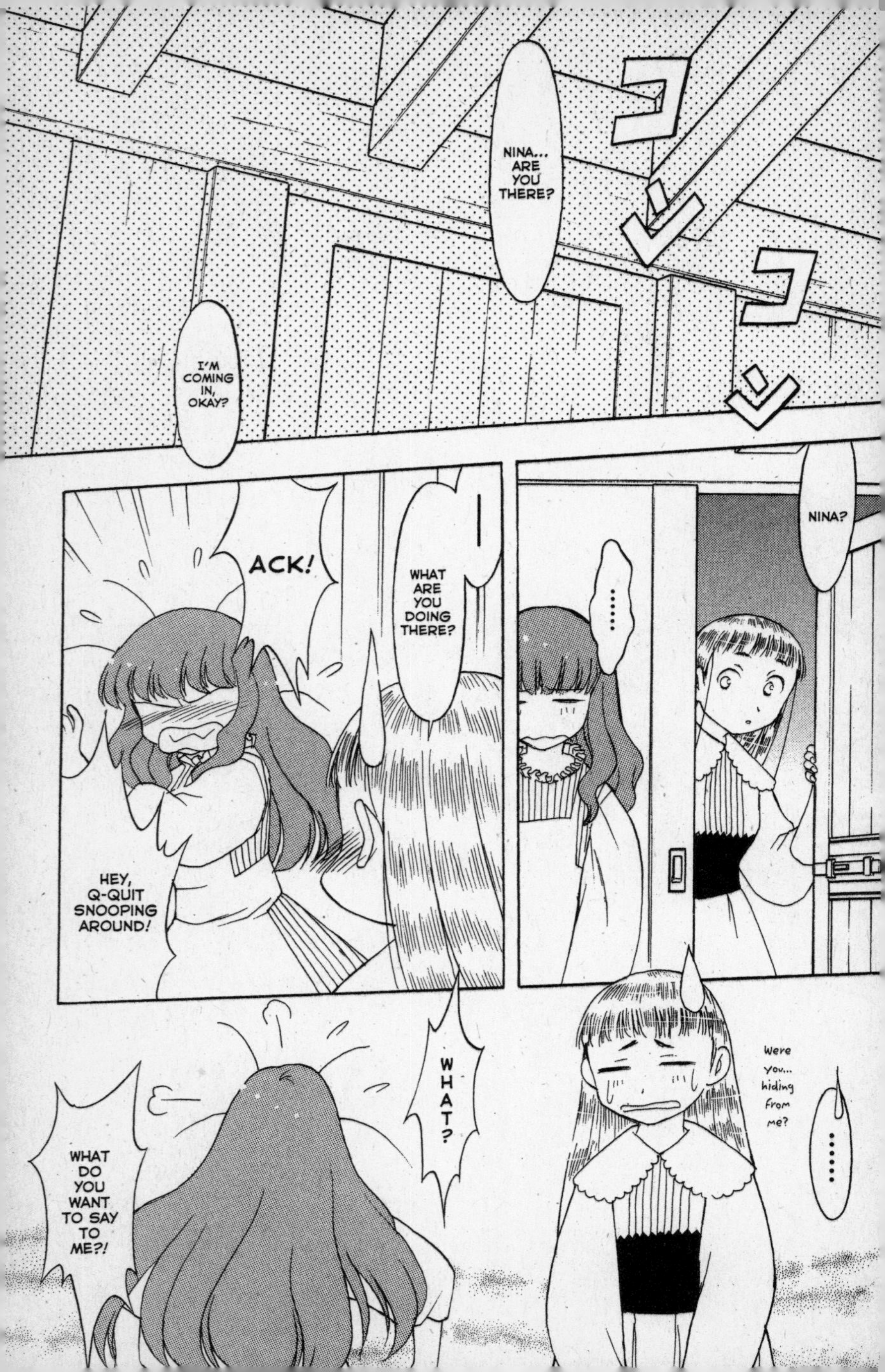
コン
NINA... ARE YOU THERE?
コン
I'M COMING IN, OKAY?
NINA?
......
WHAT ARE YOU DOING THERE?
ACK!
HEY, Q-QUIT SNOOPING AROUND!
......
Were you... hiding from me?
WHAT?
WHAT DO YOU WANT TO SAY TO ME?!

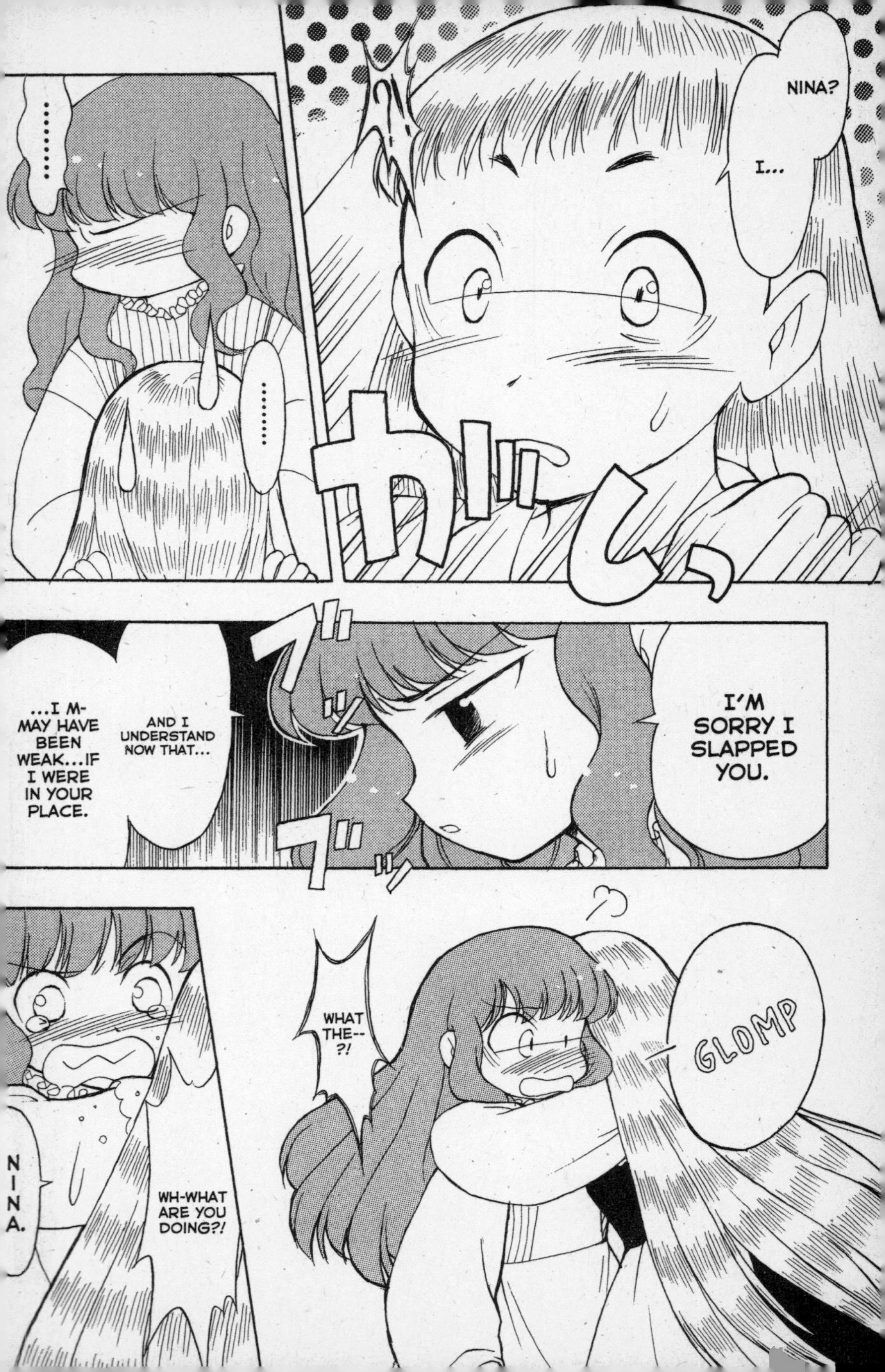
NINA?
I...
?!
......
......
I'M SORRY I SLAPPED YOU.
AND I UNDERSTAND NOW THAT...
...I M-MAY HAVE BEEN WEAK...IF I WERE IN YOUR PLACE.
GLOMP
WHAT THE-- ?!
WH-WHAT ARE YOU DOING?!
NINA.

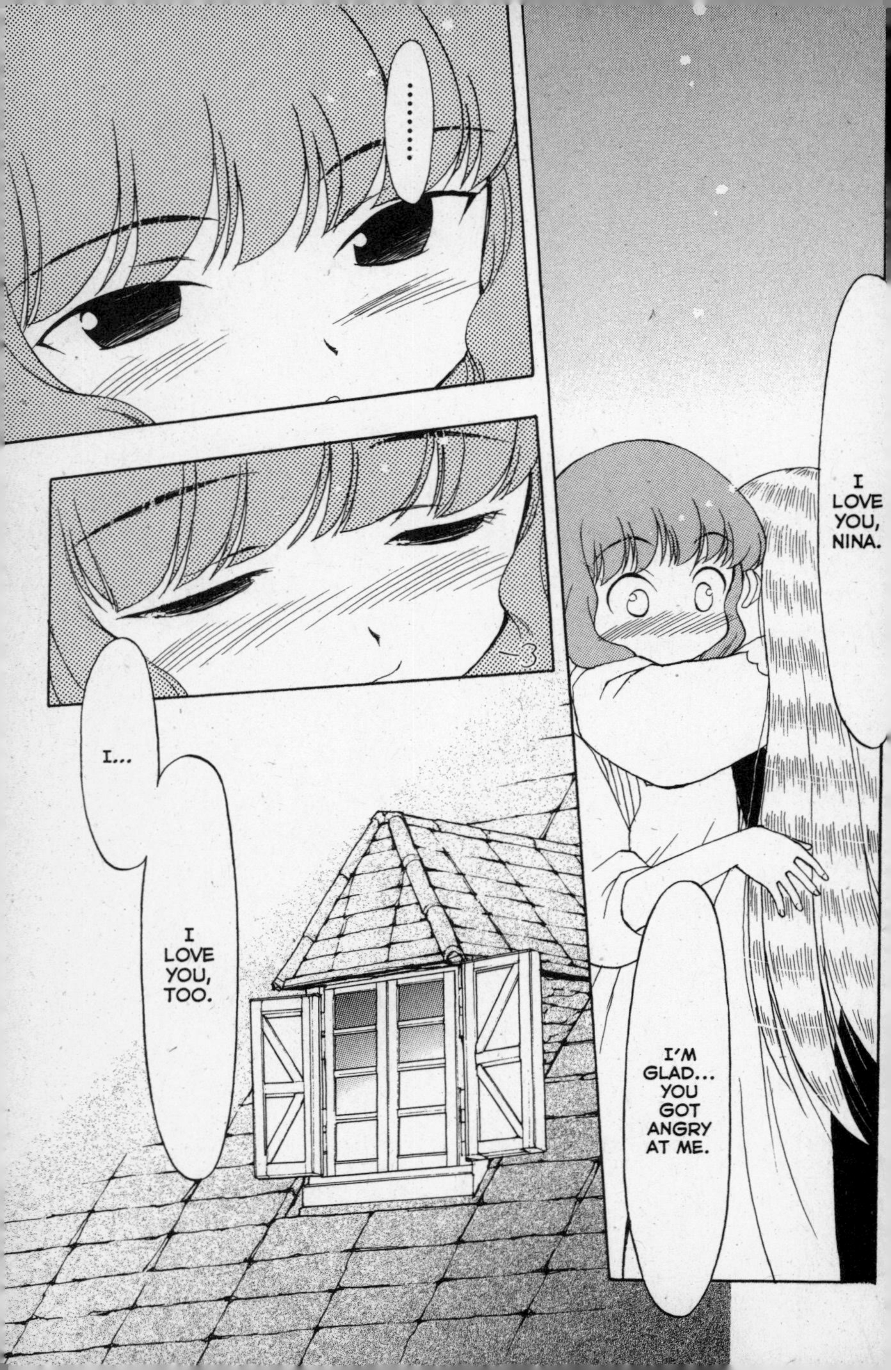
I LOVE YOU, NINA.
I'M GLAD... YOU GOT ANGRY AT ME.
......
I...
I LOVE YOU, TOO.

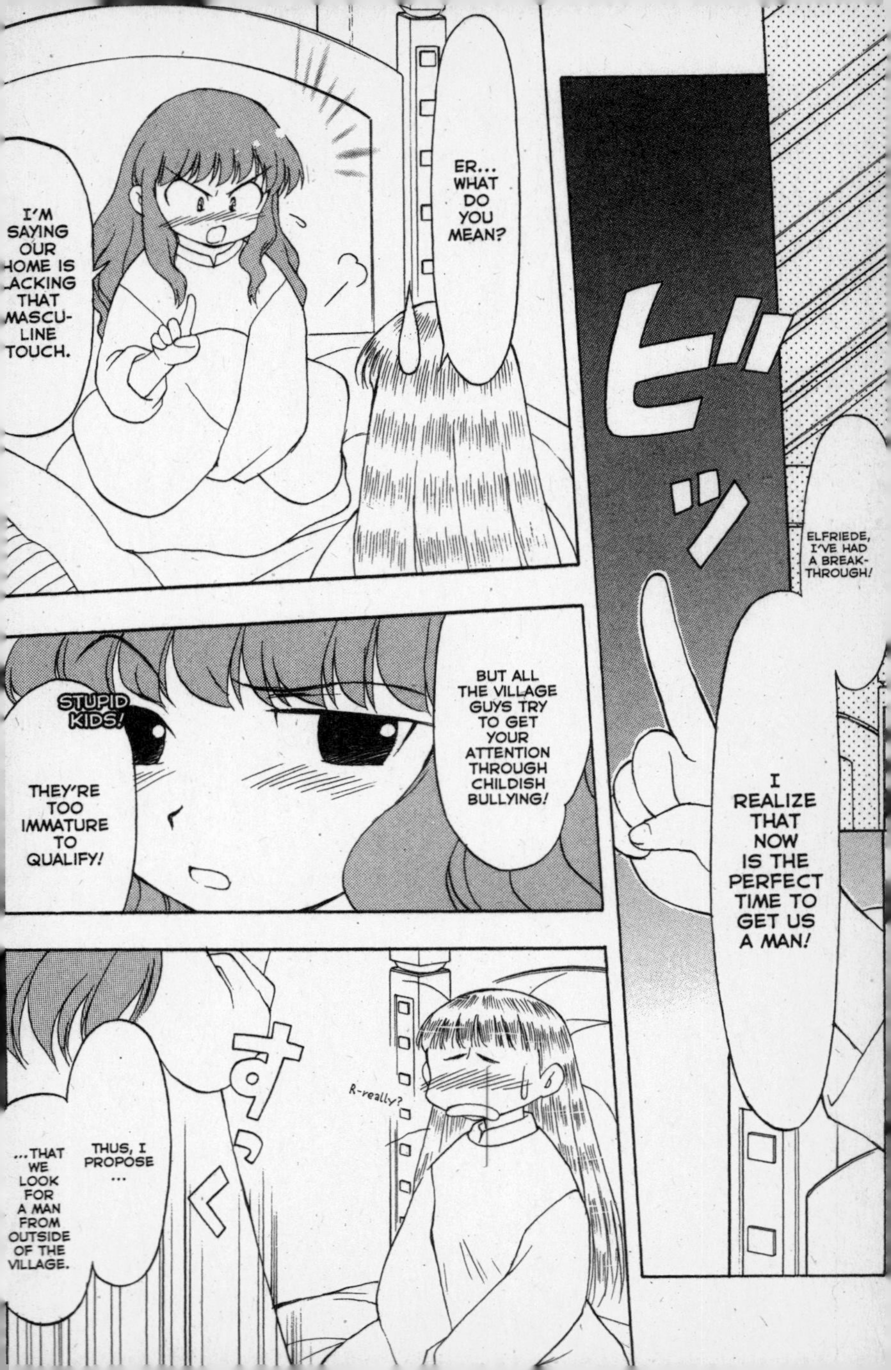
ビッ
ELFRIEDE, I'VE HAD A BREAK-THROUGH!
I REALIZE THAT NOW IS THE PERFECT TIME TO GET US A MAN!
ER... WHAT DO YOU MEAN?
I'M SAYING OUR HOME IS LACKING THAT MASCU-LINE TOUCH.
BUT ALL THE VILLAGE GUYS TRY TO GET YOUR ATTENTION THROUGH CHILDISH BULLYING!
STUPID KIDS!
THEY'RE TOO IMMATURE TO QUALIFY!
R-really?
すっく
THUS, I PROPOSE...
...THAT WE LOOK FOR A MAN FROM OUTSIDE OF THE VILLAGE.

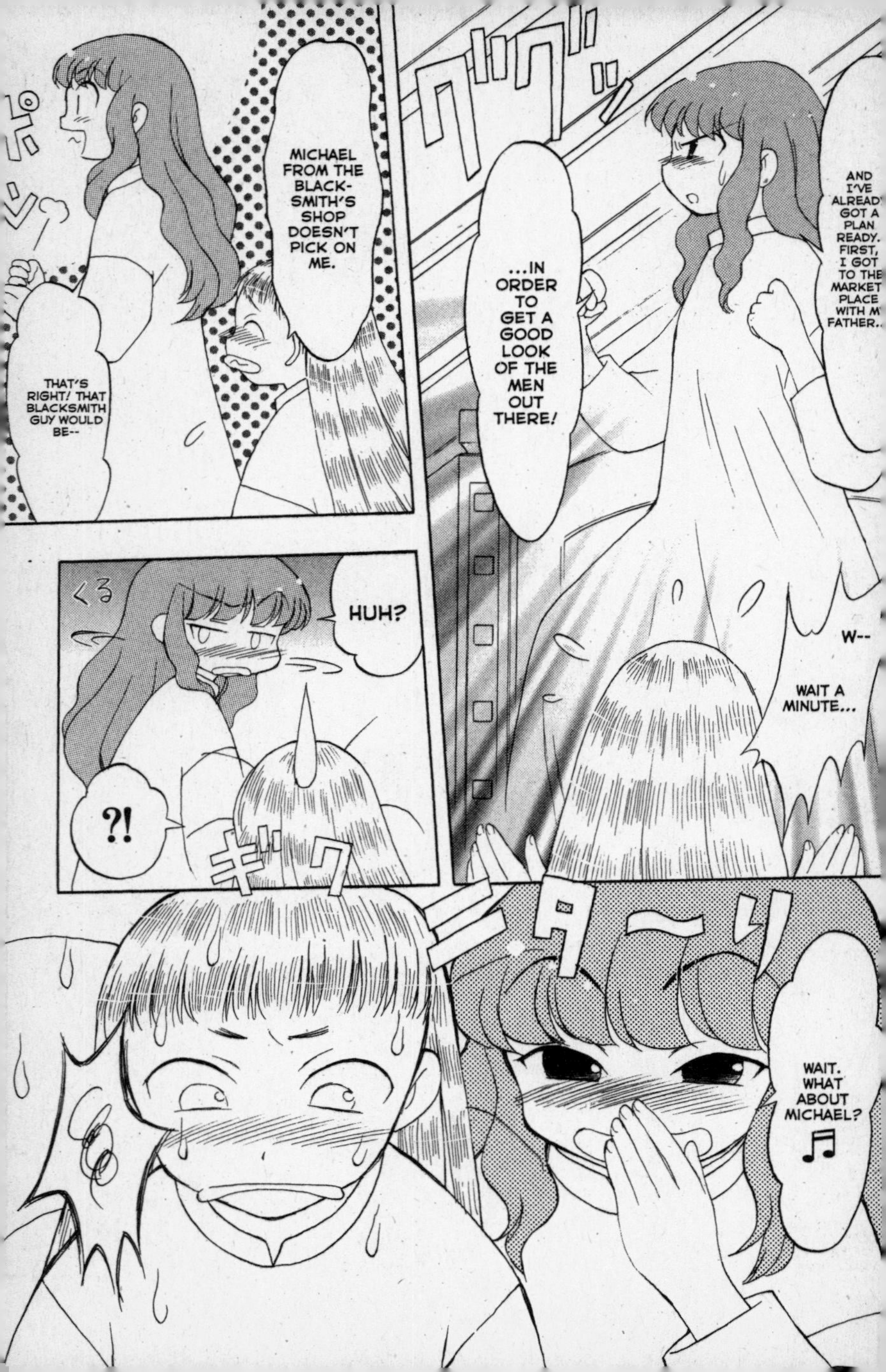
AND I'VE ALREAD GOT A PLAN READY. FIRST, I GOT TO THE MARKET PLACE WITH M' FATHER...
...IN ORDER TO GET A GOOD LOOK OF THE MEN OUT THERE!
W--
WAIT A MINUTE...
MICHAEL FROM THE BLACK-SMITH'S SHOP DOESN'T PICK ON ME.
THAT'S RIGHT! THAT BLACKSMITH GUY WOULD BE--
くる
HUH?
?!
WAIT. WHAT ABOUT MICHAEL? ♪

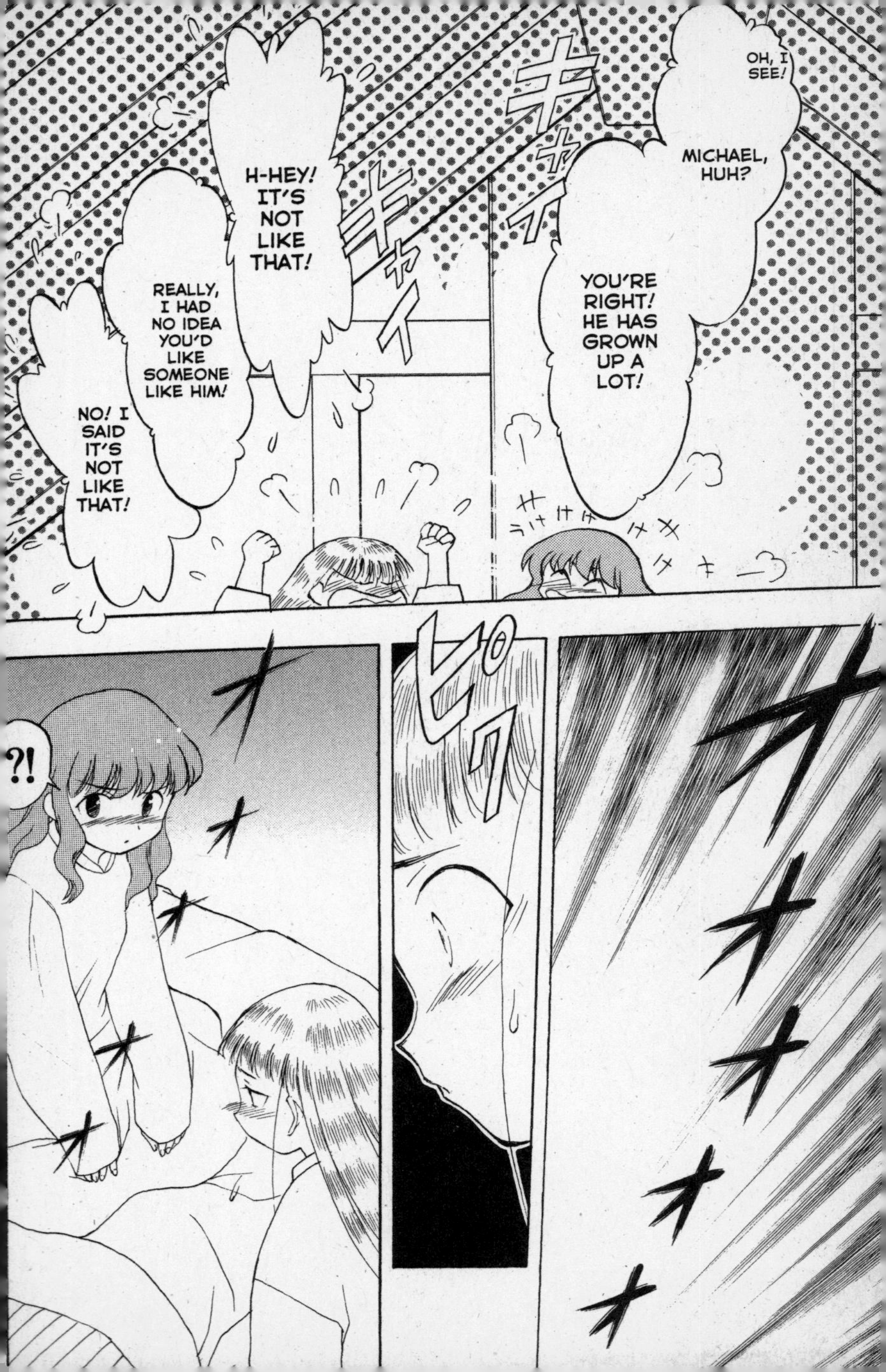
OH, I SEE!
MICHAEL, HUH?
YOU'RE RIGHT! HE HAS GROWN UP A LOT!
H-HEY! IT'S NOT LIKE THAT!
REALLY, I HAD NO IDEA YOU'D LIKE SOMEONE LIKE HIM!
NO! I SAID IT'S NOT LIKE THAT!
?!

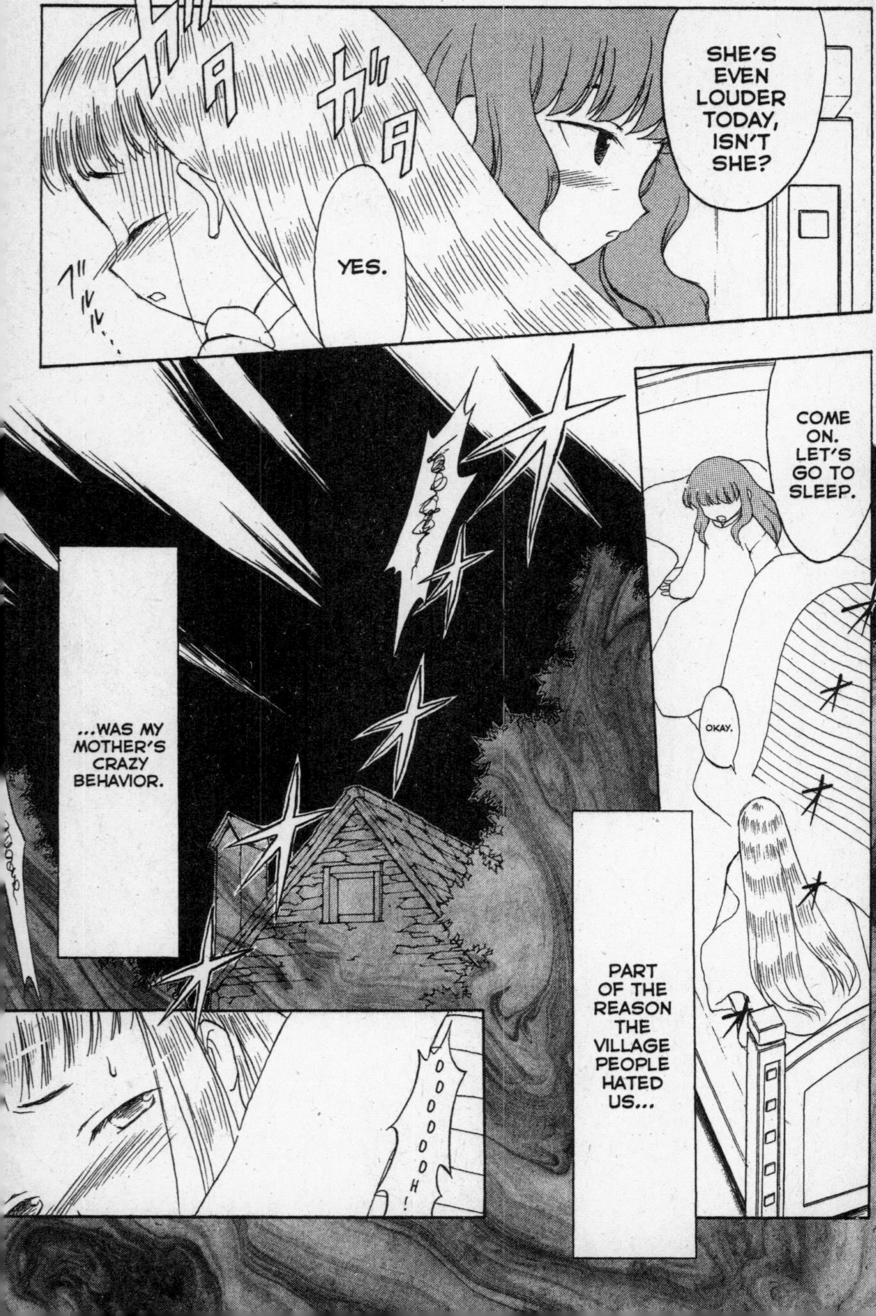
SHE'S EVEN LOUDER TODAY, ISN'T SHE?
ガタ
ガタ
YES.
ブルル…
COME ON. LET'S GO TO SLEEP.
OKAY.
PART OF THE REASON THE VILLAGE PEOPLE HATED US...
...WAS MY MOTHER'S CRAZY BEHAVIOR.
OOOOOOH!

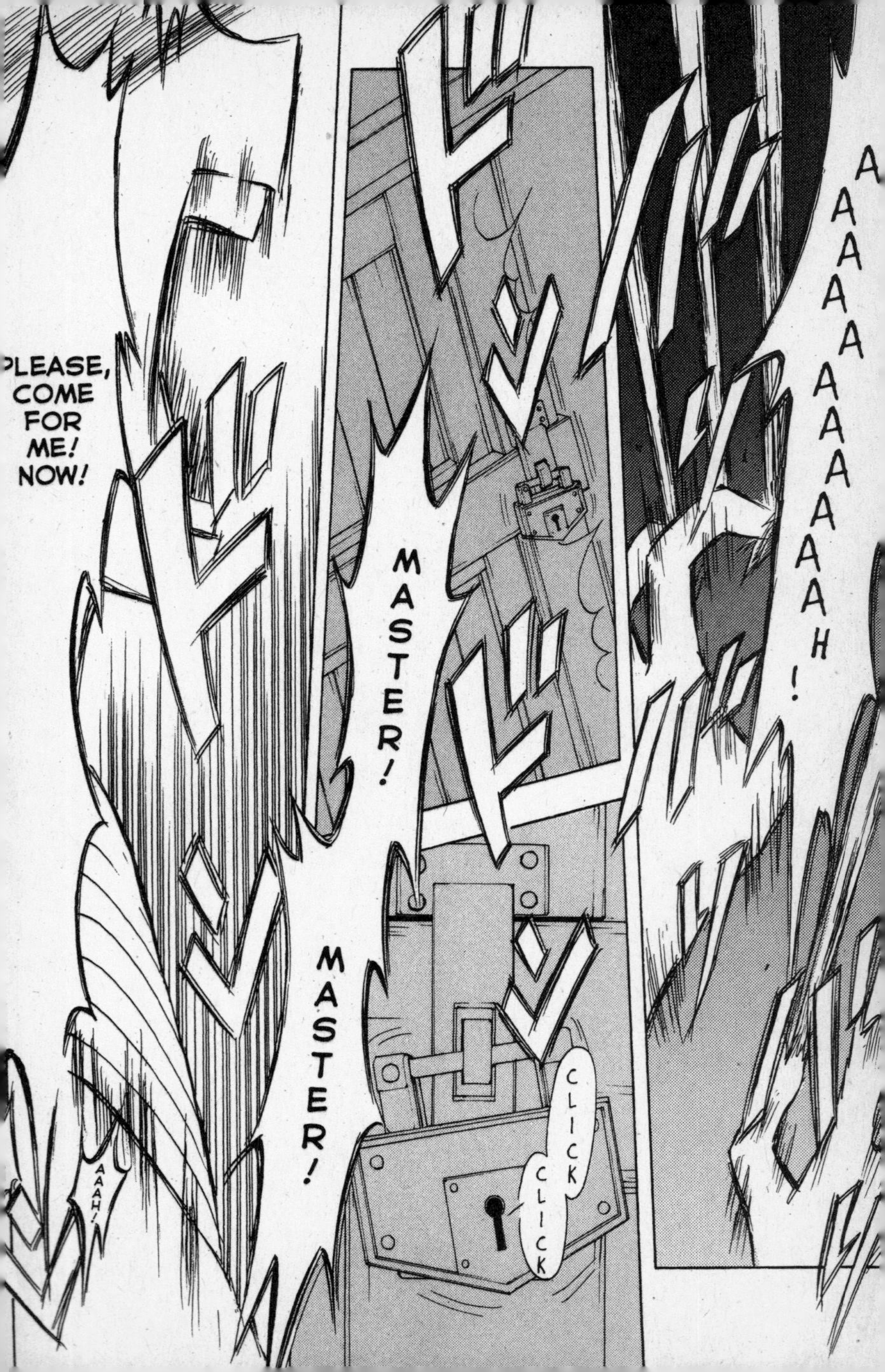
AAAAAAAAAAAH!
MASTER!
MASTER!
CLICK
CLICK
PLEASE, COME FOR ME! NOW!
AAAH!

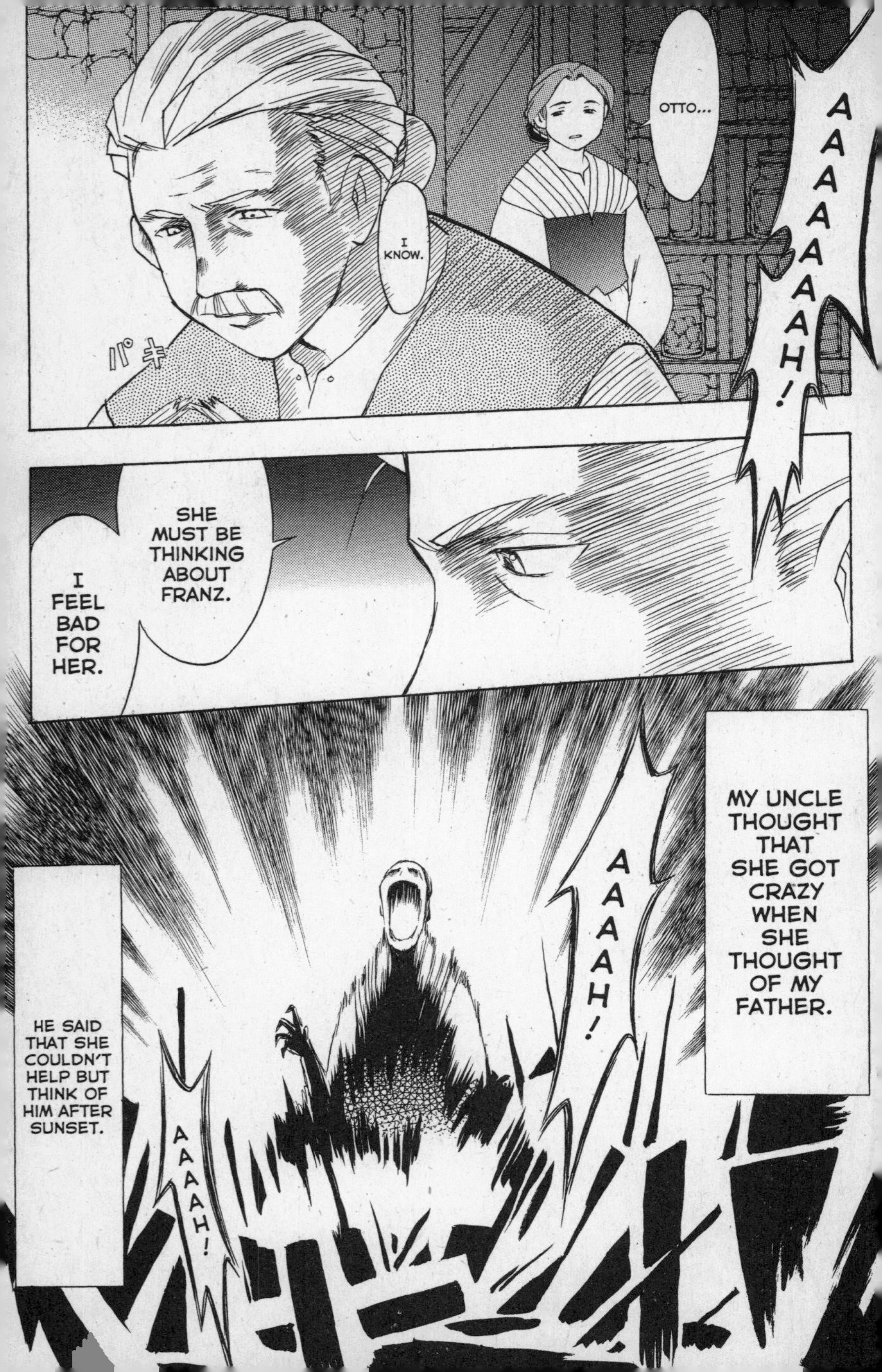
AAAAAAAH!
OTTO...
I KNOW.
パキ
SHE MUST BE THINKING ABOUT FRANZ.
I FEEL BAD FOR HER.
MY UNCLE THOUGHT THAT SHE GOT CRAZY WHEN SHE THOUGHT OF MY FATHER.
AAAAH!
AAAAH!
HE SAID THAT SHE COULDN'T HELP BUT THINK OF HIM AFTER SUNSET.

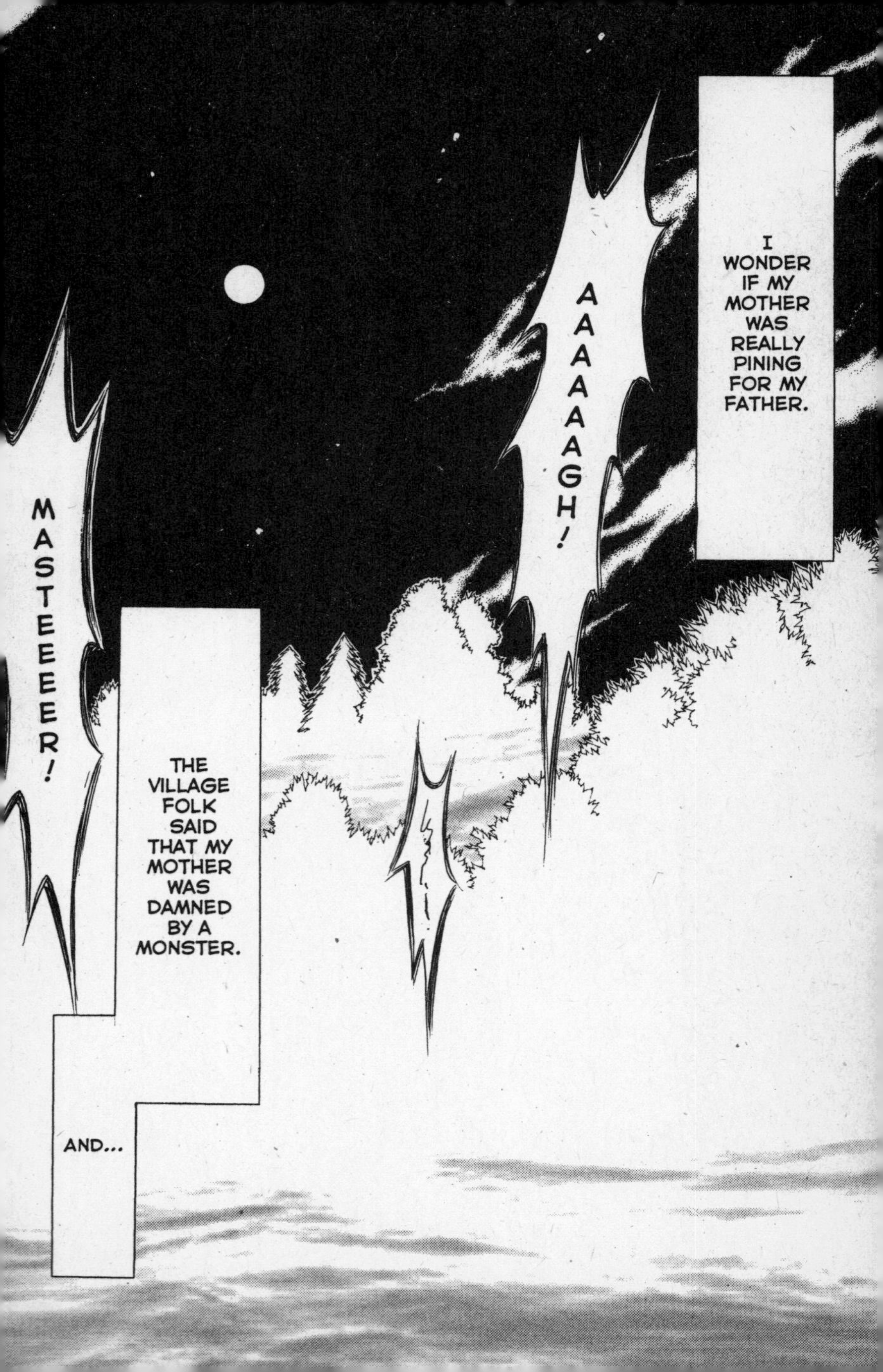
I WONDER IF MY MOTHER WAS REALLY PINING FOR MY FATHER.
AAAAAAAGH!
MASTEEEER!
THE VILLAGE FOLK SAID THAT MY MOTHER WAS DAMNED BY A MONSTER.
AND...

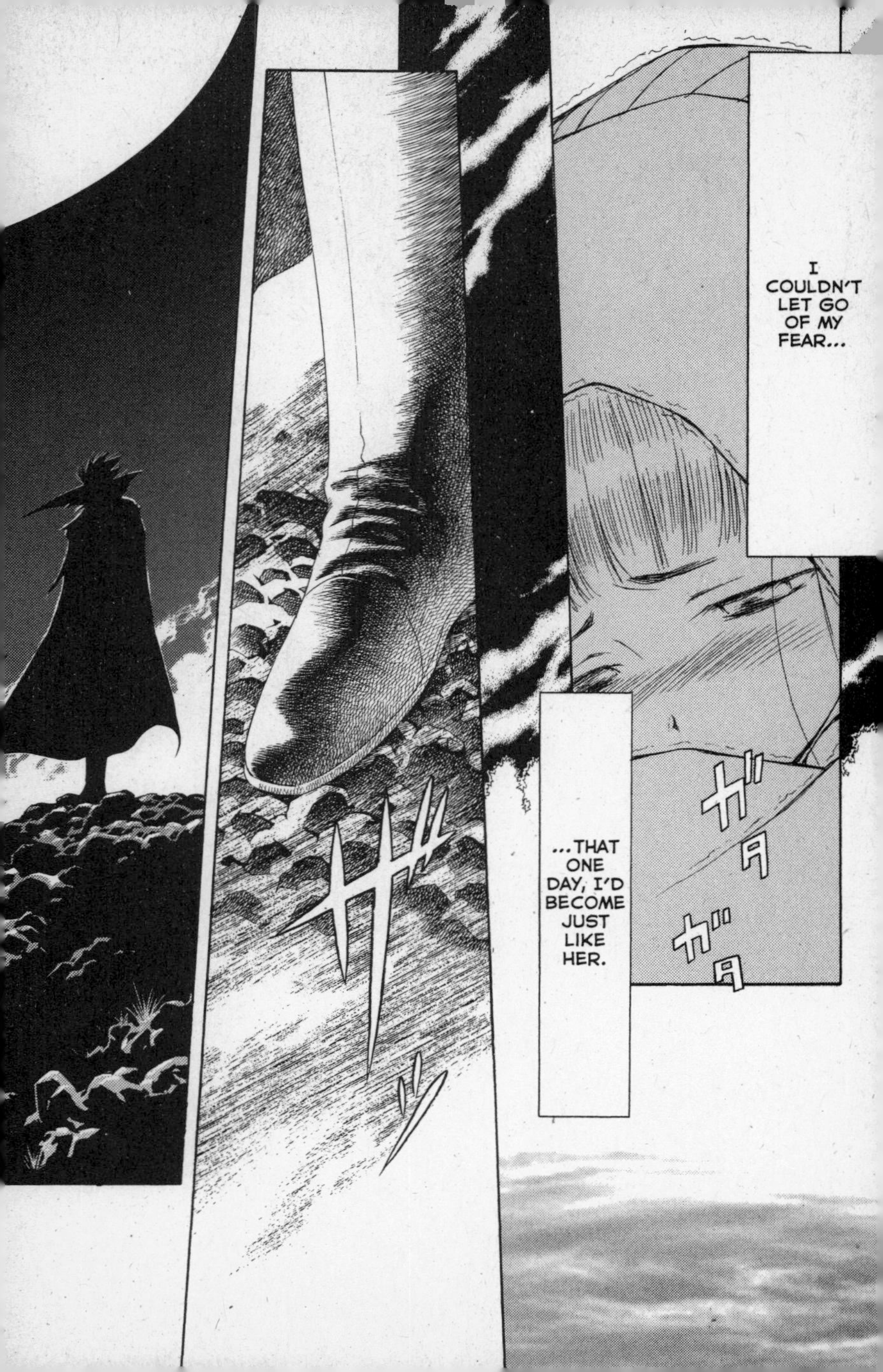
I COULDN'T LET GO OF MY FEAR...
...THAT ONE DAY, I'D BECOME JUST LIKE HER.
ガタ
ガタ
ザッ

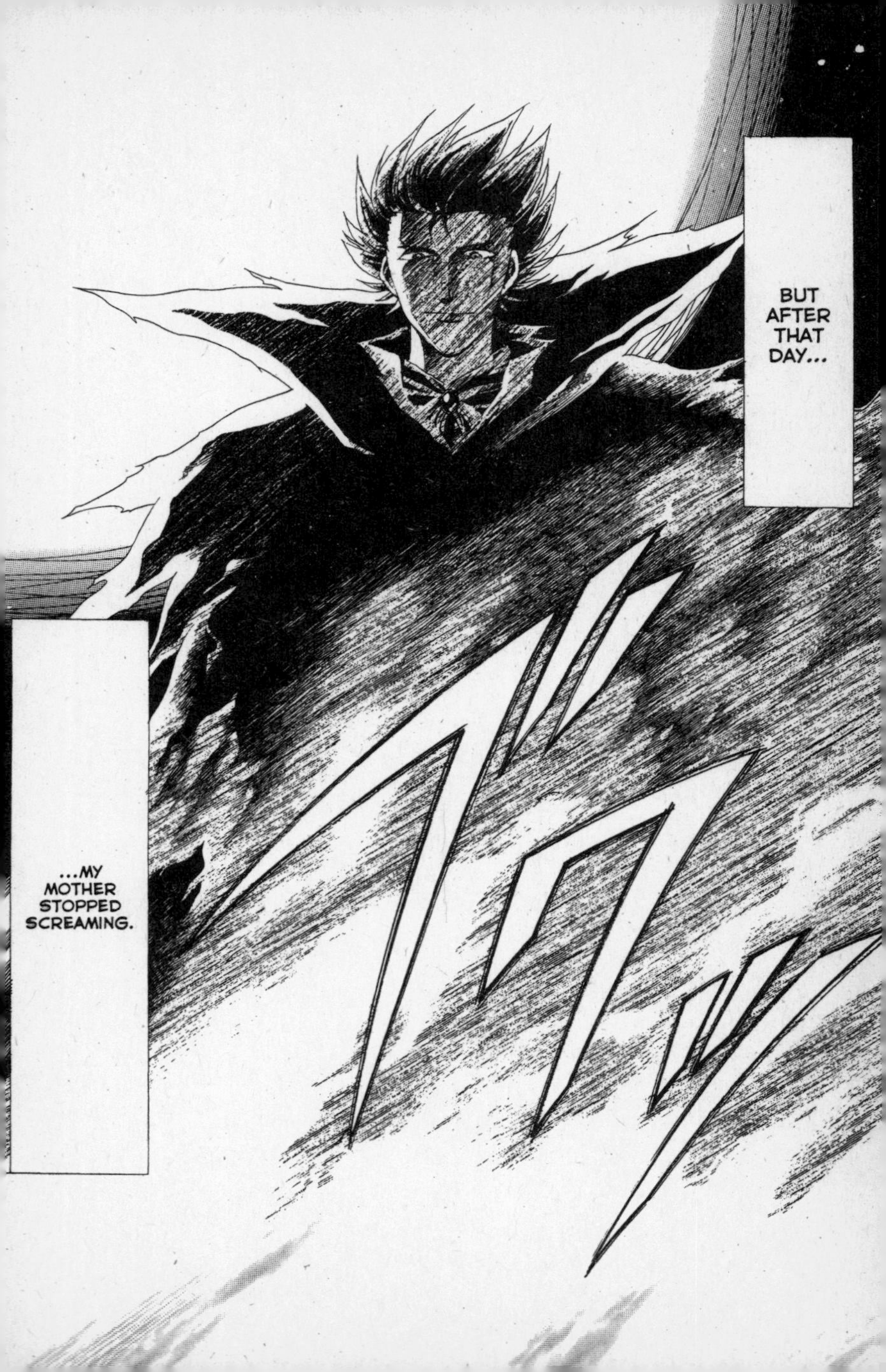
BUT AFTER THAT DAY...
...MY MOTHER STOPPED SCREAMING.

MOON 月詠 PHASE

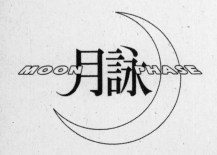

THE HOGWARTS EXPRESS! (HA!)

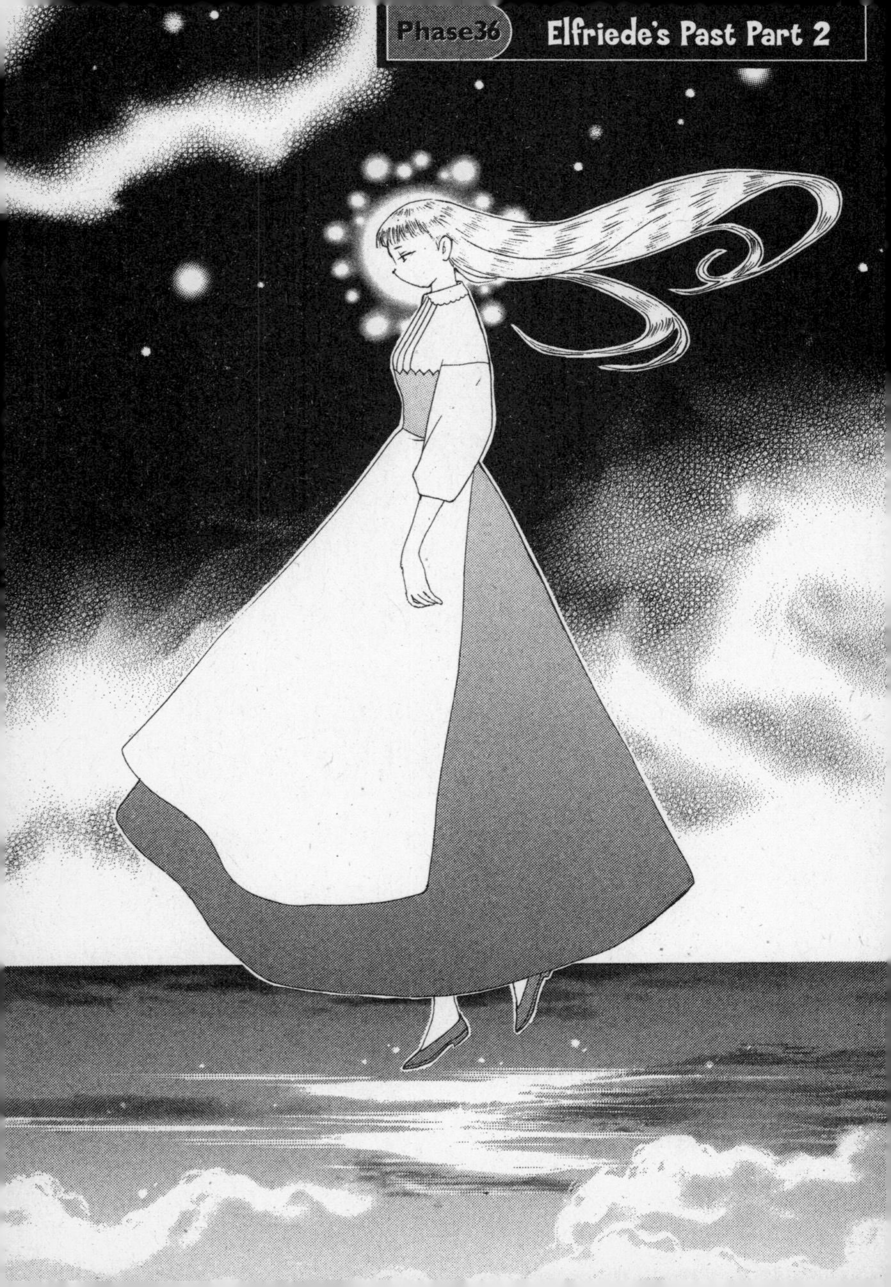
Phase36
Elfriede's Past Part 2

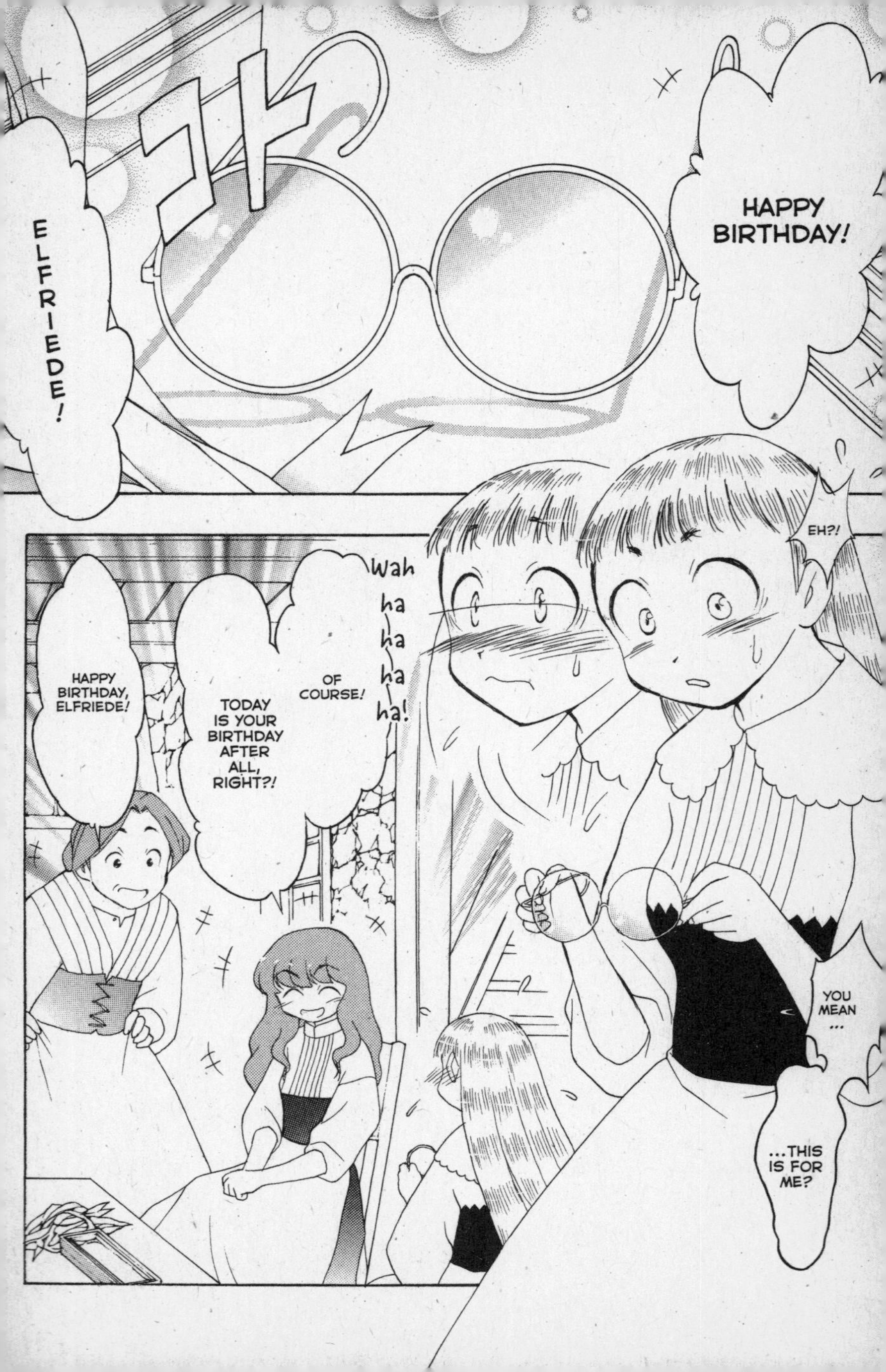
HAPPY BIRTHDAY!
コト
ELFRIEDE!
EH?!
YOU MEAN ...
...THIS IS FOR ME?
Wah ha ha ha ha!
OF COURSE!
TODAY IS YOUR BIRTHDAY AFTER ALL, RIGHT?!
HAPPY BIRTHDAY, ELFRIEDE!

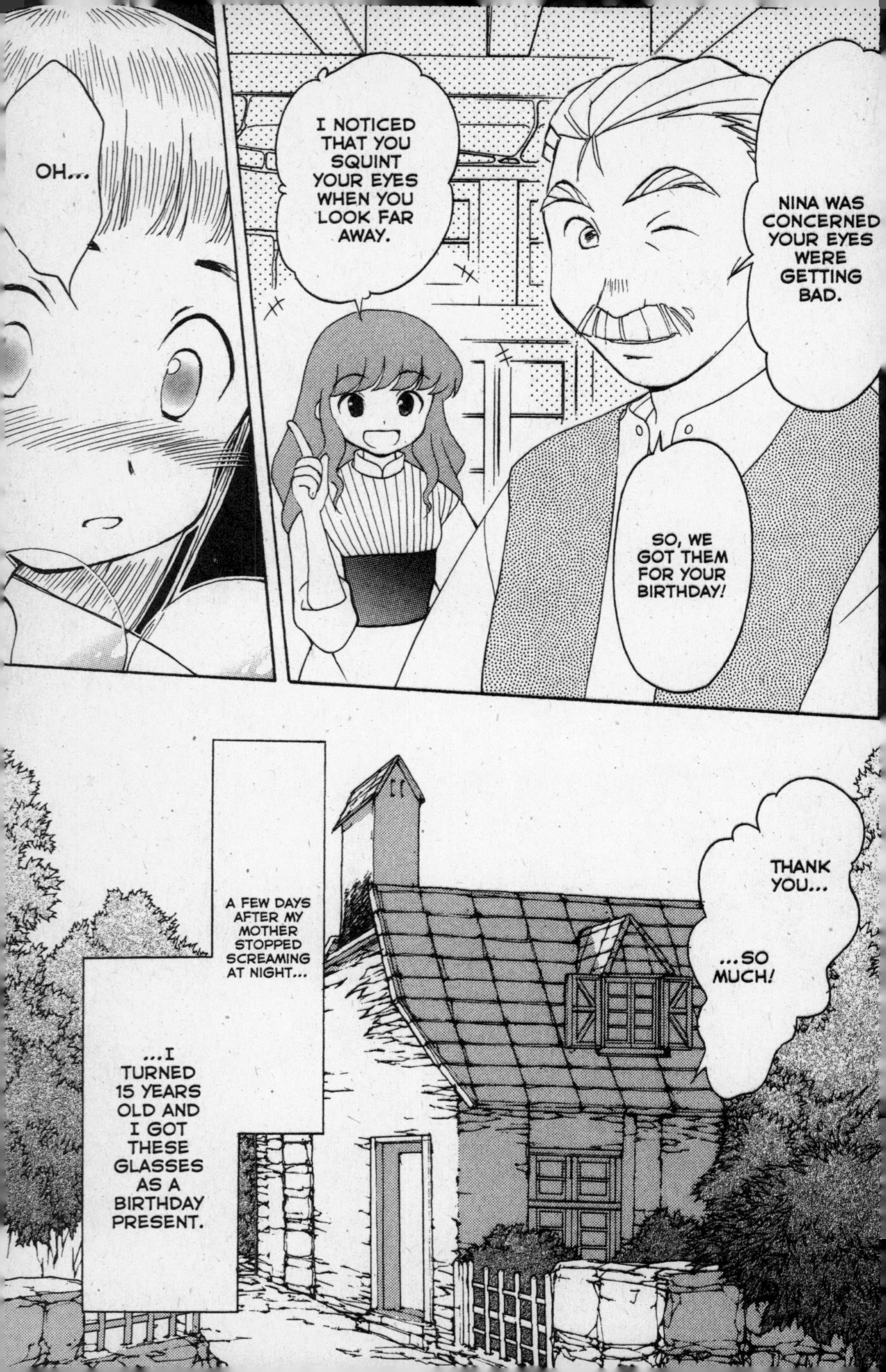
NINA WAS CONCERNED YOUR EYES WERE GETTING BAD.
I NOTICED THAT YOU SQUINT YOUR EYES WHEN YOU LOOK FAR AWAY.
SO, WE GOT THEM FOR YOUR BIRTHDAY!
OH...
THANK YOU...
...SO MUCH!
A FEW DAYS AFTER MY MOTHER STOPPED SCREAMING AT NIGHT...
...I TURNED 15 YEARS OLD AND I GOT THESE GLASSES AS A BIRTHDAY PRESENT.

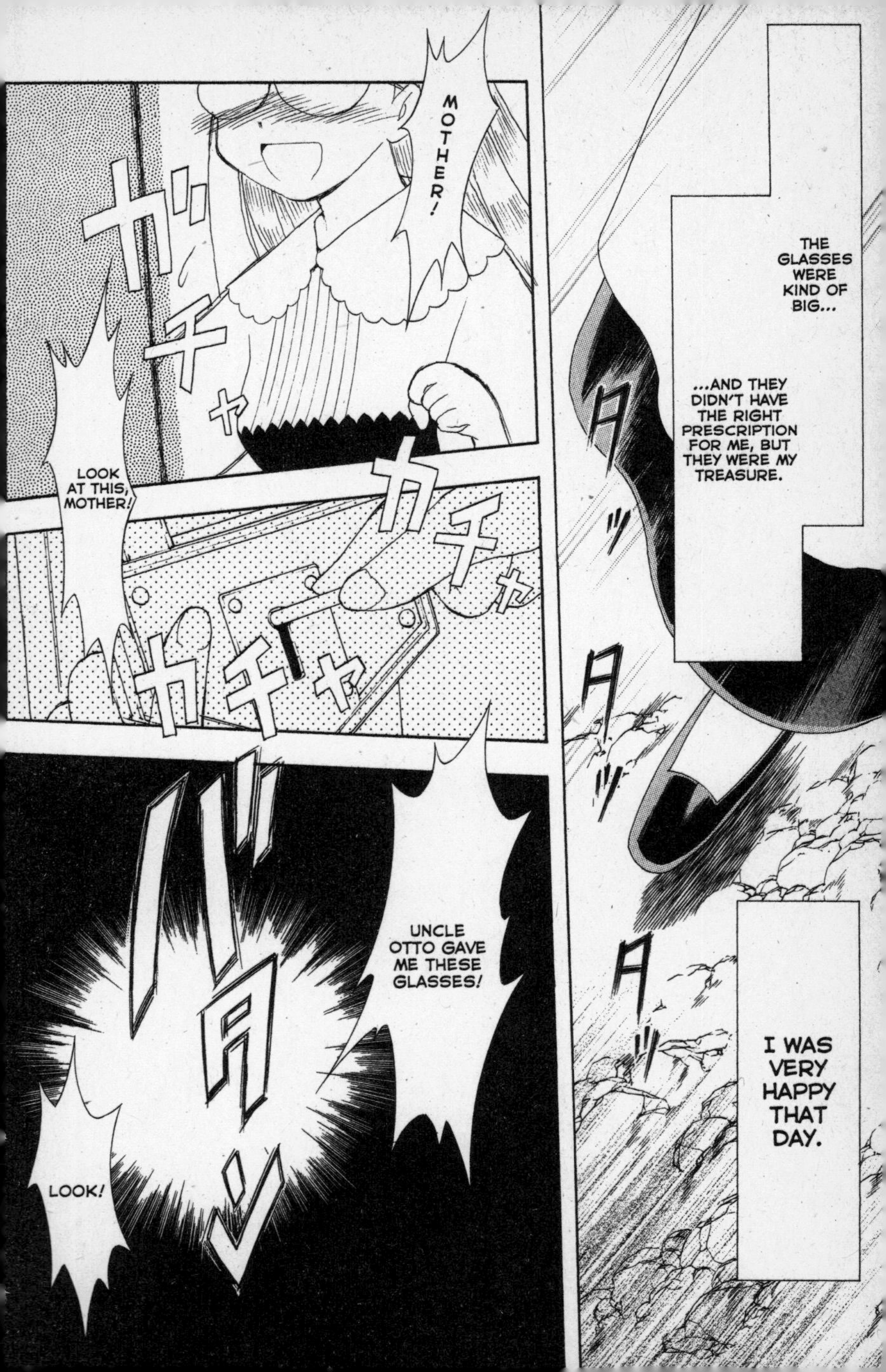
THE GLASSES WERE KIND OF BIG...
...AND THEY DIDN'T HAVE THE RIGHT PRESCRIPTION FOR ME, BUT THEY WERE MY TREASURE.
タッ
タッ
タッ
I WAS VERY HAPPY THAT DAY.
MOTHER!
ガチャ
LOOK AT THIS, MOTHER!
カチャ
カチャ
UNCLE OTTO GAVE ME THESE GLASSES!
LOOK!

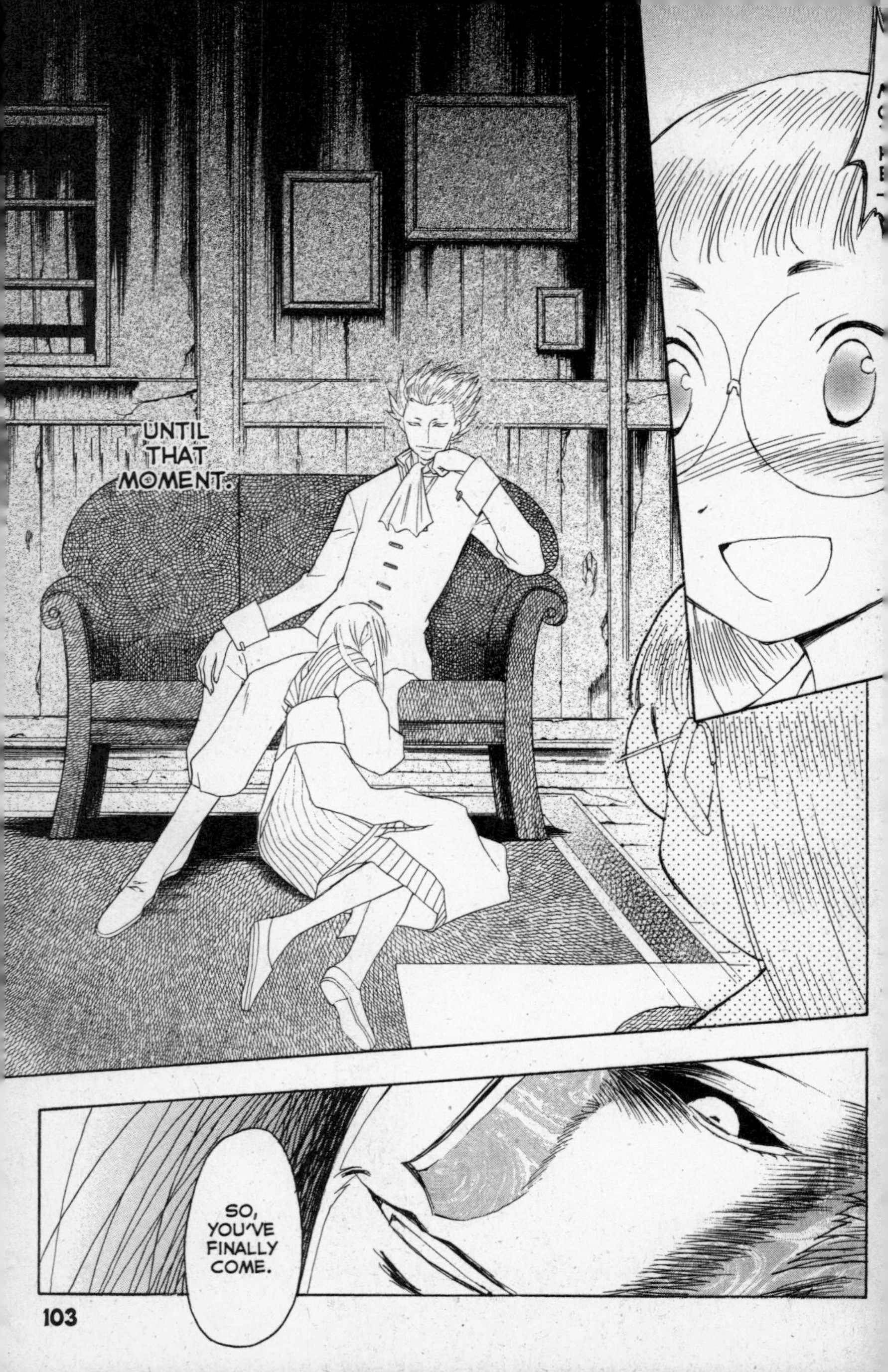
UNTIL THAT MOMENT.
SO, YOU'VE FINALLY COME.

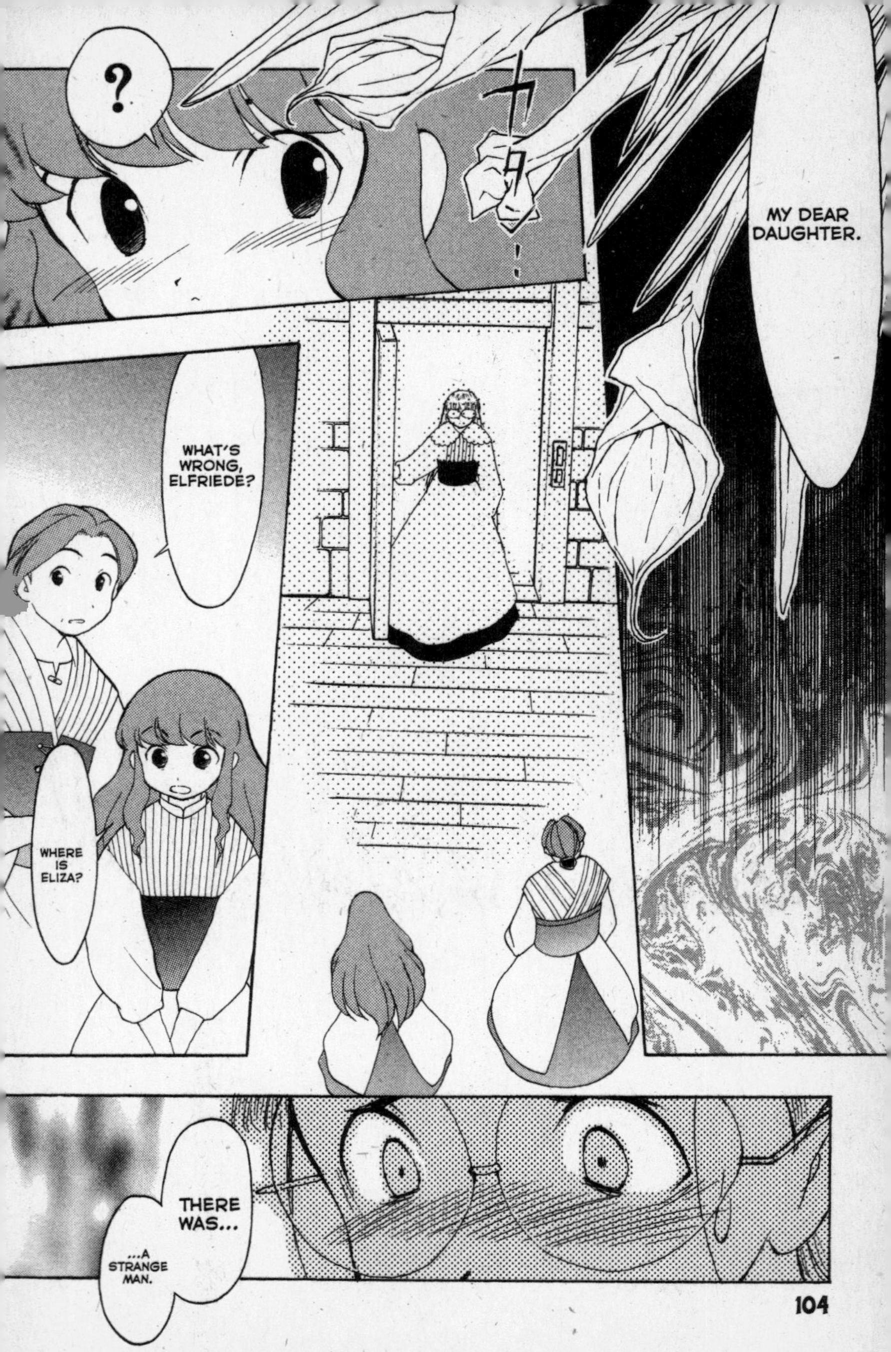
MY DEAR DAUGHTER.
?
カタ
WHAT'S WRONG, ELFRIEDE?
WHERE IS ELIZA?
THERE WAS...
...A STRANGE MAN.

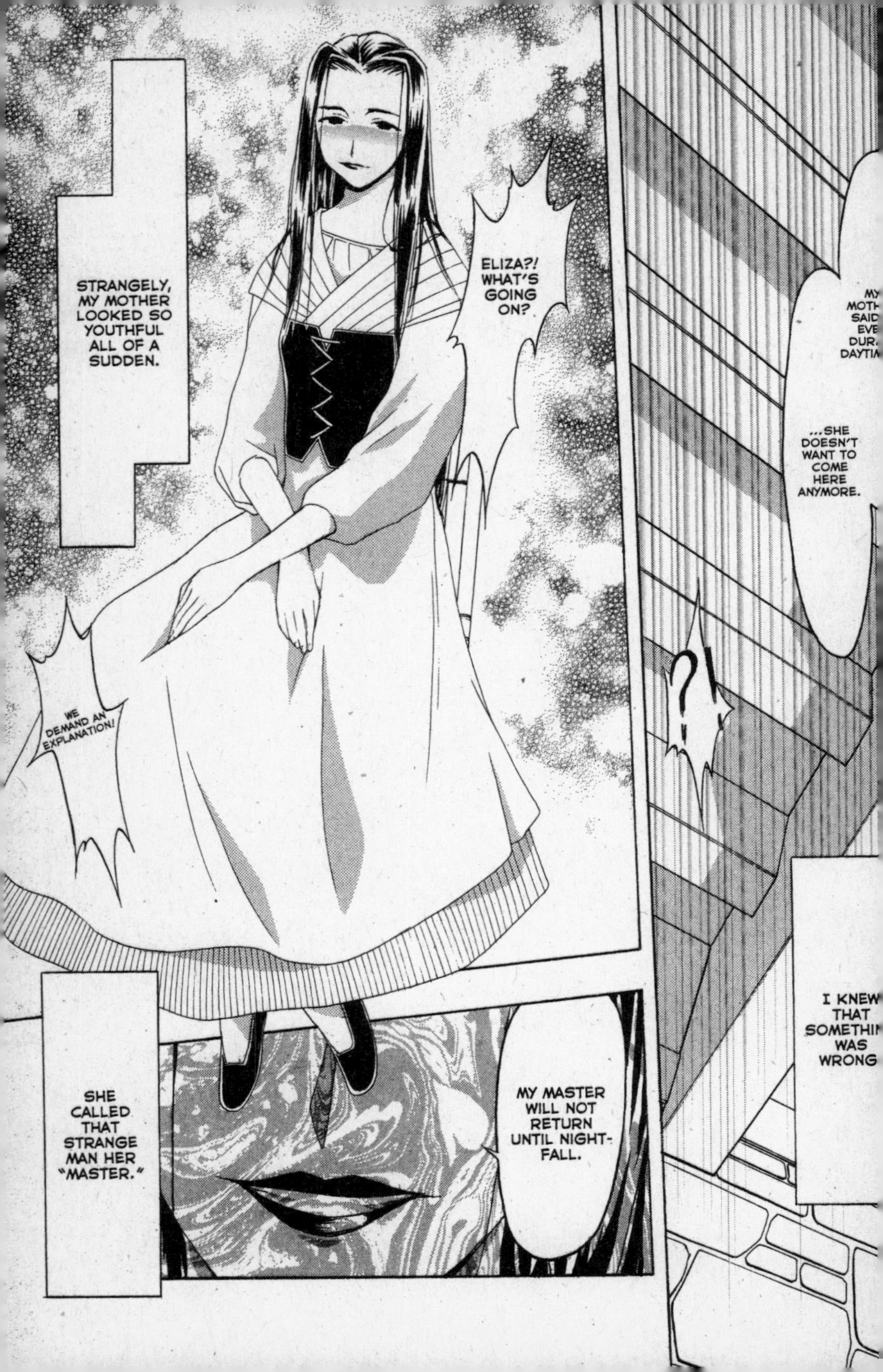
MY MOTH SAID EVE DUR. DAYTIM
...SHE DOESN'T WANT TO COME HERE ANYMORE.
?!
I KNEW THAT SOMETHIN WAS WRONG
ELIZA?! WHAT'S GOING ON?
STRANGELY, MY MOTHER LOOKED SO YOUTHFUL ALL OF A SUDDEN.
WE DEMAND AN EXPLANATION!
MY MASTER WILL NOT RETURN UNTIL NIGHT-FALL.
SHE CALLED THAT STRANGE MAN HER "MASTER."

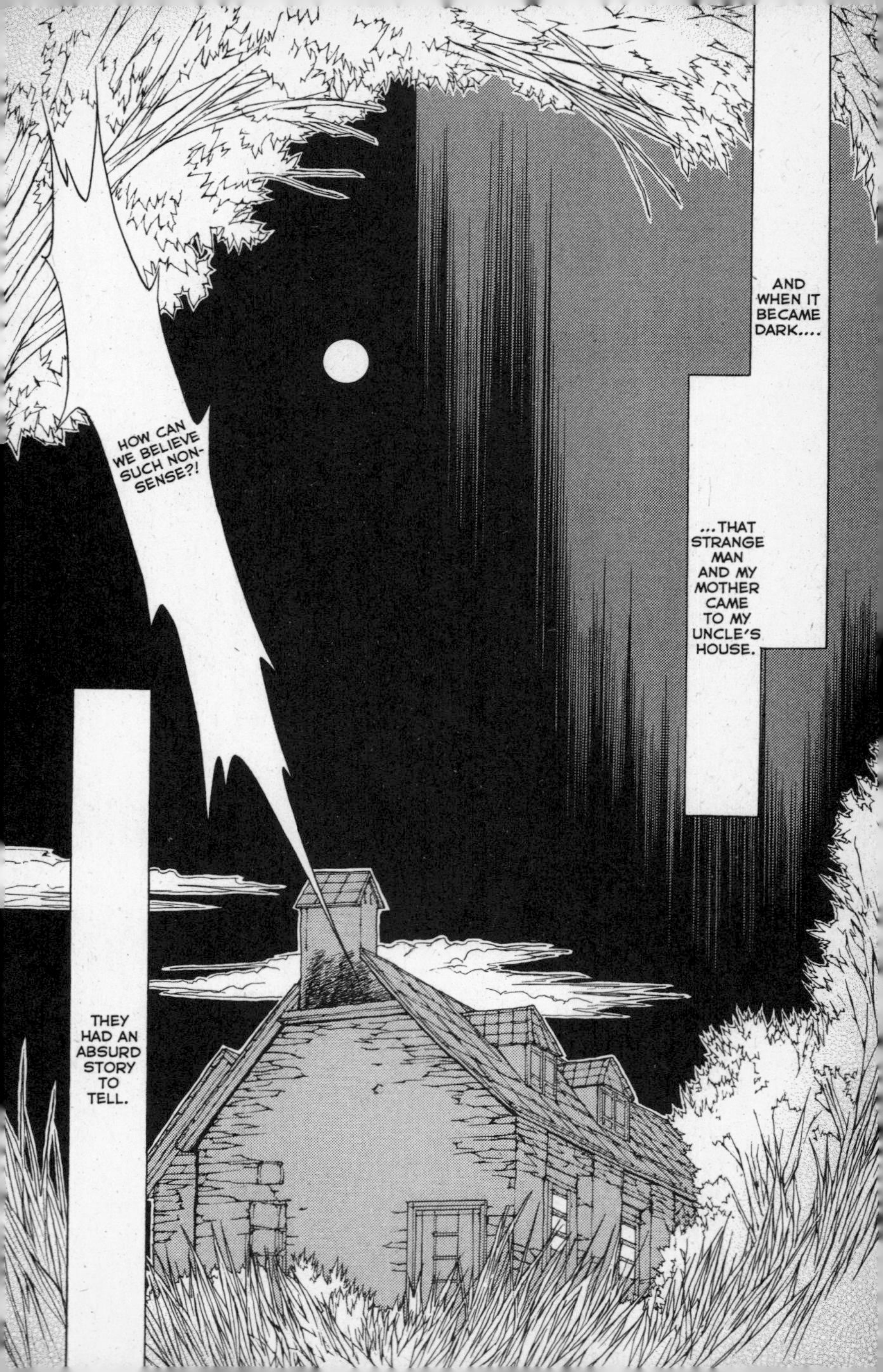
AND WHEN IT BECAME DARK....
...THAT STRANGE MAN AND MY MOTHER CAME TO MY UNCLE'S HOUSE.
THEY HAD AN ABSURD STORY TO TELL.
HOW CAN WE BELIEVE SUCH NON-SENSE?!

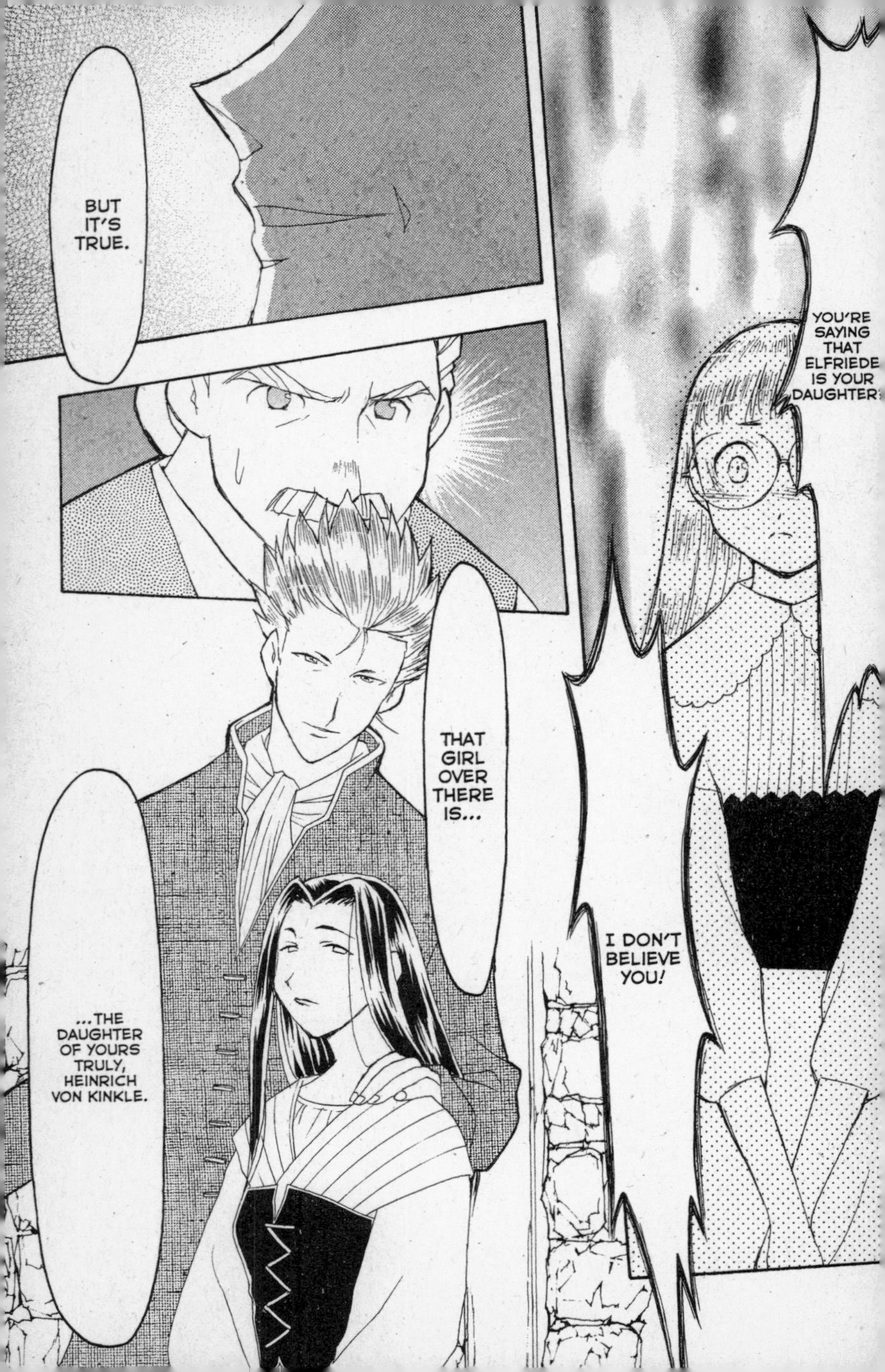
YOU'RE SAYING THAT ELFRIEDE IS YOUR DAUGHTER?
I DON'T BELIEVE YOU!
BUT IT'S TRUE.
THAT GIRL OVER THERE IS...
...THE DAUGHTER OF YOURS TRULY, HEINRICH VON KINKLE.

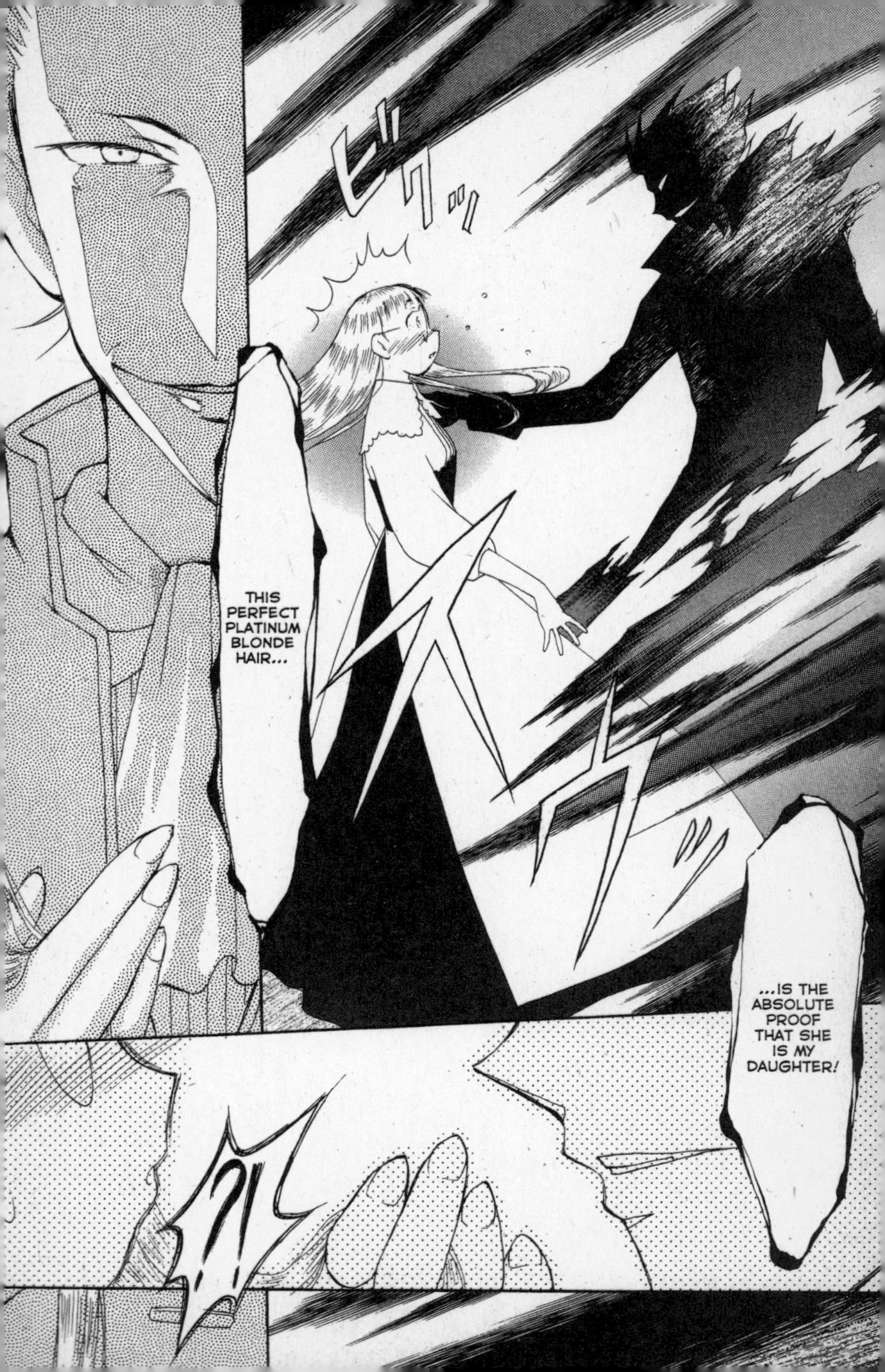
THIS PERFECT PLATINUM BLONDE HAIR...
...IS THE ABSOLUTE PROOF THAT SHE IS MY DAUGHTER!
?!

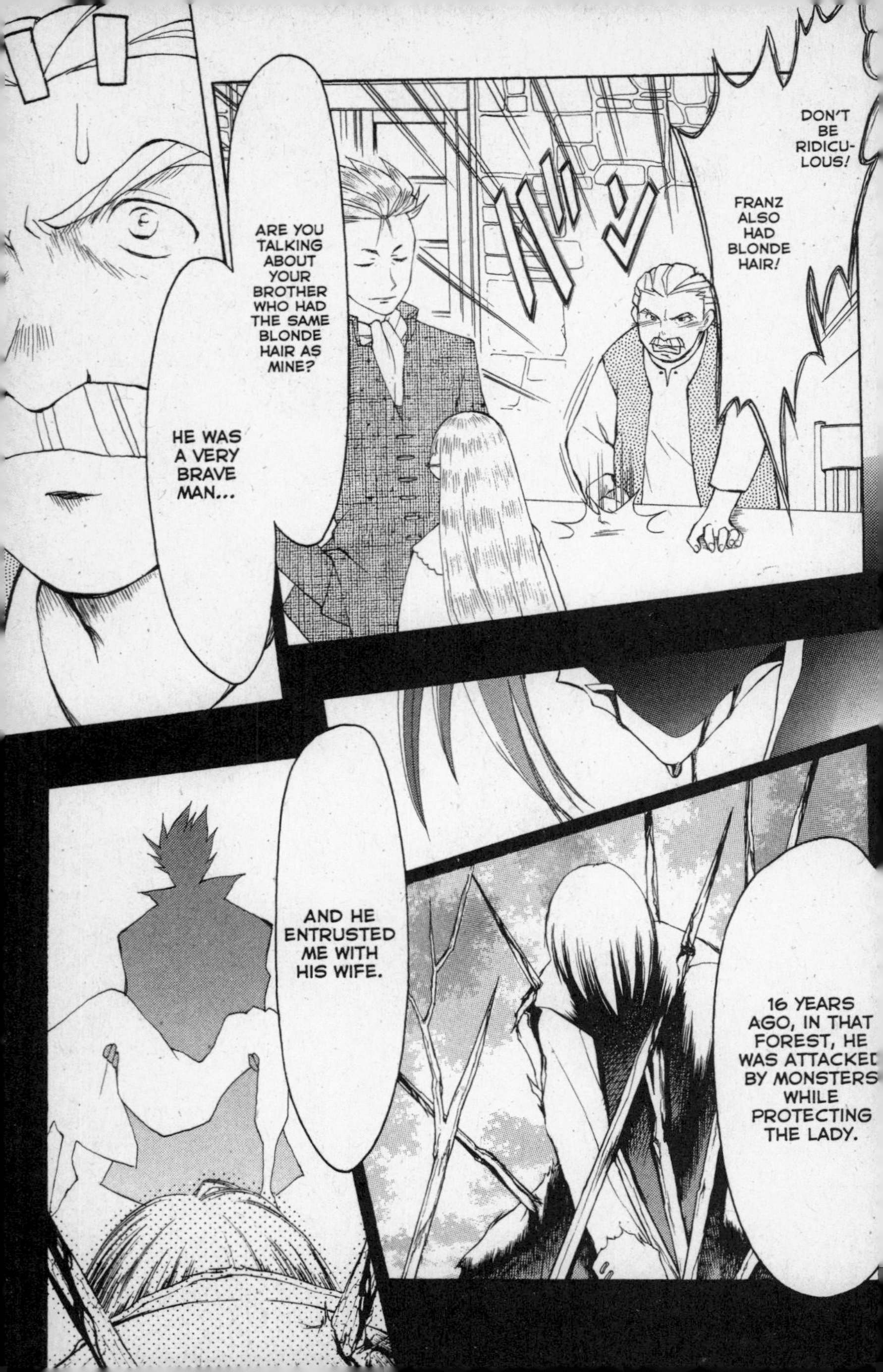
DON'T BE RIDICU-LOUS!
FRANZ ALSO HAD BLONDE HAIR!
ARE YOU TALKING ABOUT YOUR BROTHER WHO HAD THE SAME BLONDE HAIR AS MINE?
HE WAS A VERY BRAVE MAN...
16 YEARS AGO, IN THAT FOREST, HE WAS ATTACKED BY MONSTERS WHILE PROTECTING THE LADY.
AND HE ENTRUSTED ME WITH HIS WIFE.

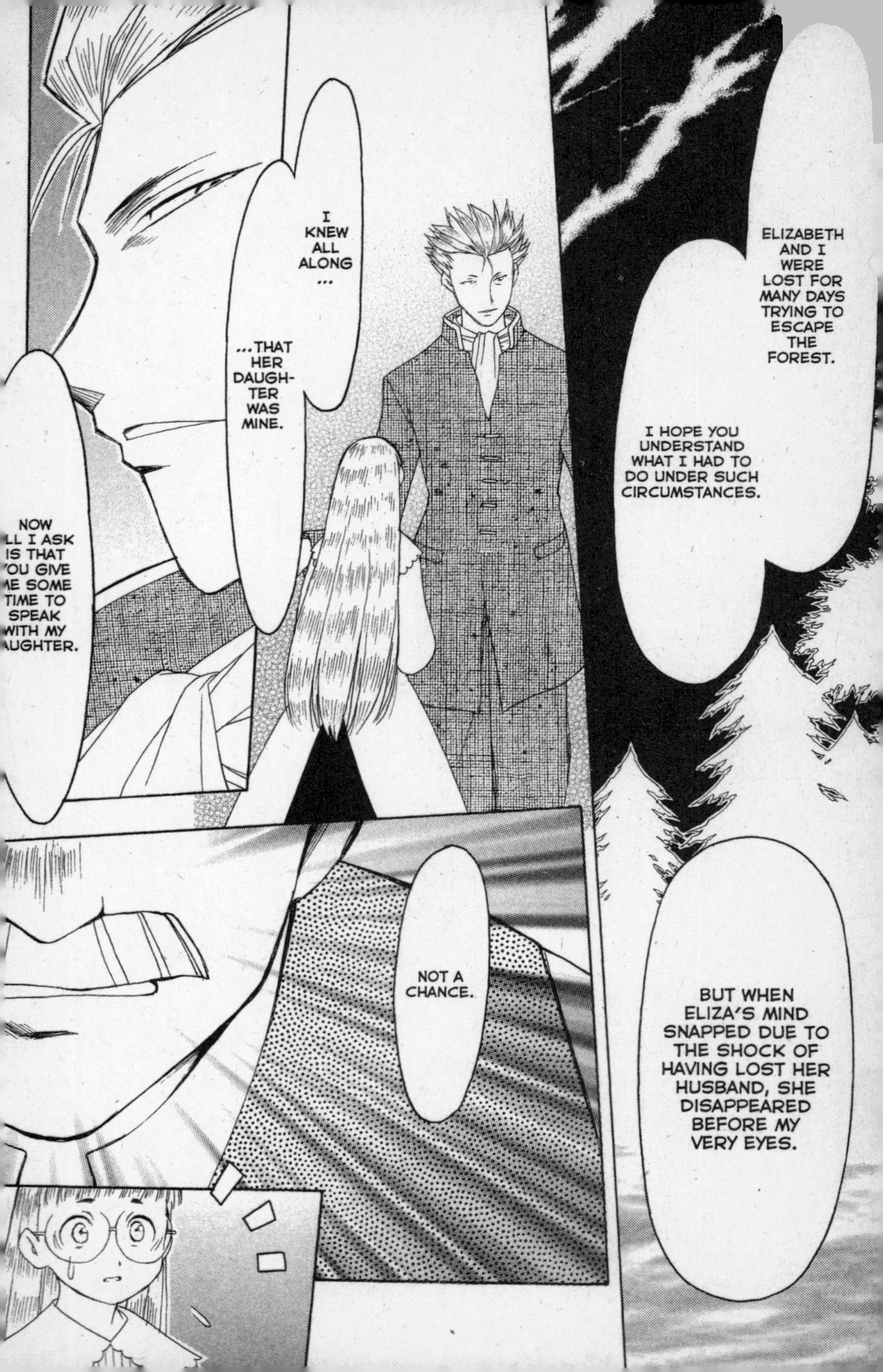
ELIZABETH AND I WERE LOST FOR MANY DAYS TRYING TO ESCAPE THE FOREST.
I HOPE YOU UNDERSTAND WHAT I HAD TO DO UNDER SUCH CIRCUMSTANCES.
BUT WHEN ELIZA'S MIND SNAPPED DUE TO THE SHOCK OF HAVING LOST HER HUSBAND, SHE DISAPPEARED BEFORE MY VERY EYES.
I KNEW ALL ALONG ...
...THAT HER DAUGHTER WAS MINE.
NOW LL I ASK IS THAT OU GIVE E SOME TIME TO SPEAK WITH MY AUGHTER.
NOT A CHANCE.

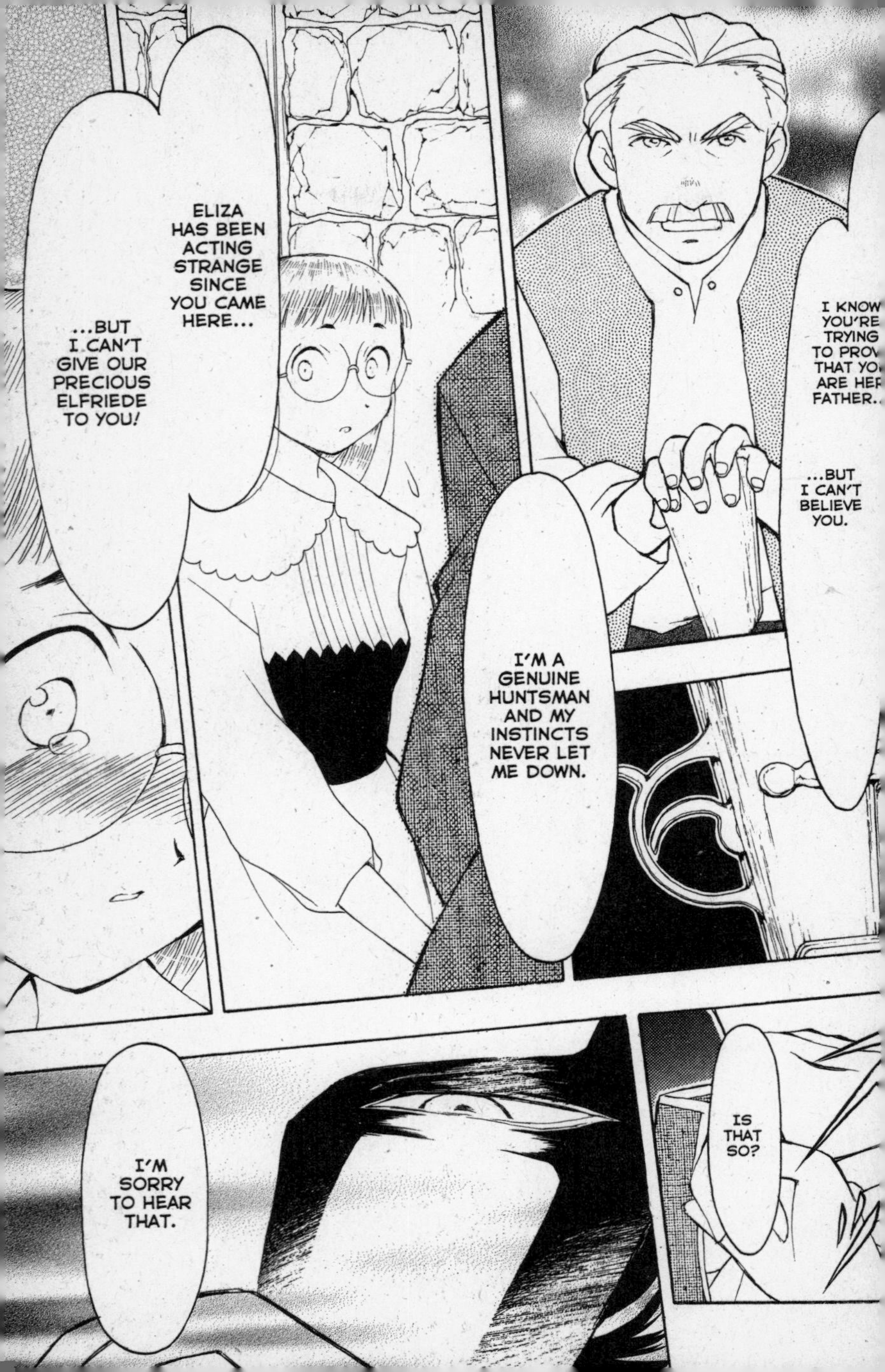
I KNOW YOU'RE TRYING TO PROV THAT YO ARE HER FATHER...
...BUT I CAN'T BELIEVE YOU.
I'M A GENUINE HUNTSMAN AND MY INSTINCTS NEVER LET ME DOWN.
ELIZA HAS BEEN ACTING STRANGE SINCE YOU CAME HERE...
...BUT I CAN'T GIVE OUR PRECIOUS ELFRIEDE TO YOU!
IS THAT SO?
I'M SORRY TO HEAR THAT.

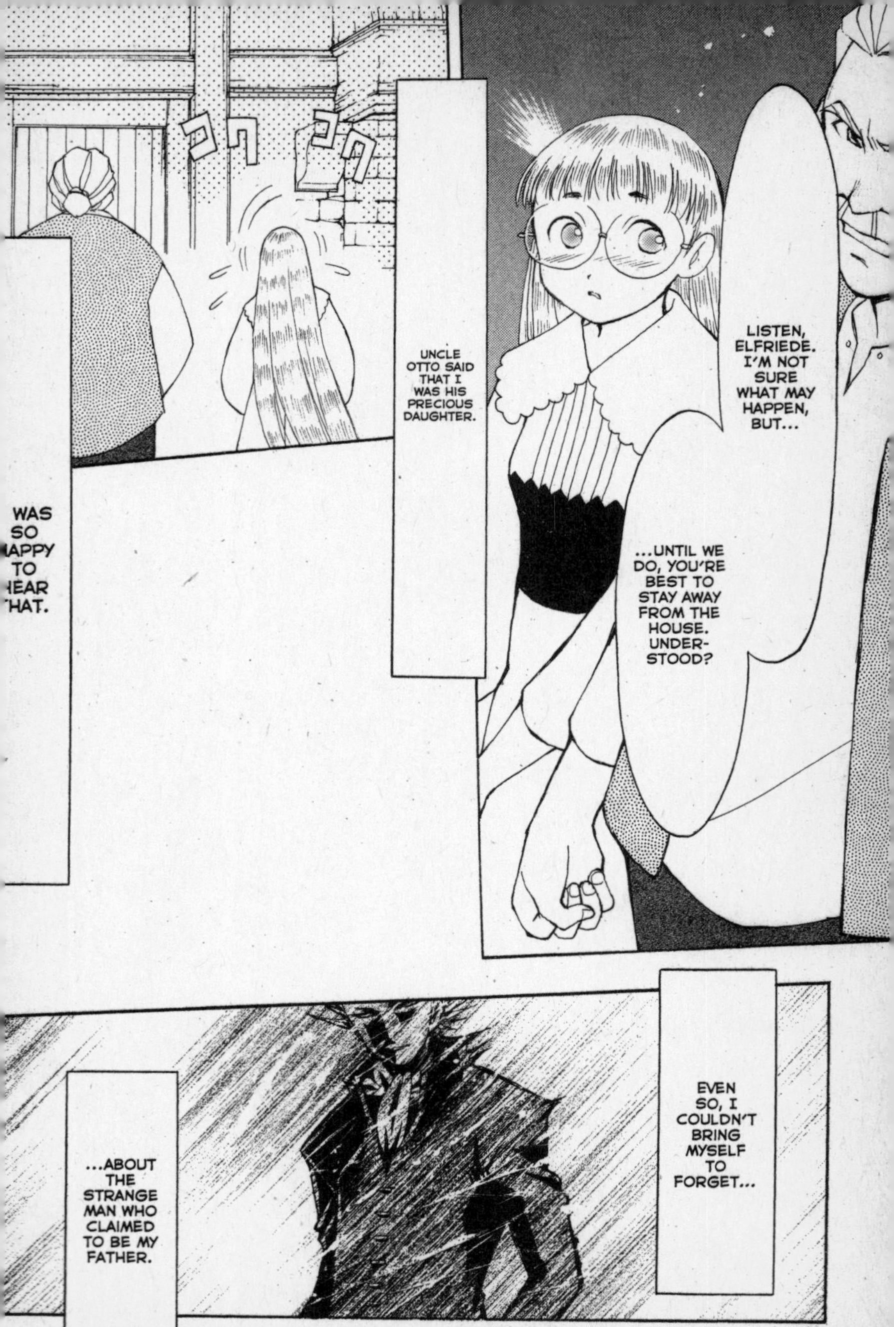
LISTEN, ELFRIEDE. I'M NOT SURE WHAT MAY HAPPEN, BUT...
...UNTIL WE DO, YOU'RE BEST TO STAY AWAY FROM THE HOUSE. UNDER-STOOD?
UNCLE OTTO SAID THAT I WAS HIS PRECIOUS DAUGHTER.
WAS SO APPY TO EAR HAT.
EVEN SO, I COULDN'T BRING MYSELF TO FORGET...
...ABOUT THE STRANGE MAN WHO CLAIMED TO BE MY FATHER.

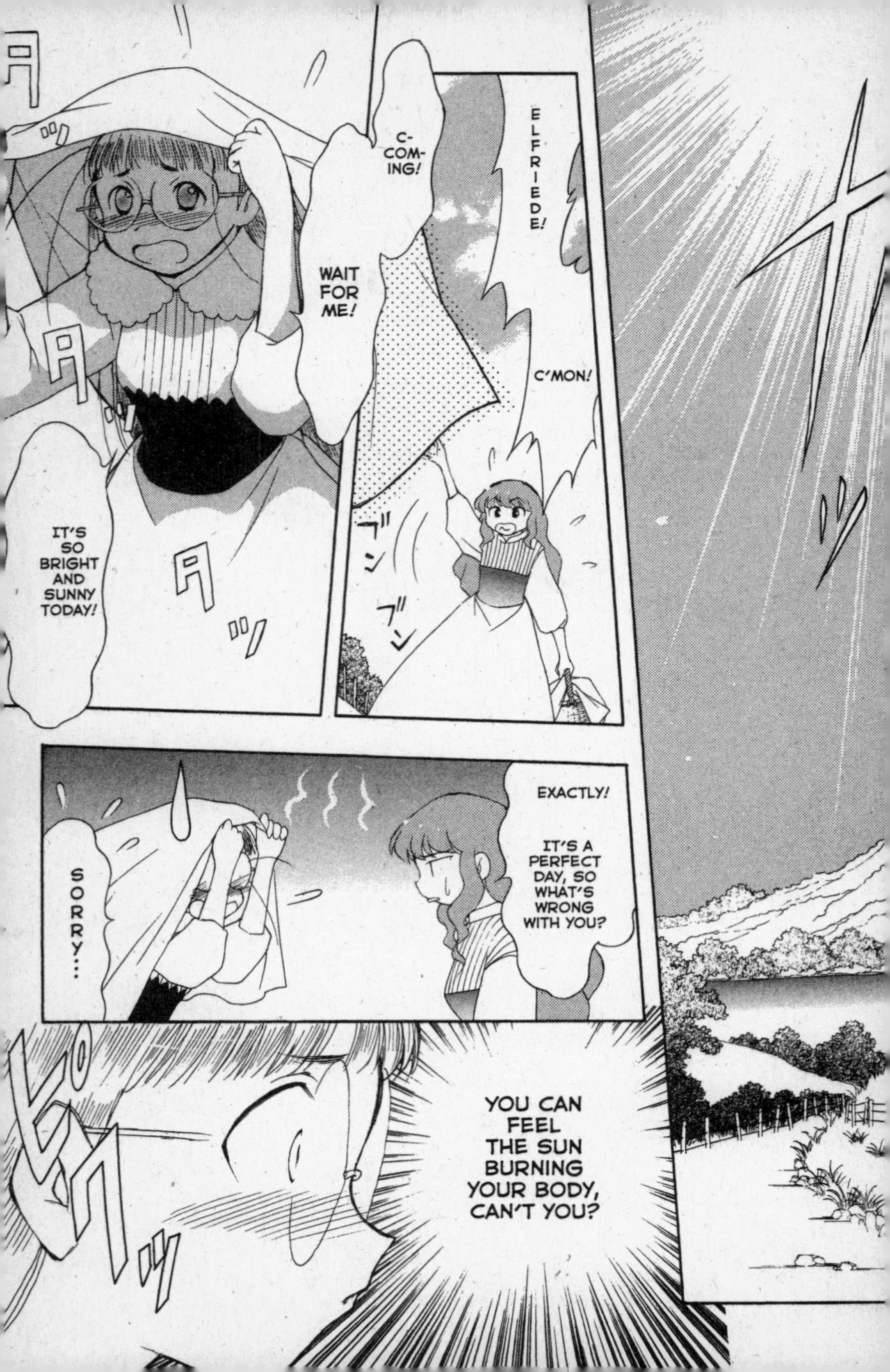
ELFRIEDE!
C'MON!
C-COMING!
WAIT FOR ME!
IT'S SO BRIGHT AND SUNNY TODAY!
EXACTLY!
IT'S A PERFECT DAY, SO WHAT'S WRONG WITH YOU?
SORRY...
YOU CAN FEEL THE SUN BURNING YOUR BODY, CAN'T YOU?

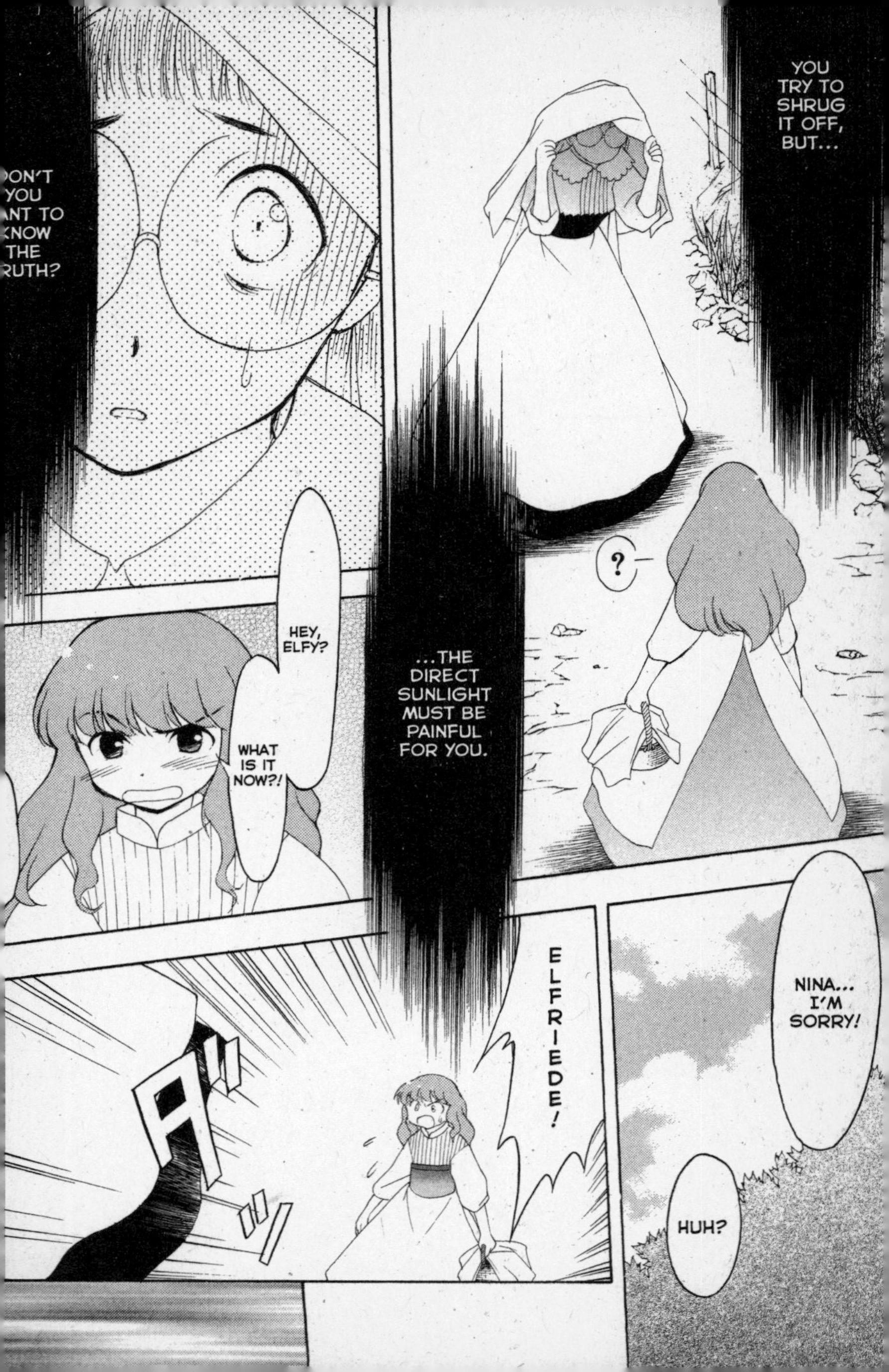
YOU TRY TO SHRUG IT OFF, BUT...
?
...THE DIRECT SUNLIGHT MUST BE PAINFUL FOR YOU.
ON'T YOU ANT TO NOW THE RUTH?
HEY, ELFY?
WHAT IS IT NOW?!
NINA... I'M SORRY!
HUH?
ELFRIEDE!

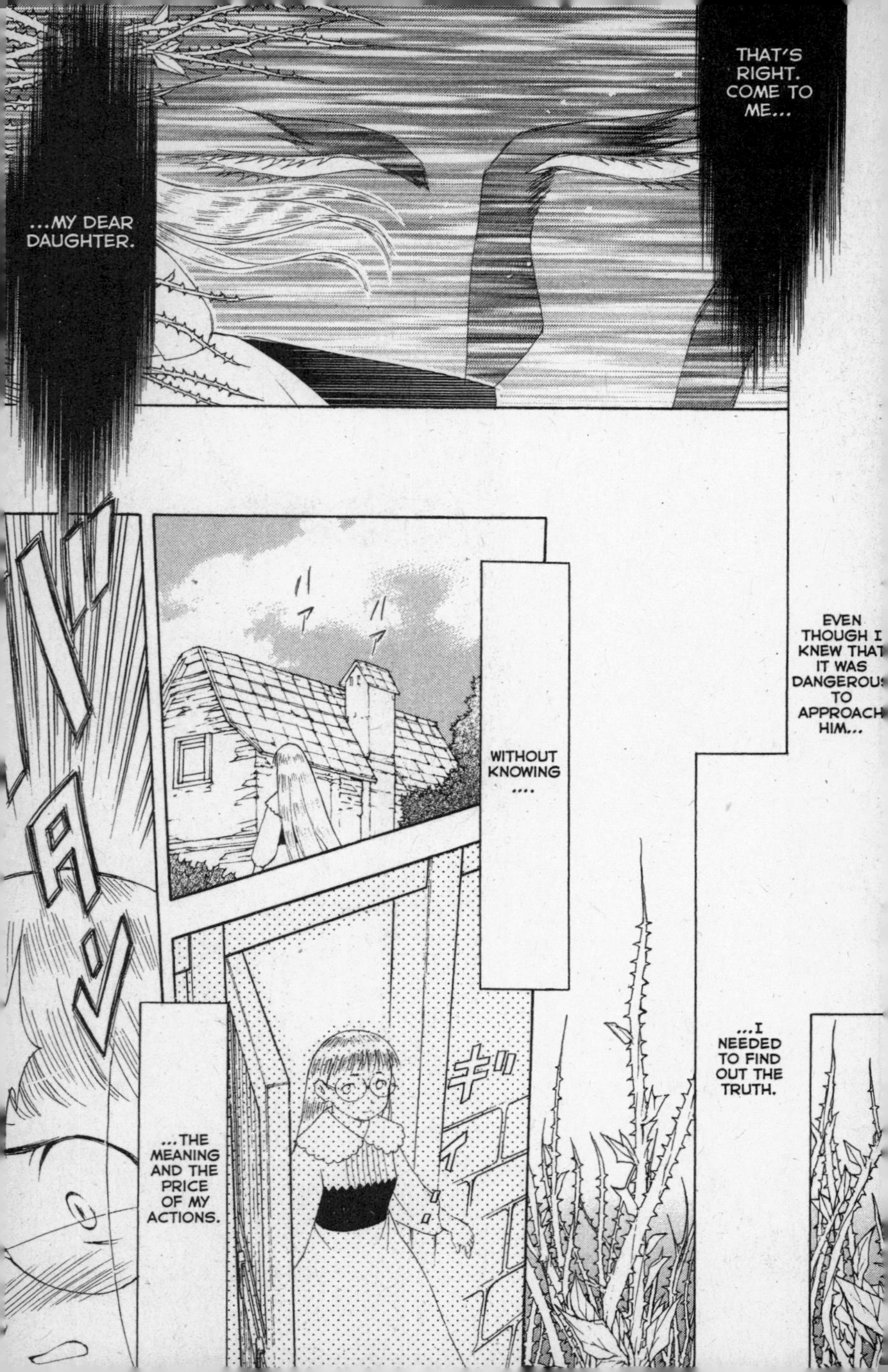
THAT'S RIGHT. COME TO ME...
...MY DEAR DAUGHTER.
EVEN THOUGH I KNEW THAT IT WAS DANGEROUS TO APPROACH HIM...
...I NEEDED TO FIND OUT THE TRUTH.
ハア
ハア
WITHOUT KNOWING ....
キィ
...THE MEANING AND THE PRICE OF MY ACTIONS.

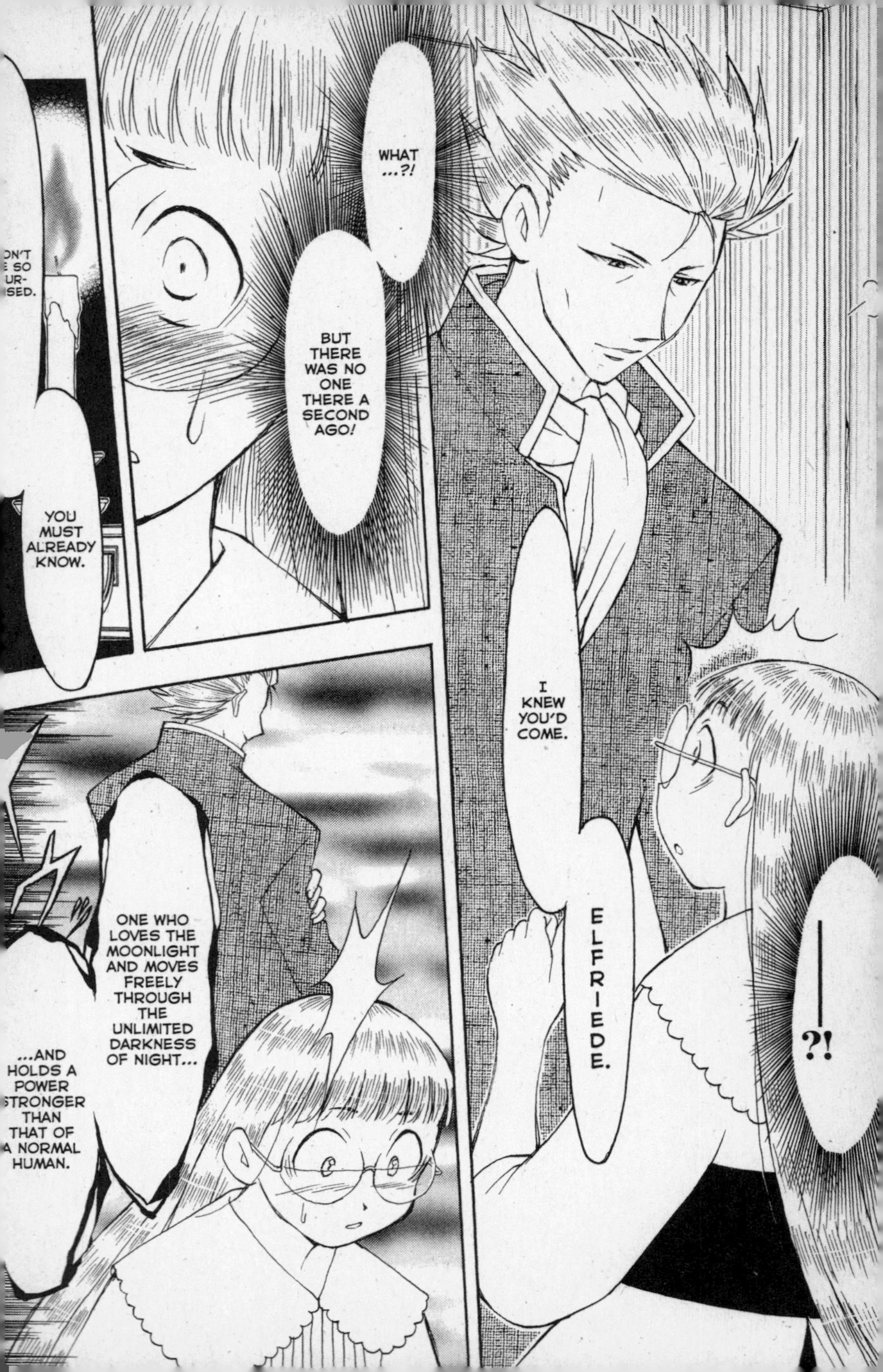
I KNEW YOU'D COME.
ELFRIEDE.
—?!
WHAT ...?!
BUT THERE WAS NO ONE THERE A SECOND AGO!
ON'T E SO UR- ISED.
YOU MUST ALREADY KNOW.
ONE WHO LOVES THE MOONLIGHT AND MOVES FREELY THROUGH THE UNLIMITED DARKNESS OF NIGHT...
...AND HOLDS A POWER STRONGER THAN THAT OF A NORMAL HUMAN.

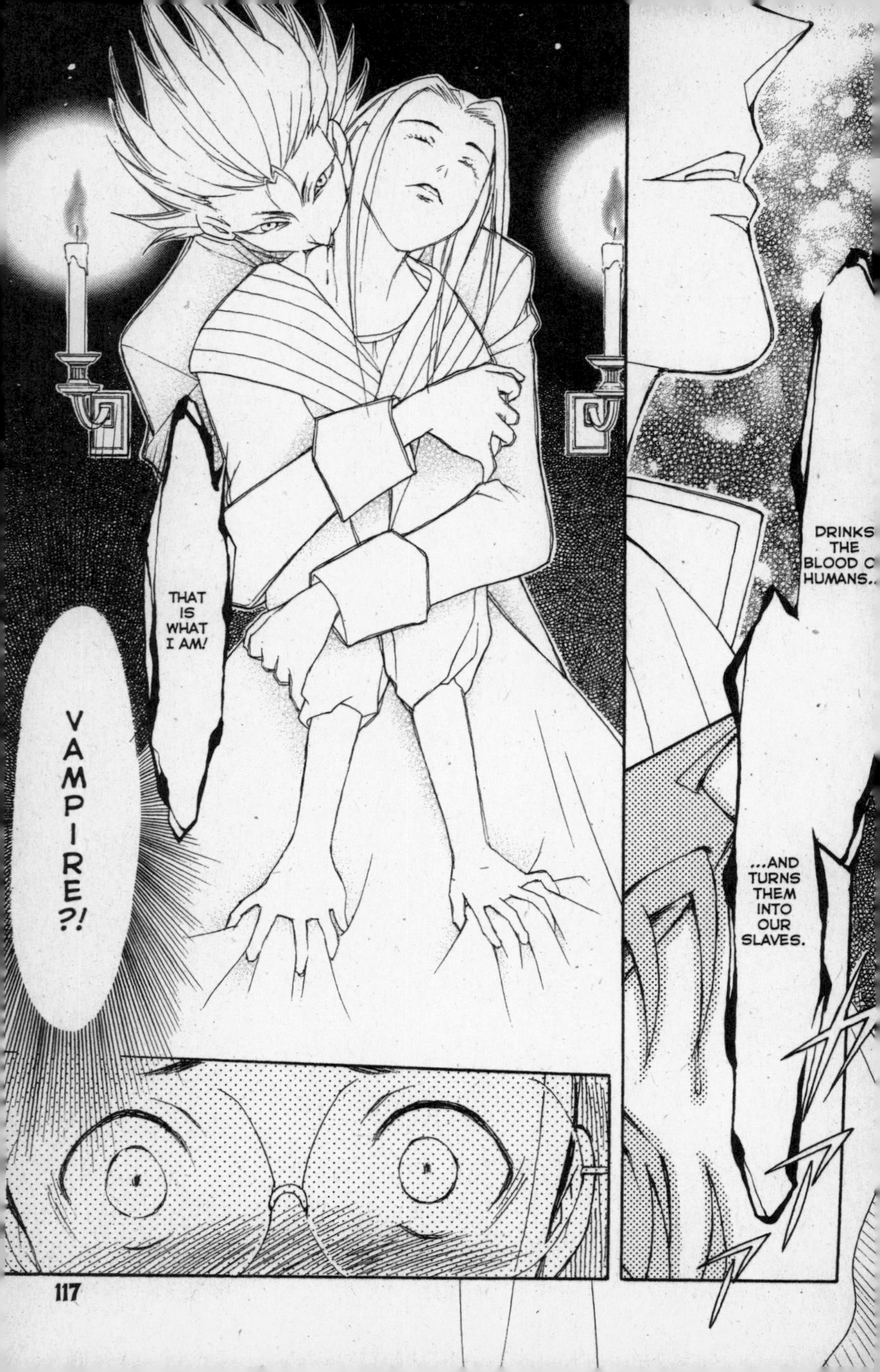
DRINKS THE BLOOD O HUMANS...
...AND TURNS THEM INTO OUR SLAVES.
THAT IS WHAT I AM!
VAMPIRE?!

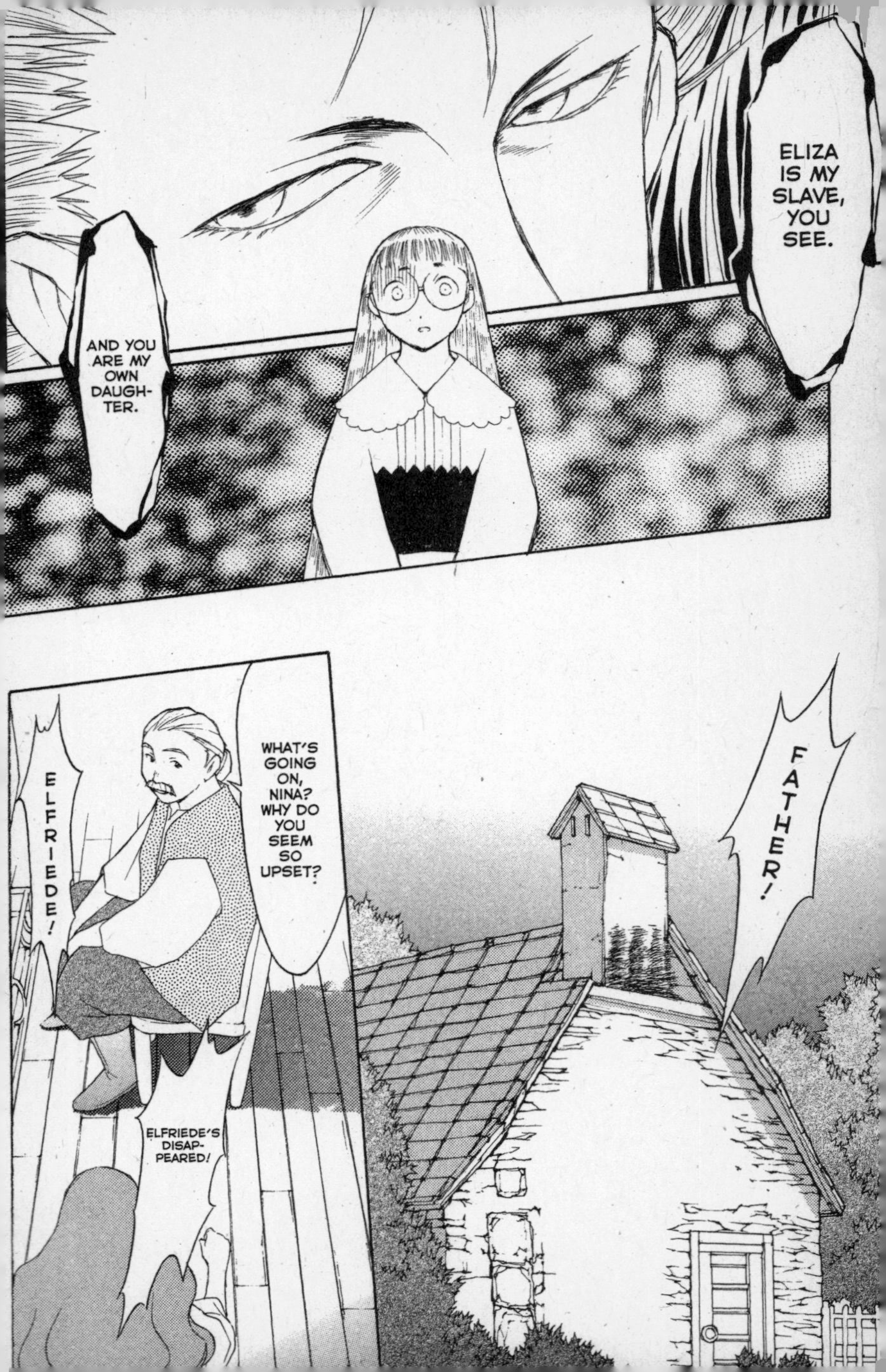
ELIZA IS MY SLAVE, YOU SEE.
AND YOU ARE MY OWN DAUGH-TER.
FATHER!
WHAT'S GOING ON, NINA? WHY DO YOU SEEM SO UPSET?
ELFRIEDE!
ELFRIEDE'S DISAP-PEARED!

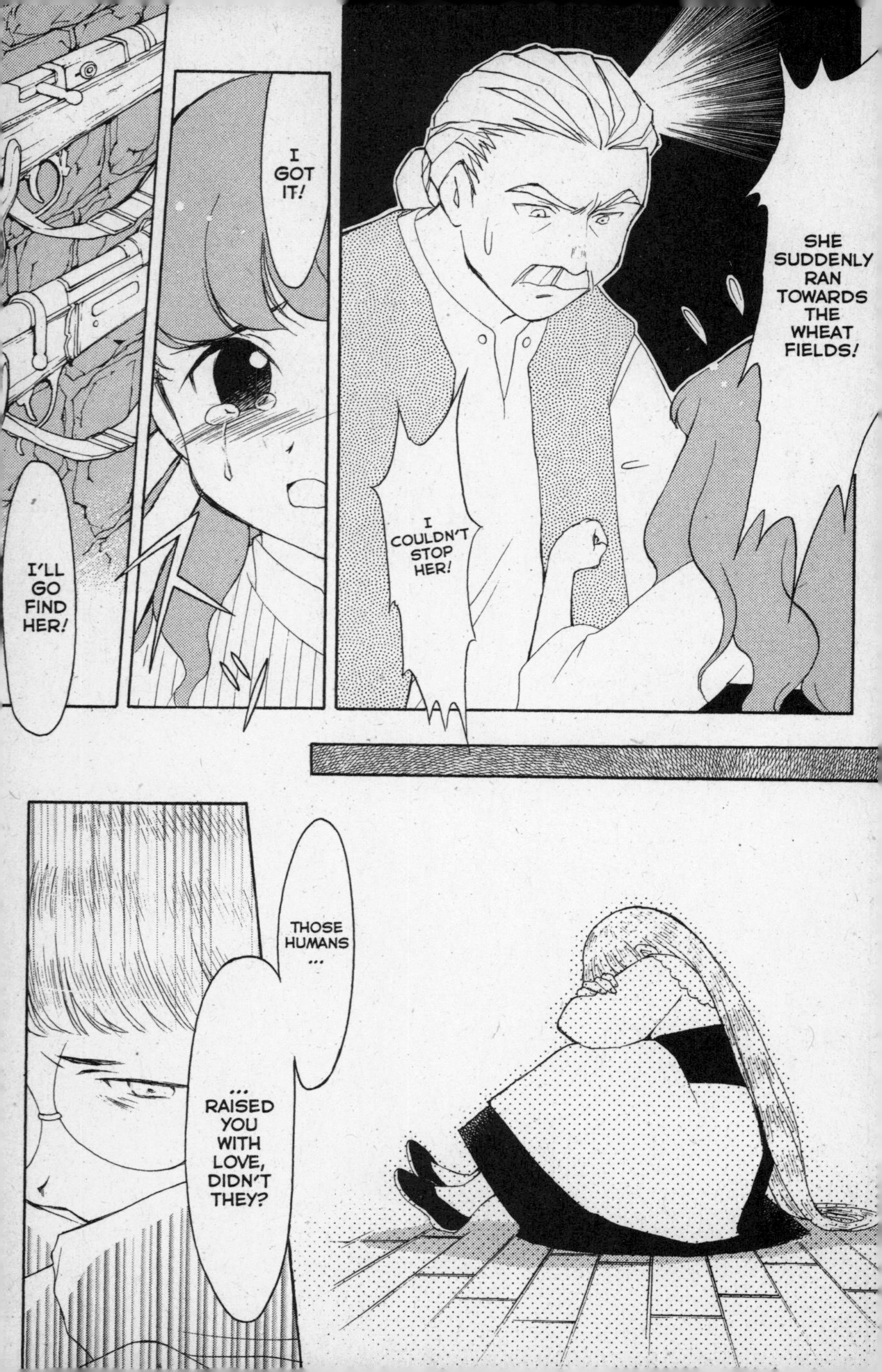
SHE SUDDENLY RAN TOWARDS THE WHEAT FIELDS!
I COULDN'T STOP HER!
I GOT IT!
I'LL GO FIND HER!
THOSE HUMANS ...
... RAISED YOU WITH LOVE, DIDN'T THEY?

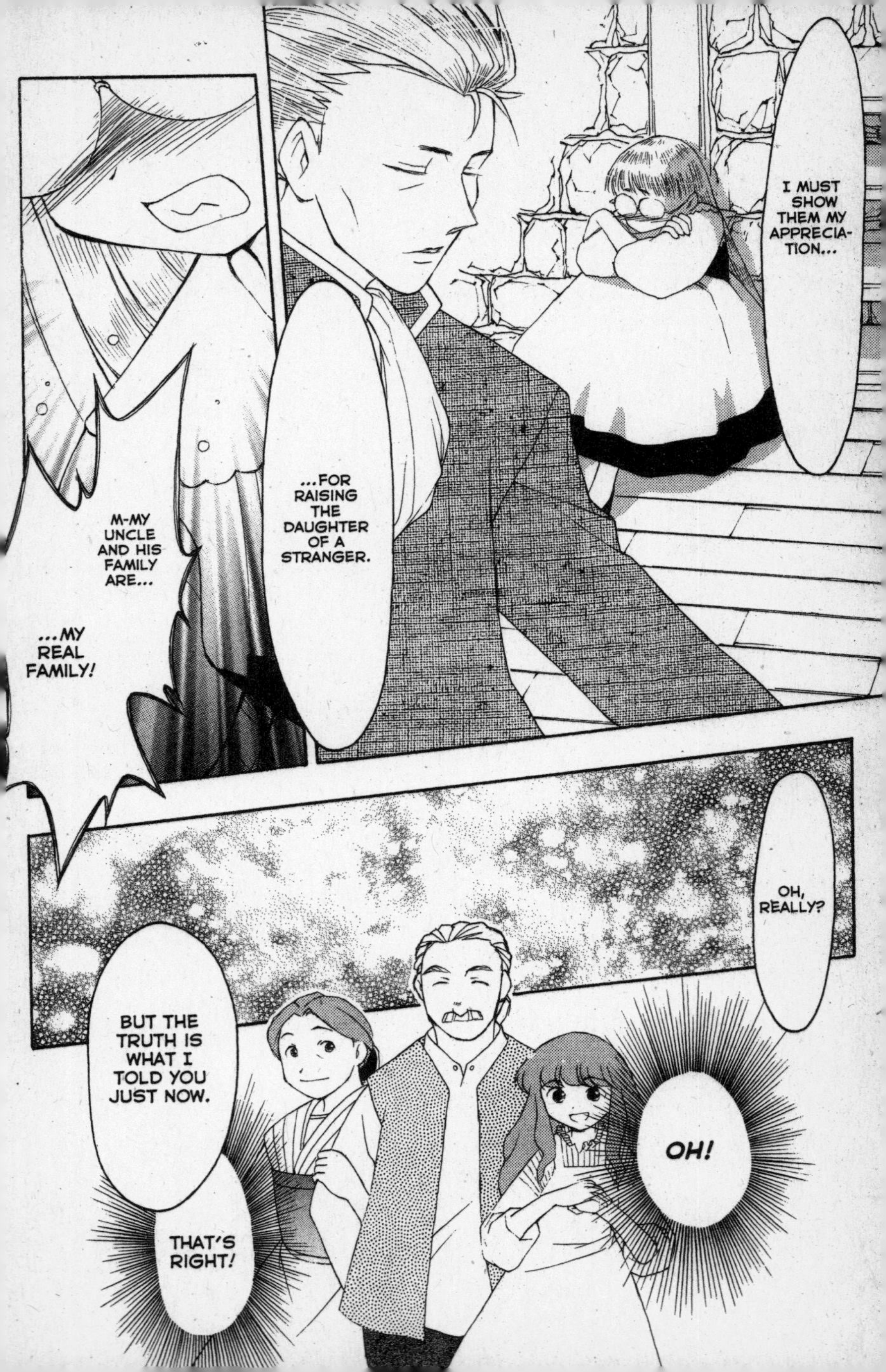
I MUST SHOW THEM MY APPRECIATION...
...FOR RAISING THE DAUGHTER OF A STRANGER.
M-MY UNCLE AND HIS FAMILY ARE...
...MY REAL FAMILY!
OH, REALLY?
BUT THE TRUTH IS WHAT I TOLD YOU JUST NOW.
OH!
THAT'S RIGHT!

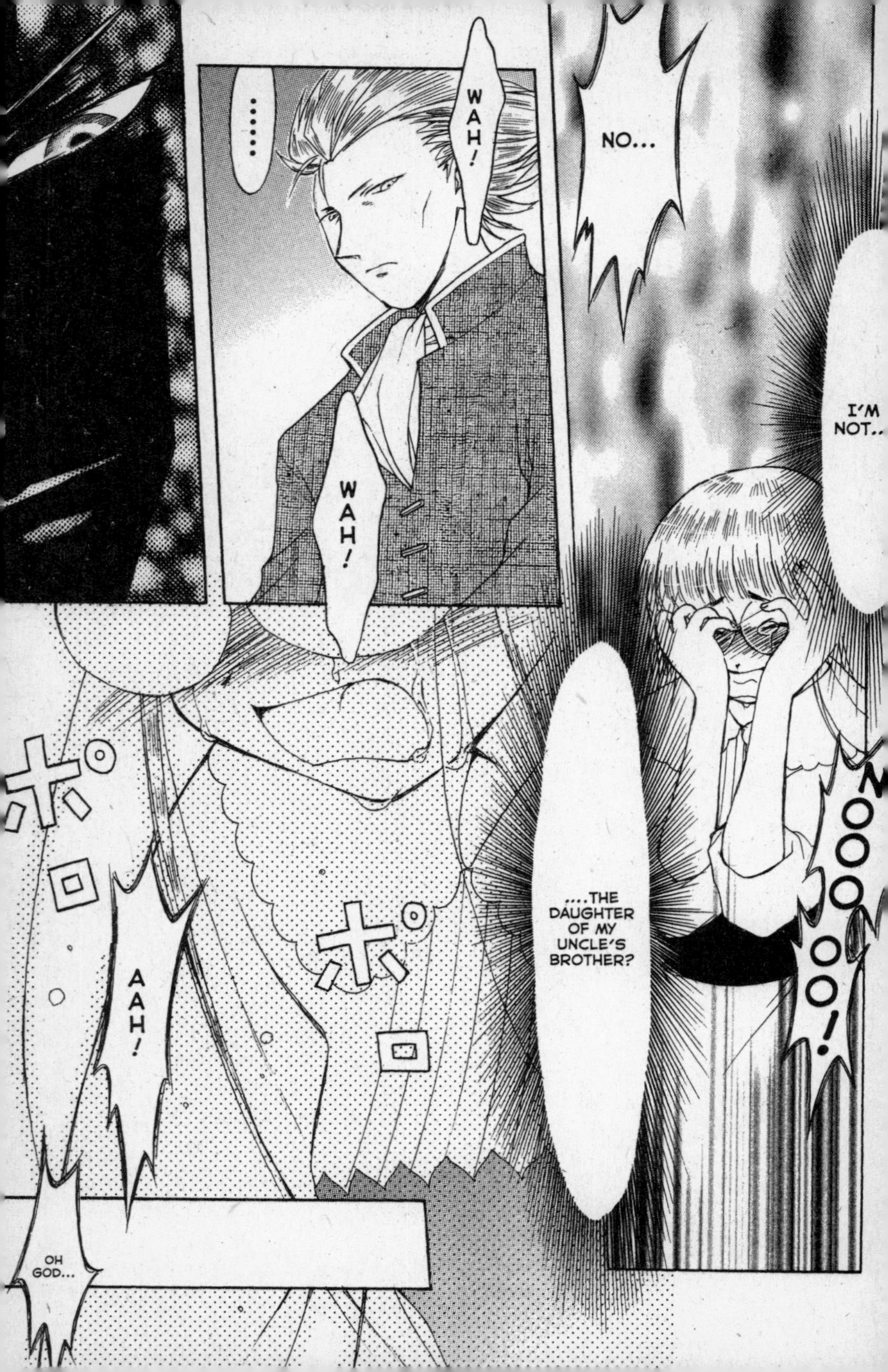
NO...
I'M NOT..
....THE DAUGHTER OF MY UNCLE'S BROTHER?
NOOOOOOO!
WAH!
......
WAH!
ポロ
AAH!
ポロ
OH GOD...

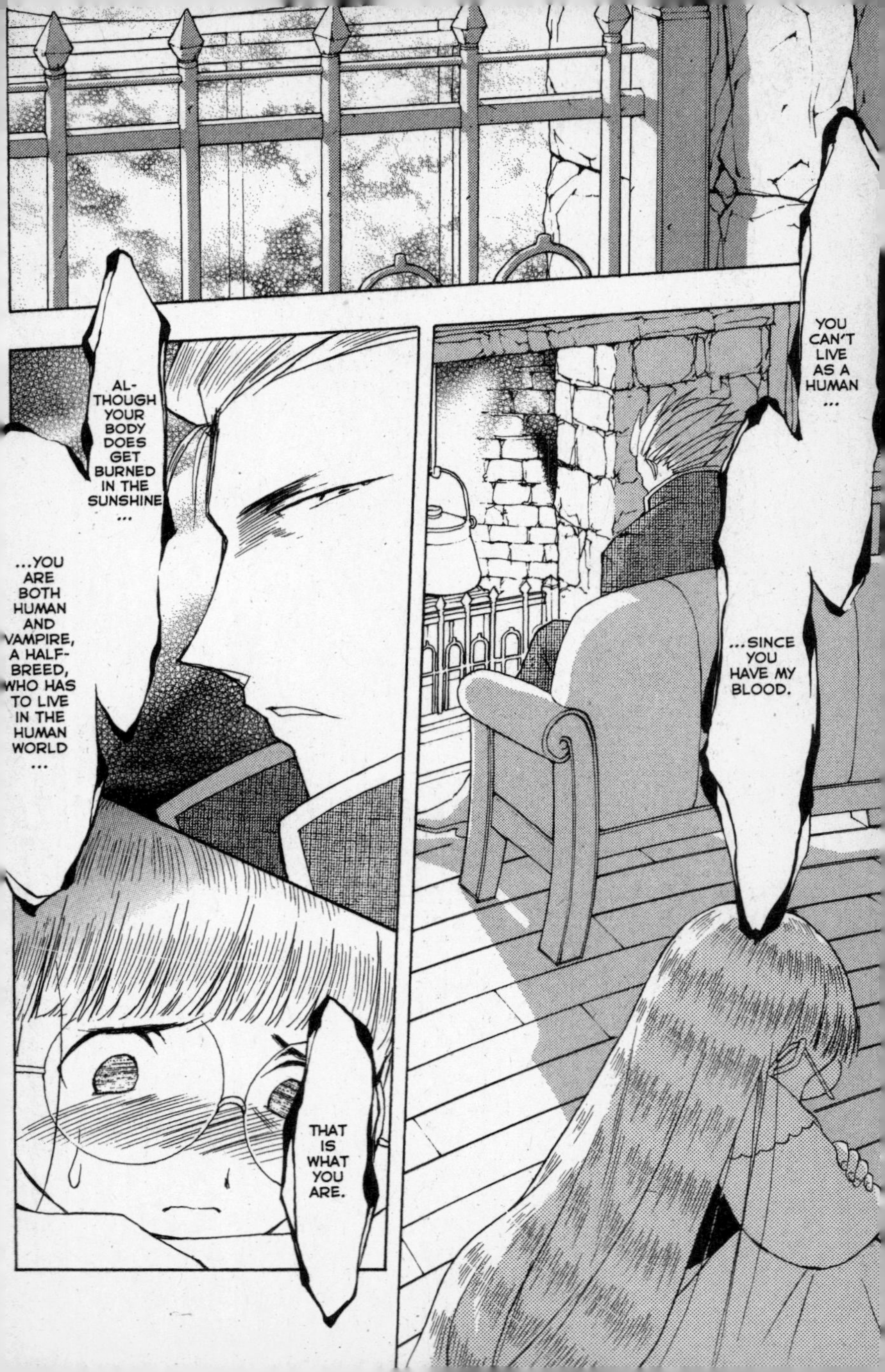
YOU CAN'T LIVE AS A HUMAN ...
...SINCE YOU HAVE MY BLOOD.
AL-THOUGH YOUR BODY DOES GET BURNED IN THE SUNSHINE ...
...YOU ARE BOTH HUMAN AND VAMPIRE, A HALF-BREED, WHO HAS TO LIVE IN THE HUMAN WORLD ...
THAT IS WHAT YOU ARE.

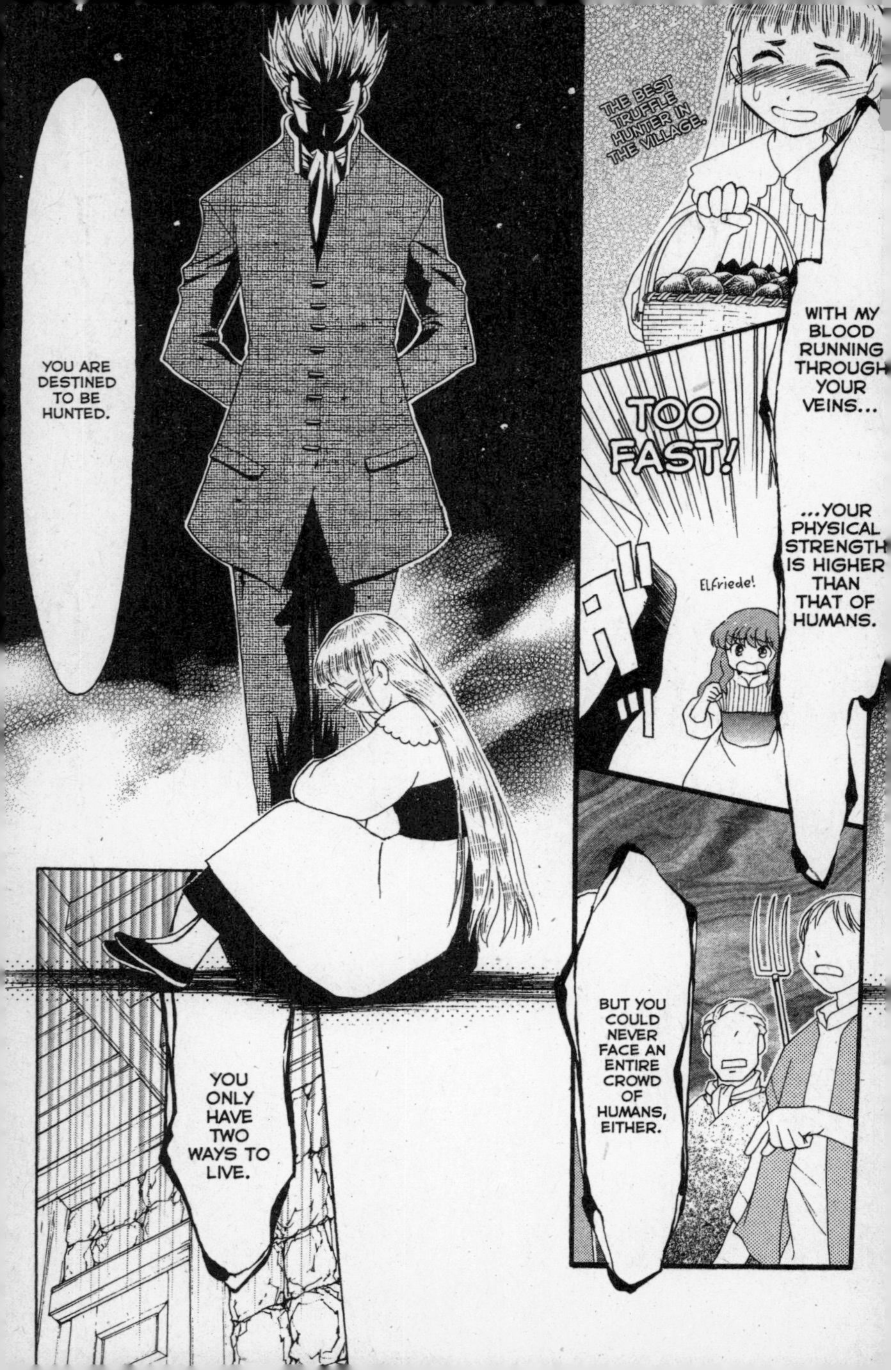
THE BEST TRUFFLE HUNTER IN THE VILLAGE.
WITH MY BLOOD RUNNING THROUGH YOUR VEINS...
TOO FAST!
Elfriede!
...YOUR PHYSICAL STRENGTH IS HIGHER THAN THAT OF HUMANS.
BUT YOU COULD NEVER FACE AN ENTIRE CROWD OF HUMANS, EITHER.
YOU ARE DESTINED TO BE HUNTED.
YOU ONLY HAVE TWO WAYS TO LIVE.

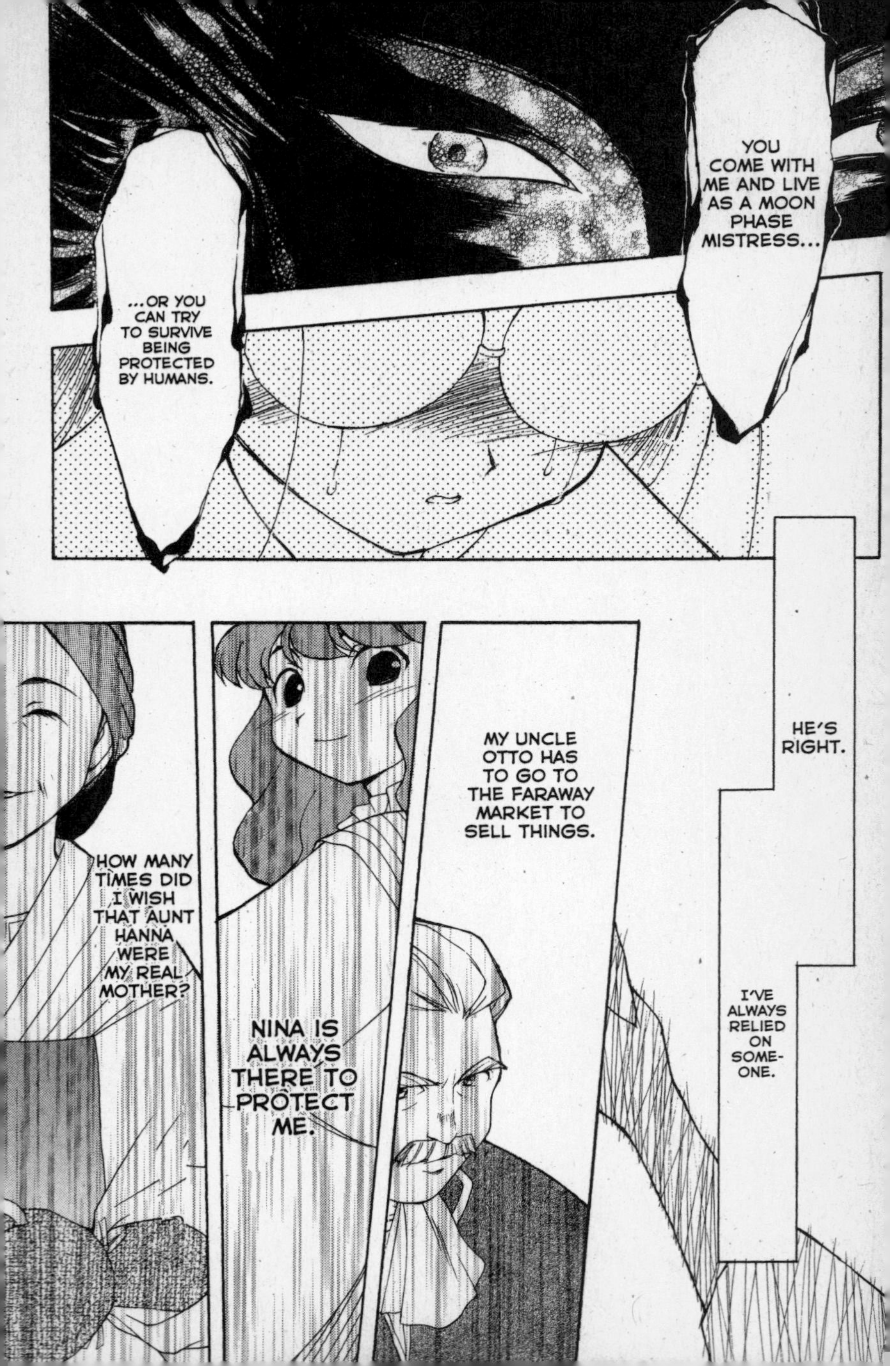
YOU COME WITH ME AND LIVE AS A MOON PHASE MISTRESS...
...OR YOU CAN TRY TO SURVIVE BEING PROTECTED BY HUMANS.
HE'S RIGHT.
I'VE ALWAYS RELIED ON SOME-ONE.
MY UNCLE OTTO HAS TO GO TO THE FARAWAY MARKET TO SELL THINGS.
NINA IS ALWAYS THERE TO PROTECT ME.
HOW MANY TIMES DID I WISH THAT AUNT HANNA WERE MY REAL MOTHER?

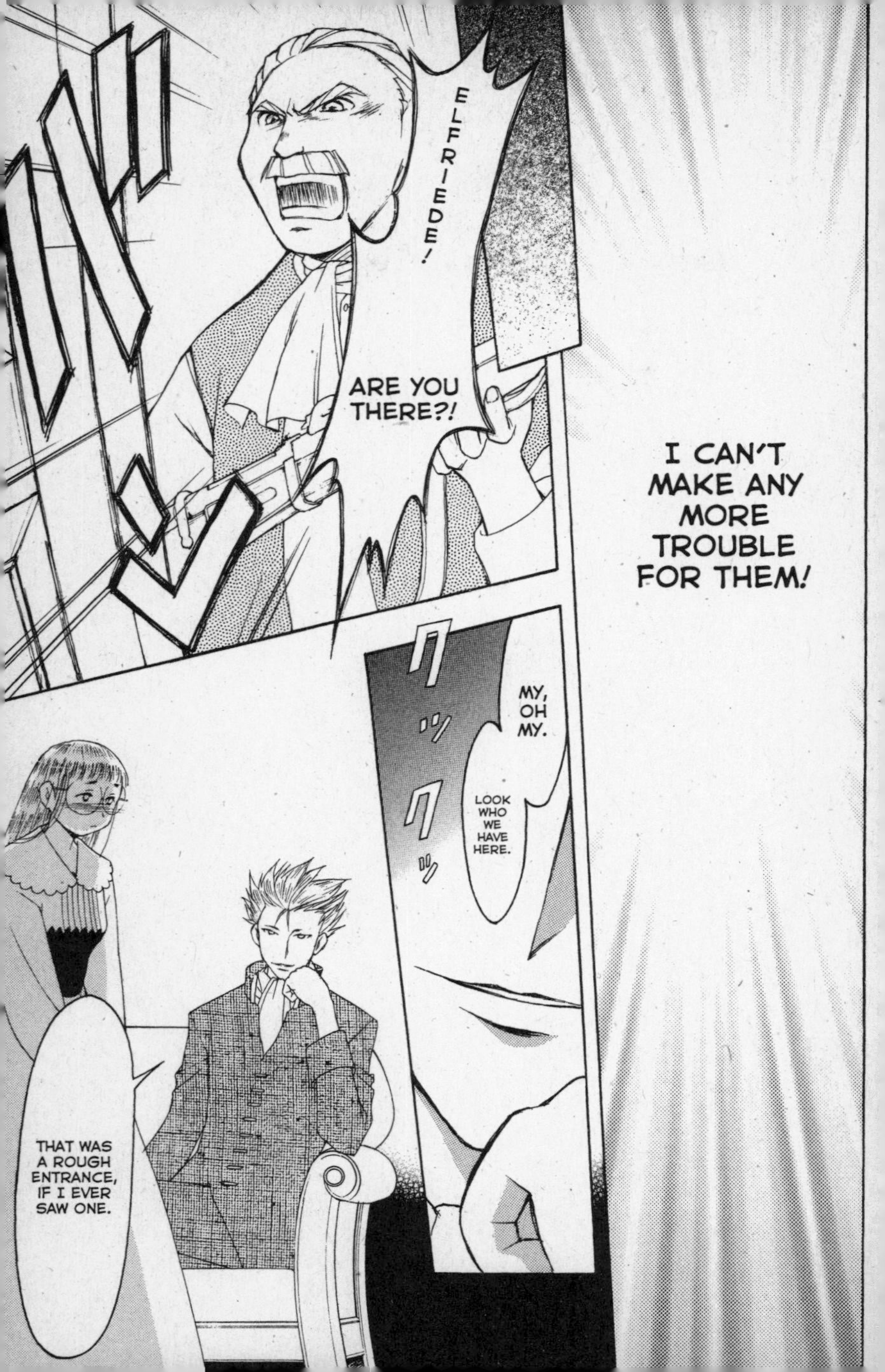
I CAN'T MAKE ANY MORE TROUBLE FOR THEM!
ELFRIEDE!
ARE YOU THERE?!
クックッ
MY, OH MY.
LOOK WHO WE HAVE HERE.
THAT WAS A ROUGH ENTRANCE, IF I EVER SAW ONE.

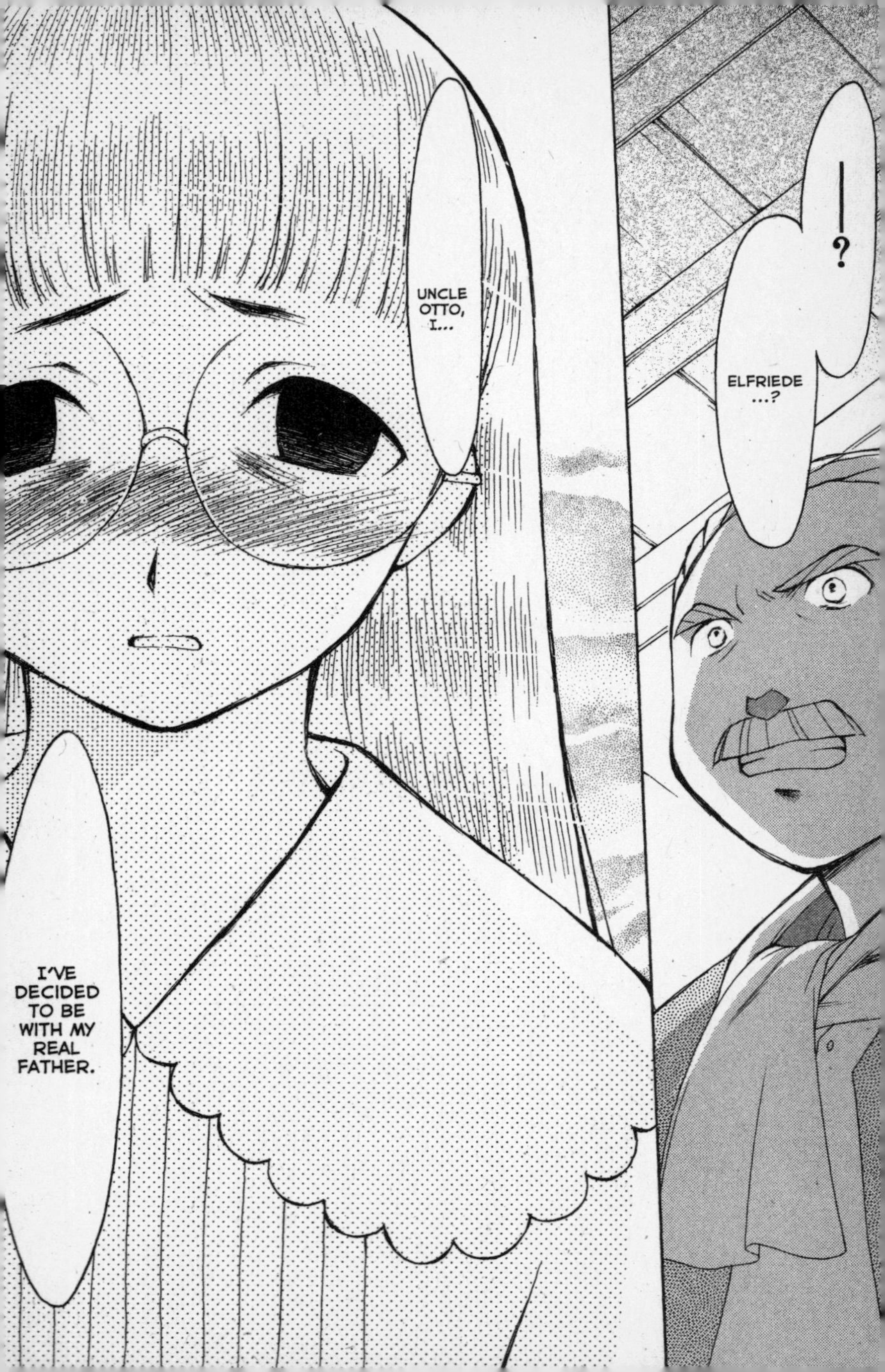
—?
ELFRIEDE ...?
UNCLE OTTO, I...
I'VE DECIDED TO BE WITH MY REAL FATHER.

MOON 月詠 PHASE

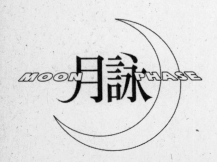

HIGHLANDS SCENERY

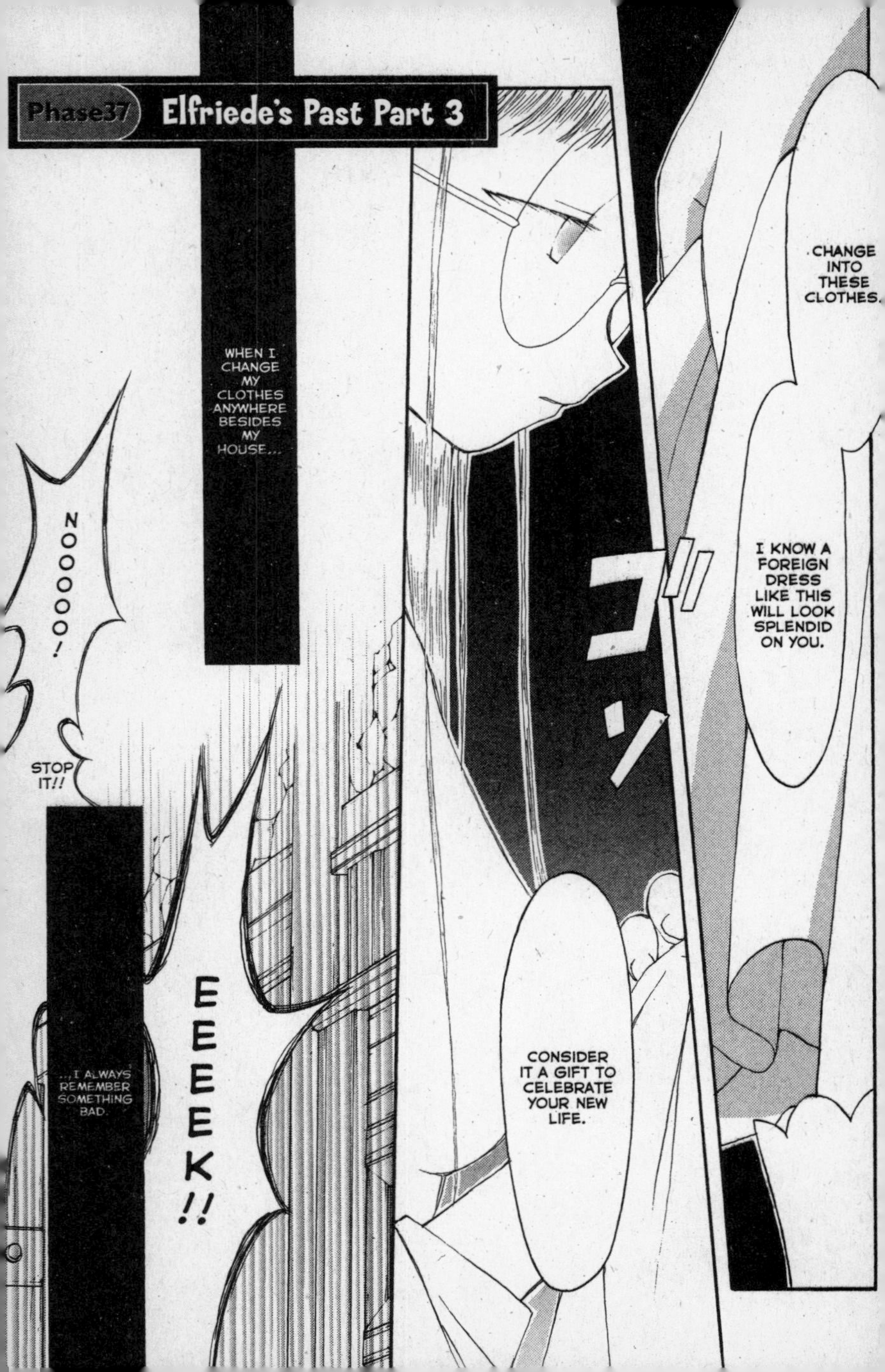
Phase37 Elfriede's Past Part 3
CHANGE INTO THESE CLOTHES.
I KNOW A FOREIGN DRESS LIKE THIS WILL LOOK SPLENDID ON YOU.
CONSIDER IT A GIFT TO CELEBRATE YOUR NEW LIFE.
WHEN I CHANGE MY CLOTHES ANYWHERE BESIDES MY HOUSE...
NOOOOO!
STOP IT!!
EEEEK!!
...I ALWAYS REMEMBER SOMETHING BAD.

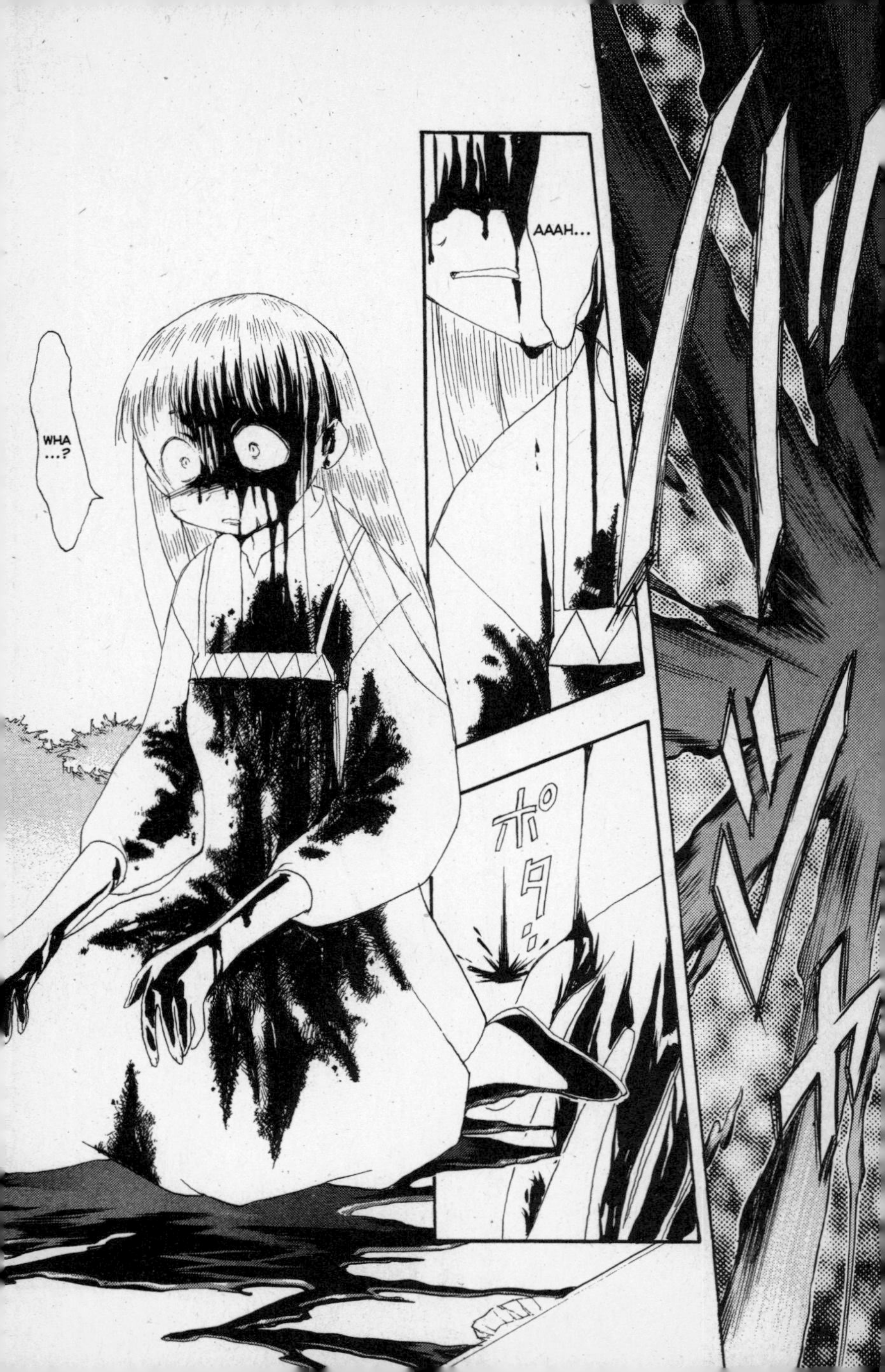
AAAH...
ポタ...
WHA ...?

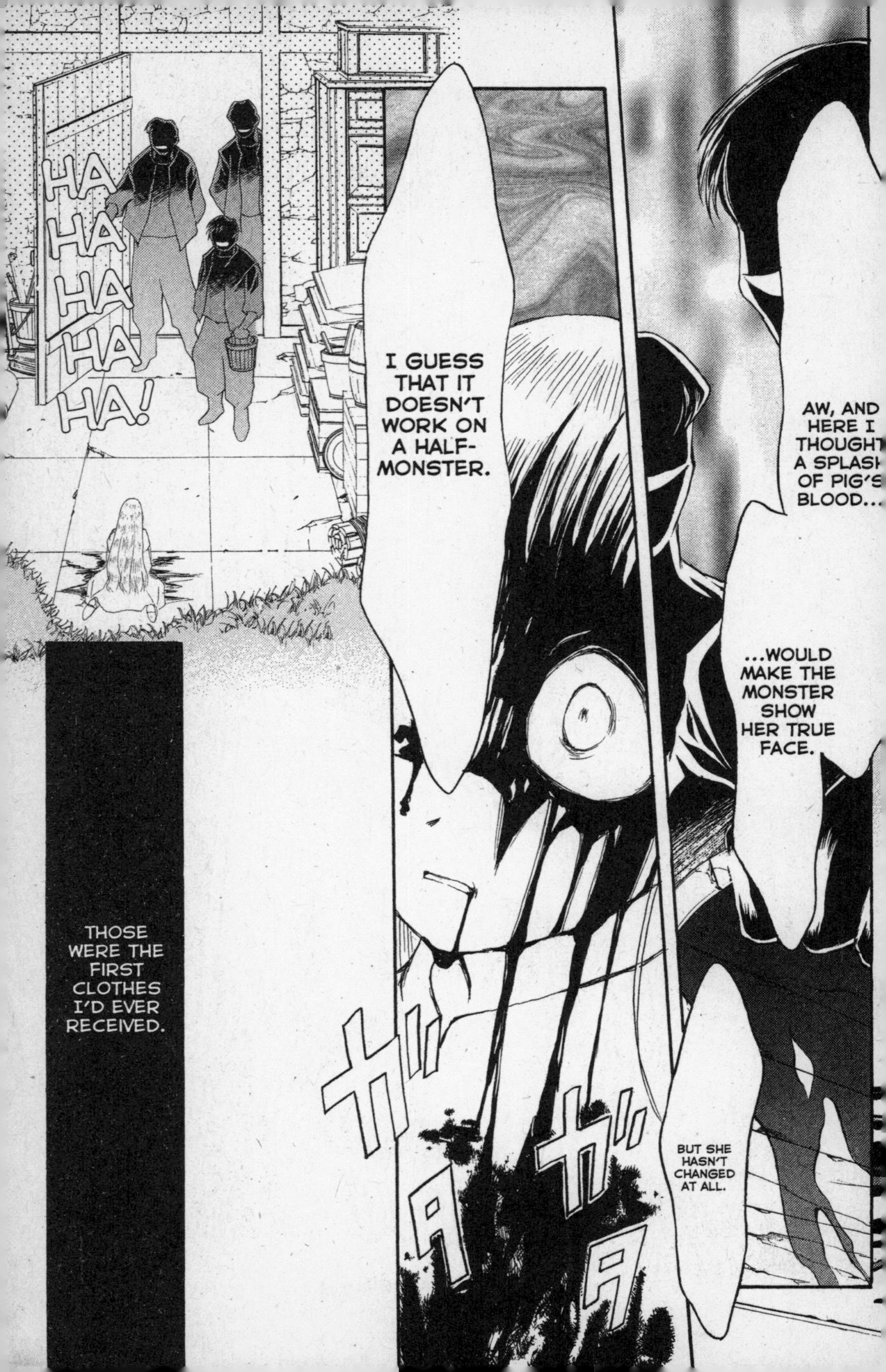
AW, AND HERE I THOUGHT A SPLASH OF PIG'S BLOOD...
...WOULD MAKE THE MONSTER SHOW HER TRUE FACE.
I GUESS THAT IT DOESN'T WORK ON A HALF-MONSTER.
BUT SHE HASN'T CHANGED AT ALL.
HA HA HA HA HA!
THOSE WERE THE FIRST CLOTHES I'D EVER RECEIVED.

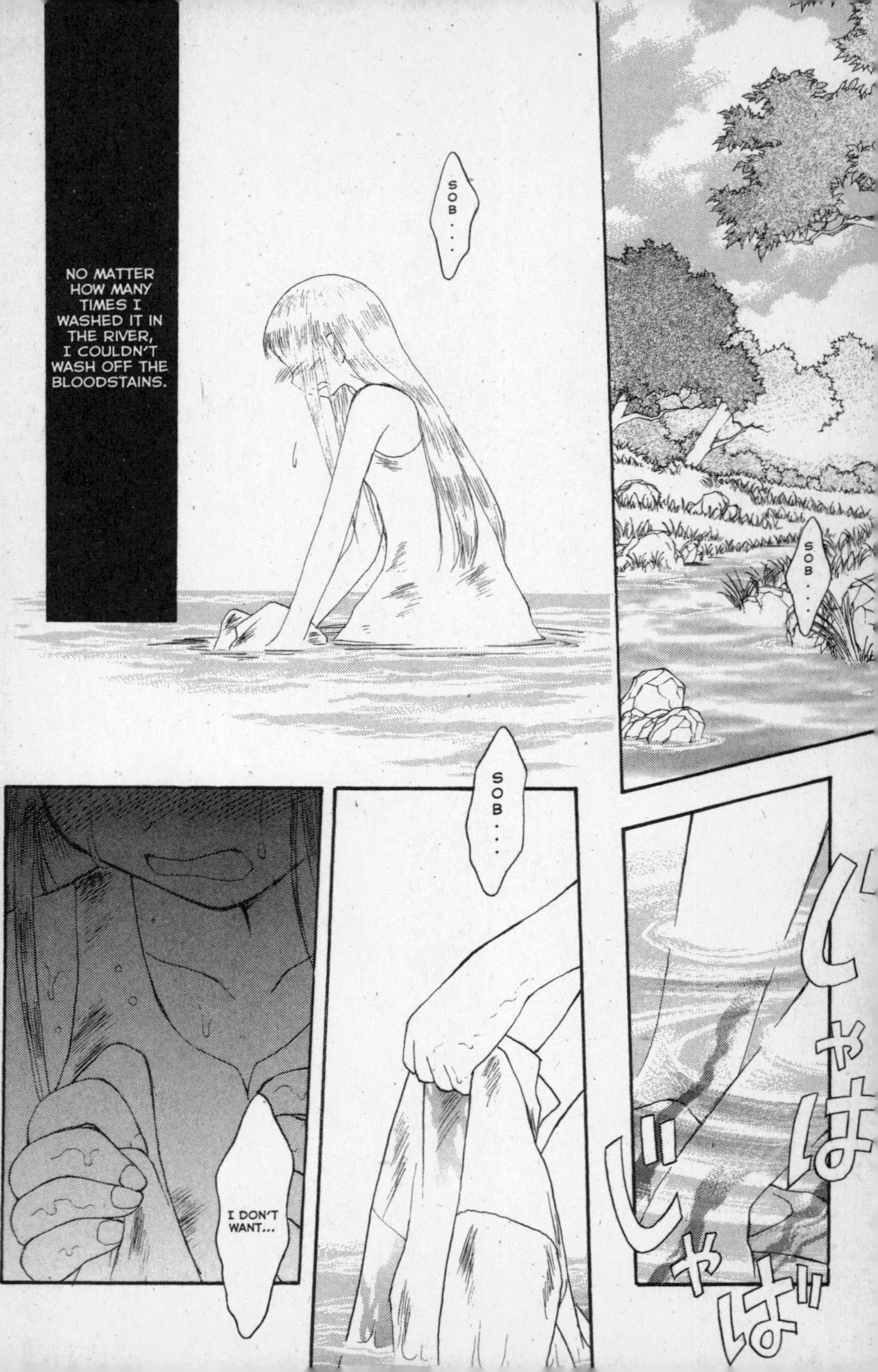
SOB...
NO MATTER HOW MANY TIMES I WASHED IT IN THE RIVER, I COULDN'T WASH OFF THE BLOODSTAINS.
SOB...
SOB...
I DON'T WANT...

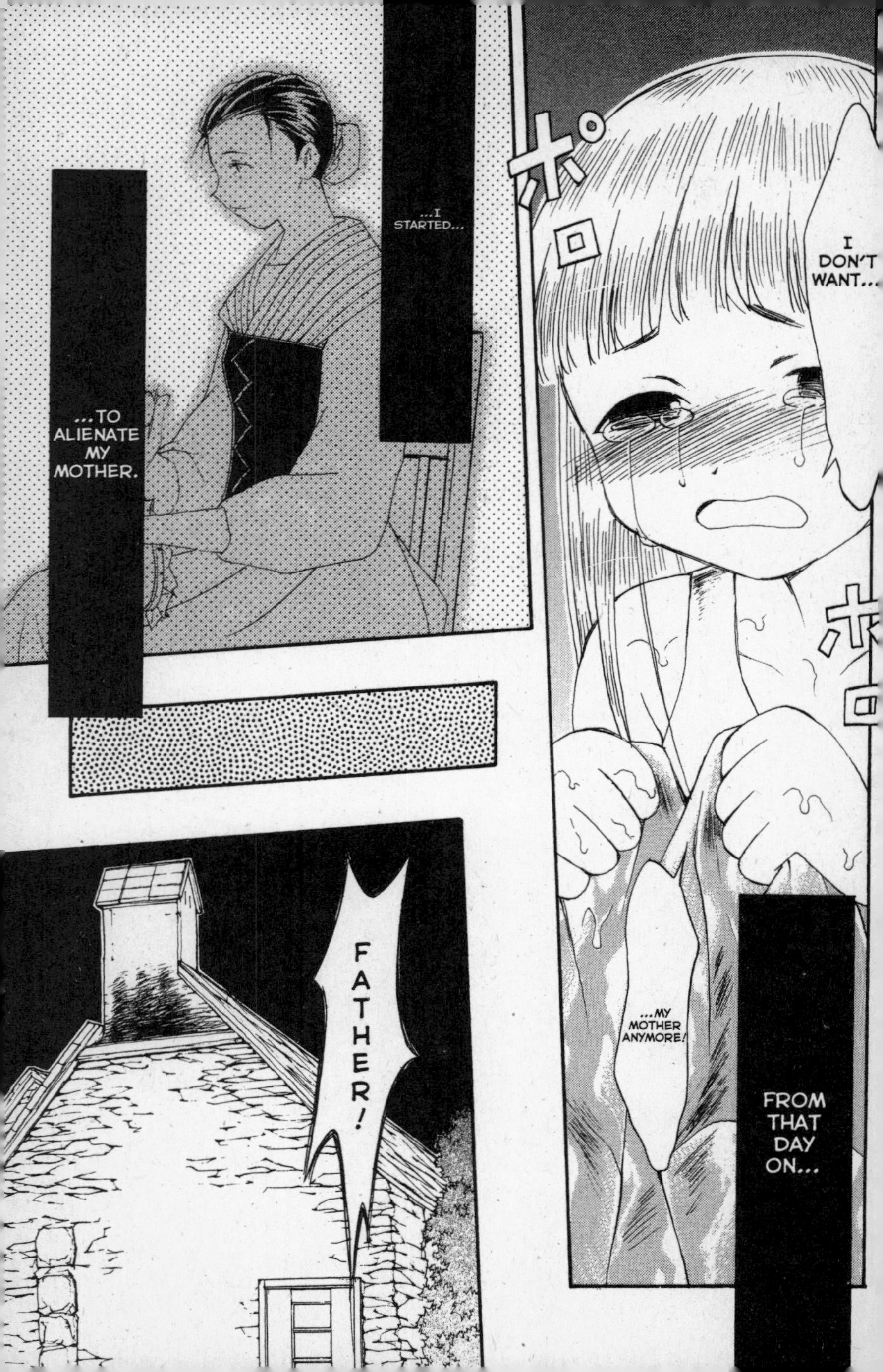
ポロ
I DON'T WANT...
ポロ
...MY MOTHER ANYMORE!
FROM THAT DAY ON...
...I STARTED...
...TO ALIENATE MY MOTHER.
FATHER!

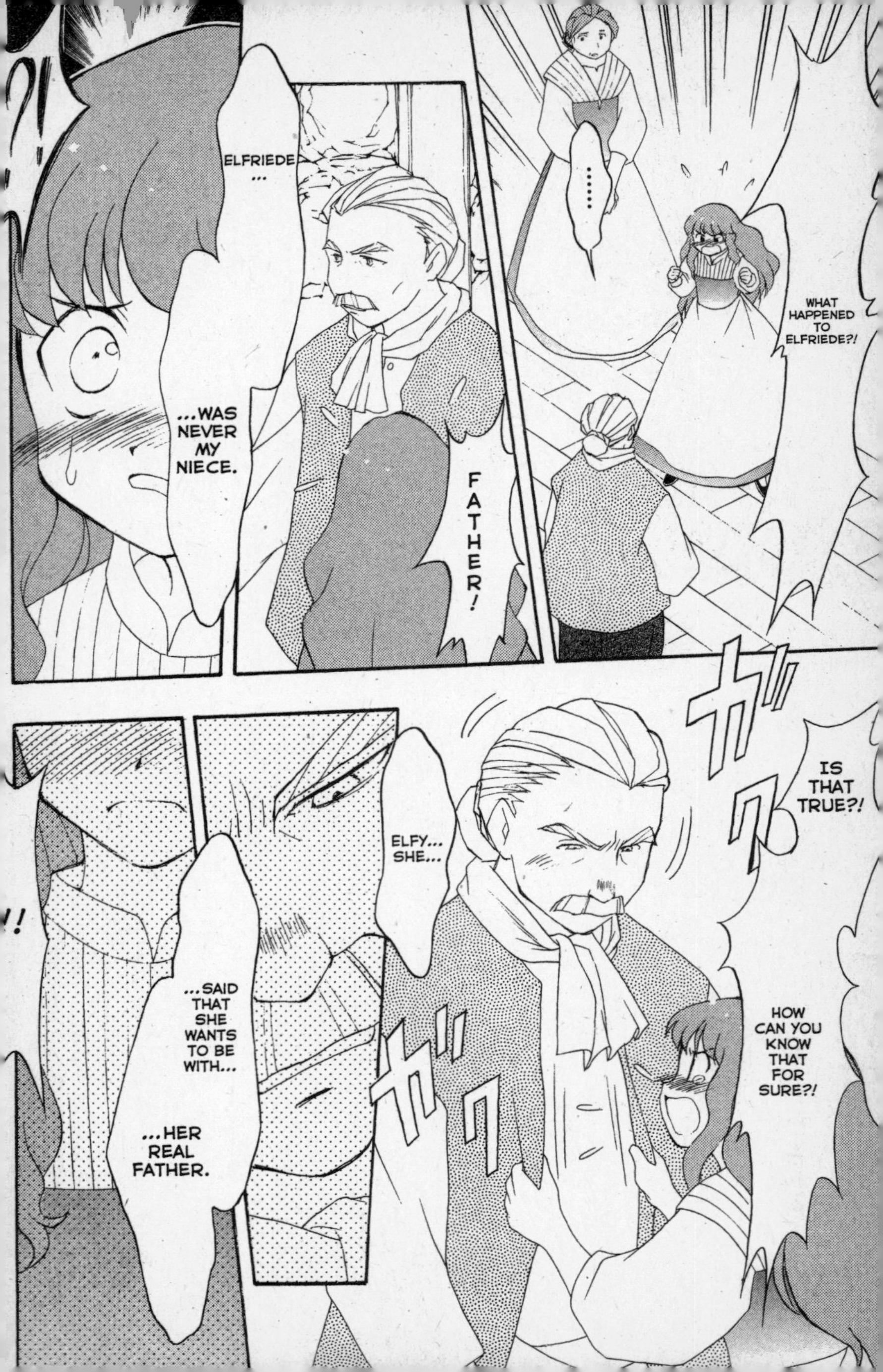
WHAT HAPPENED TO ELFRIEDE?!
......
FATHER!
?!
ELFRIEDE ...
...WAS NEVER MY NIECE.
ガク
IS THAT TRUE?!
HOW CAN YOU KNOW THAT FOR SURE?!
ガク
ELFY... SHE...
...SAID THAT SHE WANTS TO BE WITH...
...HER REAL FATHER.
!!

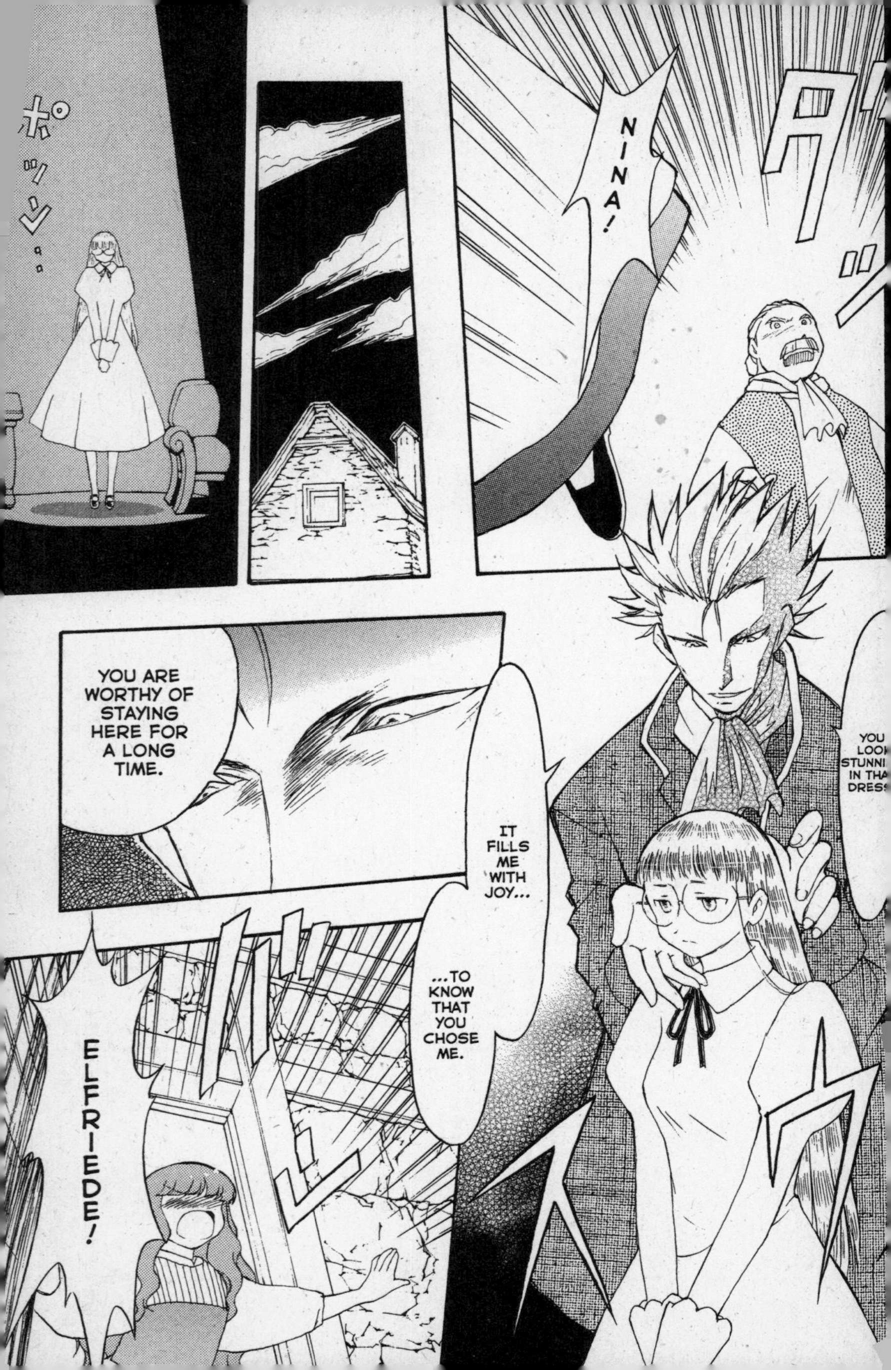
NINA!
YOU LOOK STUNNI IN THA DRESS
IT FILLS ME WITH JOY...
...TO KNOW THAT YOU CHOSE ME.
YOU ARE WORTHY OF STAYING HERE FOR A LONG TIME.
ELFRIEDE!

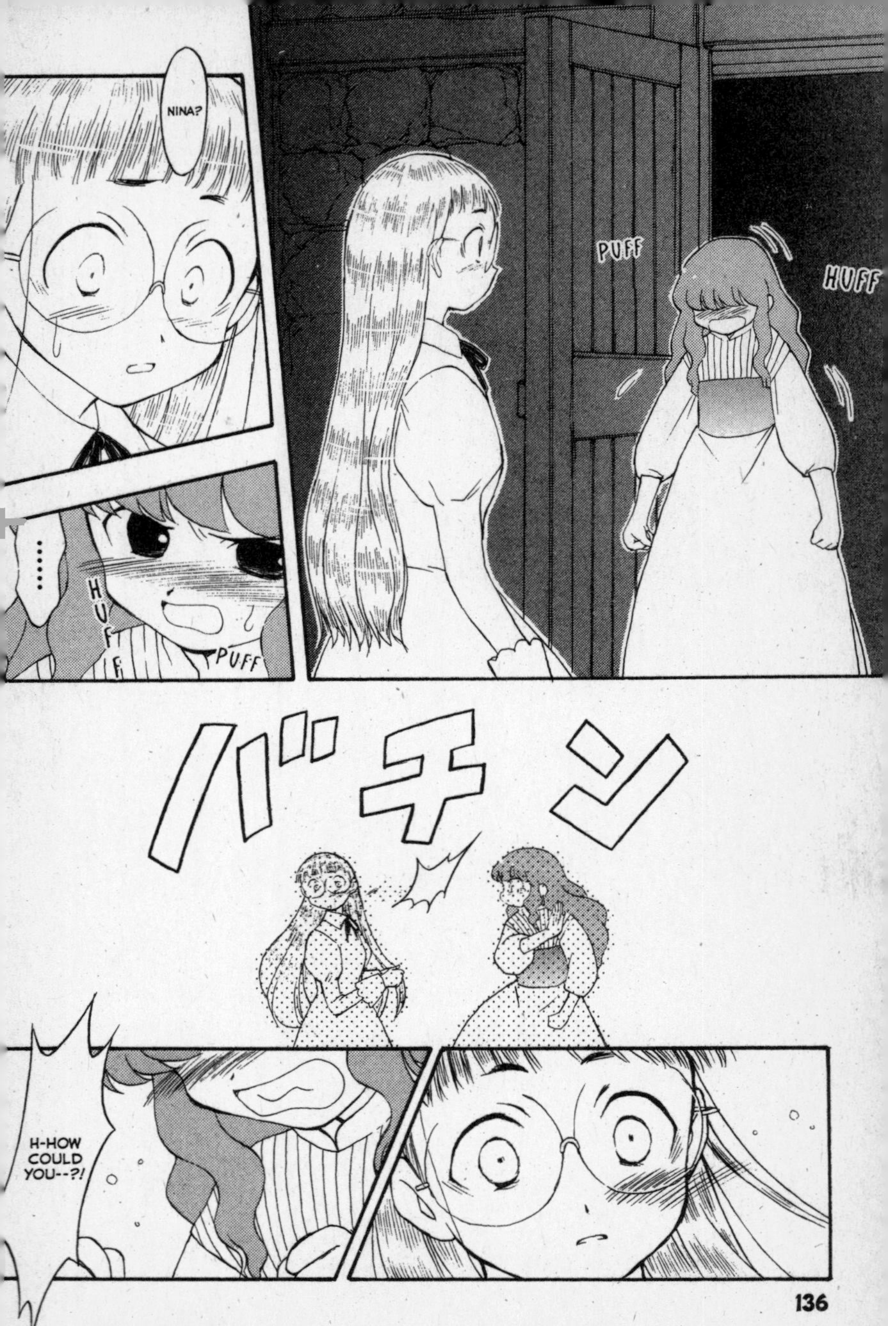
HUFF
PUFF
NINA?
......
HUFF
PUFF
バチン
H-HOW COULD YOU--?!

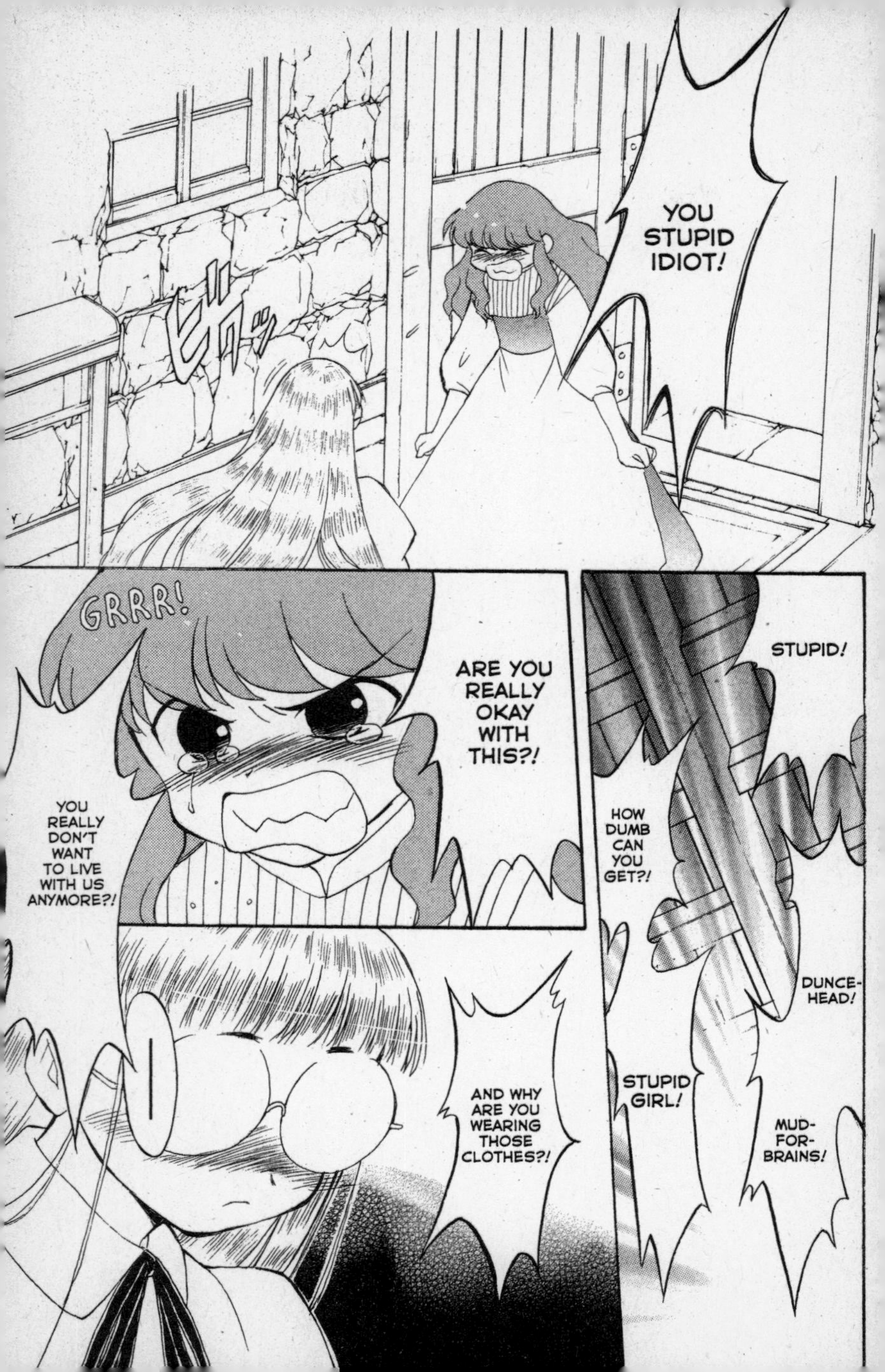
YOU STUPID IDIOT!
ビクッ
STUPID!
HOW DUMB CAN YOU GET?!
DUNCE-HEAD!
STUPID GIRL!
MUD-FOR-BRAINS!
GRRR!
ARE YOU REALLY OKAY WITH THIS?!
YOU REALLY DON'T WANT TO LIVE WITH US ANYMORE?!
AND WHY ARE YOU WEARING THOSE CLOTHES?!

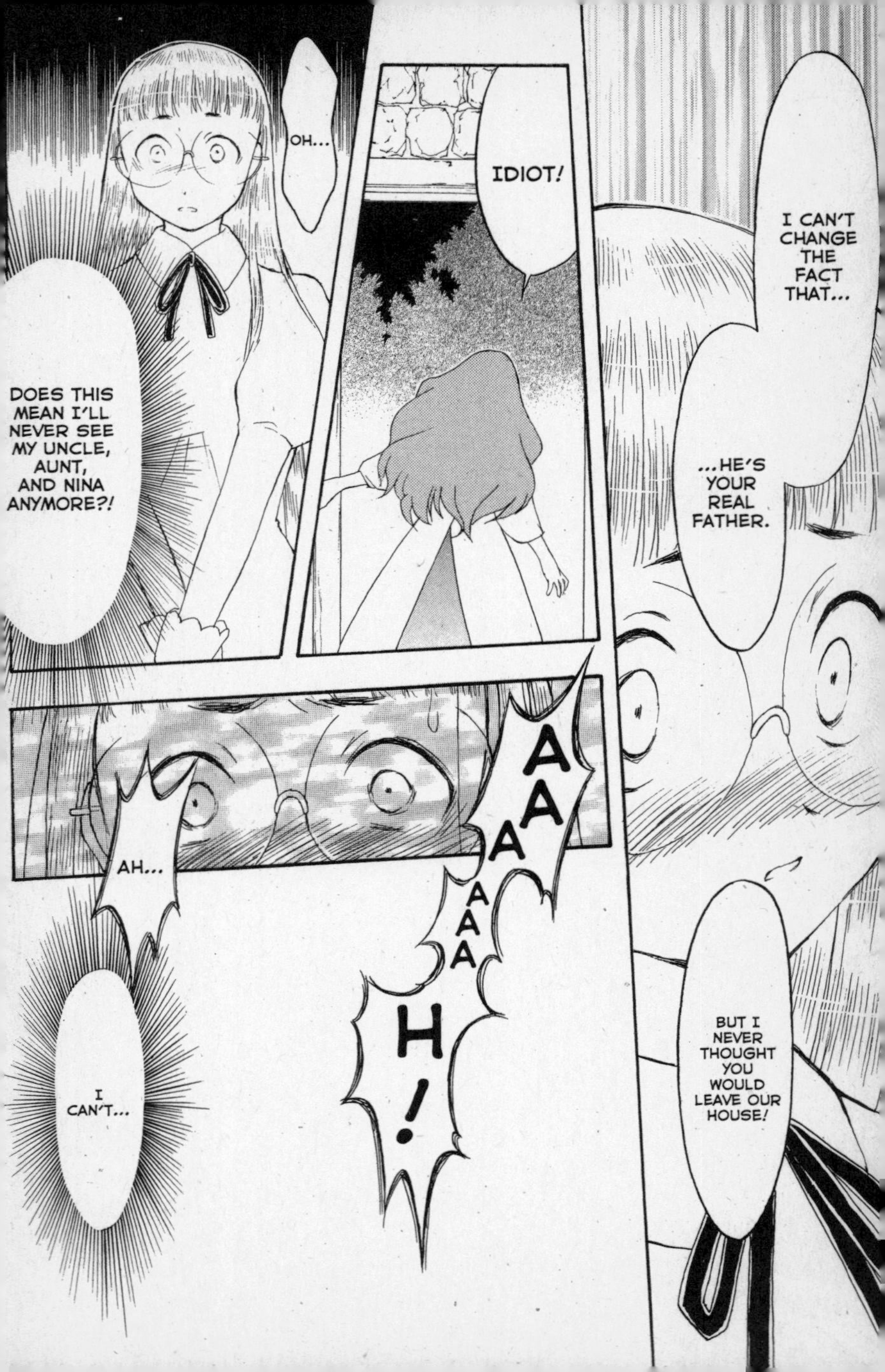
I CAN'T CHANGE THE FACT THAT...
...HE'S YOUR REAL FATHER.
BUT I NEVER THOUGHT YOU WOULD LEAVE OUR HOUSE!
IDIOT!
OH...
DOES THIS MEAN I'LL NEVER SEE MY UNCLE, AUNT, AND NINA ANYMORE?!
AAAAAAAH!
AH...
I CAN'T...

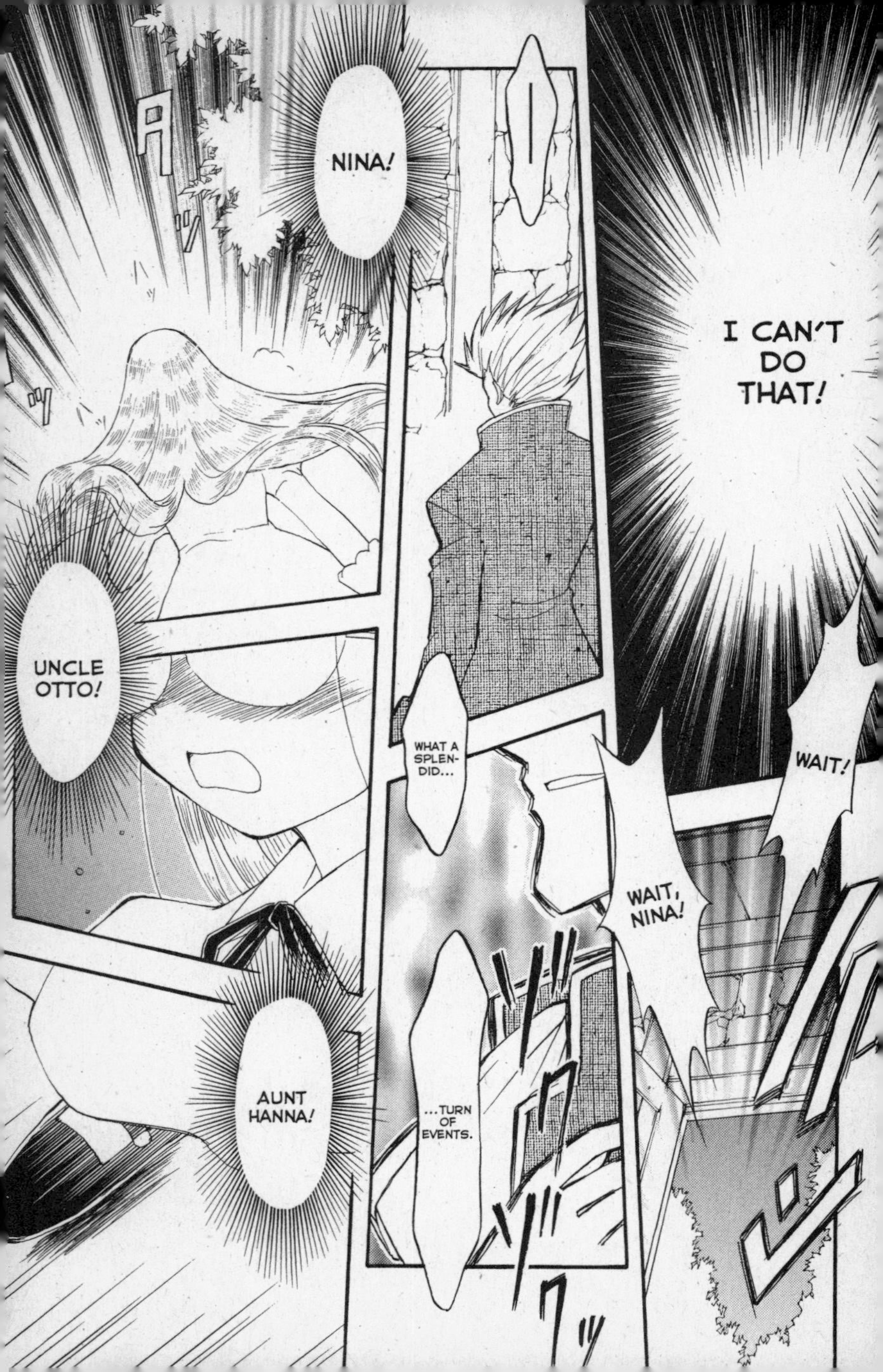
I CAN'T DO THAT!
WAIT!
WAIT, NINA!
WHAT A SPLENDID...
...TURN OF EVENTS.
NINA!
UNCLE OTTO!
AUNT HANNA!

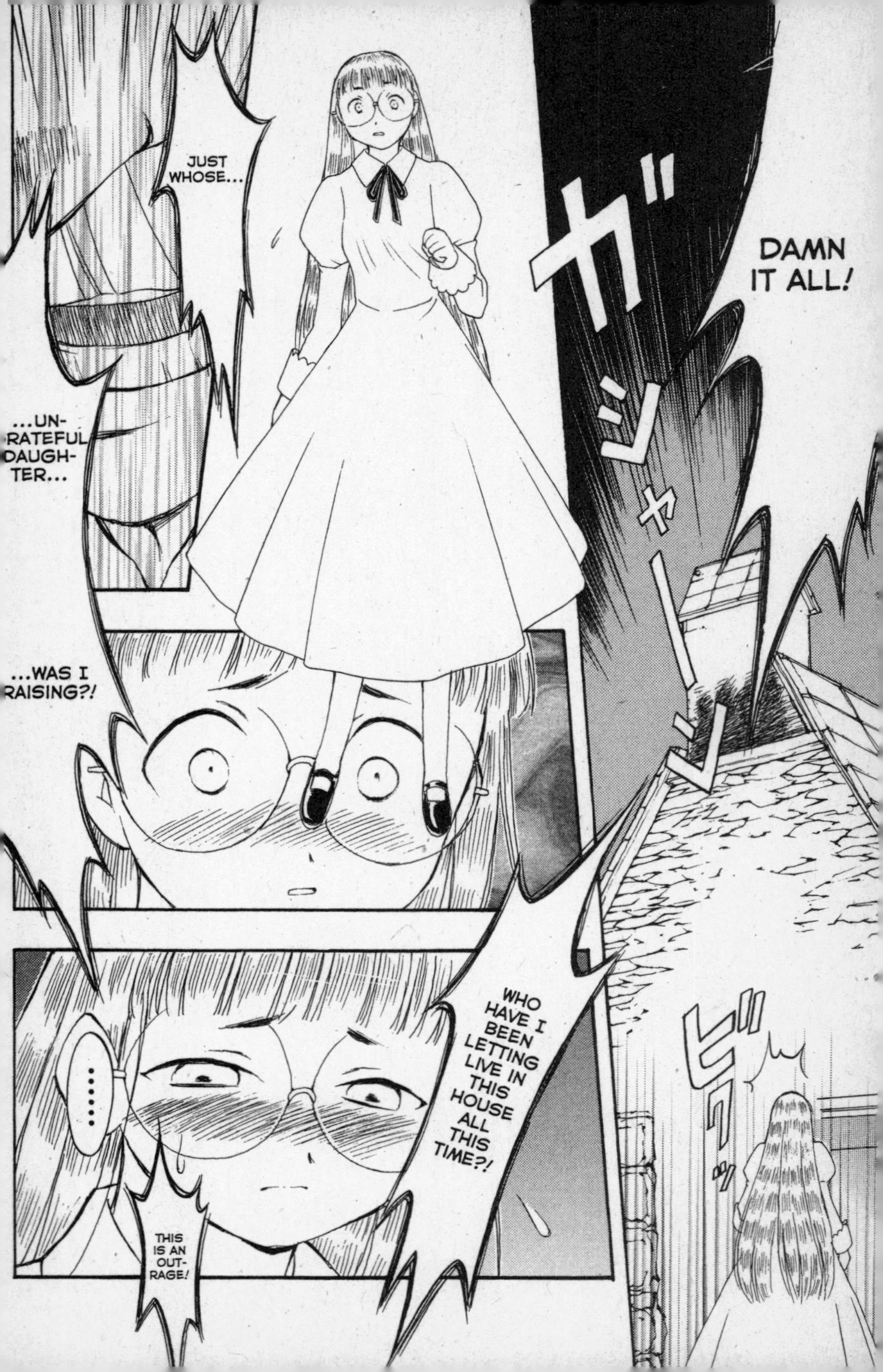
ガシャーン
DAMN IT ALL!
ビクッ
JUST WHOSE...
...UN-RATEFUL DAUGH-TER...
...WAS I RAISING?!
WHO HAVE I BEEN LETTING LIVE IN THIS HOUSE ALL THIS TIME?!
......
THIS IS AN OUT-RAGE!

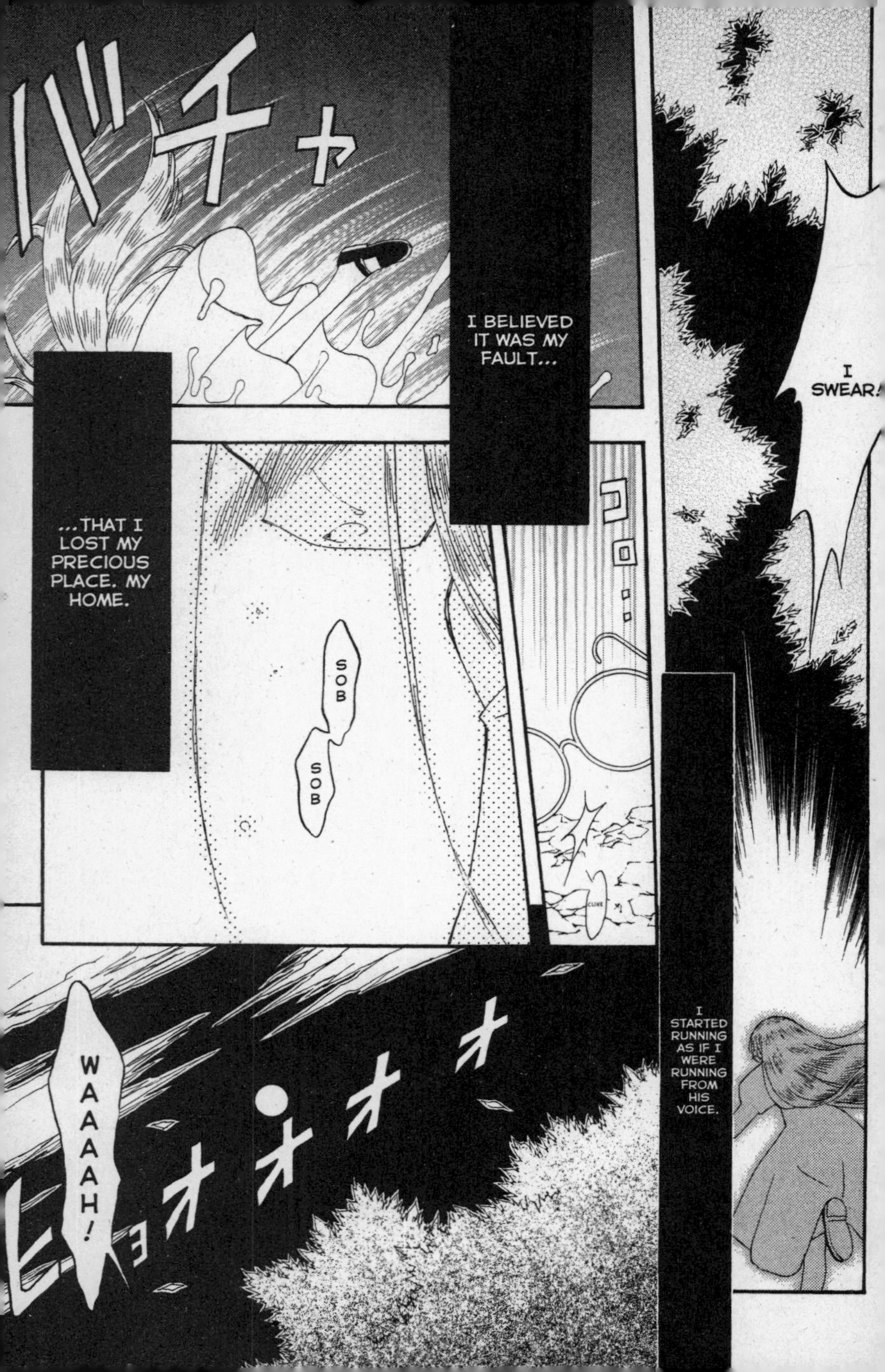
I SWEAR!
I STARTED RUNNING AS IF I WERE RUNNING FROM HIS VOICE.
I BELIEVED IT WAS MY FAULT...
バチャ
...THAT I LOST MY PRECIOUS PLACE. MY HOME.
コロ・・
CLINK
SOB SOB
ヒョオオオオオ
WAAAAAH!

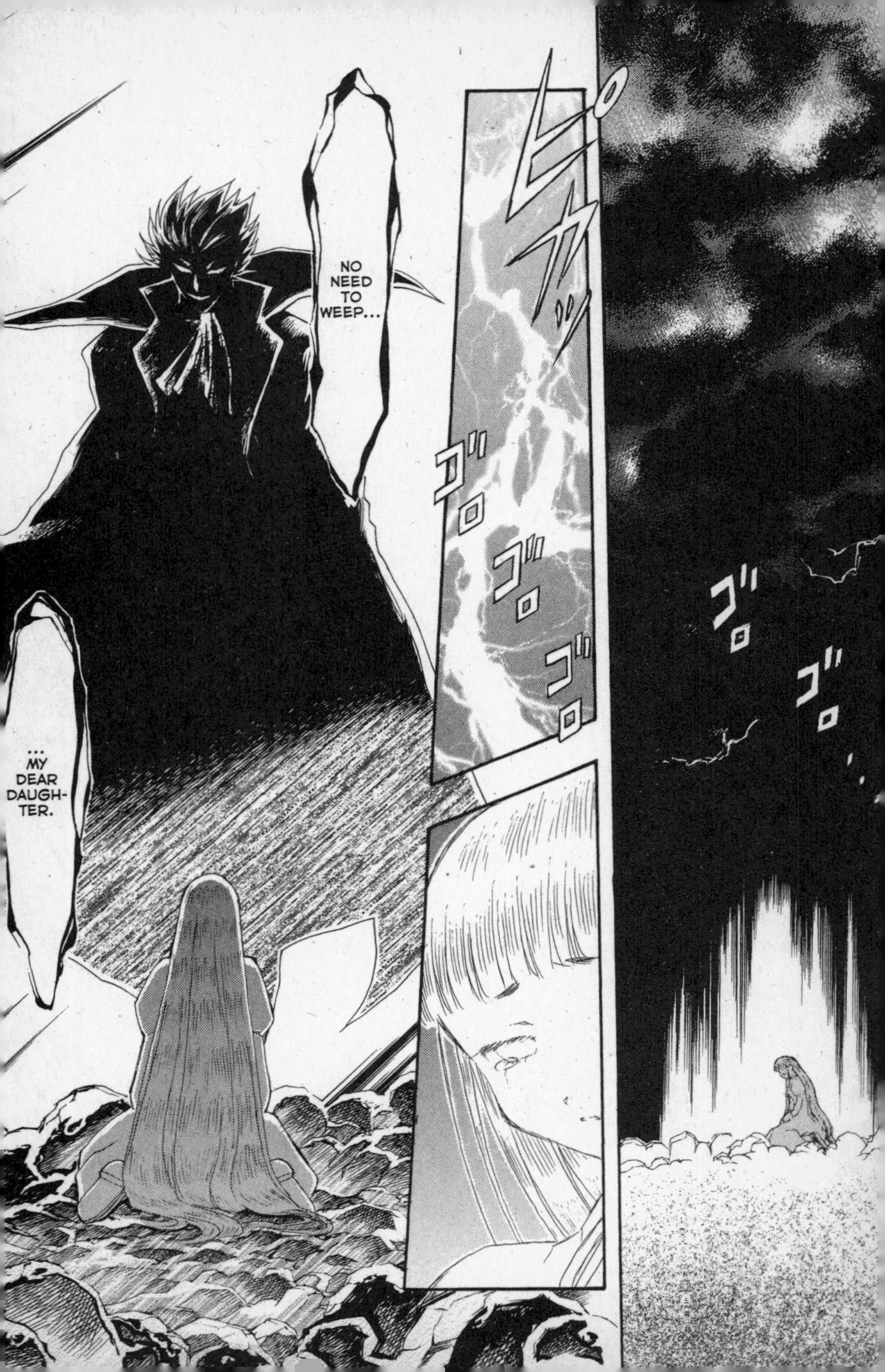
ゴロ
ゴロ
ピカッ
ゴロ
ゴロ
ゴロ
NO NEED TO WEEP...
... MY DEAR DAUGH-TER.

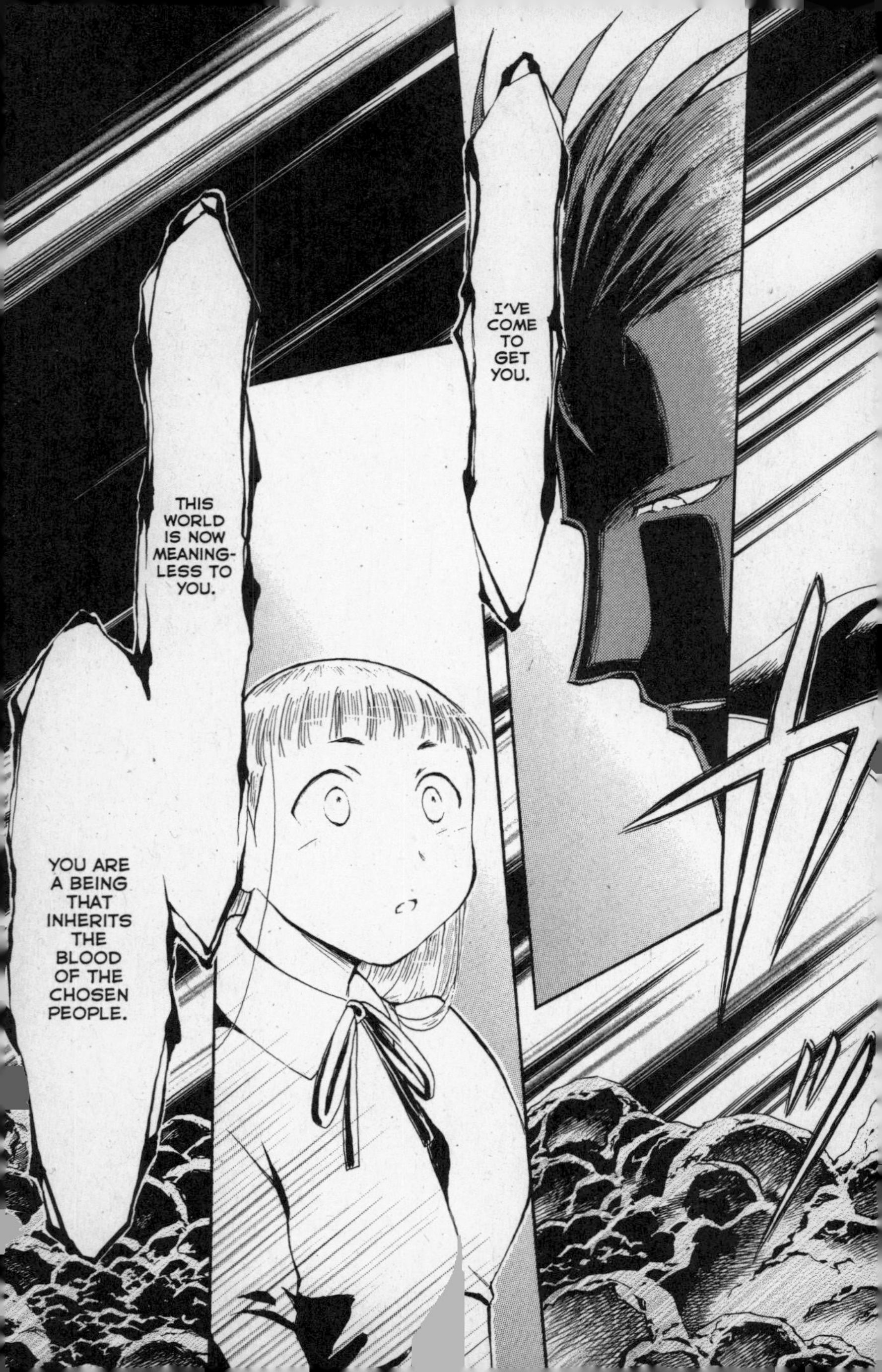
I'VE COME TO GET YOU.
THIS WORLD IS NOW MEANING-LESS TO YOU.
YOU ARE A BEING THAT INHERITS THE BLOOD OF THE CHOSEN PEOPLE.

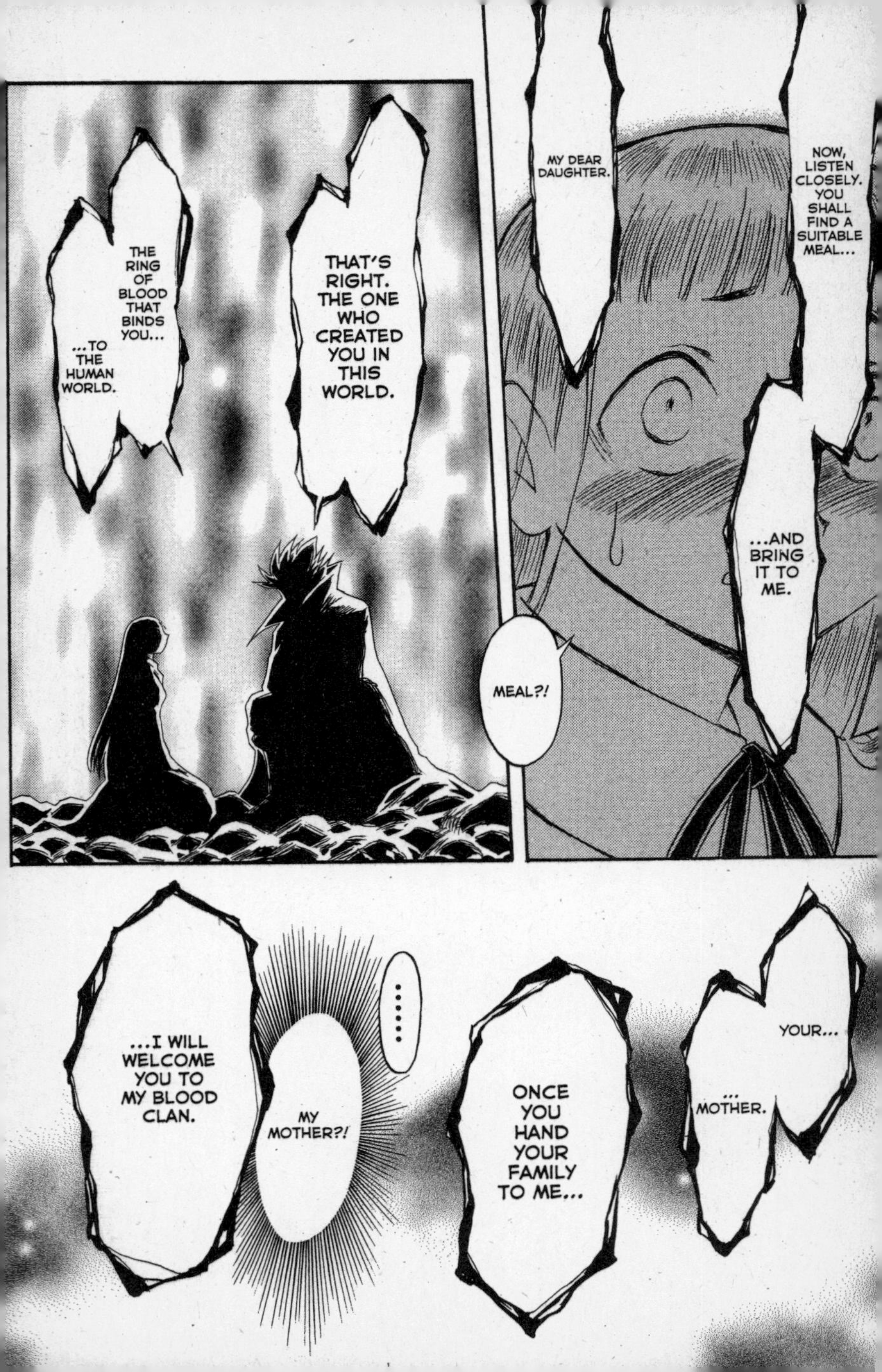
NOW, LISTEN CLOSELY. YOU SHALL FIND A SUITABLE MEAL...
MY DEAR DAUGHTER.
...AND BRING IT TO ME.
MEAL?!
THAT'S RIGHT. THE ONE WHO CREATED YOU IN THIS WORLD.
THE RING OF BLOOD THAT BINDS YOU...
...TO THE HUMAN WORLD.
YOUR...
...MOTHER.
ONCE YOU HAND YOUR FAMILY TO ME...
......
MY MOTHER?!
...I WILL WELCOME YOU TO MY BLOOD CLAN.

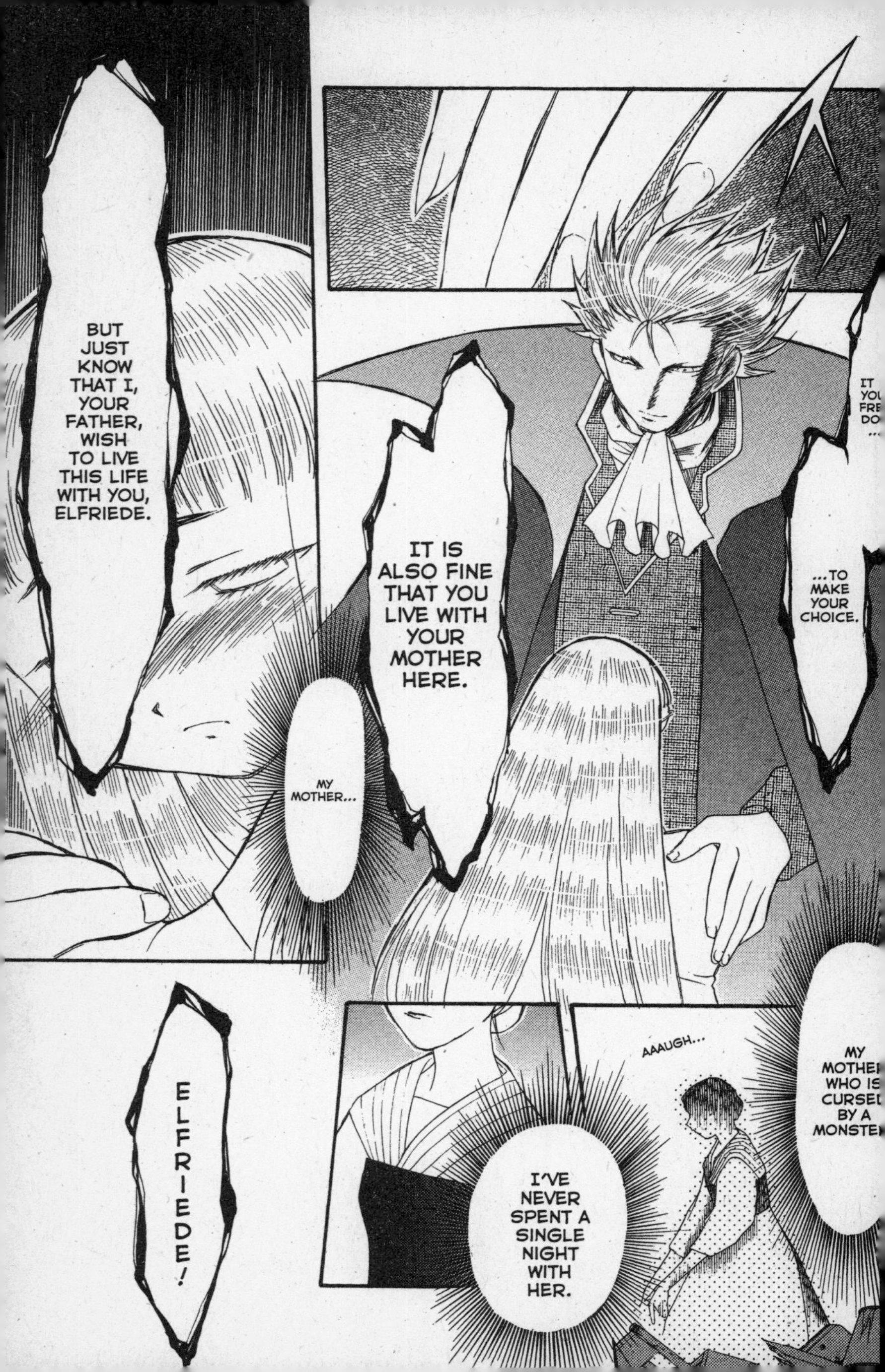
IT YOU FRE DO ...
...TO MAKE YOUR CHOICE.
IT IS ALSO FINE THAT YOU LIVE WITH YOUR MOTHER HERE.
MY MOTHER...
BUT JUST KNOW THAT I, YOUR FATHER, WISH TO LIVE THIS LIFE WITH YOU, ELFRIEDE.
MY MOTHE WHO IS CURSE BY A MONSTE
AAAUGH...
I'VE NEVER SPENT A SINGLE NIGHT WITH HER.
ELFRIEDE!

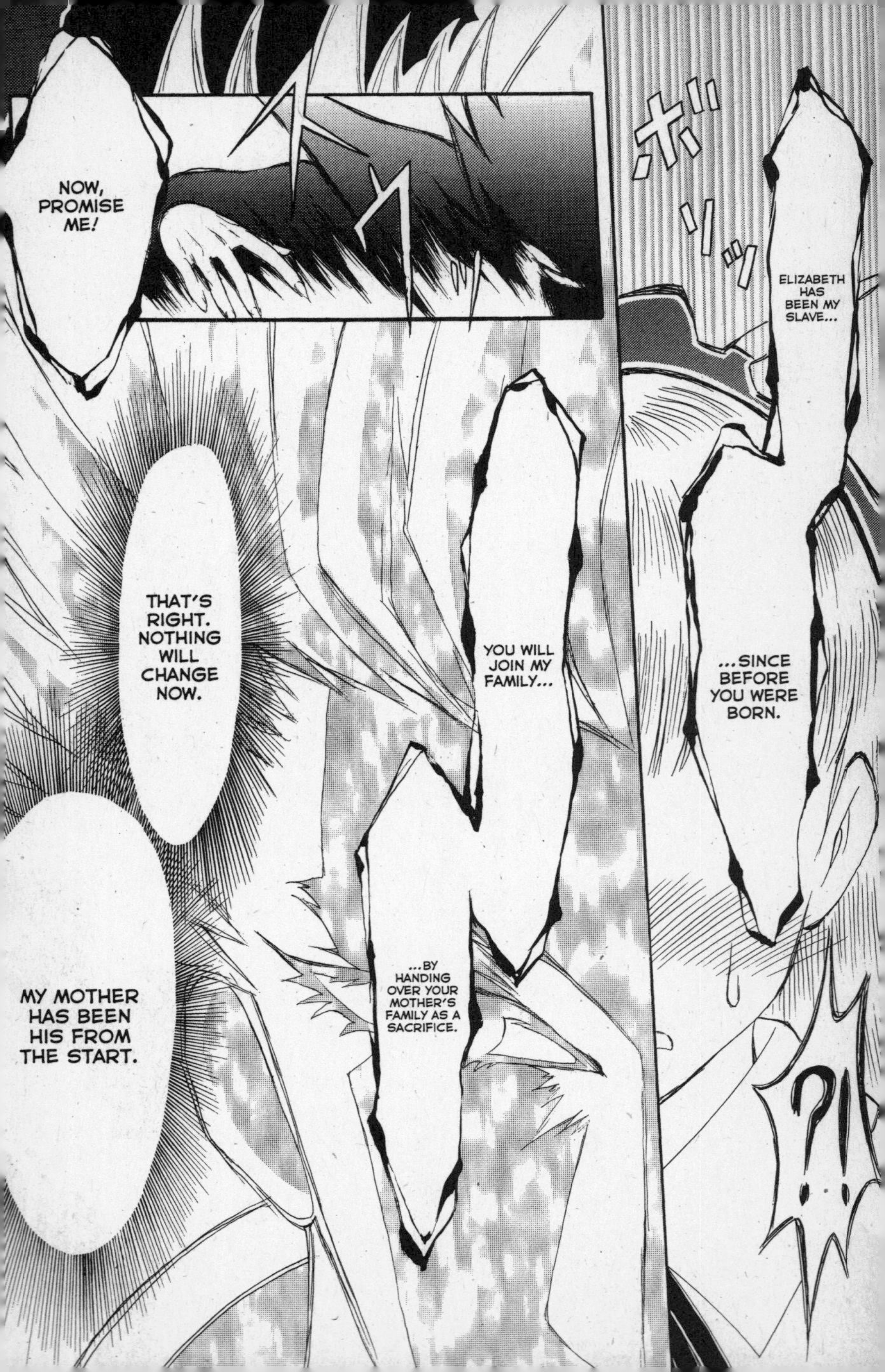
ELIZABETH HAS BEEN MY SLAVE...
...SINCE BEFORE YOU WERE BORN.
?!
NOW, PROMISE ME!
YOU WILL JOIN MY FAMILY...
...BY HANDING OVER YOUR MOTHER'S FAMILY AS A SACRIFICE.
THAT'S RIGHT. NOTHING WILL CHANGE NOW.
MY MOTHER HAS BEEN HIS FROM THE START.

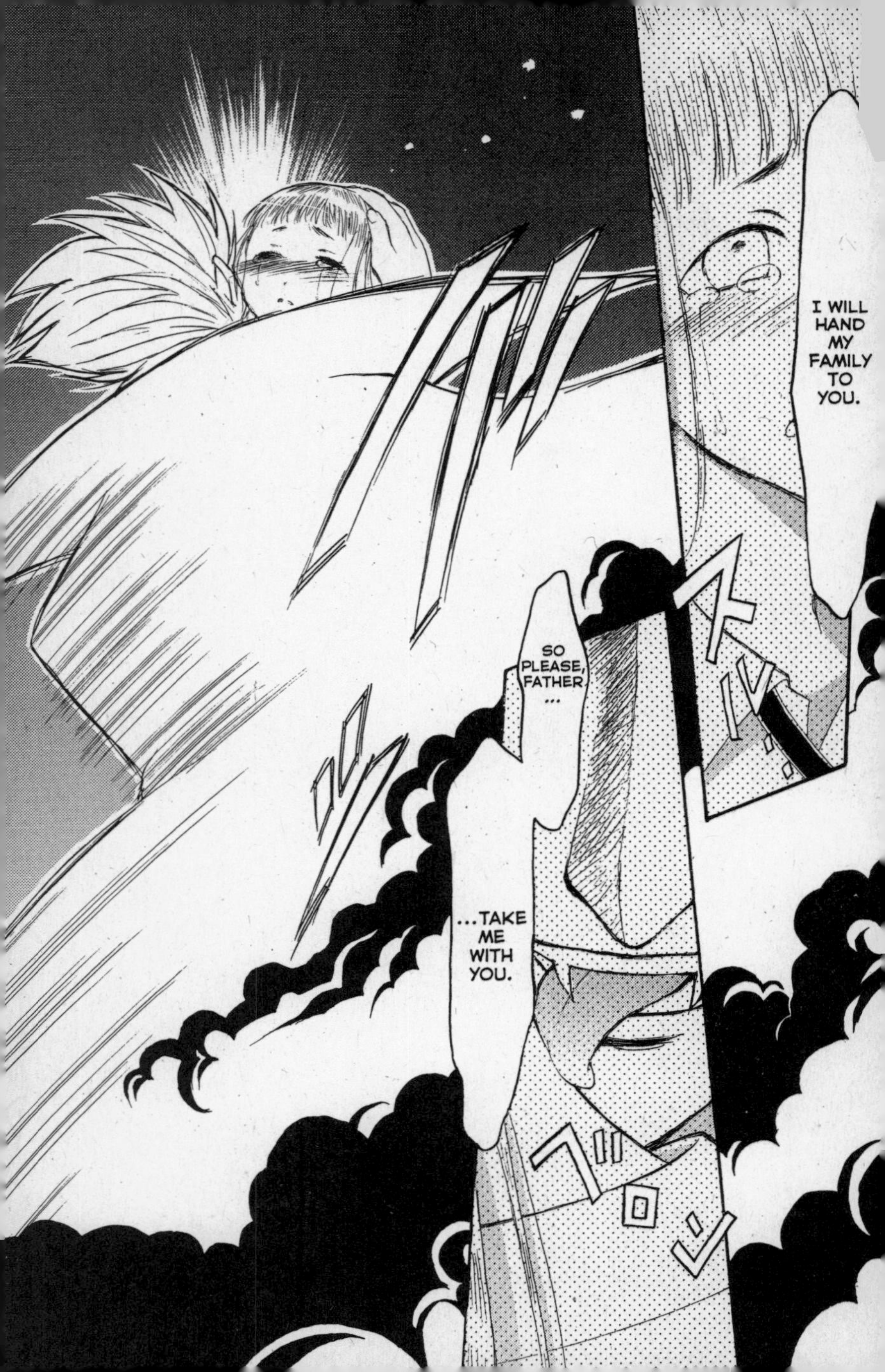
I WILL HAND MY FAMILY TO YOU.
SO PLEASE, FATHER...
...TAKE ME WITH YOU.

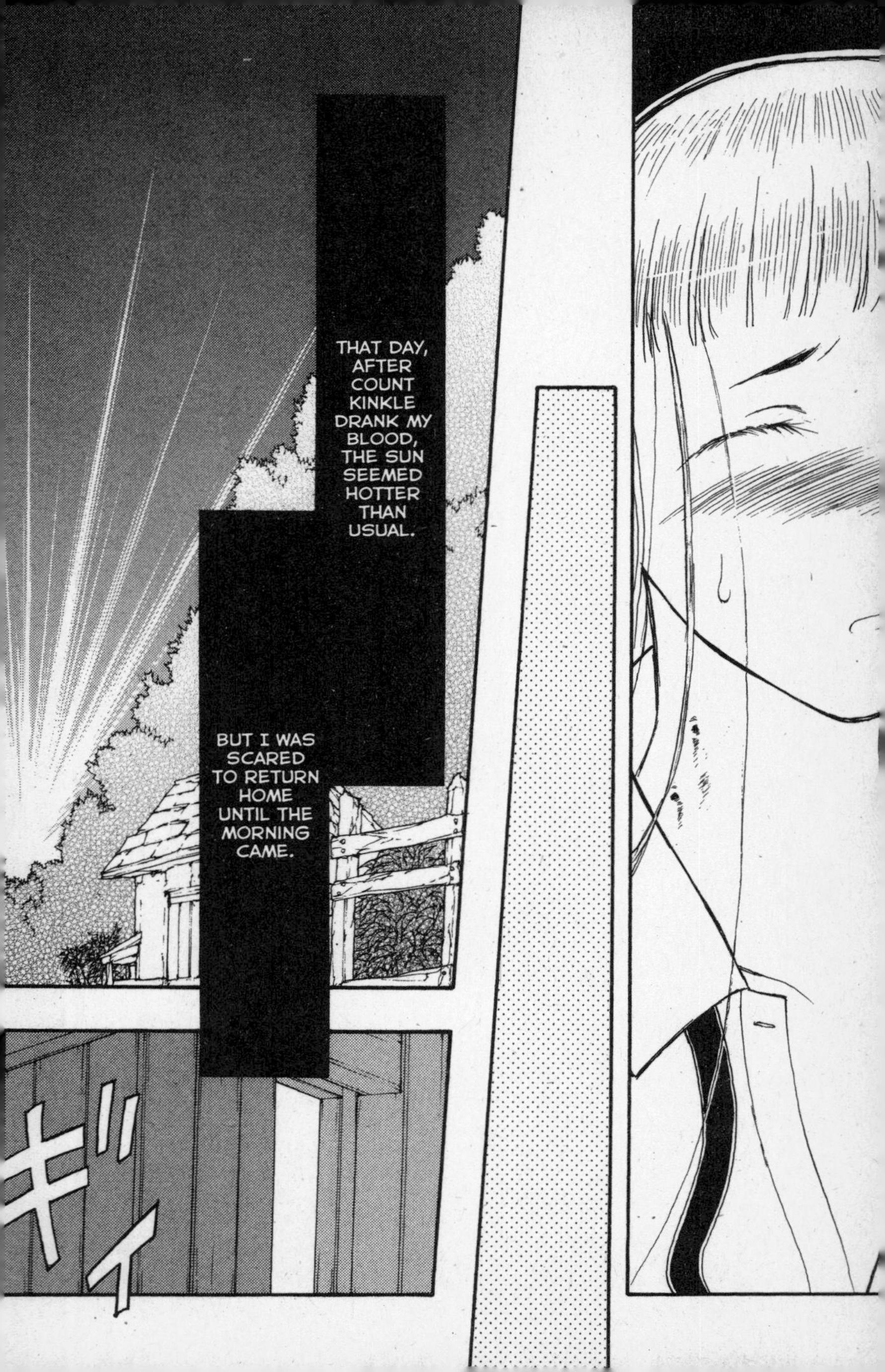
THAT DAY, AFTER COUNT KINKLE DRANK MY BLOOD, THE SUN SEEMED HOTTER THAN USUAL.
BUT I WAS SCARED TO RETURN HOME UNTIL THE MORNING CAME.
ギィ

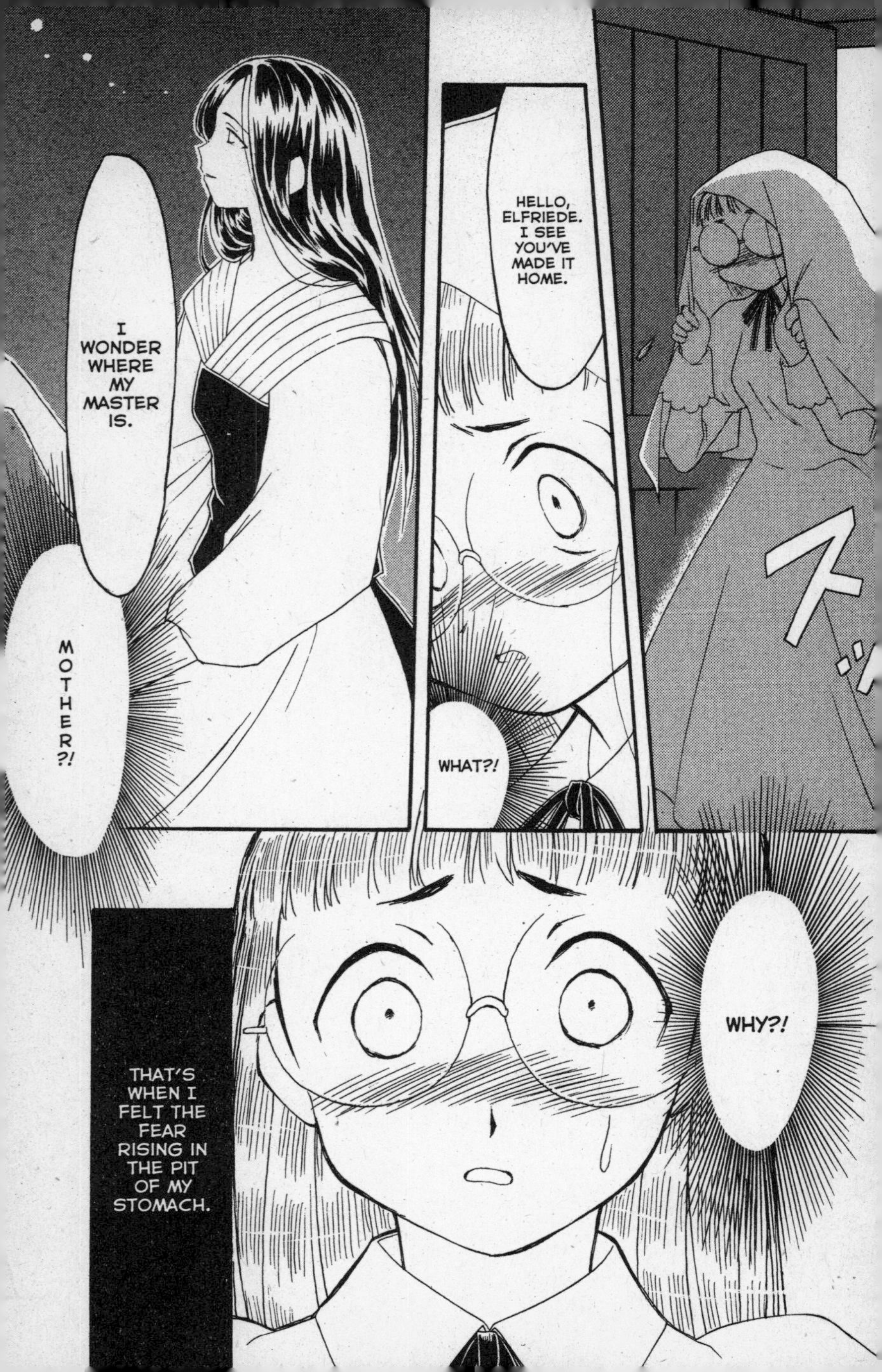
HELLO, ELFRIEDE. I SEE YOU'VE MADE IT HOME.
WHAT?!
I WONDER WHERE MY MASTER IS.
MOTHER?!
WHY?!
THAT'S WHEN I FELT THE FEAR RISING IN THE PIT OF MY STOMACH.

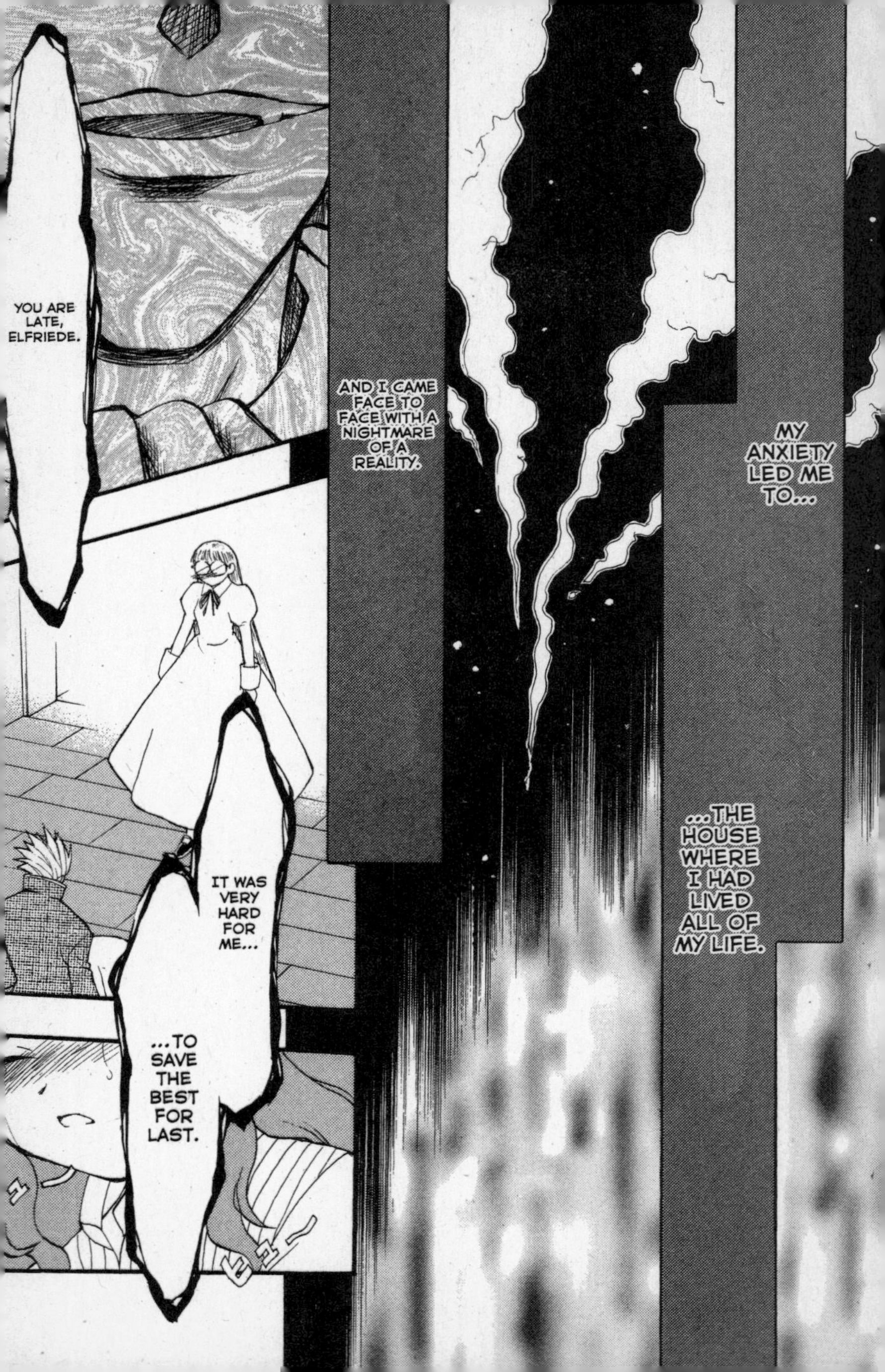
MY ANXIETY LED ME TO...
...THE HOUSE WHERE I HAD LIVED ALL OF MY LIFE.
AND I CAME FACE TO FACE WITH A NIGHTMARE OF A REALITY.
YOU ARE LATE, ELFRIEDE.
IT WAS VERY HARD FOR ME...
...TO SAVE THE BEST FOR LAST.

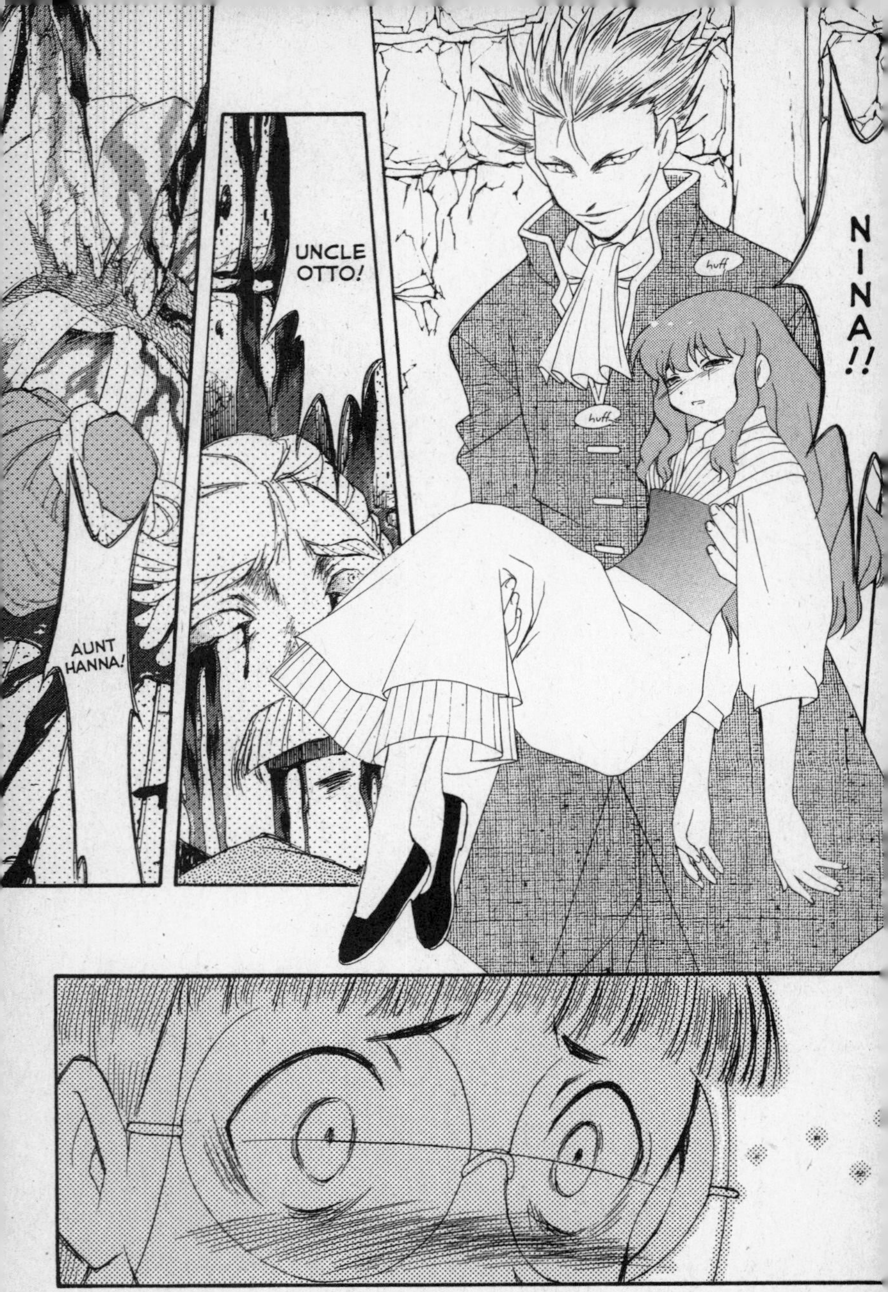
NINA!!
huff
huff
UNCLE OTTO!
AUNT HANNA!

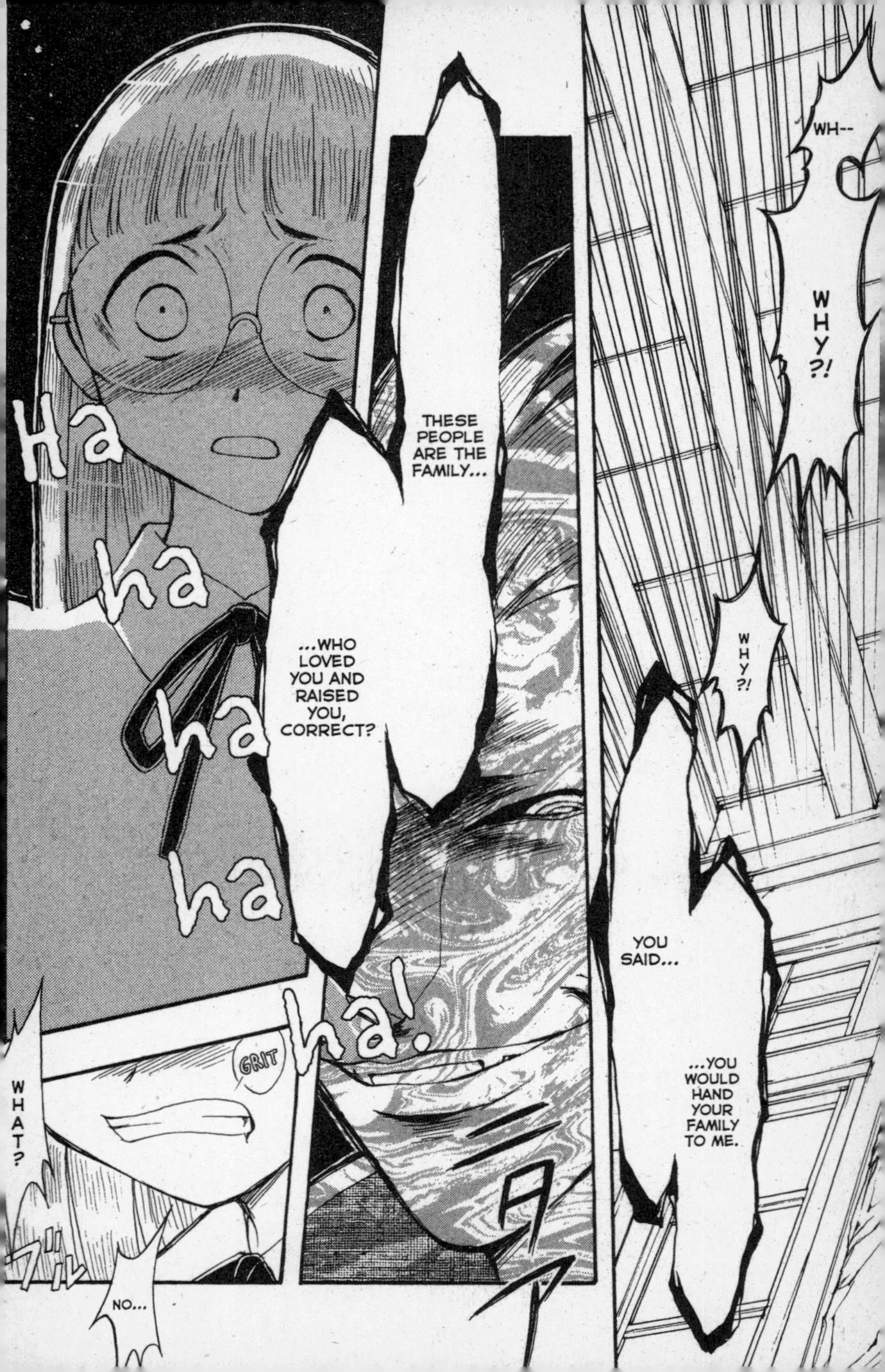
WH--
WHY?!
WHY?!
YOU SAID...
...YOU WOULD HAND YOUR FAMILY TO ME.
THESE PEOPLE ARE THE FAMILY...
...WHO LOVED YOU AND RAISED YOU, CORRECT?
Ha ha ha ha ha!
GRIT
WHAT?
NO...

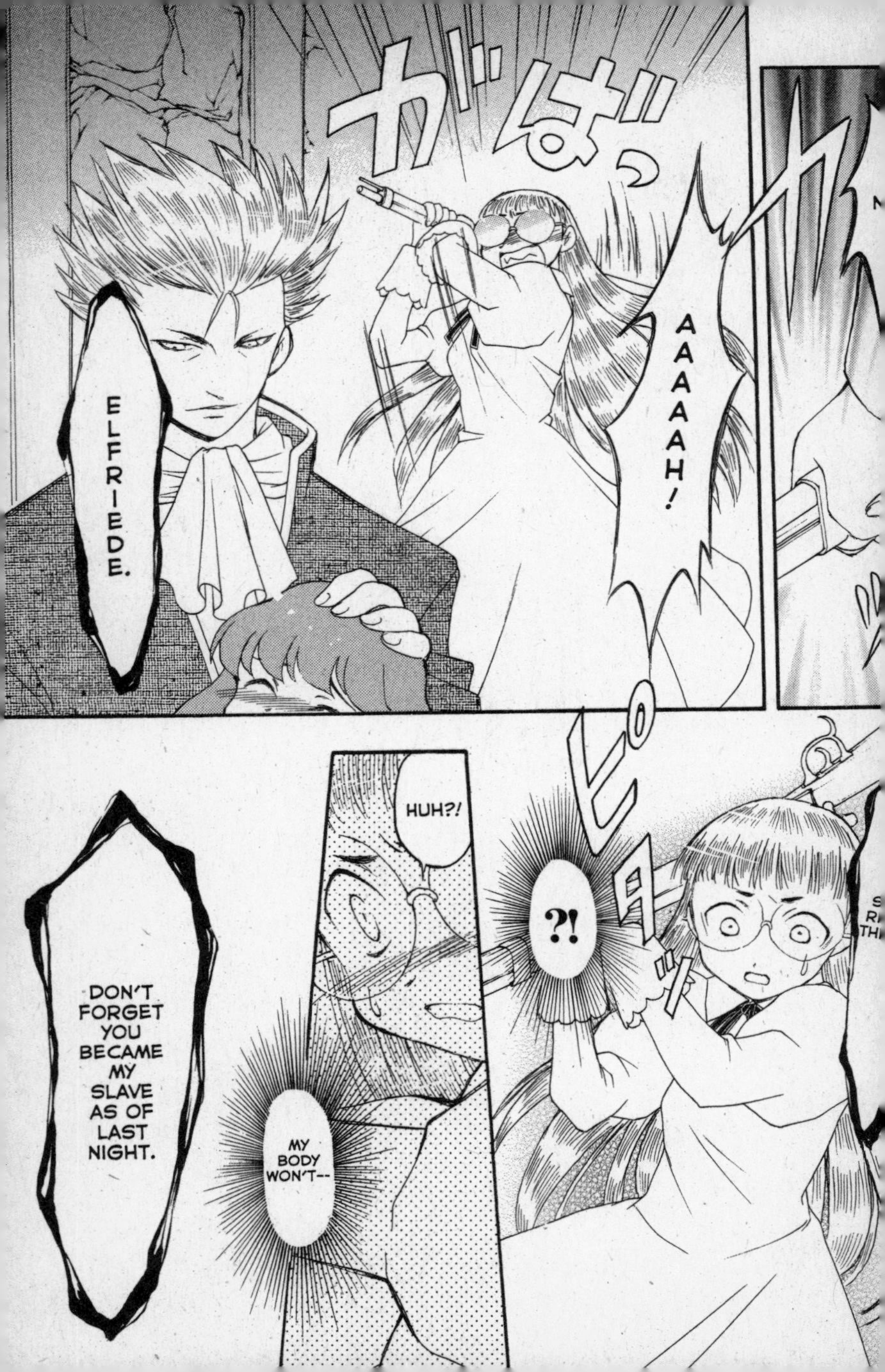

がばっ
AAAAAAH!
ELFRIEDE.
ピタ
?!
HUH?!
MY BODY WON'T--
DON'T FORGET YOU BECAME MY SLAVE AS OF LAST NIGHT.

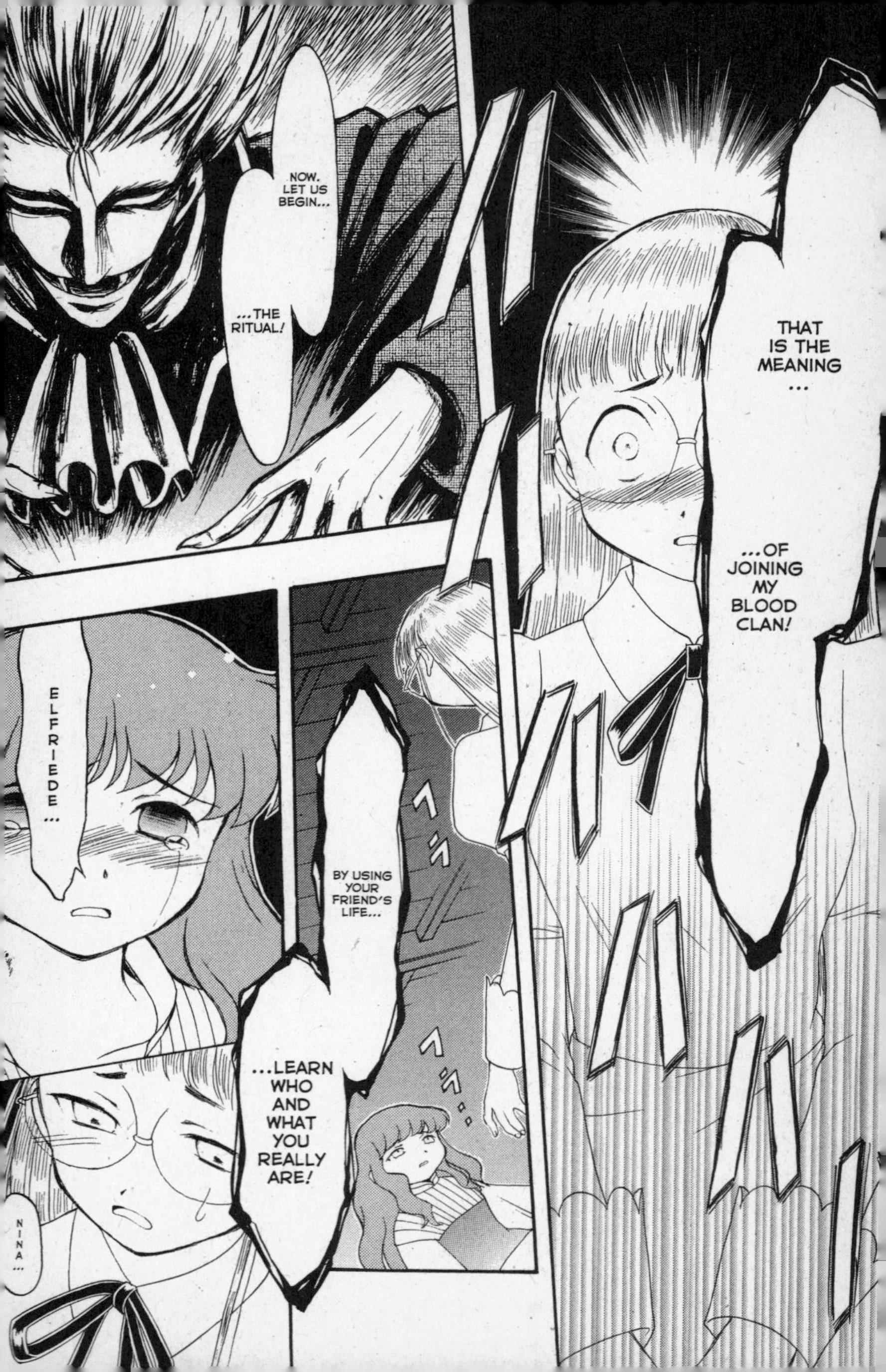
THAT IS THE MEANING ...
...OF JOINING MY BLOOD CLAN!
NOW. LET US BEGIN...
...THE RITUAL!
BY USING YOUR FRIEND'S LIFE...
...LEARN WHO AND WHAT YOU REALLY ARE!
ELFRIEDE...
NINA...

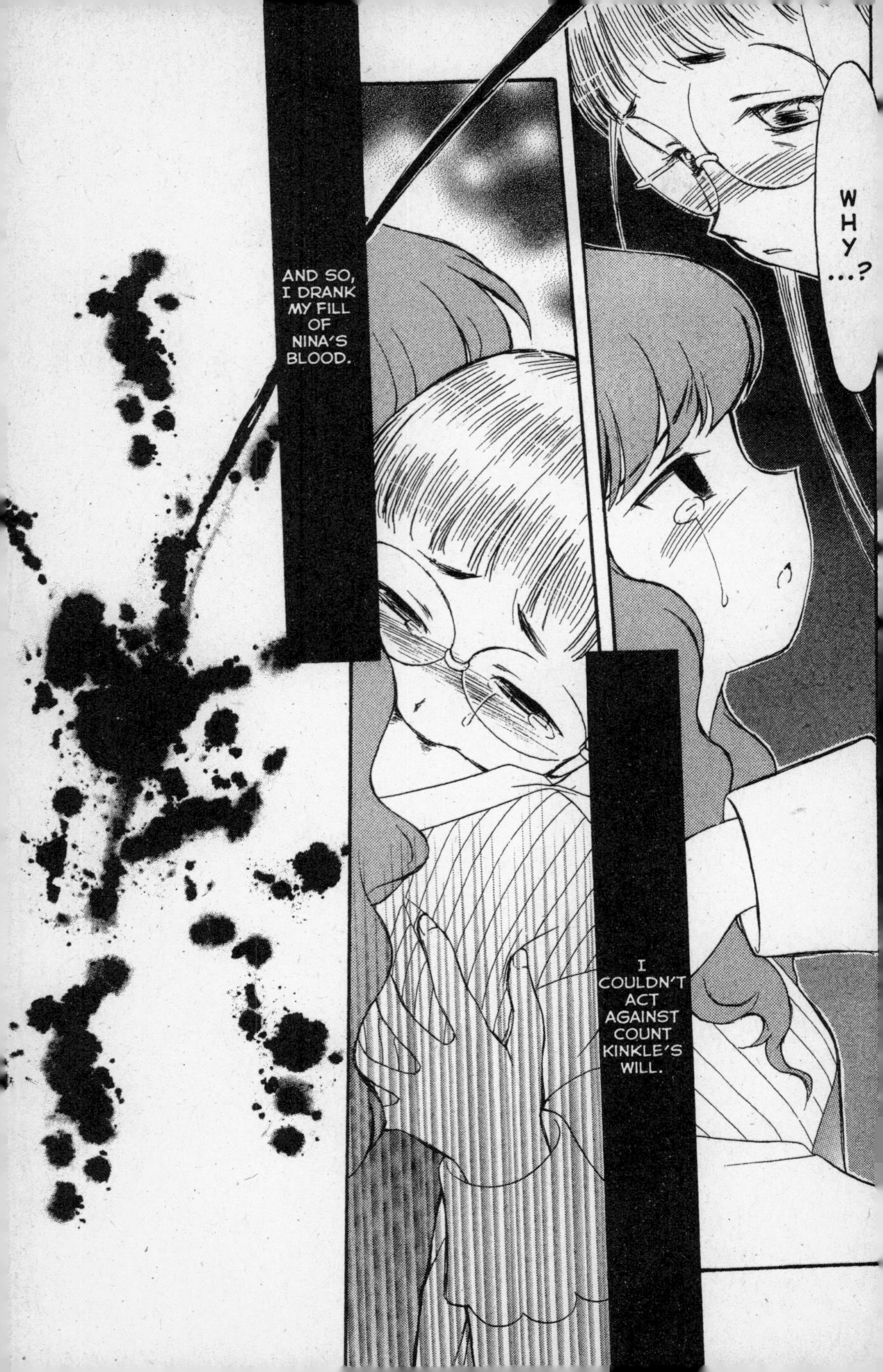
WHY...?
AND SO, I DRANK MY FILL OF NINA'S BLOOD.
I COULDN'T ACT AGAINST COUNT KINKLE'S WILL.

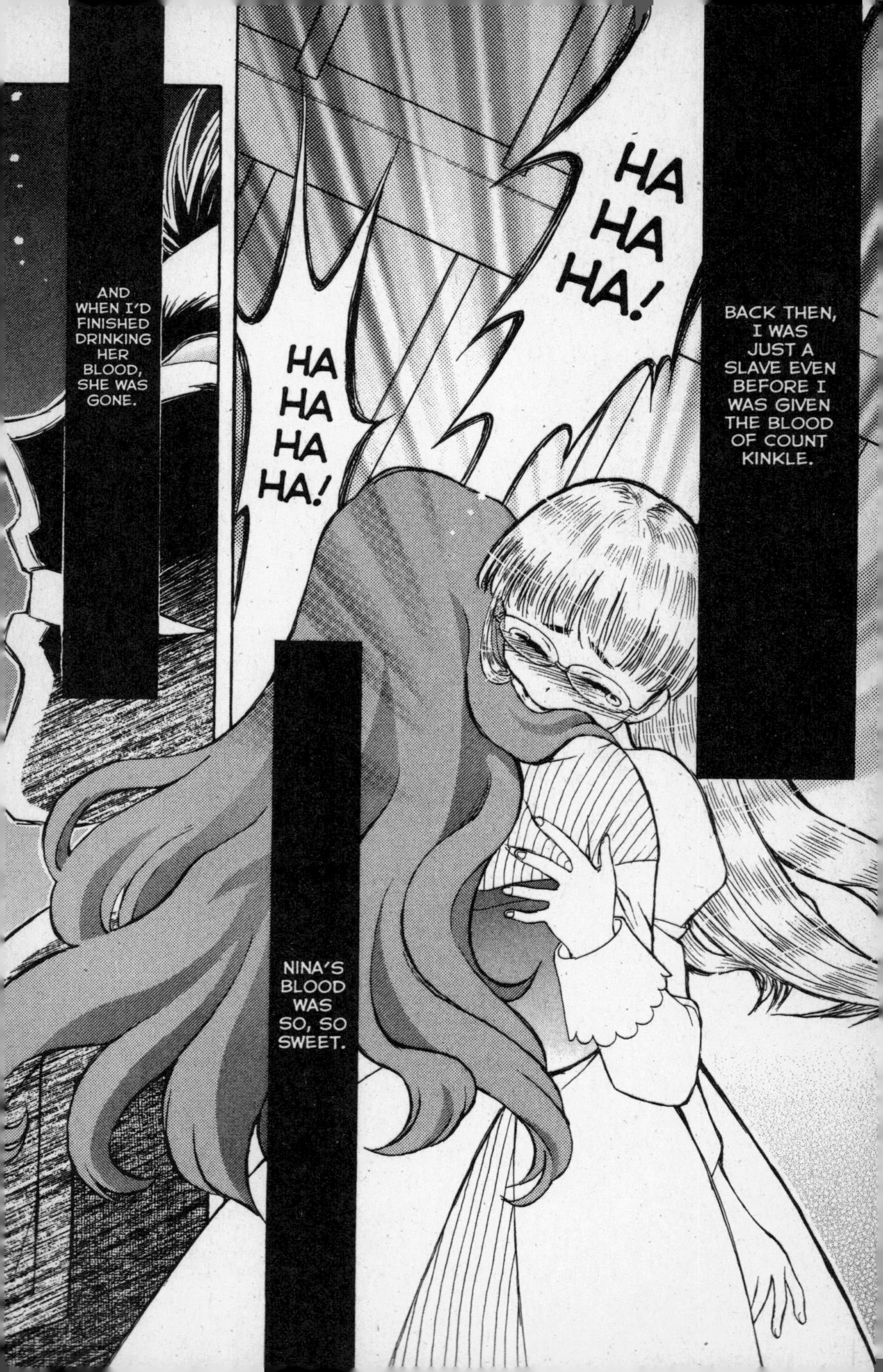
BACK THEN, I WAS JUST A SLAVE EVEN BEFORE I WAS GIVEN THE BLOOD OF COUNT KINKLE.
HA HA HA!
HA HA HA HA!
NINA'S BLOOD WAS SO, SO SWEET.
AND WHEN I'D FINISHED DRINKING HER BLOOD, SHE WAS GONE.

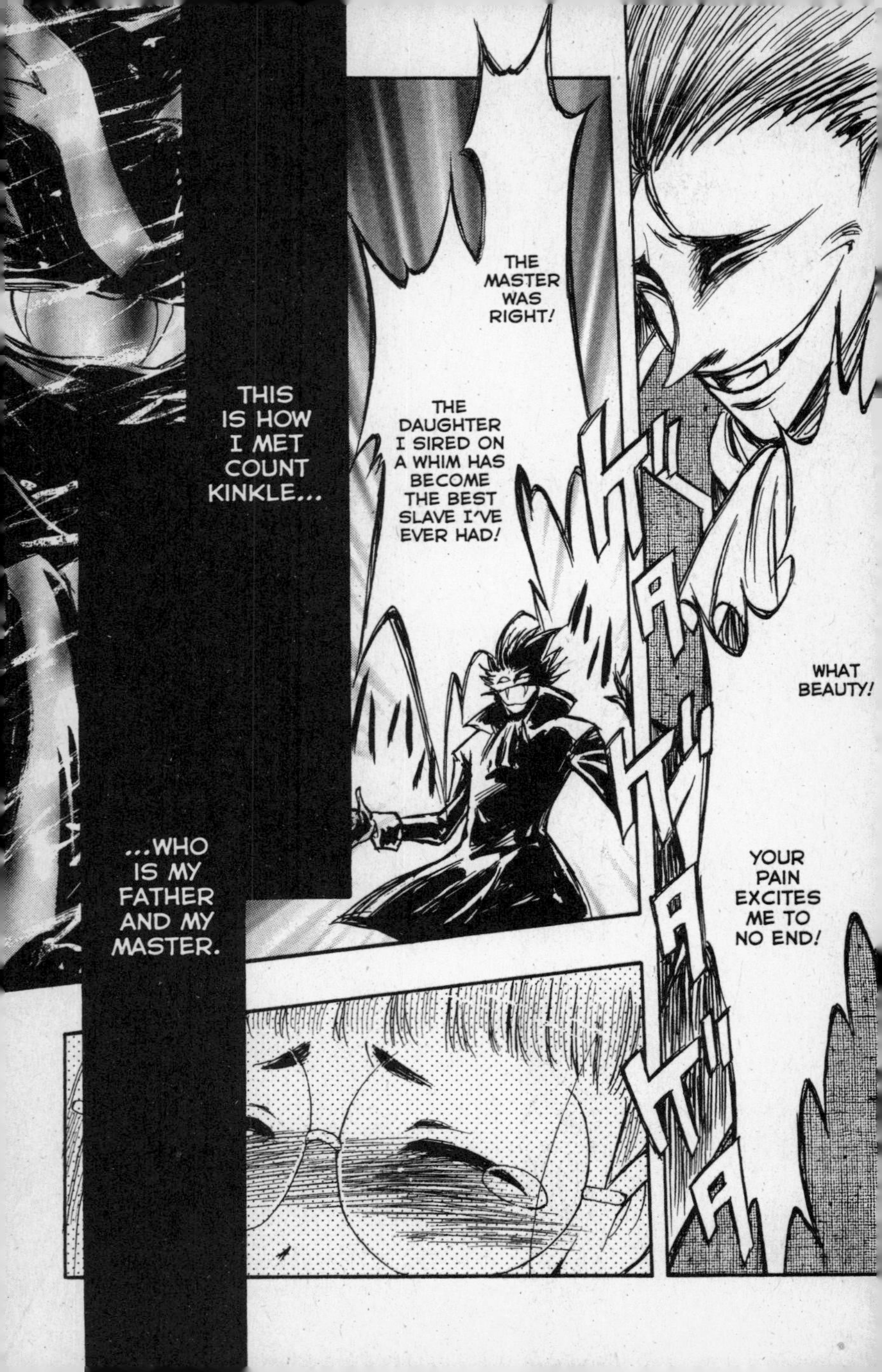
WHAT BEAUTY!
YOUR PAIN EXCITES ME TO NO END!
HA.. HA.. HA
THE MASTER WAS RIGHT!
THE DAUGHTER I SIRED ON A WHIM HAS BECOME THE BEST SLAVE I'VE EVER HAD!
THIS IS HOW I MET COUNT KINKLE...
...WHO IS MY FATHER AND MY MASTER.

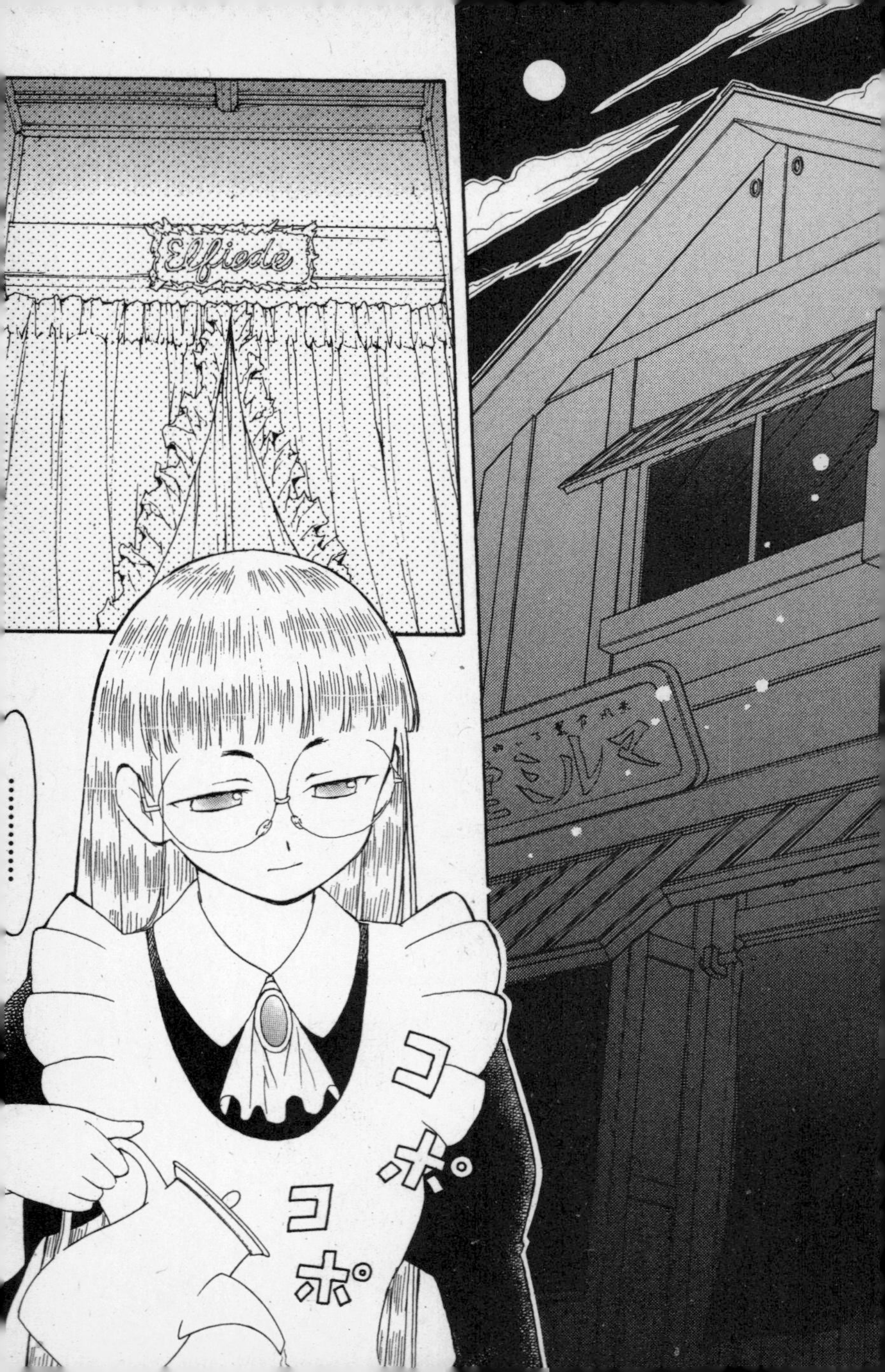
Elfiede
……
コポコポ

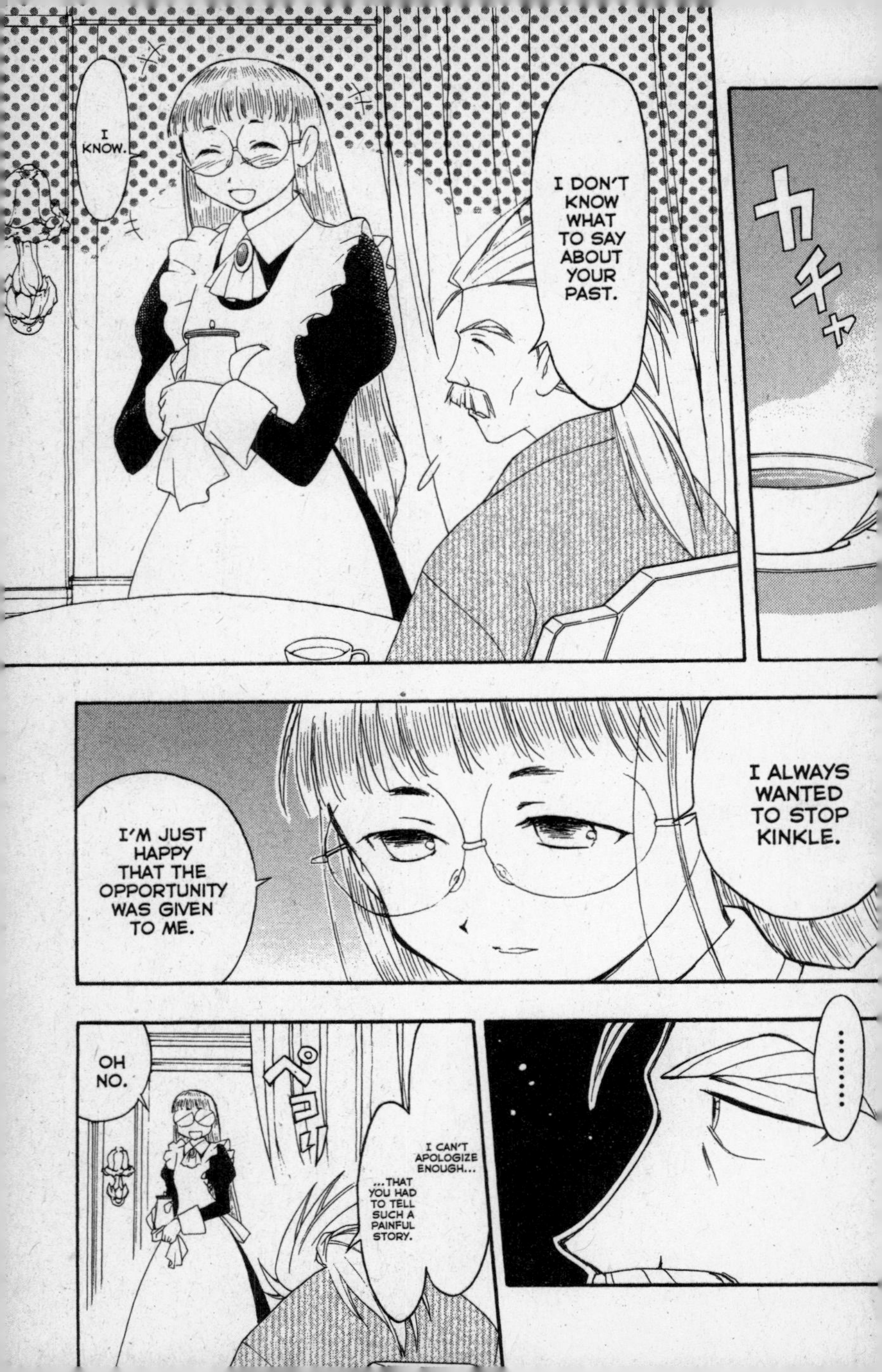
カチャ
I DON'T KNOW WHAT TO SAY ABOUT YOUR PAST.
I KNOW.
I ALWAYS WANTED TO STOP KINKLE.
I'M JUST HAPPY THAT THE OPPORTUNITY WAS GIVEN TO ME.
......
I CAN'T APOLOGIZE ENOUGH...
...THAT YOU HAD TO TELL SUCH A PAINFUL STORY.
ペコ
OH NO.

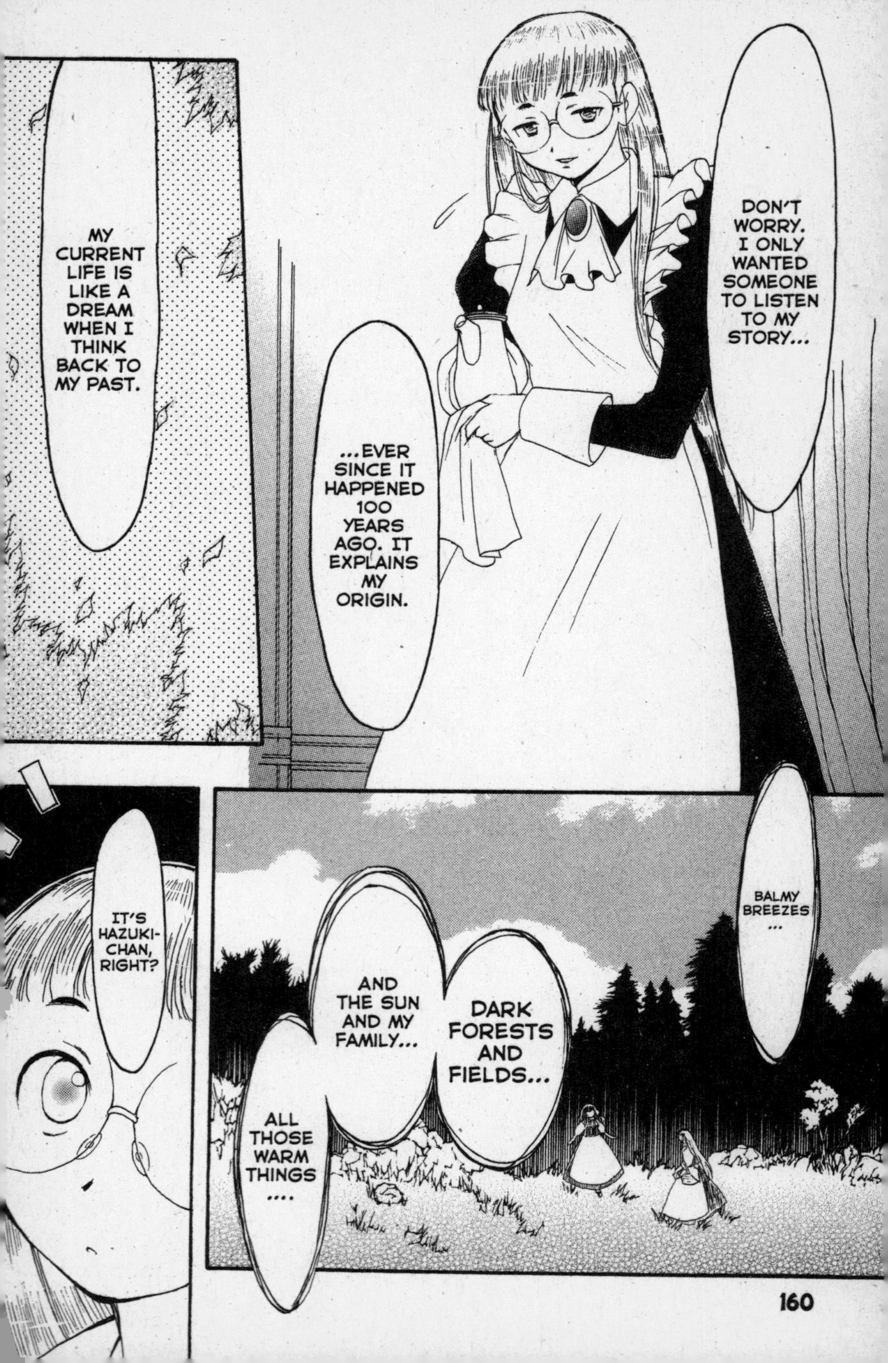
DON'T WORRY. I ONLY WANTED SOMEONE TO LISTEN TO MY STORY...
...EVER SINCE IT HAPPENED 100 YEARS AGO. IT EXPLAINS MY ORIGIN.
MY CURRENT LIFE IS LIKE A DREAM WHEN I THINK BACK TO MY PAST.
BALMY BREEZES ...
DARK FORESTS AND FIELDS...
AND THE SUN AND MY FAMILY...
ALL THOSE WARM THINGS ....
IT'S HAZUKI-CHAN, RIGHT?

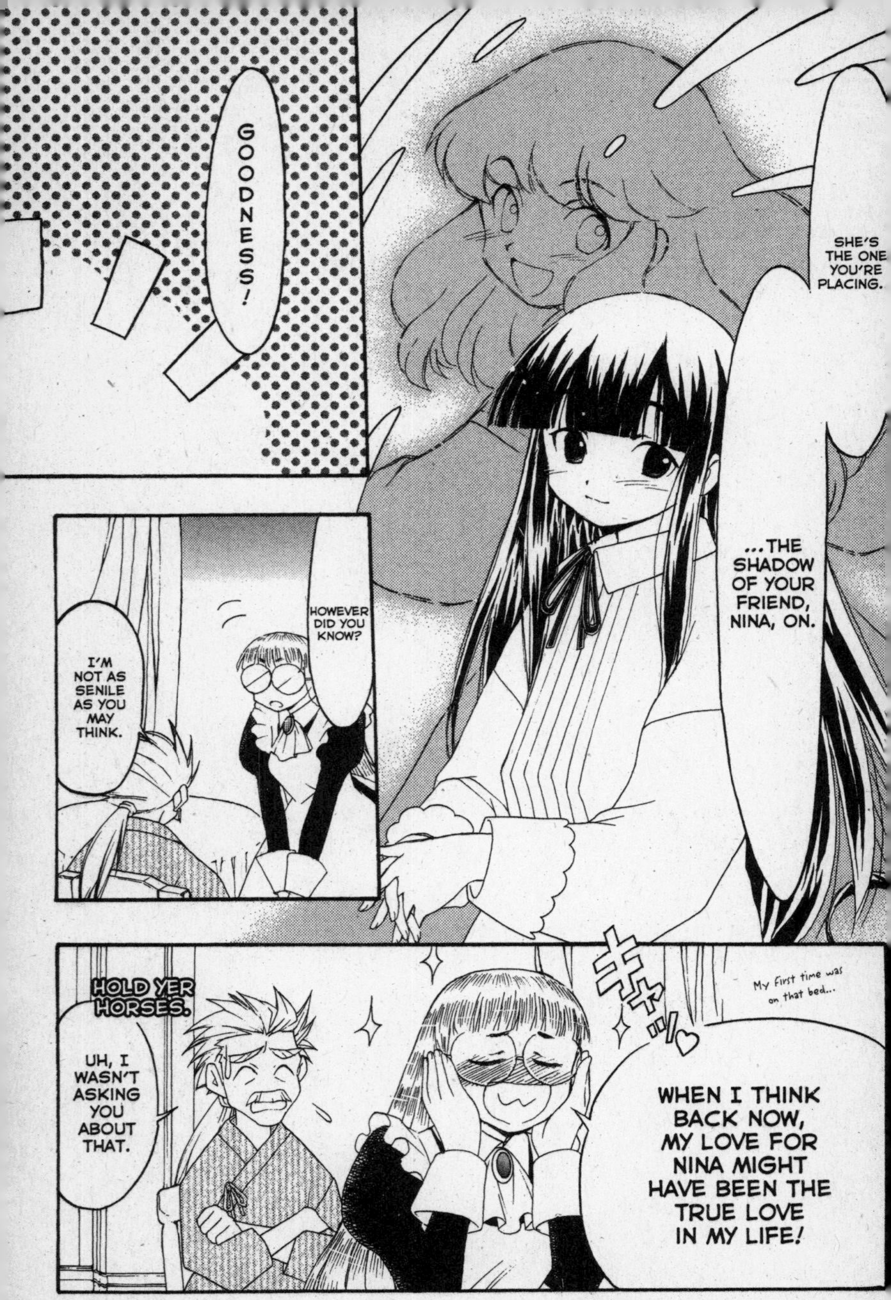
SHE'S THE ONE YOU'RE PLACING.
...THE SHADOW OF YOUR FRIEND, NINA, ON.
GOODNESS!
HOWEVER DID YOU KNOW?
I'M NOT AS SENILE AS YOU MAY THINK.
My first time was on that bed...
WHEN I THINK BACK NOW, MY LOVE FOR NINA MIGHT HAVE BEEN THE TRUE LOVE IN MY LIFE!
UH, I WASN'T ASKING YOU ABOUT THAT.
HOLD YER HORSES.

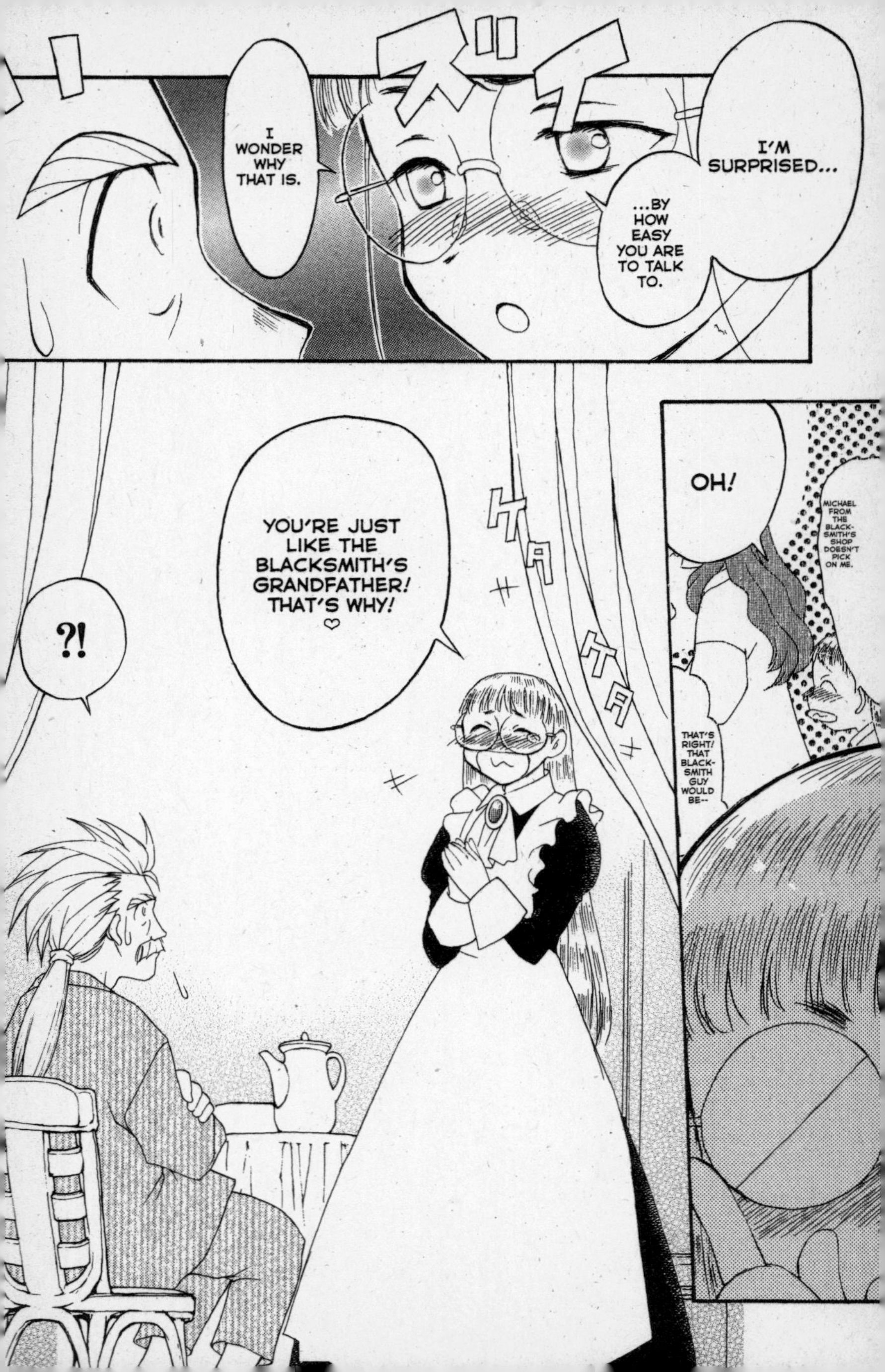
ズイ
I'M SURPRISED...
...BY HOW EASY YOU ARE TO TALK TO.
I WONDER WHY THAT IS.
OH!
MICHAEL FROM THE BLACKSMITH'S SHOP DOESN'T PICK ON ME.
THAT'S RIGHT! THAT BLACKSMITH GUY WOULD BE--
ケタケタ
YOU'RE JUST LIKE THE BLACKSMITH'S GRANDFATHER! THAT'S WHY! ♡
?!

MOON 月詠 PHASE

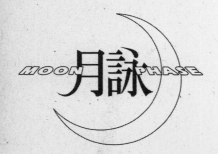

THE CASTLE WITH THE FAIRY FLAG.

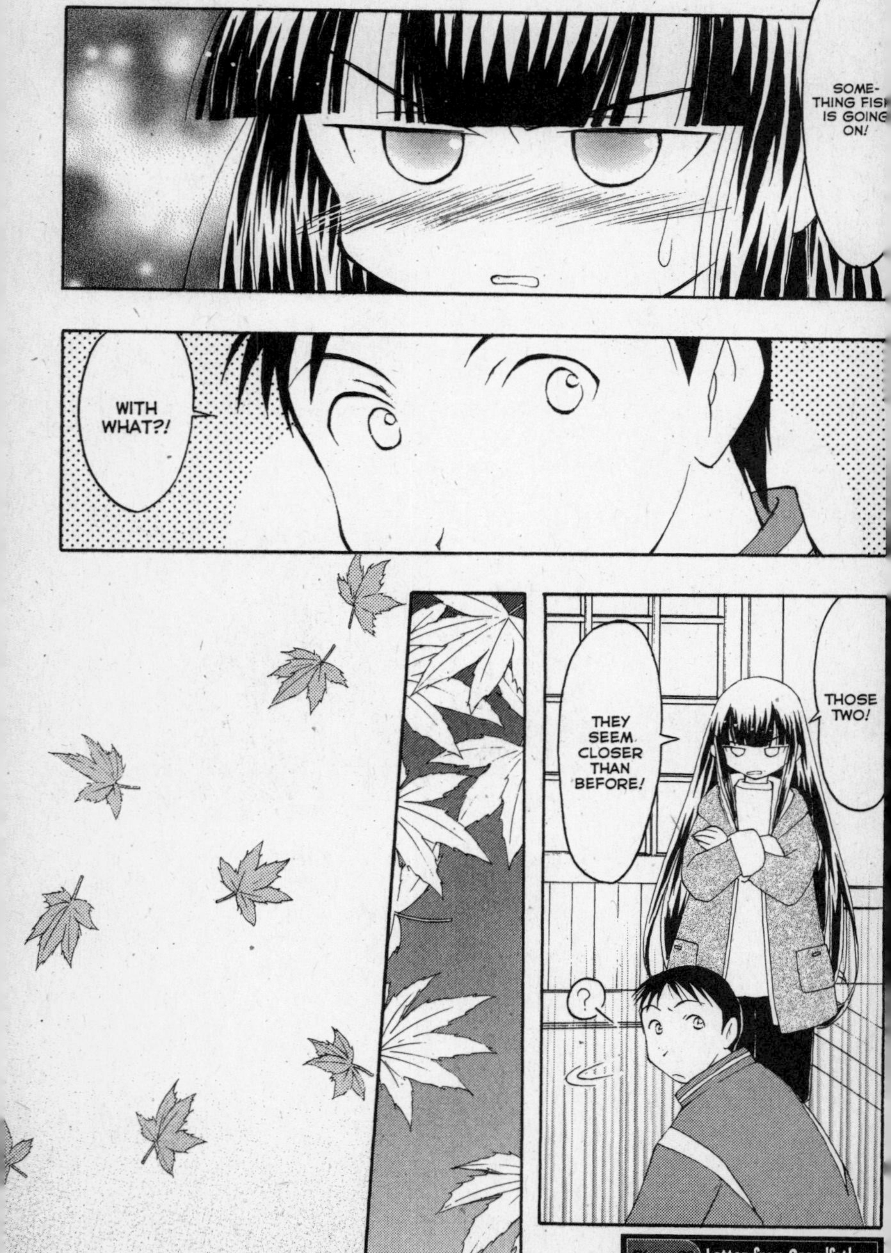
SOME-THING FIS IS GOING ON!
WITH WHAT?!
THOSE TWO!
THEY SEEM CLOSER THAN BEFORE!
?
Phase38 Letter from Grandfather

Phase38 Letter from Grandfather

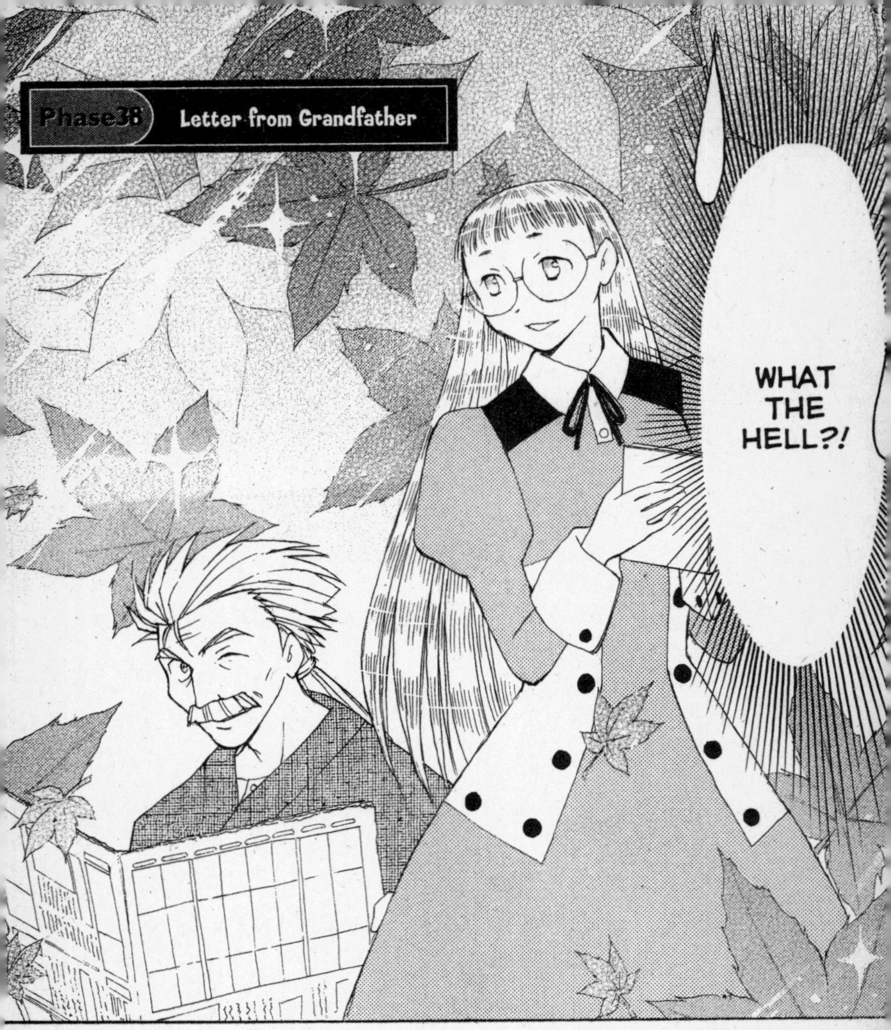
WHAT THE HELL?!

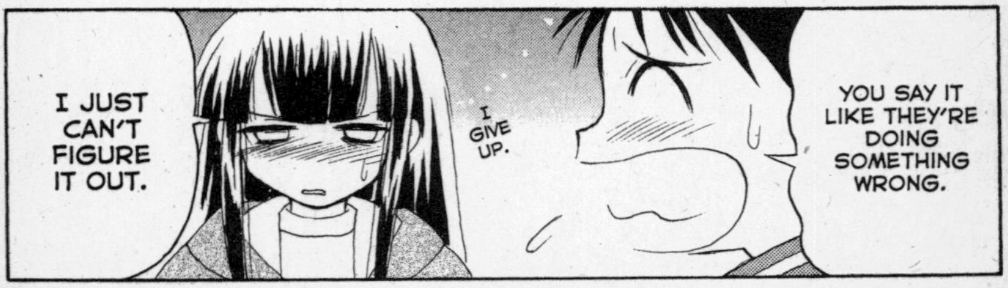
YOU SAY IT LIKE THEY'RE DOING SOMETHING WRONG.
I GIVE UP.
I JUST CAN'T FIGURE IT OUT.

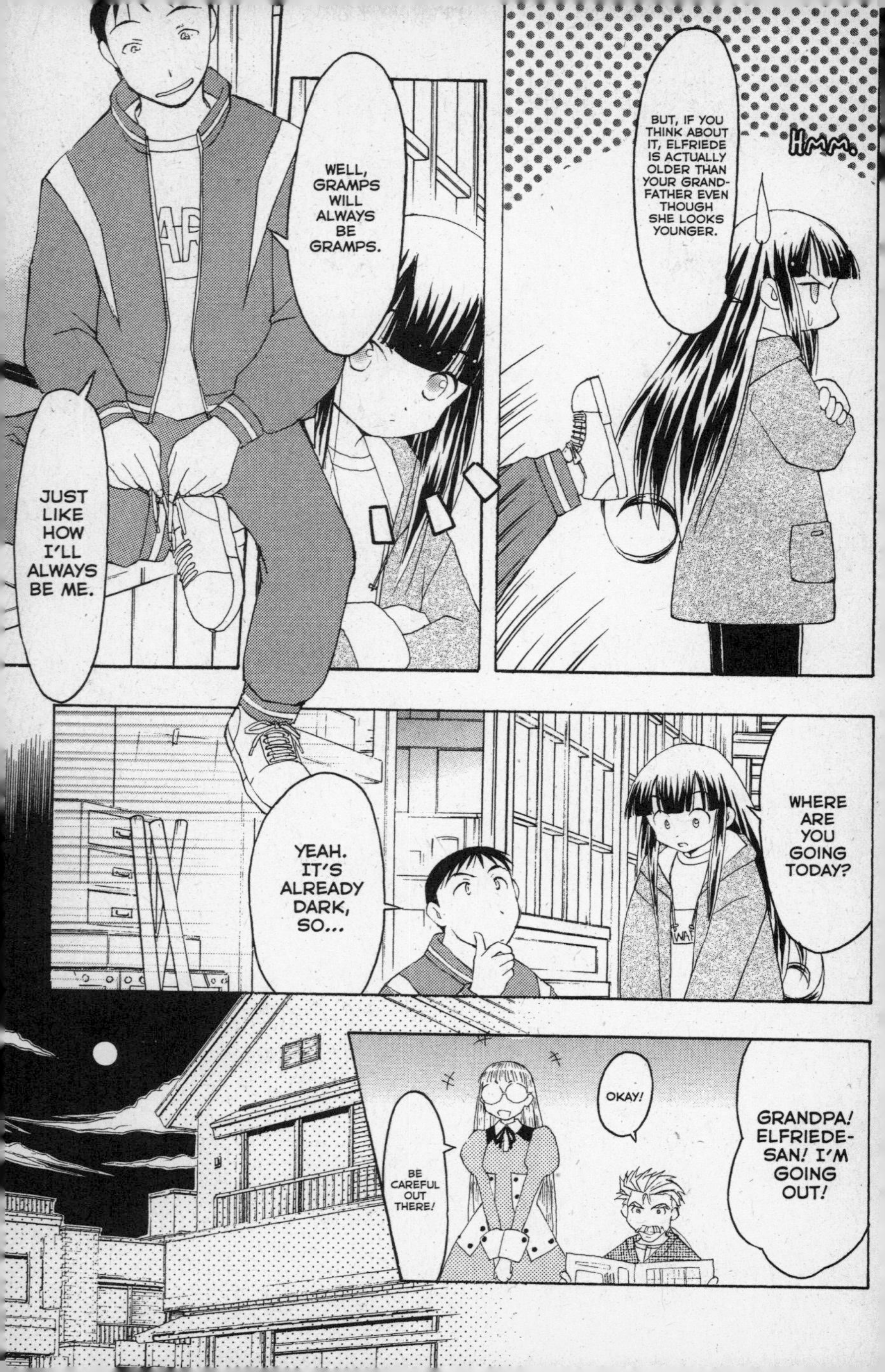
HMM.
BUT, IF YOU THINK ABOUT IT, ELFRIEDE IS ACTUALLY OLDER THAN YOUR GRAND-FATHER EVEN THOUGH SHE LOOKS YOUNGER.
WELL, GRAMPS WILL ALWAYS BE GRAMPS.
JUST LIKE HOW I'LL ALWAYS BE ME.
WHERE ARE YOU GOING TODAY?
YEAH. IT'S ALREADY DARK, SO...
GRANDPA! ELFRIEDE-SAN! I'M GOING OUT!
OKAY!
BE CAREFUL OUT THERE!

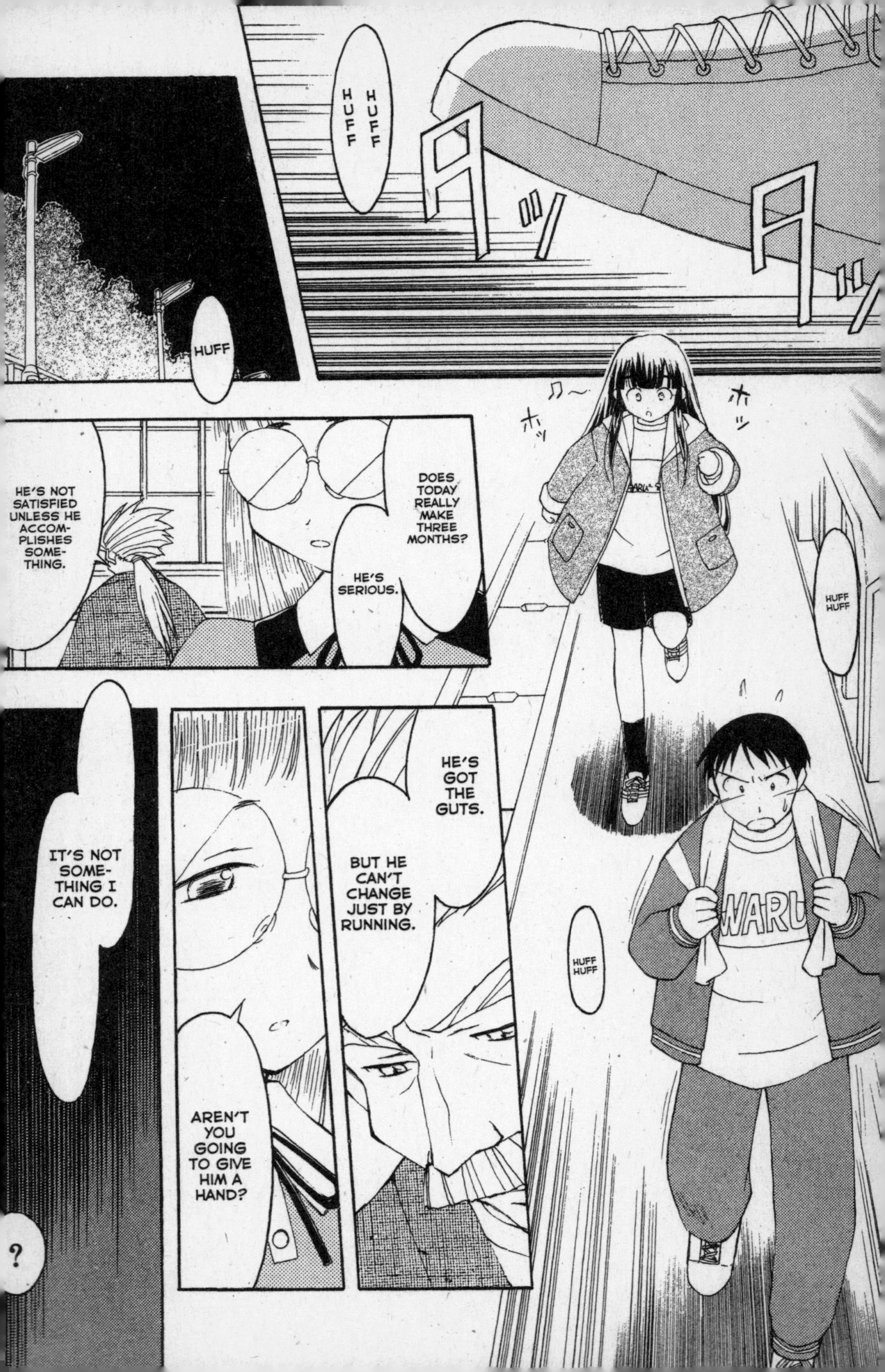
HUFF HUFF
HUFF
HUFF HUFF
HUFF HUFF
DOES TODAY REALLY MAKE THREE MONTHS?
HE'S SERIOUS.
HE'S NOT SATISFIED UNLESS HE ACCOMPLISHES SOMETHING.
HE'S GOT THE GUTS.
BUT HE CAN'T CHANGE JUST BY RUNNING.
AREN'T YOU GOING TO GIVE HIM A HAND?
?
IT'S NOT SOMETHING I CAN DO.

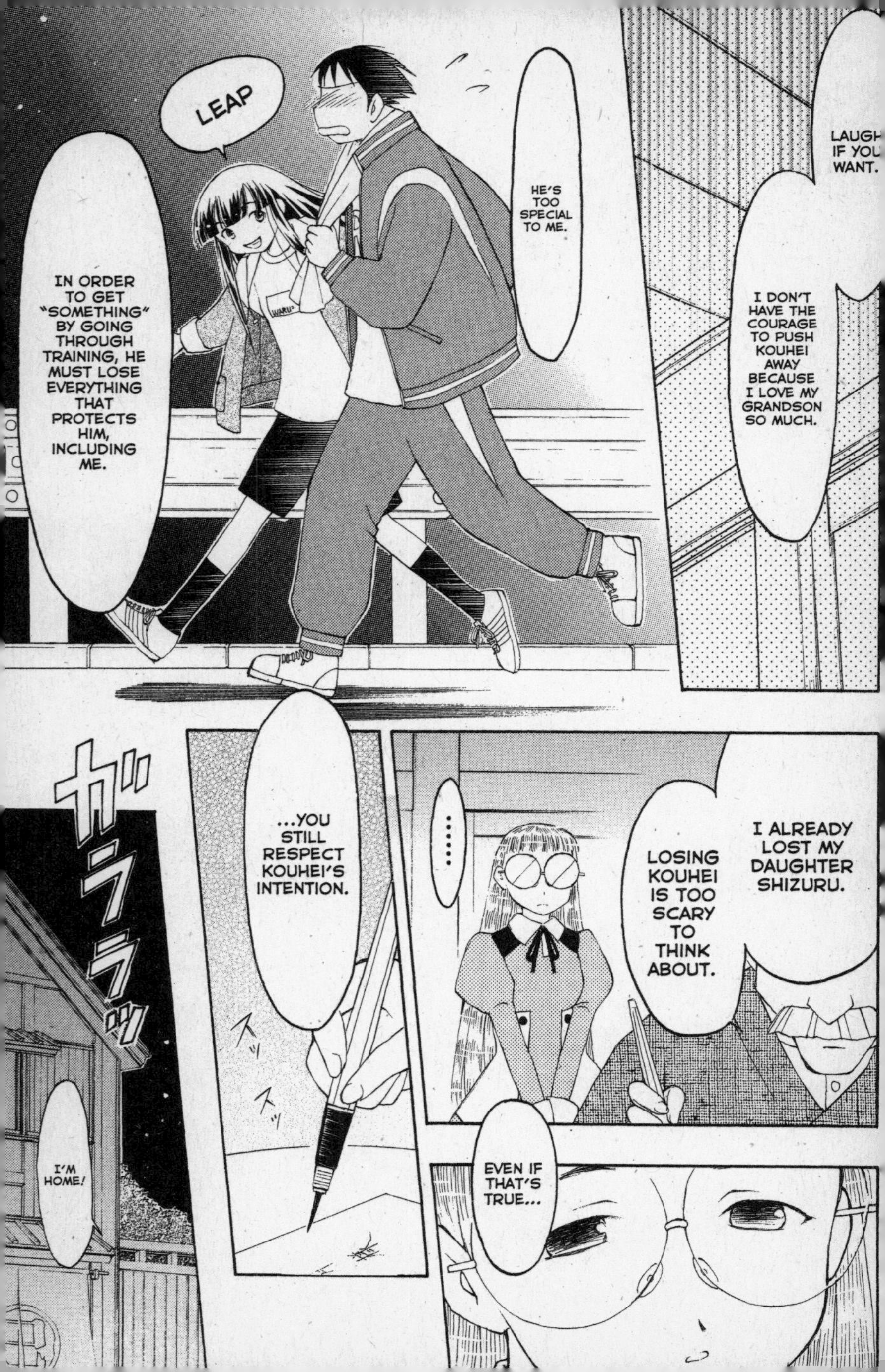
LAUGH IF YOU WANT.
I DON'T HAVE THE COURAGE TO PUSH KOUHEI AWAY BECAUSE I LOVE MY GRANDSON SO MUCH.
HE'S TOO SPECIAL TO ME.
LEAP
IN ORDER TO GET "SOMETHING" BY GOING THROUGH TRAINING, HE MUST LOSE EVERYTHING THAT PROTECTS HIM, INCLUDING ME.
I ALREADY LOST MY DAUGHTER SHIZURU.
LOSING KOUHEI IS TOO SCARY TO THINK ABOUT.
......
EVEN IF THAT'S TRUE...
...YOU STILL RESPECT KOUHEI'S INTENTION.
スッ
スッ
ガラララッ
I'M HOME!

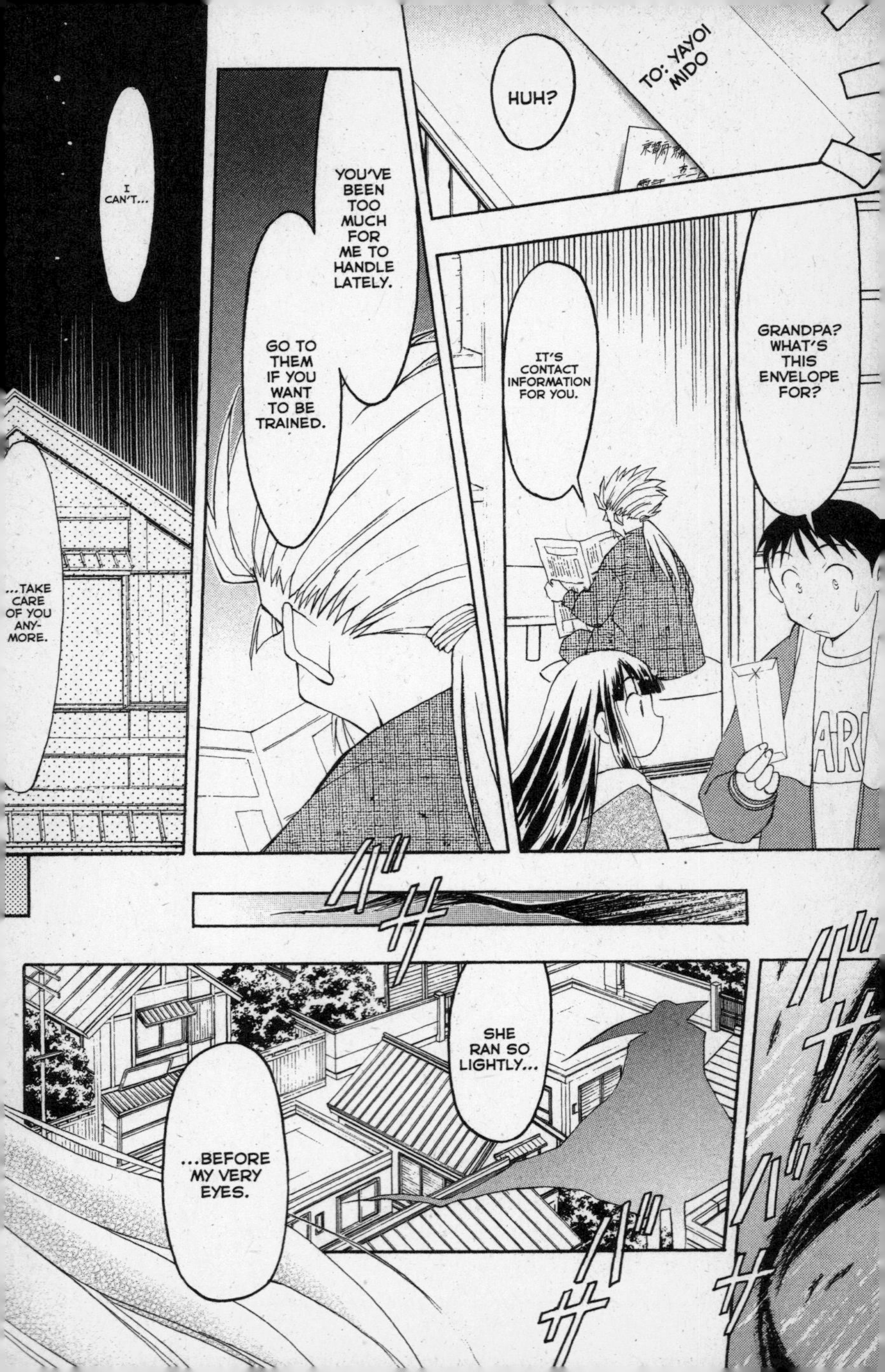
TO: YAYOI MIDO
HUH?
GRANDPA? WHAT'S THIS ENVELOPE FOR?
IT'S CONTACT INFORMATION FOR YOU.
YOU'VE BEEN TOO MUCH FOR ME TO HANDLE LATELY.
GO TO THEM IF YOU WANT TO BE TRAINED.
I CAN'T...
...TAKE CARE OF YOU ANYMORE.
SHE RAN SO LIGHTLY...
...BEFORE MY VERY EYES.

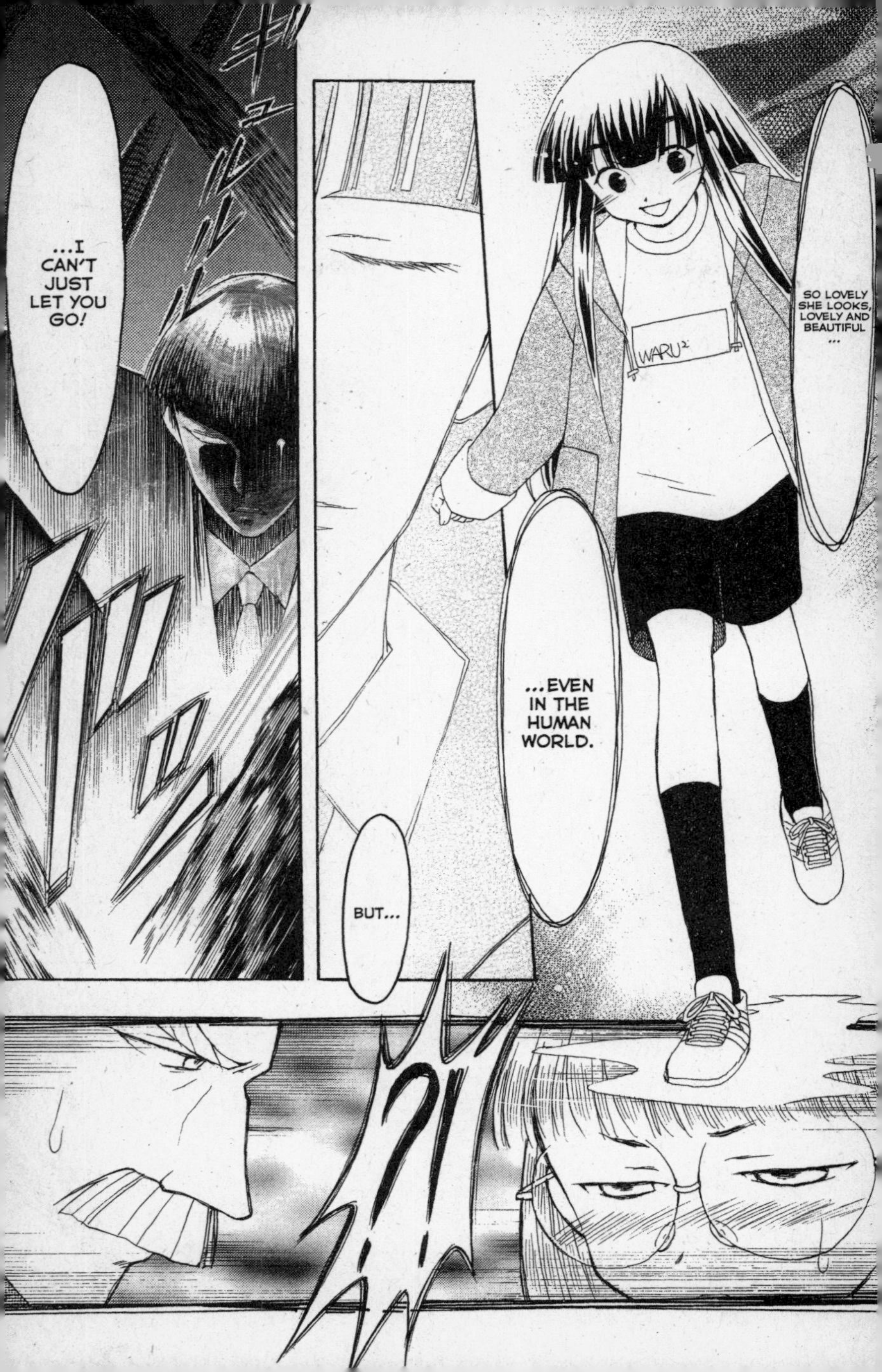
SO LOVELY SHE LOOKS, LOVELY AND BEAUTIFUL ...
...EVEN IN THE HUMAN WORLD.
BUT...
...I CAN'T JUST LET YOU GO!
?!

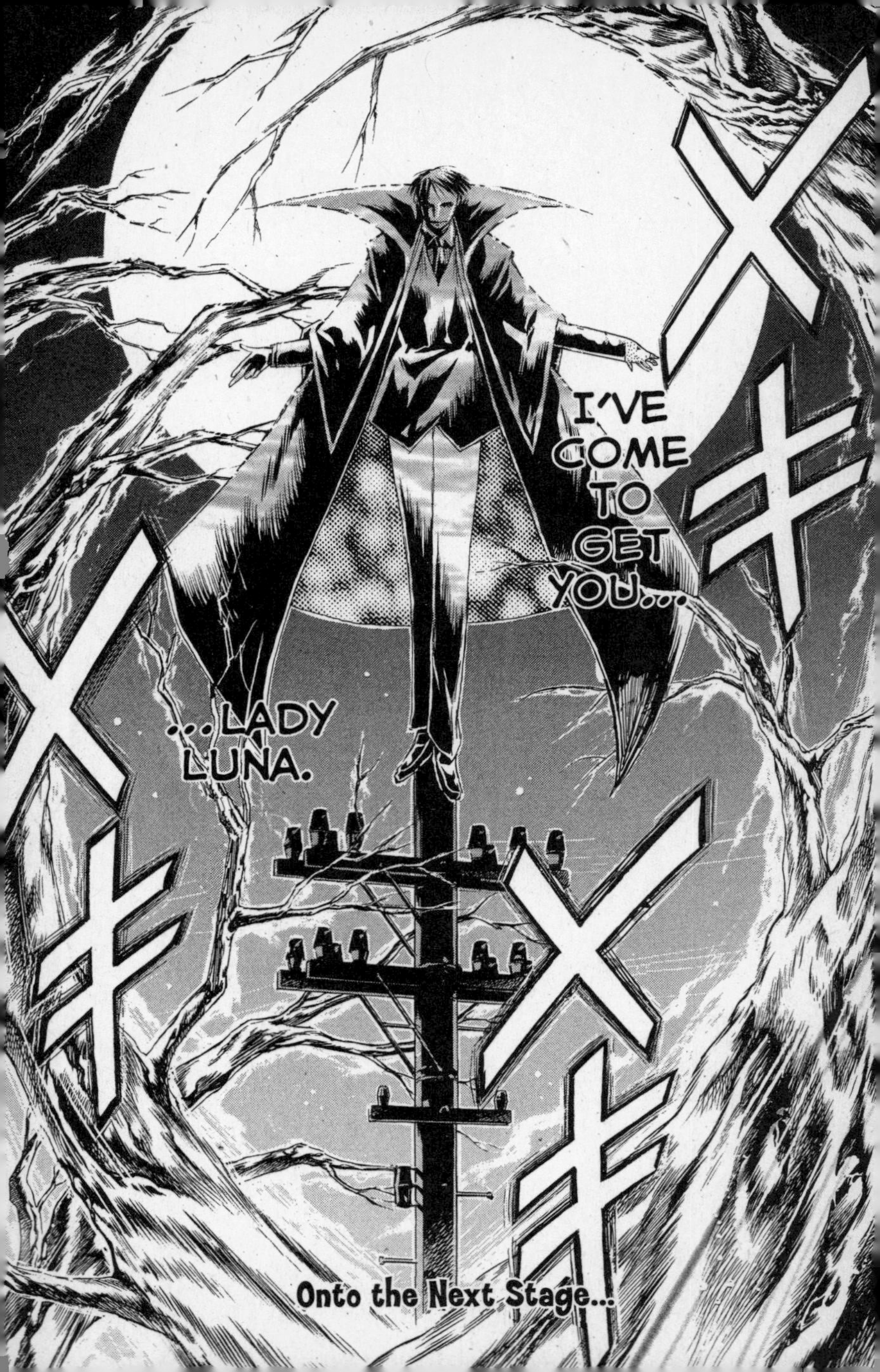
I'VE COME TO GET YOU...
...LADY LUNA.
Onto the Next Stage...

MOON 月詠 PHASE

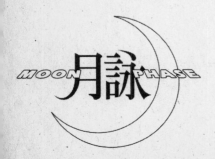

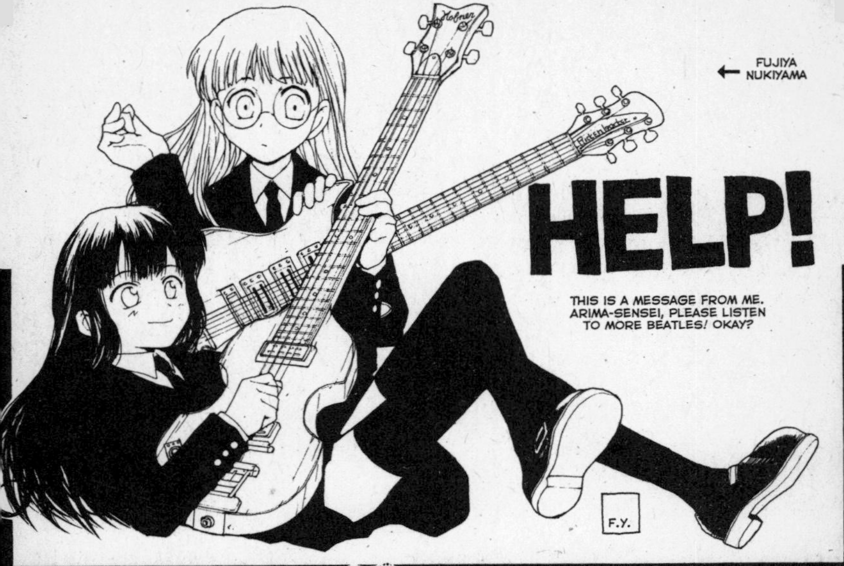
← FUJIYA NUKIYAMA
HELP!
THIS IS A MESSAGE FROM ME. ARIMA-SENSEI, PLEASE LISTEN TO MORE BEATLES! OKAY?
F.Y.

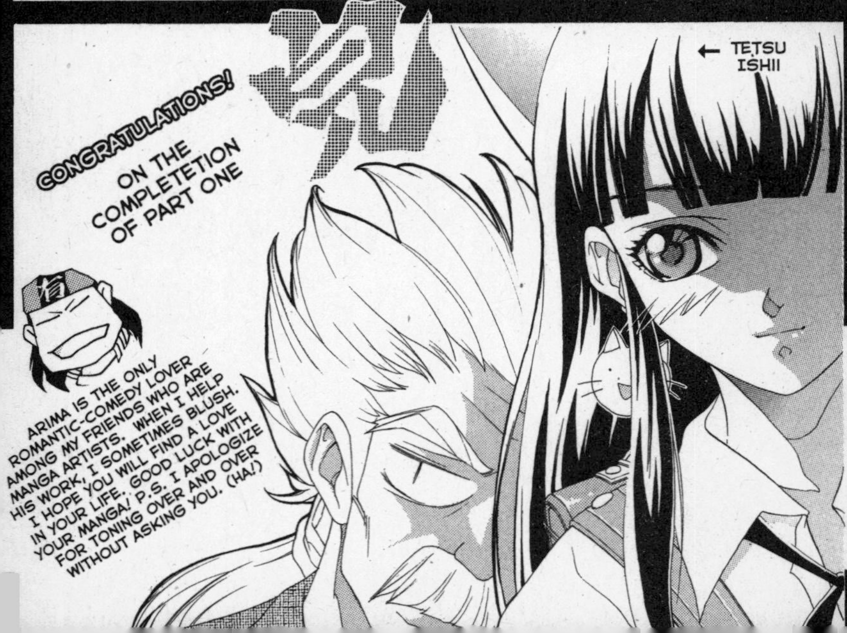
← TETSU ISHII
CONGRATULATIONS!
ON THE COMPLETETION OF PART ONE
ARIMA IS THE ONLY ROMANTIC-COMEDY LOVER AMONG MY FRIENDS WHO ARE MANGA ARTISTS. WHEN I HELP HIS WORK, I SOMETIMES BLUSH. I HOPE YOU WILL FIND A LOVE IN YOUR LIFE. GOOD LUCK WITH YOUR MANGA! P.S. I APOLOGIZE FOR TONING OVER AND OVER WITHOUT ASKING YOU. (HA!)

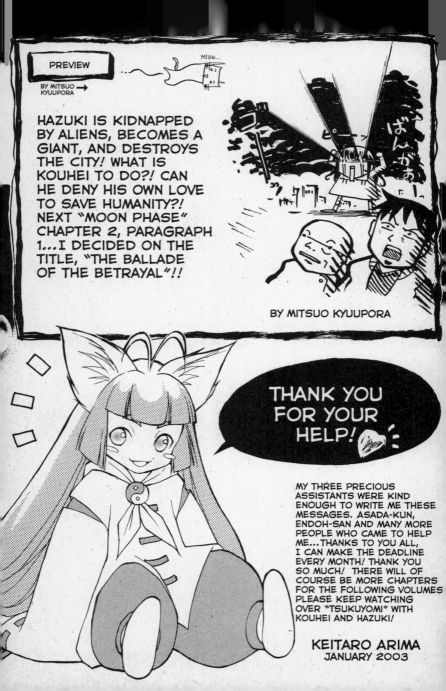

PREVIEW

BY MITSUO KYUUPORA →

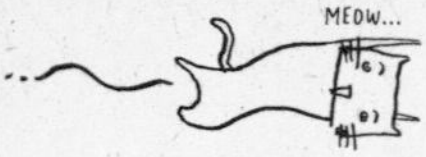
MEOW...

HAZUKI IS KIDNAPPED BY ALIENS, BECOMES A GIANT, AND DESTROYS THE CITY! WHAT IS KOUHEI TO DO?! CAN HE DENY HIS OWN LOVE TO SAVE HUMANITY?! NEXT "MOON PHASE" CHAPTER 2, PARAGRAPH 1...I DECIDED ON THE TITLE, "THE BALLADE OF THE BETRAYAL"!!

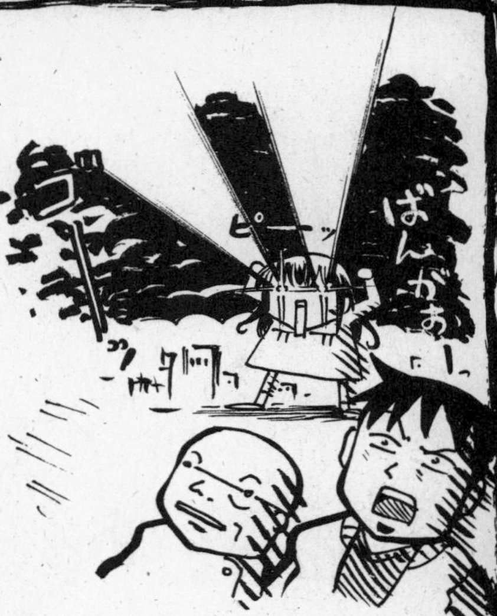
ばんがぁー!

BY MITSUO KYUUPORA

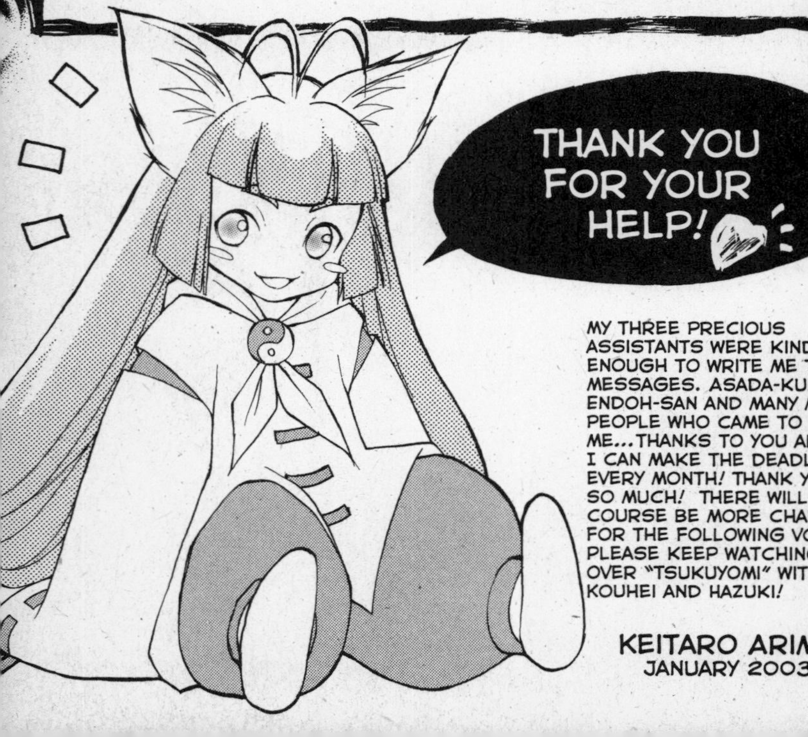
THANK YOU FOR YOUR HELP!

MY THREE PRECIOUS ASSISTANTS WERE KIND ENOUGH TO WRITE ME THESE MESSAGES. ASADA-KUN, ENDOH-SAN AND MANY MORE PEOPLE WHO CAME TO HELP ME...THANKS TO YOU ALL, I CAN MAKE THE DEADLINE EVERY MONTH! THANK YOU SO MUCH! THERE WILL OF COURSE BE MORE CHAPTERS FOR THE FOLLOWING VOLUMES PLEASE KEEP WATCHING OVER "TSUKUYOMI" WITH KOUHEI AND HAZUKI!

KEITARO ARIMA
JANUARY 2003

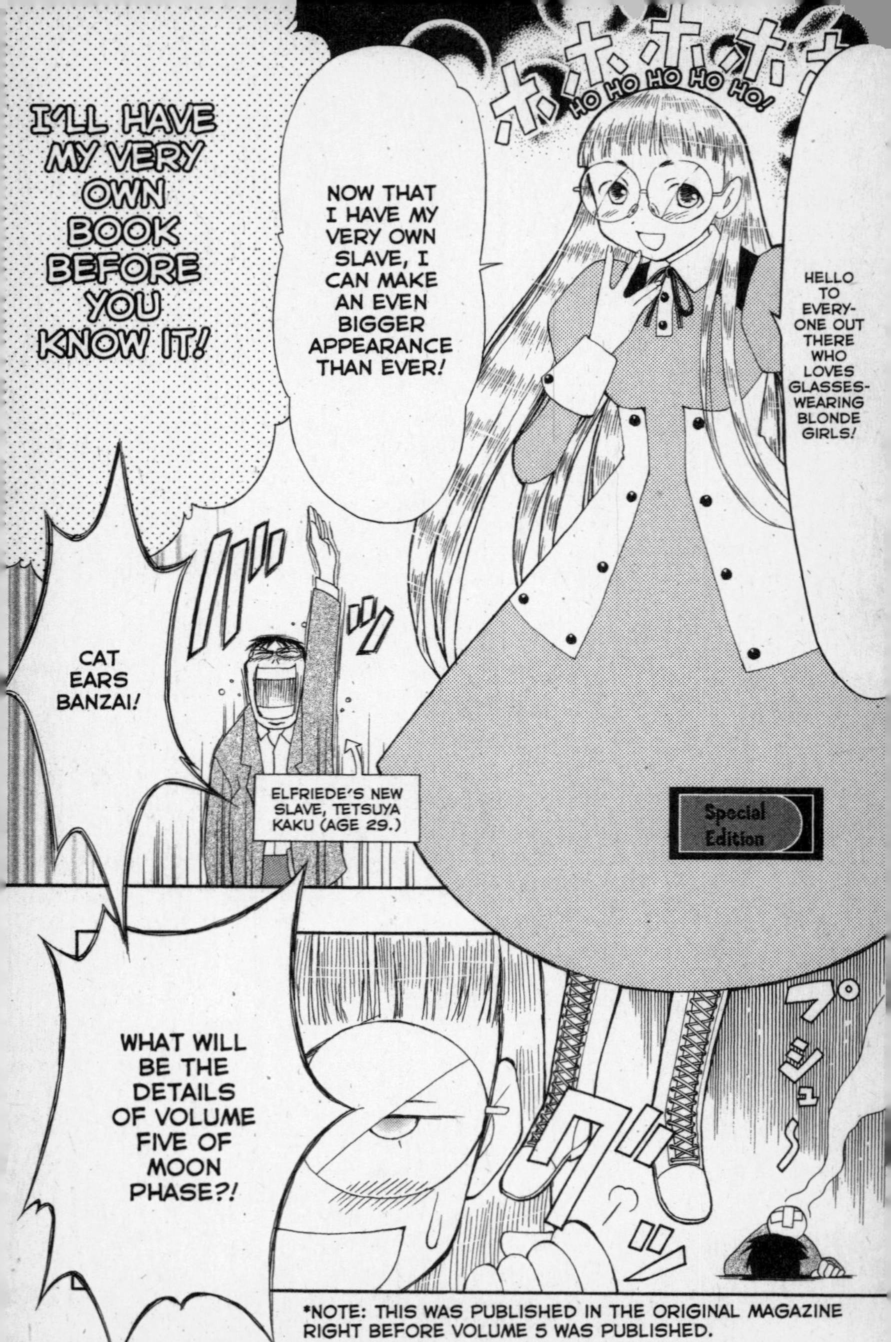
HO HO HO HO HO!
HELLO TO EVERY-ONE OUT THERE WHO LOVES GLASSES-WEARING BLONDE GIRLS!
NOW THAT I HAVE MY VERY OWN SLAVE, I CAN MAKE AN EVEN BIGGER APPEARANCE THAN EVER!
I'LL HAVE MY VERY OWN BOOK BEFORE YOU KNOW IT!
Special Edition
ELFRIEDE'S NEW SLAVE, TETSUYA KAKU (AGE 29.)
CAT EARS BANZAI!
WHAT WILL BE THE DETAILS OF VOLUME FIVE OF MOON PHASE?!

*NOTE: THIS WAS PUBLISHED IN THE ORIGINAL MAGAZINE RIGHT BEFORE VOLUME 5 WAS PUBLISHED.

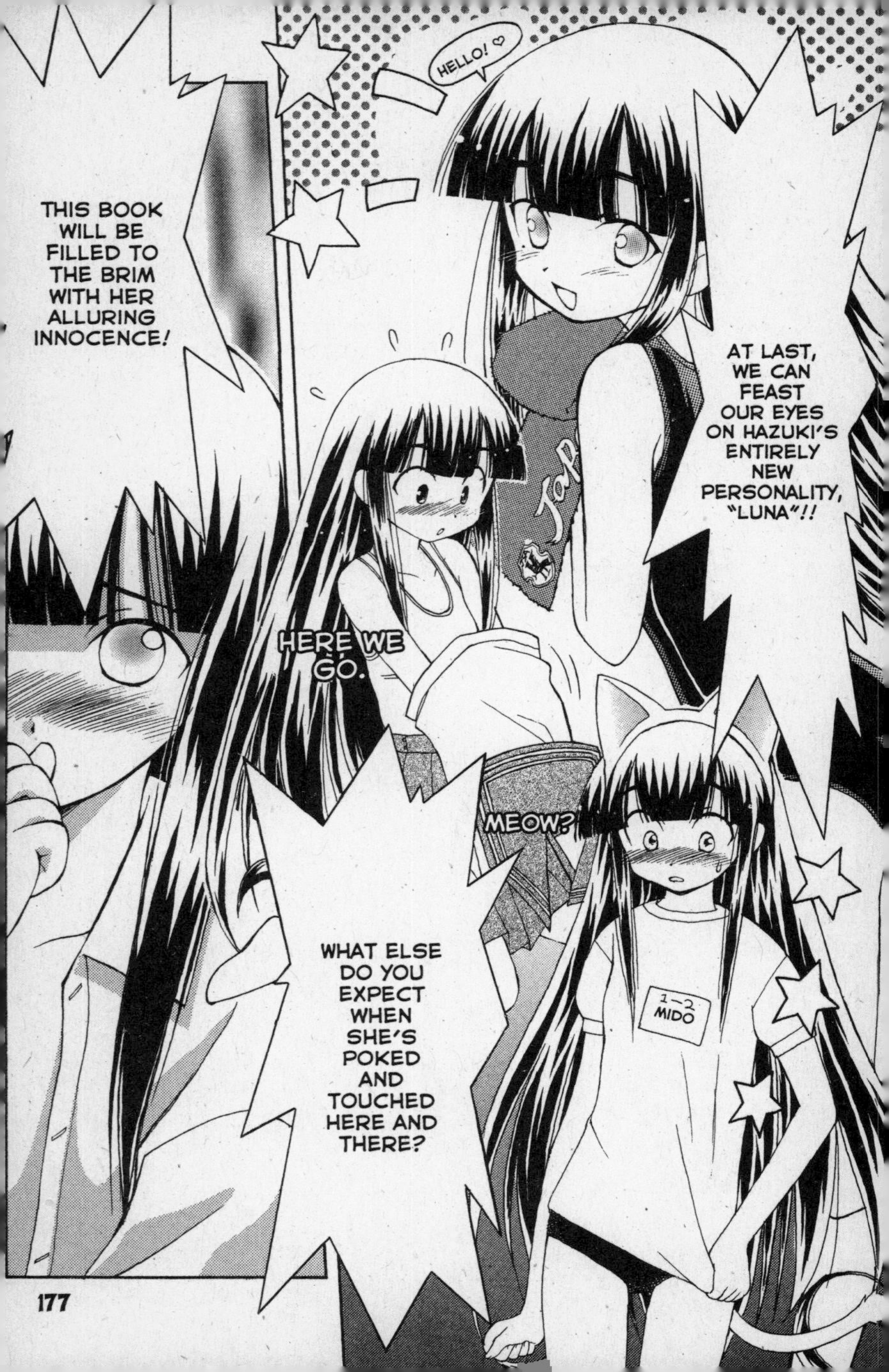
HELLO! ♡
AT LAST, WE CAN FEAST OUR EYES ON HAZUKI'S ENTIRELY NEW PERSONALITY, "LUNA"!!
THIS BOOK WILL BE FILLED TO THE BRIM WITH HER ALLURING INNOCENCE!
HERE WE GO.
MEOW?
1-2 MIDO
WHAT ELSE DO YOU EXPECT WHEN SHE'S POKED AND TOUCHED HERE AND THERE?

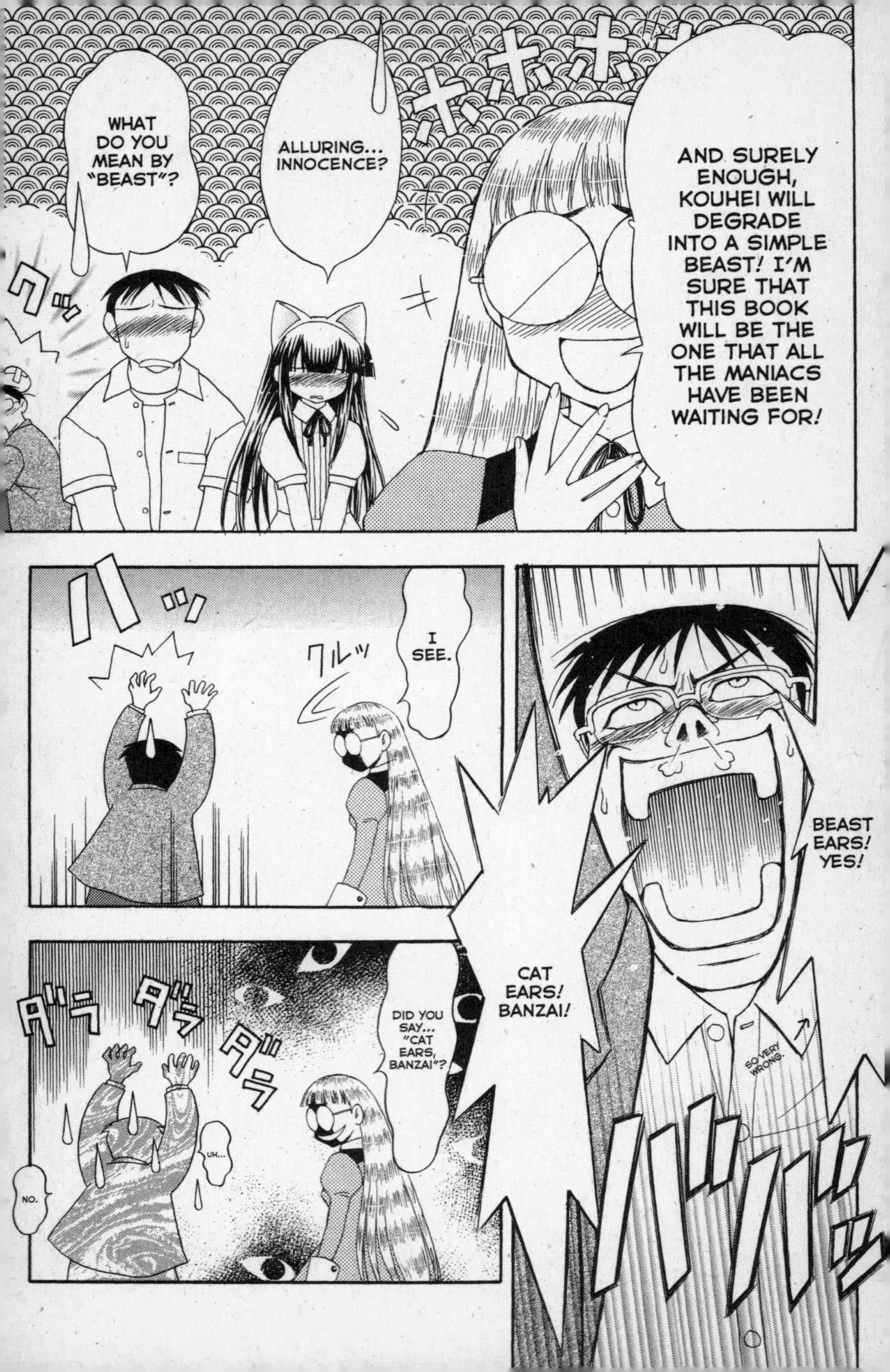

AND SURELY ENOUGH, KOUHEI WILL DEGRADE INTO A SIMPLE BEAST! I'M SURE THAT THIS BOOK WILL BE THE ONE THAT ALL THE MANIACS HAVE BEEN WAITING FOR!
ALLURING... INNOCENCE?
WHAT DO YOU MEAN BY "BEAST"?
BEAST EARS! YES!
CAT EARS! BANZAI!
SO VERY WRONG.
I SEE.
DID YOU SAY... "CAT EARS, BANZAI"?
UH...
NO.

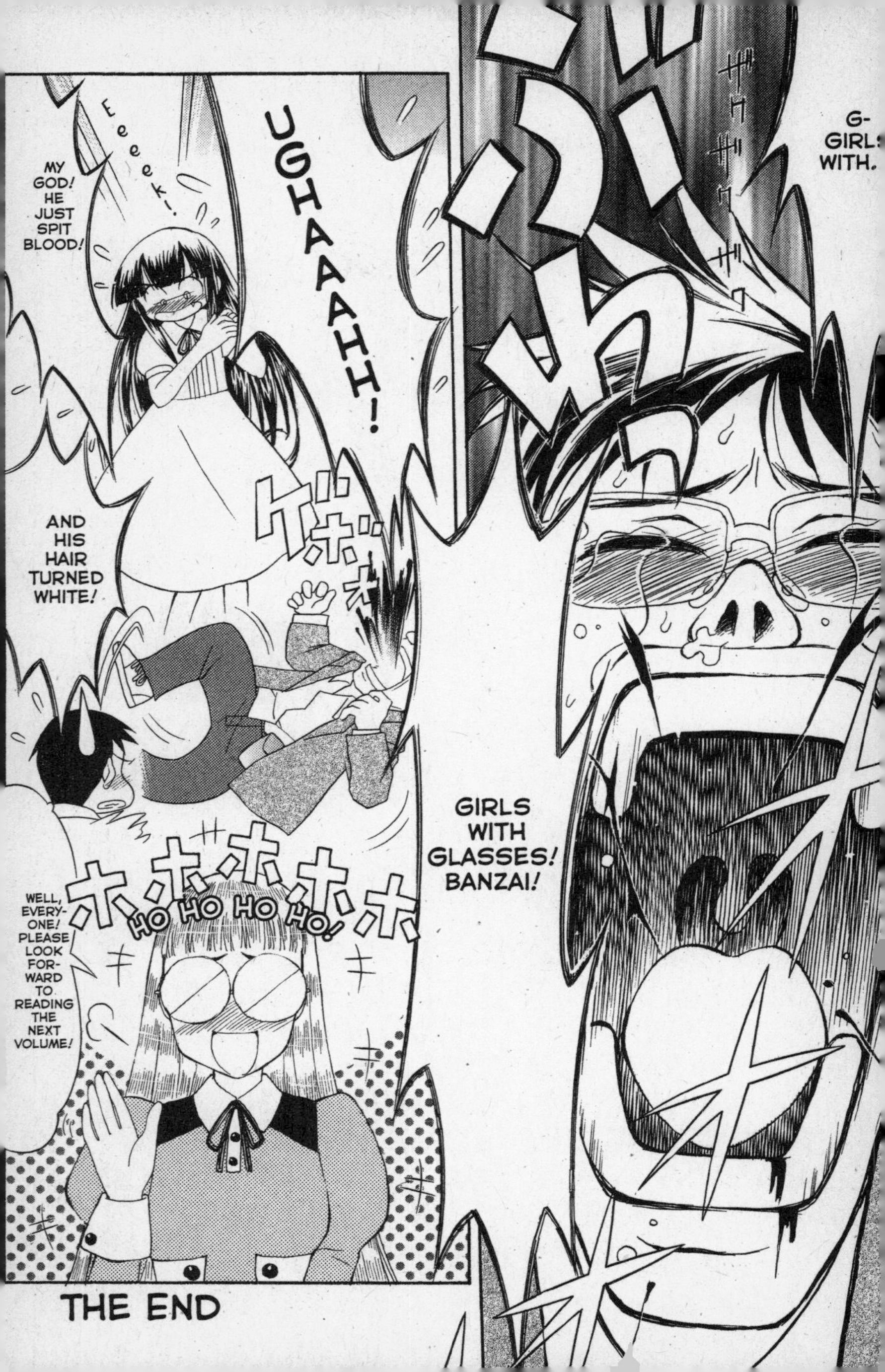
G-
GIRLS WITH.
GIRLS WITH GLASSES! BANZAI!
UGHAAAHH!
Eeeek!
MY GOD! HE JUST SPIT BLOOD!
AND HIS HAIR TURNED WHITE!
HO HO HO HO HO!
WELL, EVERY-ONE! PLEASE LOOK FOR-WARD TO READING THE NEXT VOLUME!
THE END

IN THE NEXT

TSUKUYOMI

MoonPhase 月詠

IT'S BEEN TWO YEARS SINCE OUR HEROES ENJOYED THEIR TEMPORARY PEACE AND QUIET, BUT MARIO'S ATTACK ON THE MIDO HOUSEHOLD SUDDENLY CHANGES ALL THAT. WITH THE LOSS OF THEIR DEAR AND CLOSE FRIENDS, KOUHEI AND HAZUKI SEEK REFUGE IN THE CARE OF DISTANT RELATIVES IN THE MOUNTAINS. JUST AS KOUHEI'S GRANDFATHER PROMISED, THERE IS A WAY FOR KOUHEI TO GROW STRONGER IN ORDER TO PROTECT THE ONE HE LOVES. AND HE'S ABOUT TO FIND IT UNDER THE GUIDANCE OF YAYOI MIDO AND THE ADORABLE BUT TOUGH-AS-NAILS TWINS KAORU AND HIKARU. WITH NEW ALLIES COME NEW ENEMIES, AND THIS FEARSOME DUO MAY BE OUR HERO'S GREATEST THREAT YET!

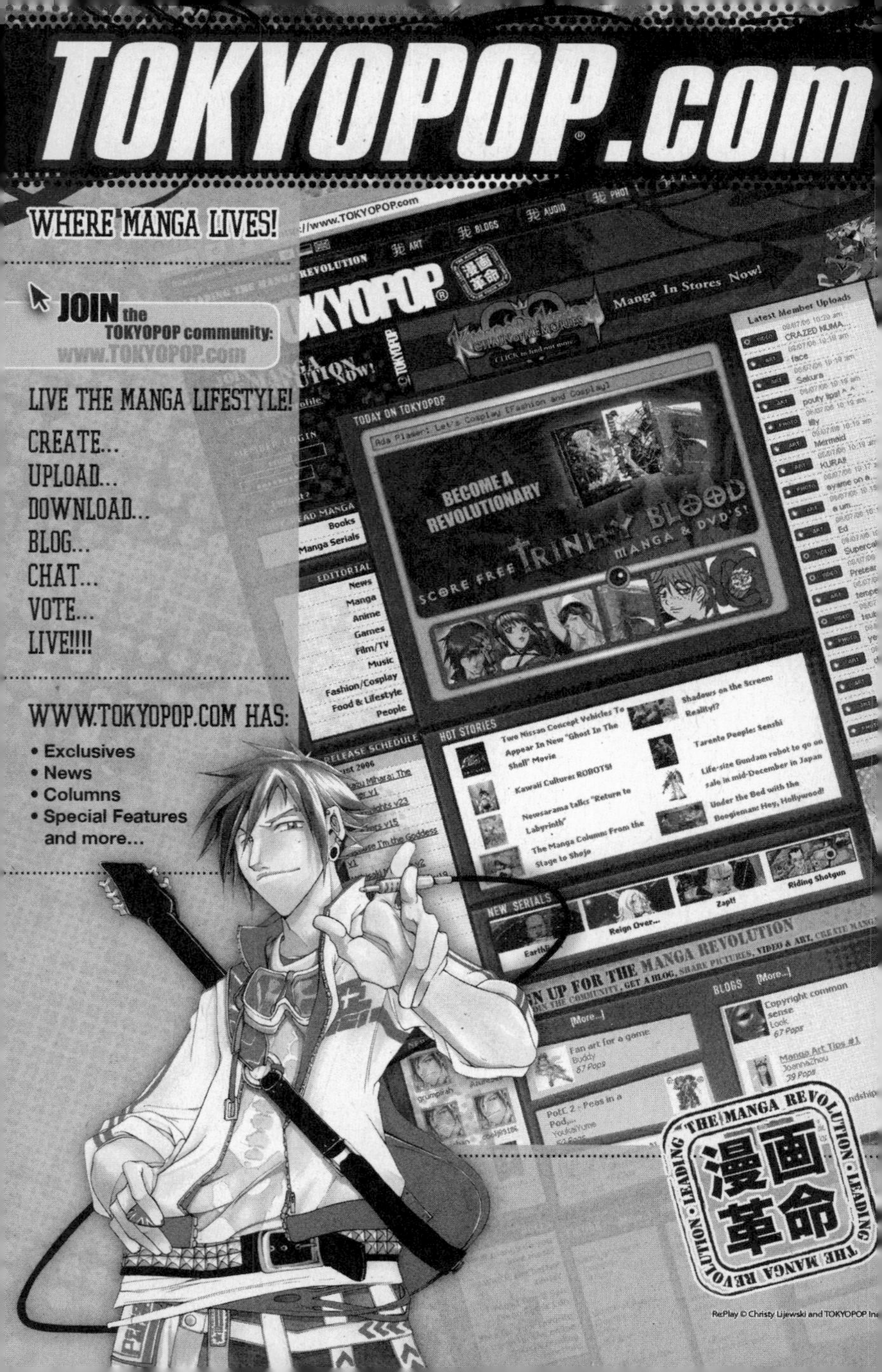
TOKYOPOP.com
WHERE MANGA LIVES!
JOIN the TOKYOPOP community:
www.TOKYOPOP.com
LIVE THE MANGA LIFESTYLE!
CREATE...
UPLOAD...
DOWNLOAD...
BLOG...
CHAT...
VOTE...
LIVE!!!!
WWW.TOKYOPOP.COM HAS:
• Exclusives
• News
• Columns
• Special Features and more...
LEADING THE MANGA REVOLUTION
漫画革命
RePlay © Christy Lijewski and TOKYOPOP Inc.

STOP!

This is the back of the book.
You wouldn't want to spoil a great ending!

This book is printed "manga-style," in the authentic Japanese right-to-left format. Since none of the artwork has been flipped or altered, readers get to experience the story just as the creator intended. You've been asking for it, so TOKYOPOP® delivered: authentic, hot-off-the-press, and far more fun!

DIRECTIONS

If this is your first time reading manga-style, here's a quick guide to help you understand how it works.

It's easy... just start in the top right panel and follow the numbers. Have fun, and look for more 100% authentic manga from TOKYOPOP®!